Mike Ashley is a leading authority on horror, fantasy and science fiction. Since 1974 he has written and edited numerous books, including *Weird Legacies, Souls in Metal, Mrs Gaskell's Tales of Mystery and Horror, Jewels of Wonder, Best of British SF, Fantasy Readers' Guide to Ramsey Campbell, Who's Who in Horror and Fantasy Fiction* and *The Complete Index to Astounding/Analog*. He is currently writing a biography of Algernon Blackwood.

He has also contributed widely to fantasy magazines and encyclopedias in Britain and America, including *Dark Horizons, Locus, Twilight Zone Magazine* and *Fantasy Tales*.

THE PENDRAGON CHRONICLES

THE PENDRAGON CHRONICLES

HEROIC FANTASY FROM THE TIME OF KING ARTHUR

EDITED BY MIKE ASHLEY

WINGS BOOKS

NEW YORK • AVENEL, NEW JERSEY

This 1994 edition is published by Wings Books, distributed by Random House Value Publishing, Inc., 40 Engelhard Avenue, Avenel, New Jersey 07001, by arrangement with Peter Bedrick Books, Inc., New York.

Random House
New York • Toronto • London • Sydney • Auckland

Printed and bound in the United States of America

Library of Congress Cataloging-in-Publication Data

The Pendragon chronicles: heroic fantasy from the time of King Arthur/
    edited by Mike Ashley.
        p.   cm.
    Includes bibliographical references.
    ISBN 0-517-09371-5
    1. Arthurian romances—Adaptations. 2. Fantastic fiction,
American. 3. Fantastic fiction, English. 4. Arthurian romances.
I. Ashley, Michael.
[PS648.A78P46 1993]
813'.0108351—dc20

10 9 8 7 6 5 4 3

CONTENTS

Copyright Acknowledgements

"Chief Dragon of the Island" by Joy Chant, © 1983 for *The High kings*; reprinted by permission of the author and Messrs Unwin Hyman Ltd, London and Bantam Books, New York.

"The Dragon's Boy" by Jane Yolen, © 1986 for *Merlin's Booke*, © 1985 for the *The Magazine of Fantasy & science Fiction* September 1985; reprinted by permission of the author and Curtis Brown Ltd, London, and Berkley Publishing Group, New York.

"The Knight With the Two Swords" by John Steinbeck, © 1977 for *The Acts of King Arthur and His Noble Knights*; reprinted by permission of Messrs William Heinemann Ltd, London and Farrar, Straus & Giroux Inc., New York.

"Morte d'Alain" by Maxey Brooke, © 1952 for *Ellery Queen's Mystery Magazine* December 1952; reprinted by permission of the author.

"King's Man" by Sasha Miller, © 1989 by Sasha Miller; first printing, used by permission of the Uwe Luserke Literary Agency.

"Sir Percivale of Wales" by Roger Lancelyn Green, © 1953 by the author for *King Arthur and His Knights of the Round Table*; reprinted by permission of Penguin Books Ltd and the author's estate.

"For To Achieve Your Adventure" by Theodore G. Roberts, © 1951 by the McCall Corporation for *Blue Book* October 1951; reprinted by permission of Mrs Dorothy Roberts Leisner.

"The King's Damosel" by Vera Chapman, © 1976 by Rex Collings Ltd; reprinted by permission of the author and Rex Collings.

"Buried Silver" by Keith Taylor, © 1977, 1981 for *Bard*; reprinted by permission of the author and Headline Publishing PLC.

"Son of the Morning" by Ian McDowell, © 1983 by Davis Publications for *Isaac Asimov's SF Magazine*; reprinted by permission of the author.

"The Lady of Belec" by Phyllis Ann Karr, © 1989 by Phyllis Ann Karr; first printing, used by permission of the Owlswick Literary Agency.

"Artos, Son of Marius" by Andre Norton, © 1972 for *Dragon Magic*; reprinted by permission of the Uwe Luserke Literary Agency.

"An Entry That Did Not Appear in Domesday Book" by John Brunner, © 1988 by TSR Inc for *Amazing Stories* March 1988; reprinted by permission of the author and the author's agents, A.M.Heath & Co. Ltd.

"Midnight, Moolight, and the Secret of the Sea" by Darrell Schweitzer, © 1981 for *We Are All Legends*; reprinted by permission of the author.

INTRODUCTION

Arthurian fiction has been with us now for 850 years and shows no sign of losing its popularity. Apart from the old romances much that has been written has been in verse or in the form of full-length novels or, in keeping with the current vogue, as trilogies. By contrast little Arthurian fiction has appeared in the short story form. Those stories which have appeared have been in diverse sources not readily available to the interested reader.

This volume brings together some of those shorter works. There are sixteen stories in all: two of them, those by Phyllis Ann Karr and Sasha Miller, seeing their first publication here. Most of the others have never been reprinted since their original appearance in books or magazines. I am particularly pleased to publish for the first time in book form one of the series of stories by Theodore Goodridge Roberts about Sir Dinadan. Often listed by bibliographies these stories have been unjustly ignored by authologists. I am also pleased to include a forgotten Arthurian romance, *Jaufry the Knight*, which you will not find amongst the usual volumes of Arthurian classics.

I have endeavoured to include varied treatments of the Arthurian myth. Some authors have chosen to update the original medieval works, as in Joy Chant's modern rendition of the life of Arthur from Geoffrey of Monmouth's *History* and John Steinbeck's retelling of the story of Sir Balin from Malory's *Morte d'Arthur*. In the same vein is Roger Lancelyn Green's retelling of the story of Sir Percivale.

Other writers have weaved new patterns into the ancient tapestry. Some have chosen the traditional form, as in the short novel by Vera Chapman, and the stories by Maxey Brooke, Theodore Goodridge Roberts and Phyllis Ann Karr. Others—Keith Taylor, Ian McDowell and André Norton—have adopted a historical setting, whilst the stories by Jane Yolen and Sasha Miller are to a design entirely their own.

1

So far as is possible I have arranged the stories in chronological order of events, starting with a general overview by Joy Chant. Owing to the authors' own treatments of the legend, a few inconsistences arise between stories, but such *is* the stuff of dreams. I have also included two post-Arthurian stories to show how the legend lives on into the medieval age.

The names of Arthurian heroes can often be confusing and are spelled in a variety of ways. I have therefore included a glossary of names to minimise confusion. I have also included a survey of the growth of Arthurian fiction up to the Victorian era, together with a bibliography of the last one hundred years.

The appeal of Arthurian fiction need not be too closely analysed. In times of need the nation frequently looks for a hero and saviour. As I show in my survey, this happened first at the time of the Norman-Plantaganet Civil War and again during the Wars of the Roses. The Arthurian revival in the Victorian age was, in part, a search for a romantic era at a time of industrial revolution and social upheaval. Today much of the interest in Arthurian (and other) fantasy may possibly be due to social unrest and anxiety related to the nuclear threat. Today, also, we appear to be looking for a hero but one to restore peace and harmony not to brandish Excalibur in battle. Perhaps we await someone with the strength to put the sword back in the stone.

Mike Ashley,
Walderslade,
November 1989

DRAMATIS PERSONAE
A guide to Arthurian characters

If like me you are easily confused by the many Arthurian characters, especially by the alternative spellings, then the following may help you avoid too many stumbles on your journey through the book. It is easy enough to remember Arthur, Merlin and Lancelot, but once we get beyond that, do you confuse Gareth and Gaheris, Lamorak and Leodegrance? And who was Gwalchmai?

Agravaine. Son of King Lot and Morgause of Orkney and brother of Gawain, Gaheris and Gareth. Sided with Mordred in the plot to reveal the adultery between Lancelot and Guinevere.

Ambrosius Aurelianius. Historically "the Last of the Romans", he governed Britain in the last half of the fifth century and helped stem the tide of Saxon advance in the days immediately prior to Arthur. In Arthurian legend he is sometimes depicted as Arthur's uncle.

Arthur/Artorius/Artos. High-King of Britain, son of Uther Pendragon and Igraine, raised as foster-son of Ector of the Forest Sauvage and foster-brother of Sir Kay. Founded the Fellowship of the Round Table, married Guinevere. By his half-sister Morgause he fathered Mordred who later waged war against him resulting in the final battle at Camlann where both Arthur and Mordred died.

Aurelianius, see Ambrosius.

Balin. A knight from Northumberland who was imprisoned by King Arthur for killing the king's cousin. He also angered the king by beheading the Lady of the Lake. He became known as The Knight of the Two Swords.

Bedivere/Bedvir/Bedwyr. One of Arthur's earliest and most trusted knights who served him as his aide. It was he who restored Excalibur to the Lady of the Lake after Arthur's death.

Bors. Son of King Bors and cousin to Sir Lancelot. He was one of the three successful knights in the search of the Holy Grail.

Brewnor/Bruno le Noir. A particularly untidy and unkempt knight who was nicknamed "La Cote Mal-Taile" by Sir Kay.

Cai/Cei, see Kay.

Dagonet. King Arthur's jester who later proves himself a valiant knight.

Dinadan. A Knight of the Round Table noted for his wit and humour.

Drustan, see Tristan.

Ector de Maris. Cousin of Sir Lancelot and not to be confused with **Ector of the Forest Sauvage** who was Arthur's foster-father.

Elaine. There are three Elaines in the Arthurian cycle: **Elaine of Garlot** the half-sister to King Arthur; **Elaine de Astolat** a maiden who fell in love with Sir Lancelot; and **Elaine of Corbenic** daughter of King Pelles and by Lancelot the mother of Sir Galahad.

Ewen, see Owain.

Gaheris. Third son of King Lot and brother to Agravaine, Gareth and Gawain and half-brother of Mordred.

Galahad. Son of Sir Lancelot and Elaine of Corbenic and the purest of all the Knights of the Round Table. With Sir Bors and Sir Perceval, he was one of the successful Grail Knights. He was the only knight able to sit at the "Seige Perilous" seat of the Round Table.

Galahaut. A prince and enemy of King Arthur but later befriended by Sir Lancelot and arranged the first secret meeting between Lancelot and Guinevere.

Gareth. The youngest son of King Lot of Orkney and brother of Gawain, Gaheris and Agravaine. He first arrived anonymously at Camelot and was given the nickname "Beaumains" by Sir Kay owing to his fine hands.

Gawain/Gwalchmai. The eldest son of King Lot of Orkney and one of the strongest of the Knights of the Round Table. He features in the earliest legends of Arthur and appears in the Celtic texts as Gwalchmai, meaning the Hawk of May. He undertook the challenge of the Green Knight, Sir Bertilak and later married Dame Ragnell.

Geoffrey, see Jaufry.

Gorlas/Gorlois. Duke of Cornwall, husband of Igraine and father of Morgan le Fay, Morgause and Elaine of Garlot.

Griflet/Gryfflet, see Jaufry.

Guinevere/Gwenhywfar/Gwynhwfar. Daughter of Leode-grance, King of Cameliard and wife of King Arthur. Her adultery with Sir Lancelot causes the downfall of the Fellowship of the Round Table. She was condemned to death by Arthur but rescued by Lancelot and ended her days in a nunnery.

Gwalchmai, see Gawain.

Igraine/Igerna/Ygraine. Wife of Duke Gorlois of Cornwall and by him mother of Morgan le Fay, Morgause and Elaine. Seduced by Uther Pendragon and became mother of Arthur. Later married Uther.

Iseult/Isolde/Isolt/Yseult/Ysolt. Wife of King Mark of Cornwall but lover of her husband's nephew Tristan of Lyonesse.

Not to be confused with **Iseult** of Britanny whom Tristan later marries after his banishment from Cornwall.

Jaufry/Geoffrey/Griflet/Gryfflet. One of Arthur's earliest and youngest knights who is wounded by King Pellenore. He recovers and becomes the hero of his quest with Brunissende.

Kay/Kai/Cai/Cei/Quex. Son of Sir Ector and foster-brother of Arthur. He becomes the king's High Seneschal and is noted for his bad humour and sour temperament. In the earlier legends, Kay is an heroic knight, but in later versions he becomes Arthur's irascible steward.

Lamorack of Gaul. Son of King Pellinore and one of the strongest knights of the Round Table. He became the lover of Morgause after the death of King Lot and was killed by Gawain and his brothers.

Lancelot/Lancelet/Launcelot/Lancot. Son of King Ban and greatest of the knights of the Round Table. His love for Guinevere led to the downfall of the Fellowship of the Round Table. After the deaths of Arthur and Guinevere he became a hermit. His castle was called the Joyous Gard.

Leodegrance. King of Cameliard and father of Guinevere.

Linet, see Lynette.

Lot. King of Orkney who opposed Arthur for the crown of Britain. He was the husband of Arthur's half-sister Morgause and father of Gawain, Agravaine, Gaheris and Gareth. He was killed by King Pellinore and his sons.

Lynette/Linet/Lunet. Sister of Lady Lyonesse and Sir Gringamore of the Castle Perilous who led Sir Gareth on his first quest. Although she later falls in love with Gareth she is given in marriage to his brother Gaheris. In Celtic myth she is the mistress of the Lady of the Fountain.

Margawse, see Morgause.

Mark/Marc. King of Cornwall and husband of Iseult.

Marrok. A knight who through enchantment was turned into a wolf and could not return to human shape until he had regained his clothing.

Medraut, see Mordred.

Merlin/Merdyn/Myrddyn. Magician and adviser of King Arthur. He was the offspring of a girl and a demon of the air and was raised in a nunnery. His prophecies began in the last days of King Vortigern. He later raised Stonehenge. He put a glamour on Igraine so that she mistook Uther Pendragon for her husband Gorlois. Merlin became guardian to the young Arthur and later contrived the episode of the sword in the stone so that Arthur was recognised as the future king of England. He created the Round Table. He became enamoured of enchantress Niniane who imprisoned him in a cave.

Mordred/Medraut/Modred. The incestuous child of Arthur and his half-sister Morgause. He later attempted to seduce Guinevere and claimed the throne of Britain. He met in mortal combat with Arthur at Camlann.

Morgan le Fay/Morgana/Morgaine. Daughter of Gorlois and Igraine and half-sister of King Arthur. She was educated in the sorcerous arts and became Arthur's major enemy, forever seeking the downfall of the Round Table. By hiding the scabbard of Excalibur, which had previously protected Arthur, she rendered him mortal. She was the mother of Owain.

Morgause/Margawse. Daughter of Gorlois, sister of Morgan le Fay, wife of Lot of Orkney and mother by him of Gawain, Agravaine, Gaheris and Gareth. She was also the mother of Mordred by Arthur, her half-brother.

Nimue, see Niniane.

Niniane/Nimue/Nymia/Vivian/Vivayn. An enchantress who is perceived in a number of roles in the Arthurian legend. She is called the Lady of the Lake, the foster mother of Lancelot who gave Excalibur to Arthur. She also became the lover of Merlin whom she imprisoned in a cave.

Oisc/Aesc. Early king of Kent, son of the Teutonic invader Hngist, and early contemporary of Arthur. Reigned from 488–512.

Owain/Ewen/Uwaine/Yvain. Actual historical hero who, in Celtic and Arthurian legend, becomes the son of Morgan le Fay and King Urien, and later still the knight Sir Yvain.

Palomides/Palamides. A Saracen who becomes one of the greatest Knights of the Round Table. A suitor for Queen Iseult he later becomes involved in the ceaseless search for the Questing Beast.

Parsival, see Percivale.

Pelles. The King of the Grail Castle and possibly synonymous with the Fisher king. He was wounded by Sir Balin. He was also the grandfather of Sir Galahad and is sometimes named as the brother of King Pellinore.

Pellinore. King of the Isles and one of the mightiest of the Knights of the Round Table who, in an early episode, overpowered Arthur and would have killed him had he not been enchanted by Merlin. He was involved in the search for the Questing Beast. He was the father of Sir Lamorack and, in some versions, also of Sir Percivale. He killed King Lot and was in turn killed by Sir Gawain.

Percivale/Parsival/Parzival/Peredur. The knight most closely associated with quest for the Holy Grail. Early legends have him raised in the wilds of Wales, but later legends link him with King Pellinore.

Peredur, see Percivale.

Quex, see Kay.

Taliesin. A legendary bard and prophet who has become closely linked with Merlin.

Tristan/Tristram/Drustan. The son of King Meliodas of Lyonesse and nephew of Mark of Cornwall whose wife, Iseult, he fell in love with. Banished from Cornwall he entered King Arthur's court as one of the mightiest knights, until forced to flee to Brittany where he married another Iseult.

Uther Pendragon. King of Britain and father of Arthur by Igraine.

Uwaine, see Owain.

Vivian/Vivayn, see Niniane.

Vortigern. King of Britain whose reign precedes Ambrosius in the mid-fifth century. He invited Hengist to Britain to rid the land of Saxons, but Hengist in turn conquered Kent. Merlin first appears in Vortigern's reign.

Yseult, see Iseult.

Yvain, see Owain.

CHIEF DRAGON OF THE ISLAND
by Joy Chant

We start our journey through the Pendragon Chronicles with a survey of Arthur's life and deeds adapted freely from the History of Geoffrey of Monmouth by Joy Chant. It comes from her magnificently illustrated book The High Kings *(1983) which retells the lives of the early kings of Britain as first recorded by Geoffrey, and the life of Arthur forms the final chapter. Joy Chant (1945–), formerly a librarian, is best known for her fantasy trilogy set in the land of Vandarei:* Red Moon and Black Mountain *(1970),* The Grey Mane or Morning *(1977) and* When Voiha Wakes *(1983). She has also written a study of* Fantasy and Allegory in Literature for Children and Young People *(1971).*

O f all the Kings of the Island of the Mighty, three are foremost: Dunvallo the Lawgiver, Bran the Blessed, and Arthur the Soldier. These are the Three Pillars of the Island; and the greatest of them is Arthur.

His mother Igerna was sister to the High King Ambrosius. She was the loveliest of women, wooed by many, and won at last by Gorlas of Cornwall. For the length of a winter they were happy together, until on the eve of Beltain, Gorlas learned from a wise woman that if Igerna should ever bear a child, her husband would not live out the day of its birth.

From that moment Gorlas never lay with Igerna again, and when he was not in her company he kept her prisoned on the rock

10

of Tintagel with none but women about her. The neck of land to that stronghold was closed by a gate, and night and day a woman warrior was portress there so that none but Gorlas might enter.

There came a day that the High King Ambrosius Aurelianus was talking with his friend and counsellor Merdyn, and lamenting that there was no child of his house to be his heir. "It is not my fate have a wife," he said, "but I grieve that my sister Igerna is barren."

"Maybe she is not so," Merdyn soothed his Lord.

"Seven years she has been the wife of Gorlas, and she has not conceived."

"Yet do not despair, for I foretell that a son of Igerna shall be High King after you."

Ambrosius rejoiced, for there was never a foretelling of Merdyn that proved false. He was the wisest of men and of great powers; it was said of him that he no earthly father. He was the bard of Ambrosius, and he had is called one of the Three Foremost Bards of Britain; the others are Guidion son of Don, and Taliesin the bard of Arthur. By his great knowledge Merdyn found the truth of Igerna's barrenness, and he was angry with Gorlas. He left the court of Ambrosius for a while, and no man knew where he had gone. Nor has any man ever known all the deeds of Merdyn, nor all his journeyings.

Gorlas had a mistress, and one summer's eve he set out to visit her; but before he reached their tryst he came to a lake, and by it was a troop of fair and merry people of unearthly beauty. They called to him, laughing, and said, "Come with us, handsome brown-curled man, to our court within the lake."

They took him by the hand and led him below the water, and there was a hall fairer than any he had ever seen, full of light and music. In the chief place was a dark-haired woman of great beauty, who rose and coming to Gorlas kissed him and bade him take the place at her side. Presently she led him away to her own chamber, and that night he lay with her.

On that same night a little after sunset a man with the likeness of Gorlas came to Tintagel, and the portress admitted him. The man sought Igerna, and as soon as he was alone with her he said, "Beloved, at Beltain it is not good for lovers to lie apart!"

Igerna looked at him both astonished and angry. She replied coldly, "I marvel that you speak so to me! Seven years and a winter have I been your wife, and since this night seven years ago not one word of love have I had from you. You have caused me to be reproached for barrenness throughout Cornwall and shamed me in my own house. Seven times has

Beltain come, but not you to me. What miracle brings you tonight?"

He answered gently, "Alas, it was not my choice that you should lie down and not I at your side. A fate has been on me, that I might neither enjoy your love nor tell you of the reason for it; hard I have found it. But tonight I am freed of my bonds; therefore let us forget sorrow."

And he talked tenderly and persuasively to her, until Igerna forgot her anger; and because of his sweetness she remembered her love for Gorlas, and welcomed him to her. They passed the night of Beltain together in great joy; and that night Arthur was conceived.

But when the sun fell across their bed and they woke, the man rose up in his own form, and Igerna saw that he was not her husband. And though he was handsome with an unearthly beauty she covered her face and lamented her dishonour.

"There is no dishonour here," said the man, "for I am a King among my own people, and the child that shall be born of this night shall bring you more honour than ever belonged to a woman of Britain. And while you go with child none shall know of it, lest Gorlas seek to harm you; for his death is near when you bear your son, and that is why he has kept from you." Then he kissed her, saying, "Have no shame of our love, for you had no sin in it." And he departed as he had come.

Three times the time that is customary the child was in her womb, yet Gorlas was in the fortress with her when her time came, and she feared his knowledge of it. But in the same hour that the child first strove to be born there came a red-eared white stag to the gates of Tintagel; its calling was sweeter than any music, and when it shook its antlers brightness fell from them. Gorlas and his companions spilled from the fortress in such haste to hunt it they heeded nothing else, and the woman warrior went with them leaving the gate open. Then Igerna fled into the woods to bear her child there. But she came upon a hut where were three old women and they cried out, "In your belly is a gold-torqued prince!" and taking her in they tended her. The child was delivered without the pains of childbirth. The afterbirth they took and cast into a fire by the door.

Igerna bore a son, a boy strong and beautiful and bright as fire; when he came from the womb he raised a shout. The woman who received him first cried, "Here is a Dragon! He shall be the terror or Britain's foes!" Peering into the baby's face her sister said, "Here is the comfort of the weak, the protector of Britain!"

And the third prophesied, "Here is the King to surpass all earthly Kings, the glory of his people! His name shall be a joy and a comfort to the Britons so long as it is spoken." Then they gave the child to Igerna to nurse, and she was full of joy.

But Gorlas had returned to Tintagel and finding her gone he pursued her in great anger. When he found her in the hut with the child at her breast, his terror was as great as his rage: he snatched the baby from her and took him to the shore to drown him. Yet as he raised the boy in his hands to cast him in, fear of the deed came over him: so rather than kill with his own hands he took a little boat and set the child in it, and cast the boat out to sea.

The fire where the afterbirth had been cast had burned down, and among the ashes there was an egg; and out of the eggs broke a worm. The worm ate the shell of the egg and the ashes and embers of the fire, and it grew to the size of a lizard, then of a cat, then of a hound, then of a horse; then it spread its wings and rose into the air. The dragon sped down to the beach, and found Gorlas coming up from it. It swooped over him and enveloped him in its fiery poisonous breath, so that he smothered and scorched in it, and so died.

After that the dragon flew above Britain, and many saw it and cried out in wonder and fear. But Merdyn said to Ambrosius, "The child I foretold to you is born!" The High King went eagerly to his sister, and he found Igerna in distraction and the child gone, and Gorlas dead. In sorrow and bewilderment he took her to his own house, and although Merdyn bade them be hopeful they were full of grief. As for the dragon, it came to land in the mountains, and found a cave among rocks, secret from men; and there it lay down to sleep quietly.

The little boat was borne to shore in the lands of Cunomor King of Cornwall, and the child was brought to him. He was amazed to see his beauty and strength, marvelling that a child so young should come unharmed from the sea. He said to his wife, "What shall be done with him?"

His wife was a sister of Igerna through their father Andblaud; her name was Morvith, and she also had lately borne a son. She looked at the baby and instantly said, "My heart yearns over him; give him to me, and I shall nurse him with our son Custenhin."

They named the boy Arthur, and he was raised in the court of Cunomor until he was seven years old. At that time he was the leader of all the boys in the place, even those of twice his age. At four years old he could outrun grown lads and cast a spear, at five he could ride a warhorse and swim the fastest river, at six he could leap up to the roof crest and down again and ride at the mark. The King and Queen were often in fear for him because of his daring.

When Arthur was seven Cunomor said, "It is time this boy was fostered!" He took the boy with him when he next went to the High King's court. Ambrosius saw him there, at sport with the other boys, foremost among the best, and his heart stirred in him.

He said to Merdyn, "Whose son is the little bronze-haired lad? For I feel my heart drawn to him, as if he were my own kin."

"That is no wonder," replied Merdyn, "for he is the son of Igerna your sister!"

Ambrosius was amazed and Merdyn now revealed to him the story of the boy's birth. Then Ambrosius summoned Arthur and talked with him, and he was delighted at the alertness and courtesy of the boy, and by the understanding that he showed. When he heard that Cunomor was seeking a foster father for him the High King said, "How would it seem to you to remain here and have your fostering of me?"

"What should I learn here?" asked Arthur.

"To be a King."

"That would delight me!"

From that time Arthur was fostered in the court of Ambrosius, and when his birth was made known Igerna, now married again, hastened joyfully to see her son. The High King was not the only one to have a hand in his rearing. Part of the year Arthur passed with Cunomor and Morvith, another part in the household of Igerna's husband Rica Chief Elder of Cornwall. No man in the realm had such wealth as Rica, nor dispensed it with such an open hand. He fostered the sons of many noble men; Gai was Arthur's foster brother there. Merdyn taught Arthur all the lore of Britain, and other learning he had of Saint Illtud who was his cousin. But Ambrosius, his mighty uncle, taught him the skills of a warrior, and all that was needful for a King to know; and the boy's heart belonged to him above all others.

When Arthur was near to manhood the Saxons made war again in the east of the Island. Ambrosius gathered his warband in haste and rode out at the head of them. Arthur saw it as he was returning from hunting with Gai his foster brother and Custenhin his cousin. He said to Merdyn, "What news has come, to cause my uncle to lead out his warriors?"

"That the breed of Ronnwen are healed of the hurts he gave them, and rise again to plague us."

"By the dragon born with me," cried Arthur, "it is time I rode with him!"

Merdyn replied, "Indeed it is; for the victory of the Britons follows at your heels. But the weapons to arm you are not in this court."

"Where shall I find them then?"

"Come with me," said Merdyn.

He took Arthur into Cornwall, and to a lake; it was very fair, with a wood of oak and hazel on its shore and an island in the middle of it. Merdyn said, "There is the place you will find your weapons. Go now, and I will await you here."

Arthur went down into the wood, and a girl met him on the path. She was tall and slender, the nine braids of her black hair fastened with silver pins, with a garment of green silk and a crimson mantle over it. Her brow and arms were white as the blackthorn blossom, and when she smiled at Arthur her red lips disclosed teeth of pearl, and the beam of lovemaking shone in her bright eyes. Arthur dismounted from his horse to greet her, and the brightness of his eyes and his smile was like her own.

The maiden said, "Who you are I know, and why you come. You shall have what you ask; and I will give you counsel that might gain you more, if I might have the thing I ask."

"And what is that?"

"Your company this night, and your side against my side."

"By my friend's hand, it is no hardship to grant that!"

He went with the girl into her green bower; and that was his first knowledge of women. In the morning she said to him, "And now for my counsel. Upon that island you will find a rock, and behind it the way to the place you seek; but so much I was sent here to tell you. Here is my own word to you. The lord and lady of that place will arm you, and whatever spear they offer you, whatever shield and helmet and dagger, accept them; but refuse any sword they offer you until you see an old plain sword with hilts of brass and a sheath of pigskin to it. Take that; for that is Caledvolc. That sword would draw blood from the wind, it would divide the thought from the word. So long as Caledvolc, the hard falcon of battle, is in your hand, there shall be no warrior who can withstand you; and while its sheath is at your side there will be no hurt upon you. Go now; and return to me tonight."

"Every word I shall remember, but none so clear as that!" said Arthur. He took her in his arms and gave her many sweet kisses before he went across to the island. He found the rock and the door, he found the hall Gorlas had seen, and there was the lady of surpassing beauty who ruled in the place.

She said, "You are welcome here. Long have we waited for you, Dragon of the Island!"

Arthur answered, "A blessing on this place, and on the lady of his place. I thank you for your greeting, but as for the name you give me, I have yet to earn it. It is a poor warrior who lacks weapons."

"Those you shall have," said the lady.

Weapons were fetched and she armed him, setting a helmet on his head and a fine shield on his arm, a dagger in his belt and a spear in his hand. But when she fetched him a sword all inlaid with bright enamel, and an enamelled sheath to it, he said, "That is not the sword for me."

"Then you shall have another," she said, and a finer was fetched; but Arthur gave the same answer, and so he did to every one however splendid, until they fetched out an old sword with a dark blade and brass hilts to it, in a worn pigskin sheath. That he laid hold of, saying, "This is the sword for me!"

"There is a good eye for a sword!" said the lady. "You have that from your father."

Then the lord of the place came in and greeted Arthur smiling. He said, "I think you were taught that asking; but take the sword that was mine, as is fitting, and smite the enemies of Britain with it." A horse was brought in, all of white with glittering red ears, and a red-eared white dog as big as a calf, and the lord put the bridle of the horse and the leash of the dog into Arthur's hand. Also he gave him a mantle, saying "Here is one of the Treasures of the Island; for whoever wears this mantel sees everything and is seen of no one."

After that Arthur left the glorious hall, and on the shore of the lake Merdyn was waiting. When he saw Caledvolc in Arthur's hand he smiled, and said, "You are well armed indeed, if your father gave you his own sword!"

Arthur was surprised. "Was the lord there my father?"

"He was: the same who came to your mother in the form of Gorlas her husband. It was well done to get Caledvolc of him; I would not have thought it could be done, unless by help of the lady or of her daughter."

Remembering the lovely girl in the green bower, a great dread filled Arthur. Slowly he said, "I had counsel. Who is the maiden here?"

"Then there is less wonder, for that is your sister Morgen."

At that a great horror fell on Arthur, and when he saw the girl coming toward him he cried out, "No! No nearer! When I think of the sin we have shared, my heart is turned to ice!"

Morgen drew back angrily. "I see no sin," she said, "but great discourtesy! Go then! Break your tryst and lose the luck of it: for there is a price for your faithlessness. In might and glory no man shall equal you, and Britain shall never forget your fame; but this fate also is on you—that you shall never have the love of a woman, and never one to keep faith with you, and never peace in the arms of one, until you lie in my lap again!" Then she whirled away from them and went down into the lake.

Merdyn looked grave. "That were ill-fortune, indeed."

But Arthur raised his head and said, "How so? Are might and glory not mine, and a name to be remembered? It is time I sought them all; therefore tell me where I may find this battle!"

So mounting the red-eared white mare, and with the hound at his side, Arthur rode like the wind in pursuit of Ambrosius and his warband; and he found them, for the horse and the hound were two battle-smellers. The host of Ronnwen's people was great, and the Britons were hard pressed, until Arthur came. He went into battle as a reaper goes into a barley field; as a harsh wind comes to strip the orchard of its blossom, so was the descent of Arthur upon the Saxons. Back and forth he charged, Caledvolc a bloody scythe in his mighty arm, crushed bone and death beneath every hoofprint of the white mare, while the great hound hurled himself at any attacker who came from the rear. But soon none came—those that survived the battle-mad companions fled. Then on the ghastly battlefield Arthur and Ambrosius met, and dismounting from their horses they embraced.

Arthur said, "I have my weapons, Head of the Island."

The High King threw back his head and laughed aloud. "Dragon of the Britons, the word has spread!"

Thus was Arthur born of the gods, weaponed by them and blessed by them with glory and might and powers not human. But the fate put on him by his sister flawed his strength and followed him all his days.

The time came when Ambrosius died, and bitter was the grief of Arthur. But in a while he came to remember his heritage. At Easter Arthur was acclaimed High King of Britain and there was rejoicing throughout the Island that they had such a mighty man to lead them. For there never was a King to compare with Arthur.

His court in Camalod was of great splendour, and there bards

and warriors from all Britain gathered to him, men of art and
men of craft and noble ladies, and all found a generous welcome.
The laws were kept in Arthur's time; then the strong man dared
not oppress the weak, and there was no dissension among the
princes of the Island. Britain knew safety from the foreigner.
When Arthur rode to battle, gaily clad, with Caledvolc in his
hand his mare Leaping Silver under him and his dog Cabal at
his side, there was no withstanding him. In twelve great battles
he defeated the Saxons, and in the last of them at Mount Badon
he crushed them utterly. He was winter to his foes, but summer
to the Britons.

Many are the marvellous deeds of King Arthur; only a few are
told here, for the measure of his glory is well-told elsewhere. In
the first days of his kingship a giant called Ritto sent an insolent
message to him: "My cloak is trimmed with the beards of Kings,
and I would have the beard of the King of the Britons, if his cheek
could grow one!"
Arthur was incensed; with Gai his foster brother he sought the
giant, but he climbed the mountain to the mouth of the cavern
alone, and called mockingly, "Here is Arthur of the Britons; and
his beard also, if your razor is sharp enough to get it!"
Ritto rushed out, the beard-fringed cloak on him, and they
fought until Arthur was victorious. He came down the mountain with the cloak on his shoulder and the head of Ritto in his
hand. Gai raised a shout, but Arthur only said, "Speak softly of
the deed; it is not for my honour to kill a barber!"

The women of Britain smiled on Arthur, perfect in face and
form, with his hair like shining bronze and the blue-green iris
of each eye pleating about the pupil like the Cornish sea about
a rock. Many was the tryst he kept with a garland of sweet-
mouthed girls. Yet better to him than the love of women was
the comradeship of his friends.
Dearest of all to him were Gai and Bedvir. Gai the Tall had
been his foster brother in childhood. As a man in battle he was a
joyous host at Arthur's side: courage was his heart and laughter
his head. As for Bedvir, the Britons called him the Perfect Man.
Beautiful and fair-spoken was he, the swift eagle of war. Between
these two and Arthur was great love, and he did many deeds in
their company. But he did not set his desire on one girl more than
another, until one year at apple-harvest.
Riding alone he came upon a wood of wild apple trees, and he

was confounded, thinking it was an orchard of the Ever Young, because of the exceeding beauty of the maiden he saw there. She was straight and slender as a pear, though supple and graceful in her movements. Her unbraided hair was the colour of dark honey, and the sheen and ripple of it was like the sun passing over a field of barley; the eyes under her fine brows were the colour of violets, the red of the rose hip was her lip. There were no words to tell of her beauty; a summer day was in her face. She wore a tunic of saffron silk with a bright enamel belt, and she held up the skirt to gather apples in the lap of it, showing her slender ankles and delicate feet.

Arthur watched her, marvelling; the girl turned her head and saw him, but she did not speak, only looked at him smiling and then veiled her eyes with the lashes. At that, love for her filled every limb on him, so that he blushed red and sprang from his horse to go to her. But she slipped out of his sight, and though he sought he could not find her nor a sign of her passing. He cast about calling to her, and when he knew she was gone indeed anguish filled him; he felt there was no good in the world for him any more, if he could not see that slim perfect girl again and take her in his arms.

He returned with haste to Camalod and sought Merdyn. He said, "Wisest of men, here is a puzzle for you! Who is the woman I saw under the apple trees, with the bearing of a Queen and the aspect of a morning in May, her auburn hair brighter than any gold I ever saw?"

Merdyn answered, "You have seen Gueneva, daughter of the Giant Ogran."

"I must find her again," he declared, "for nothing will content me but to have her love."

Merdyn laughed, saying, "Are there not bright-eyed girls enough in Britain, that you must seek a tryst with a giant's daughter?"

"There is no woman in the world could content the man who had seen Gueneva!" said the King. "Moreover, it is not my arm about her waist only that I desire, but to make her my wife and Queen of the Island of the Mighty; for nothing less is fitting for her."

Merdyn was dismayed but still he used soft words. Gently he said, "Though the maiden is indeed lovelier than any now living, though she has the beauty of Eve and Helen, still the Chief Dragon of the Island must use wisdom in selecting a Queen. This lady is not the wife you should choose."

But Arthur answered hotly, "By the Dragon, I *have* chosen her! And if I do not have her I shall have none!"

"Even that would be better for you," Merdyn replied shortly.

Then a quarrel arose between the young King and his counsellor. Arthur would not yield. And Merdyn in his wisdom could not; nor would Merdyn tell Arthur where he should seek Ogran the Giant. He said only, "You will get no help from me in this matter; for by my counsel you will not seek this maiden."

"Then I will seek her against it, and find her despite you!" cried Arthur; and they parted in anger.

Arthur donned the mantle that the lord under the lake had given him, and went back to the wood apple trees. Three days he waited and when next saw Gueneva he followed her to her father's stronghold. They came to an old grey fortress hewn from the mountain, with nine gates into it and every one guarded by a giant. Now Arthur threw off his mantle, broke down each gate and slew every porter. He won at last to a vast hall where Ogran sat in darkness, and he a deeper darkness within the gigantic shadows.

Then a great rumble filled the chamber, and it was the voice of Ogran. "Who knocks so roughly, and why does he come?"

"Arthur of Britain, Chief Dragon of the Island, and he comes requesting that your daughter Gueneva shall be his wife, and Queen of the Island of the Mighty!"

"A bold asking! But a guest is not to be denied. Come here, Gueneva!"

Into the room came three young women, and they brought their own light with them. Arthur caught his breath at sight of them for each was as like to the others as one drop of water is to another.

With malicious politeness Ogran said, "There are my three daughters, my three Guenevas. Which is the one you love? Choose now; but if you choose wrong, I shall have your head!"

Arthur gazed at the three Guenevas before him, and strove to see a difference, so that he might choose the only true soul he loved among the three. Yet he could not choose. He said to himself, "By my head, this is a harder trial than battle." Then Ogran laughed, and waved the girls away and they walked towards the door; and as the last of the three passed Arthur, he caught from her swinging skirt the scent of apples. Triumph filled him; he seized her hand and cried, "Here is the bride of my choice!"

The girl laughed and her sisters vanished away. But Ogran said, "A bad choice; your death and mine is in it. Yet take her since you choose her, and keep her if you can!" As he spoke he rose up and struck at Arthur out of the darkness. But Arthur cast his mantle about himself and Gueneva and drew Caledvolc and cut off the giant's head.

Then he fled with Gueneva, and she came gladly. When they were in the sun she cast her arms about his neck and kissed him, and said, "I feared the man did not live who could win me from my father!"

Arthur reassured her, "So long as I have Caledvolc in my hand, even a giant cannot withstand me."

So he took her to Camalod, and all his court marvelled at her great beauty. Only Merdyn did not rejoice. He said to Arthur, "Now you have what you have chosen. Well is she named Fair Enchantment; for no man now living shall see her equal. Yet she is one to cause the breaking of spears and therefore if you will heed me, you will not make her your wife."

"In this I will not heed you," declared the King.

Merdyn rose and said, "I have never prophesied falsely, nor advised you ill; yet since you prefer a girl's kisses to my counsel I will burden you with no more of it."

Arthur was grieved, yet in those first days it was hard for him to repent of what parted them, so joyous his victory over the giant, so sweet the company of Gueneva and the delight he found in her arms.

In Arthur's time Huarwor the hungry man came as a plague on the Island; he had never found a table that could feed him, yet at Arthur's court he was satisfied. Also there came Paluc Cat, that ate nine score warriors at a meal, until Arthur killed it; he covered his shield with its hide and its hairs gave spear-points for a host.

But of all his deeds, the boldest was the raid he made upon the Land of Promise, to capture the Cauldron of Plenty. He wished to win that Cauldron to be a Treasure of the Island in the Cauldron of Rebirth that Bran had given to Ireland. For Arthur felt a rivalry between himself and Bran.

Yet that venture was not much more fortunate than the hosting of Bran into Ireland. For they sailed to the shores of the Land of Youth, Arthur in his ship Pridwen and other ships behind; and Arthur went alone to seek the Cauldron and found it. But when he laid hold of it he found he could not so much as tilt its rim; and when he would have left it, he found his hands stuck fast to it. There he was held until the people of that place came to release him, and they freed him from the Cauldron only to bind him in Oeth and Anoeth. Manadan, great in craft, had built that prison; it is made all of human bones mortared together, and within it is a labyrinth of little cells. Its name means, Difficult and Very Difficult; Wonderful and Very Wonderful; Strange and Very Strange.

Three nights and three days Arthur lay there, and the Prison of Bone had held him forever, had there been lesser men in his company. But Custenhin his cousin and Bedvir found him, and getting on the roof of Oeth and Anoeth they dug down until they broke open the House of Bones and disclosed all its prisoners. They were curled like young bees in the cells of a hive. Arthur came out unhurt, but he did not speak for a night and a day; then he wept like a child, and after was whole again. But the host of the Otherworld fell upon them, and when that host was driven back, only six men remained to escape with Arthur in his ship. Seven times the fullness of Pridwen was the host that sailed with Arthur; seven men only returned. Yet though the victory was costly, it went to the Britons; and no other victory was ever gained by mortals in battle by the Ever Young.

It was after that raid that Arthur dug up the Head of Bran from its place of concealment in London. That is one of the Three Unhappy Disclosures, when the head of Bran the Blessed was revealed, and no more set its face against the foreign people. If King Arthur had not shunned a sharer in his glory, but had joined with his strength the strength of Bran, then surely the Island would have been a possession of the Britons to the end. But Arthur scorned the idea that Britain needed any defence but his; and he did not wish that the protection of the Marvellous Head should lessen the praise of his valour.

Indeed, as King and warrior Arthur was triumphant, though he also found the other fate Morgen foretold. There was never a woman faithful to him, but every path he trod was trodden by others. Although Gueneva his Queen was never matched for grace and beauty, it was not long he was happy at her side; and as for her, her eye and smile were readier for any man than for him: a cold bed he found with her. After he fetched her back from the City of Glass, where Melwas King of the Summer Country had taken her, Arthur never lay with her again. He had many mistresses, and these are the chief of them: Garwen, daughter of Henin the Old; Guil daughter of Gendaut; and Indeg, by whom he was the father of Lachu the glorious hero. Each was famed for beauty, but he did not find a steadfast love among them. Thus the curse of Morgen worked against Arthur all his life, nor was this worst of the tragedy attending their union.

A youth came to Camalod, and asked a place among those who learned war there; and when his lineage was told, he was the son of Arthur that Morgen bore him, and his name was Amros. He was admired of all; not one of the youths or boys of Camalod surpassed him, not even Arthur's son Lachu of marvellous promise.

Arthur made the boy welcome and called him his son before the court; but when the youth declared his parentage the heart of the High King grew sick. For learning Amros was unequalled, also for eloquence; yet Arthur took no delight in him or his fine spirit, nor was he pleased by the lad's comeliness; the day he did not see Amros was a good day to him.

When the day came for the boy to be a warrior he proved himself his father's son in his deeds, yet still the King could not rejoice in it. And the end of it was bitter, the greatest sin of Arthur's life. He was riding alone with his son in the lands about Severn, and after their meal Amros sang to his father, and when the song was done he looked at him laughing; and his eyes and smile were like another Arthur had seen, so that he was filled with love and horror, and rose up and killed Amros with his own hands.

When he saw the young man lifeless on the ground, all the love Arthur had never felt for him came upon him at once; he was overwhelmed with grief and shame. He cried aloud, "Alas, Amros, for my fault and not your own I blamed you! Woe that I ever saw your mother, or that ever she sent you to me. You were the flower of the young men of the Island, young hawk of battle; no foe could overcome you. If the loss of Caledvolc would give back your life, if my right hand would buy it, I would part with them!"

Then he made Amros tomb by his own labour, and buried him where he fell. That tomb is called Licat Amros, and it has this peculiarity, that no one has ever been able to find the length of it, for it varies each time it is measured. And out of the grave of Amros grew a hazel; whoever ate of those nuts was gifted with marvellous knowledge. Such was the death of Arthur's son, and not until his last days did Arthur know grief like his grief for the killing of Amros.

There was a young man even dearer to Arthur than Amros, dearer even than Lachu. He was Modrat, eldest son of Cordav Chief Officer of Britain, whose task it was to watch over the Island whenever the King was absent. Modrat and his brothers

Kideboc and Idaug were in fosterage with Arthur, and Arthur loved him above all save Gai and Bedvir. When Modrat became a man he was as great in judgment as in battle, and Arthur endowed him with the office of Cordav his father; and when he crossed with his companions into Ireland to hunt the Boar Troit, he left Modrat to rule Britain in his place.

Modrat protested, "I would rather go with you."

"No," say Arthur "for there is no other to whom I would give the care of Britain."

Then he went in pursuit of Troit. That pig was a King who for his wickedness had been changed into the form of a boar, and his evil sons into his brood of piglings. It was a hard task to hunt him. He laid waste one of the five provinces of Ireland, and when the host of Britain came there and fought him he crossed into the Island of the Mighty and made havoc there. Arthur and his host pursued him the length and breath of Britain, and many noble men died in that chase. At last they killed all his young, but Arthur held to the trail of Troit, and in Cambria they saw the boar going fast towards Severn.

The King said to Gai and Bedvir and the men with him, "Too many men of mine have died to this boar and his vicious brood. By the fame of their valour I swear, while I live he will not go into Cornwall, but I will close with him, life for life!"

He struck heels into Leaping Silver, and the matchless horse sprang forward, and Cabal too. If it had been hard to keep Troit in sight it was harder yet to overtake him, and would not have been possible for any but Arthur's mare of surpassing leap. From Penlimon they sighted the boar, and then Leaping Silver made a day's journey at a bound, for she leapt from the top of Penlimon and did not come to ground again until the Black Mountains, although near Buelt she struck one hoof upon a stone to lengthen her leap. The stone bears the print of her hoof to this day. They caught Troit beyond Wye, near the banks of Severn.

There Arthur held him at bay for a day, until Cabal reached him. Then Cabal rushed in on Troit, and Arthur too, and Troit fought them both. All three plunged into Severn, and savage was the fight that followed. The hound hung on Troit's throat, while the King thrust his spear again and again into the heaving body, and still the beast fought; at last he slashed Cabal with his tusks and gave the great hound his death wound.

Then Arthur seized the boar's feet and rolled him over in the water, and held him there. That was a struggle like Gogmagog's with Corineus. Arthur nearly lost his life, and he did lose the sheath of Caledvolc, for it was filled with water and carried away by the river. But Arthur held Troit until the monstrous boar was drowned. Then he dragged the creature to the shore, and Gai and Bedvir were waiting there. Arthur took Caledvolc and cut off Troit's head and Gai and Bedvir loose the jaws of Cabal, in death still embedded in the torn body. Then the three of them leaned on their spears about the carcass, and looked at each other, spent and weary.

"Friends," said Arthur, "we grow old. From now on let us leave adventures to the young men."

Then he knelt by the body of the hound and stayed there for a space cradling the great head in his lap. And presently his companions had the grave ready. He laid Cabal in the earth and raise a cairn over him, and on top of the cairn he put the stone with Leaping Silver's hoofprint on it. It is called Cairn Cabal still. Then Arthur went over into Cornwall to rest at his court of Celliwic.

But in Camalod a great woe had begun for Britain, for love had sprung up between Gueneva the Queen and Modrat, Chief Officer, so strong that they did not know how to defend themselves against it. Gueneva's heart was broken with the love of the young man, and she dreaded the return of Arthur; yet neither spoke any word to the other. For Modrat was a man of flawless honour, a great champion and steadfast in his love for Arthur, and from regard for that Gueneva too kept silent; until they had word that Troit was slain and the King would soon return. Then Gueneva was filled with despair.

She said to Modrat, "I never loved a man until now, but now love has destroyed me. By the truth that is in your tongue I bid you tell me, whether or not you love me!"

He answered sadly, "Alas, for the day the King refused to take me into Ireland! This is an evil word you compel from me, that I do love you; and alas that I must speak it. Yet you have no need of my love, with the Dragon of the Island for your husband; nor may I betray him who is my King and my foster father besides. Therefore I will leave Camalod, and the company of heroes here, and King Arthur, and the sight of you."

Gueneva cried, "Then I put bonds on you, that wherever you go you take me with you! If I were given the choice of the Dragon and you, I would choose you. There is no love nor the dealings of man and wife between me and Arthur. By my two sisters I swear, I do not desire his return nor my place as Queen of the Island, only your voice in my ears and your arm under my head at night!"

Then Modrat kissed her; and after he had done so she said,
Your duty to Arthur you know best, but I have a claim also.
Therefore I bid you to come to me tonight, and never again unless
you wish it."

So Modrat went to her that night, and they lay together; and
what had been once must be again. From that time they were
lovers, as well when Arthur returned as before. Gueneva was
joyful in those days, but the heart of Modrat burned him.

After the killing of Troit no more great adventures came to
Arthur. There were no more monsters nor giants in the Island,
and the Saxons were utterly subdued. The High King began to
weary of board-game and feasting, of hunting and remembering
old deeds; and then word came to Britain that the rule of Rome
had fallen to unworthy men.

"By my head," said Arthur, "shame to me if I do not deliver the
greatest city of the world from those men!" And he resolved that
he would rule there himself.

So he gathered an army and entrusted the rule of the Island
of the Mighty again to Modrat, Chief Officer of Britain; neither
did Modrat protest at it. But the night before Arthur's departure
Gueneva went secretly to his chamber; and she took Caledvolc,
and left in its place a sword made in its likeness. And Caledvolc
she hid.

Then Arthur departed with great splendour into Gaul. There
the Gauls and the Britons of Armorica gathered to him, and they
fought against the Franks and won many victories; and though it
was not Caledvolc in Arthur's hand he did not know it, because
there was still none who could withstand him.

Gueneva was left at Celliwic, and Modrat was at Camalod.
He said to himself, "This deed I shall do now shall leave me no
honour so long as my name lives; but the Queen will be preserved
from blame by it."

He gathered his own warband and led them to Celliwic,
and there he dragged Gueneva from her chair and struck her
a blow, and carried her off. Then the people of the court rose up
in a roar, and there was fierce fighting between them and the
warriors with Modrat, and when Modrat left the place there was
great ruin in Celliwic. That was the first of the Three Costly
Ravagings of this Island; the second was the one Arthur made
in return.

Modrat said to his love, "For that battle and the men who died
in it, Arthur will not forgive me."

Guevena answered him, "You need not seek his forgiveness

while you have this at your side!" And she gave him Caledvolc that she had stolen.

Messengers left Britain, and came to Arthur with all speed. When he had heard all their tale it was hard to know if his grief or his rage was the greater. The host of Arthur returned swiftly to the Island of the Mighty, and Modrat sent a force to resist them. Then there was killing between the men of Britain, which had not been so since Vortigern died; bitter was the day. Arthur's nephew Gualcmai, his sister's son, was slain in that battle, and where the ninth wave breaks on the shore is his grave.

At his death Arthur's fury increased. He cried out, "The blow that Modrat gave my Queen was a harmful blow for Britain, as harmful as the blow Matholug the Irishman gave Branwen!"

Then he went to Modrat's house and utterly destroyed it; when he left there was nothing to show where it had stood, and neither man nor beast living there. And he killed Kideboc, who had defended the fortress, with his own hands, although the man was his foster son.

At news of his brother's death Modrat was roused to fierce enmity against Arthur; he did not make war with half a heart after that. He raised a host, and his warriors fought the warriors of Arthur in many places. The Kings and princes and chieftains of Britain were divided, some for one and some for the other, and some only to be free of any High King. Britons killed Britons, law was forgotten, and when he saw it Arthur cried aloud in pain.

After that first battle he held aloof from the strife, and in a battle in the North his son Lachu begged for the leadership of the host. Arthur said, "I have lost Anros and Gualcmai and Modrat; I would keep you at my side." But he yielded to the young man at last, and gave him the sword from his own side to bear in the battle. Then Lachu rode before the battle-horsemen; renowned in war was he, the raven of a host. But that day he fell, and Arthur's son was slain before his eyes. His heart nearly broke with bewilderment.

When they fetched the young man's body to him Arthur said, "If Lachu could be slain, it could not be with Caledvolc in his hand!" He looked at the sword closely, and perceived that it was not his own; and he understood the treachery of Gueneva. So died Lachu, the best son of great Arthur, and they buried him on the hillside.

Arthur rode away mourning. "Cabal is dead, and the girl I won from the giant betrays me, and a sword not Caledvolc is in my hand without my knowledge; I grow old."

Nor was his grief at an end, for in the next battle Guidaug, son of Menester, slew Gai. Terrible was the grief of Arthur for his foster brother, and the grief of Bedvir also. Arthur pursued Guidaug and killed him, and he was roused to a deadly wrath; he gathered all his hosts, to seek Modrat himself and compel him to battle.

Twice they came up with Modrat's host, and twice the host gave way before Arthur and would not do battle. Relentlessly the Dragon of the Island pursued them, and the third time, in the west, he penned Modrat and his host in a crooked valley from which there was no escape except by battle. The name of the place was Camlann.

In the night before the battle Modrat did not sleep, oppressed with sorrow and shame. Nor did Arthur rest; he paced with Bedvir at his side, and gazed at the host encamped opposite his own. And weariness came on him, the rage and hatred in him burned low, and he remembered how he had taught Modrat, how he had watched his growing and loved him. He thought of Britain, her strength wasted, laid open to her foes, and he said to Bedvir, "Gai is dead, and Lachu, with other companions of ours, and countless men of the Island of the Mighty. If war was to end now, my life would not see this harm made good. And tomorrow worse will be done."

Bedvir said, "It is a great strife for a wanton woman; yet so did Troy fall."

"I have forgotten every woman I ever loved. What is Gueneva to me, or the place where she makes her pillow, if Britain can be spared?"

He called Idaug, the third of Cordav's sons, and said, "Of three brothers, one is faithful. Will you go to your brother Modrat and give him offers of peace from me?" Idaug consented, and Arthur gave his messages for Modrat. But as he went towards his brother's host Idaug remembered Kideboc: and his heart was roused against both the enemies. So he gave Modrat not Arthur's message, but one full of insults.

"I have deserved them all," said Modrat. Sadness filled him, and he gave Idaug a courteous reply to Arthur.

Yet Idaug returning thought, "It is easy for him to forget our brother's death; and why not, since he was the cause of it? But it is hard for me." And he changed the message again, petending that Modrat had taunted Arthur with not daring to fight while another wielded Caledvolc.

Arthur's face darkened at that, and he turned away. But pres ently he said to Bedvir, "What is an insult to me, against such danger to Britain?" And he sent for Idaug again. A second time he agitator went between them, and from each received a gentle message, and to each delivered a harsh one.

"It is not for my honour to do more!" cried Arthur. Yet when the dawn wind stirred he said, "With day comes the death of Britain. Let Idaug try once more."

So again he sent a fair offer to Modrat, and again Idaug altered it. And this time he said to Modrat, "He taunts you, that you shrink from battle like a coward; and he marvels that you would make peace with the man who killed your brother. And so do I!" Then anger blazed up in Modrat, and he drew his sword. He cried, "Kideboc will be avenged before sunset!"

Idaug galloped back along the valley, and this time there was no need of a message, for the charge came behind him.

"There is no making peace with this man," said Arthur to Bedvir. "Therefore let us give thanks for all the times that are gone, and end like warriors!"

So began the battle of Camlann, the most grievous that ever befell the Island of the Mighty. All day it raged in that valley, and the din of it was heard far off, while the terror of it was felt throughout the land; in all Britain there was not a face that smiled that day. Terrible was the slaughter; ravens waded in blood there. Custenhin died that day, and Caranguen son of Gai, and many other gold-torqued lords of battle; a hundred thousand men of the Island fell there. Those who died before that day were fortunate; the last days of the world will show nothing more fearful than that battle, when the glory and the safety of Britain were cast for the sake of a faithless woman, and by the wiles of a contentious man. Such was Camlann, where Arthur and Modrat fell.

Sunset came, and of Arthur's host eight men only were living; and of Modrat's, he alone remained, but he had Caledvolc in his hand. The King's companions gathered to him, and Modrat yelled defiance at him.

"Sheathe your swords," commanded Arthur, "for he is mine."

He took Rongomiad in his hand and ran at Modrat, and the keen spear pierced him through, giving him his death wound. But Modrat struck at the shaft and sheared it through, and with the spear in him he hurled himself on Arthur, and wounded him with Caledvolc. Arthur grappled with him, and wrested the sword from his hand; then Modrat fell dead, and Arthur slid down beside him.

Seven men were left alive, and Arthur; but Arthur had a mortal wound. His few comrades gathered about him weeping, and raised him up to carry him from the field, for Leaping Silver too was dead. Arthur said, "Not far away there is a lake with an island in the midst of it; carry me there."

So they did as he asked, though it cost them hard pains, for there was not a man without a wound. They found the lake, dark and broad, and far across it an island, and on the shore of it they set the High King down. He opened his eyes and smiled at them. These were the men who were with him at the end: Bedvir and his son Ambren, the bards Taliesin and Morvran, Petroc Splintered Spear who never took up arms again but became a saint, Idaug the provoker of battle who was distracted with grief and did penance for his deed all his life after, and Cador son of Custenhin.

Arthur said, "Such Kingship as there is in Britain, let Cador have it."

Then in the twilight a boat came over the water, and in it sat a woman of surpassing beauty, and two maidens attending on her. The boat came to shore, and the woman came out of it to Arthur, and kissed his brow. She said, "Alas, my brother; why have you kept so long from me?" After that she examined his wound. "There may be help from this," she said, "but not in Britain."

She went back into the boat, and her maidens lifted Arthur lightly into it, and he laid his head on the lady's lap. His companions began to weep, but Arthur said, "Be comforted. I go to Avalon to be healed of my wound; but when my strength is restored, I will return. Let Britain watch for me!"

So Bedvir put Caledvolc in the King's hand, and the boat turned from shore and went away to the Palace of Apples, while the seven men stood watching. All wept, save Bedvir; and his heart was broken beyond tears. Thus did the King Arthur pass from mortal knowledge; nor since that day has any man seen him.

Some say he died in Avalon; others, that in the Holy Island none can die, and all wounds heal in time. No one has ever seen his grave. Who knows the truth? Maybe he sleeps, or rests in the Palace of Apples. Maybe he feasts there, with his heroes about him, awaiting the hour of Britain's need, when the Dragon shall be roused from slumber, and Arthur again shall be King.

And they told the stories of Arthur in all the realms of the Britons, from Kernow to Manau Gododdin; to the exiles in Armorica, and to Princes of Cymru. Owain ap Urien heard them, sitting with his Ravens about the campfire, and the men of Catraeth before they rode to battle. They were sung by bards in Gwynedd and Dyfed, in Elfed and Rheged and Powys.

But not in the Kingdom of Britain. For the tale of the Island of the Mighty was ended, and there was no such realm anymore.

THE DRAGON'S BOY
by Jane Yolen

Those who have seen the Walt Disney film The
Sword in the Stone, *or read the T.H. White
story on which it was based, will have one particular view of Arthur's youth. Here is another,
in which you will be interested if you have
ever wondered how Arthur and Merlin first
met. It comes from a collection of stories by
Jane Yolen called* Merlin's Booke *(1986) which
draws many pictures of Merlin throughout his
shadowy life and career. Jane Yolen (1939–)
is an extremely prolific writer with over a hundred books to her credit, the majority written
for young children. She also teaches courses in
children's literature.*

It was on a day in early spring with the clouds scudding across
a gray sky, that the boy found the cave. He had been chasing
after Lord Ector's brachet hound, the one who always slipped
her chain to go after hare. She had slipped him as well, leaving
him lost in the boggy wasteland north of the castle walls. He
had crossed and recrossed a small, meandering stream following
her, wading thigh-deep in water that—he was painfully aware
of it—would only come up to the other boys' knees. The reminder
of his height only made him crankier.

The sun was high, his stomach empty, and the brachet had
quit baying an hour earlier. She was no doubt back at the kennel
yard, slopping up her food. But she was his responsibility, and he
ad to stay out until he was sure. Besides, he was lost. Well, not

exactly lost but *bothered* a bit, which was a phrase he had picked up from the master of hounds, a whey-colored man for all that he was out of doors most of the day.

The boy looked around for a place to get out of the noon sun, for the low, hummocky swamp with its brown pools and quaking mosses offered little shelter. And then he saw a small tor mounding up over the bog. He decided to climb it a bit to see if he could find a place where he might shelter, maybe even survey the land. He'd never been quite this far from the castle on his own before and certainly had never come out into the northern fens where the peat-hags reigned, and he needed time to think about the way home. And the brachet. If the mound had been higher, he wouldn't have attempted it. The High Tor, the really large mound northwest of the manor, had somewhat of an evil reputation. But this hillock was hardly that. He needed to get his bearings and sight the castle walls or at least a tower.

He was halfway up the tor when he saw the cave.

It was only an unprepossessing black hole in the rock, as round as if it had been carved and then smoothed by a master hand. He stepped in, being careful of the long, spear-like, hanging rocks, and let his eyes get used to the dark. Only then did he hear the breathing. It was not very loud, but it was steady and rumbling, with an occasional *pop!* that served as punctuation.

He held his breath and began to back out of the cave, hit his head on something that rang in twenty different tones, and said a minor curse under his breath.

"Staaaaaaaaaay," came a low command.

He stopped. And so, for a stuttering moment, did his heart.

"Whooooooooooo are you?" It was less an echo bouncing off cave walls than an elongated sigh.

The boy bit his lip and answered in a voice that broke several times in odd places. "I am nobody. Just Artos. A fosterling from the castle." Then he added hastily, "Sir."

A low rumbling sound, more like a snore than a sentence, was all that was returned to him. It was that homey sound which freed him of his terror long enough to ask, "And who are you?" He hesitated. "Sir."

Something creaked. There was a strange clanking. Then the voice, augmented almost tenfold, boomed at him, "I am the Great Riddler. I am the Master of Wisdoms. I am the Word and I am the Light. I Was and Am and Will Be."

Artos nearly fainted from the noise. He put his right hand before him as if to hold back the sound. When the echoes had ended, he said in a quiet little voice, "Are you a hermit, sir? An anchorite? Are you a Druid? A penitent knight?"

The great whisper that answered him came in a rush of wind. "I am the Dragon."

"Oh," said Artos.

"Is that all you can say?" asked the dragon. "I tell you I am the Dragon and all you can answer is *oh?*"

The boy was silent.

The great breathy voice sighed. "Sit down, boy. It has been a long time since I have had company in my cave. A long time and a lonely time."

"But. . .but. . .but." It was not a good beginning.

"No *buts*," said the dragon.

"But. . ." Artos began again, needing greatly to uphold his end of the conversation.

"Shush, boy, and listen. I will pay for your visit."

The boy sat. It was not greed that stayed him. Rather, he was comforted by the thought that he was not to be eaten.

"So, Artos, how would you like your payment? In gold, in jewels, or in wisdom?"

A sudden flame from the center of the cave lit up the interior and, for the first time, Artos could see that there were jewels scattered about the floor as thick as pebbles. But dragons were known to be great games players. Cunning, like an old habit, claimed the boy. Like most small people, he had a genius for escape. "Wisdom, sir," he said.

Another bright flame spouted from the cave center. "An excellent choice," said the dragon. "I've been needing a boy just your age to pass my wisdom on to. So listen well."

Artos did not move and hoped that the dragon would see by his attitude that he was listening.

"My word of wisdom for the day is this: Old dragons, like old thorns, can still prick. And I am a very old dragon. Take care."

"Yes, sir," said Artos, thinking but not saying that that was a bit of wit often spoken on the streets of the village nestled inside the castle walls. But the warning by the villagers was of priests and thorns, not dragons. Aloud he said, "I will remember. Sir."

"Go now," said the dragon. "And as a reward for being such a good listener, you may take that small jewel. There." The strange clanking that Artos had heard before accompanied the extension of a gigantic foot with four enormous toes, three in the front and one in the back. It scrabbled along the cave floor, then stopped not far from Artos. Then the nail from the center toe extended peculiarly and tapped on a red jewel the size of a leek bulb.

Artos moved cautiously toward the jewel and the claw. Hesitating a moment, he suddenly leaned over and grabbed up the jewel. Then he scuttered back to the cave entrance.

"I will expect you tomorrow," said the dragon. "You will come during your time off."

"How did you know I had time off?" asked Artos.

"When you have become as wise as a dragon, you will know these things."

Artos sighed.

"There is a quick path from the back bridge. Discover it. And you will bring me stew. With *meat!*" The nail was suddenly sheathed and, quite rapidly, the foot was withdrawn into the dark center of the cave.

"To—tomorrow," promised the boy, not meaning a word of it.

The next morning at the smithy, caught in the middle of a quarrel between Old Linn the apothecary and Magnus Pieter the swordmaker, Artos was reminded of his promise. He had not forgotten the dragon—indeed the memory of the great clanking scales, the giant claw, the shaft of searing breath, the horrendous whisper had haunted his dreams. But he had quite conveniently forgotten his promise, or shunted it aside, or buried it behind layers of caution, until the argument had broken out.

"But there is never any *meat* in my gravy," whined Old Linn.

"Nor any meat in your manner," replied the brawny smith. "Nor were you mete for battle." The smith rather fancied himself a wordsman as well as a swordsman. And until Old Linn had had a fit, falling face first into his soup in the middle of entertaining the visiting High King, the smith had been spitted regularly by Old Linn's quick tongue. Now Linn was too slow for such ragging and he never told tales after meals anymore. It was said he had lost the heart for it after his teeth had left prints on the table. But he was kept on at the castle because Lord Ector had a soft heart and a long memory. And because—so backstair gossip had it—Linn had a cupboard full of strange herbs locked up behind doors covered with deep carved runes.

Artos, who had been at the smithy to try and purchase a sword with his red jewel, was caught with his bargaining only just begun. He had not even had time to show the gem to Magnus Pieter when Old Linn had shambled in and, without any prelude, started his whining litany. His complaints were always laid at the

smith's door. No one else in the castle was as old as the pair
of them. They were best of friends by their long and rancorous
association.

"My straw is ne'er changed but once a se'nnight," Linn complained. "My slops are ne'er emptied. I am given the dregs of the
wine to drink. And now I must sit, if I am to be welcomed at all,
well below the salt."

The smith smiled and returned to tapping on his piece of steel.
He had stopped when Artos had begun his inquiries. In time to
the beat of the hammer, he said, "But you have straw, though you
no longer earn it. And a pot for your slops, which you can empty
yourself. You have wine, even though you ne'er pay for it. And
even below the salt, there is gravy in your bowl."

That was when Old Linn had whined piteously, "But there is
never any *meat* in my gravy."

It was the word *meat* and Magnus Pieter's seven or eight vari-
ations on it, that rung like a knell in Artos' head. For *meat* had
been the dragon's final word.

He slunk off without even the promise of a sword, that shining
piece of steel that might make him an equal in the eyes of the other
boys, the gem still burning brightly in his tightly clenched hand.

He brought a small pot of gravy with three pieces of meat with
him. Strolling casually out the back gate as if he had all the time
in the world, nodding slightly at the guards over the portcullis,
Artos could feel his heartbeat quicken. He had walked rather
more quickly over the moat bridge, glancing at the gray-green
water where the old moat tortoise lazed atop the rusted crown
of a battle helm. Once he was across, he began to run.

It was difficult not to spill the stew, but he managed. The path
was a worn thread through a wilderness of peat-mosses and tangled brush. He even clambered over two rock outcroppings in
the path that were studded with stones that looked rather like
lumps of meat themselves. And actually climbing over the rocks
was easier than wheedling the pot of stew had been. He only had
it because Mag the scullery was sweet on him and he had allowed
her to kiss him full on the lips. She hadn't noticed how he had held
his breath, hoping to avoid the stink of her garlic, and closed his
eyes not to see her bristly mustache. And she sighed so much after
the kiss she hadn't had time to ask what he needed the stew for.
But what if the dragon wanted gravy every day and he had to give
Mag more kisses. It didn't bear thinking about, so Artos thought
instead about the path. The dragon had been right. There was

a quicker route back to the mount. Its only disadvantages were the two large rocks and the old thorny briar bushes. But they, at least, were safer than the peat pools which held bones enough way far down.

He got to the cave rather quicker than he had bargained. Breathless, he squinted into the dark hole. This time he heard no heavy dragon breathing.

"Maybe," he said aloud to himself, his own voice lending him badly needed courage, "there's no one home. So I can just leave the gravy—and go."

"Staaaaaaaaay," came the sudden rumbling.

Artos almost dropped the pot.

"I have the gravy," he shouted quickly. He hadn't meant to be so loud, but fear always made him either too quiet or too loud. He was never sure which it was to be.

"Then give it meeeeeeeee," said the voice, followed by the clanking as the great claw extended halfway into the cave.

Artos could tell it was the foot by its long shadow. This time there was no stream fire, only a hazy smoldering light from the back of the cave. Feeling a little braver then, he said, "I shall need to take the pot back with me. Sir."

"You shall take a bit of wisdom instead," came the voice.

Artos wondered if it would make him wise enough to avoid Mag's sweaty embrace. Somehow he doubted it.

"Tomorrow you shall have the pot. When you bring me more."

"*More?*" This time Artos' voice squeaked.

"Mooooooore," said the dragon. "With meat!" The nail extended, just as it had the day before, and caught under the pot handle. There was a horrible screeching as the pot was lifted several inches into the air, then slowly withdrawn into the recesses of the cave. There were strange scrabbling noises as if the dragon were sorting through its possessions, and then the clanking resumed. The claw returned and dropped something at Artos' feet.

He looked down. It was a book, rather tatty around the edges, he thought, though in the cave light it was hard to be sure.

"Wissssssssdom," said the dragon.

Artos shrugged. "It's just a book. I know my letters. Father Bertram taught me."

"Lettersssssss turn matter into sssssspirit," hissed the dragon.

"You mean it's a book of magic?"

"All booksssss are magic, boy." The dragon sounded just a bit cranky.

"Well, I can read," said Artos, stooping to pick up the book. He added a quick, "Thank you," thinking he should seem grateful. *Old thorns and old dragons. . .*he reminded himself.

"You can read *letters*, my boy, which is more than I can say for your castle contemporaries. And you can read *words*. But you must learn to read *inter linea*, between the lines."

Edging backward to the cave's mouth, Artos opened the book and scanned the first page. His fingers underlined each word, his mouth formed them. He turned the page. Then he looked up puzzled. "There is nothing written between the lines. Sir."

Something rather like a chuckle crossed with a cough echoed from the cave. "There is always something written between the lines. But it takes great wisdom to read it."

"Then why me, sir? I have little wisdom."

"Because. . .because you are here."

"Here?"

"Today. And not back at Ector's feeding his brachet or cleaning out the mews or sweating in the smithy or fighting with that pack of unruly boys. Here. For the getting of wisdom." The dragon made stretching noises.

"Oh."

There was a sudden tremendous wheezing and clanking and a strange, "Oh-oh," from the dragon.

Artos peered into the back of the cave nervously. It was all darkness and shadow and an occasional finger of fire-light. "Are you all right? Sir?"

A long silence followed during which Artos wondered whether he should go to the dragon. He wondered if he had even the smallest amount of wisdom needed to help out. Then, just as he was about to make the plunge, the dragon's voice came hissing back. "Yessssss, boy."

"Yes what, sir?"

"Yessssss I am all right."

"Well, then," said Artos, putting one foot quietly behind the other, "thank you for my wisdom."

A furious flame spat across the cave, leaping through the darkness to lick Artos' feet. He jumped back, startled at the dragon's accuracy and suddenly hideously afraid. Had it just been preparation for the dragon's dinner after all? He suddenly wished for the sword he had not yet purchased, turned, and ran out of the cave.

The dragon's voice followed him. "Sssssssssilly child. That was not the wisdom."

From a safe place alongside the outside wall of the cave, Artos peeked in. "There's more?" he asked.

"By the time I am through with you, Artos Pendragon, Arthur son of the dragon, you will read *inter linea* in people as well." There was a loud moan and another round of furious clanking, and then total silence.

Taking it as a dismissal and holding the book hard against his chest, Artos ran down the hill. Whatever else he thought about as he neared the castle walls, topmost in his mind was what he would tell Mag about the loss of the gravy pot. It might mean another kiss. That was the fell thought that occupied him all the way home.

Artos could not read the book without help, he knew it at once. The sentences were much too long and interspersed with Latin and other languages. Perhaps that was the between line the dragon had meant. The only help available was Old Linn, and he did not appear until well after dinner. Unfortunately, that was the time that Artos was the busiest, feeding the dogs, checking the jesses on the hawks, cleaning the smithy. Father Bertram might have helped had he still been alive, though somehow Artos doubted it. The dragon's book was neither Testament nor Commentary, that much he *could* read, and the good father had been fierce about what he had considered proper fare. The castle bonfires had often burned texts of which he disapproved. Even Lady Marion's *Book of Hours*, which had taken four scribes the full part of a year to set down, had gone up in Father Bertram's righteous flames because Adam and Eve had no fig leaves. This Artos had on good authority, though he had never seen it himself, for Lady Marion had complained to Lady Sylvia who had tittered about it to her serving girls who passed the news along with the gravy to young Cai who had mentioned it as a joke to his friends in the cow shed when Artos, who had been napping in the haymow, overheard them.

No, the good Father Bertram would never have helped. Old Linn, though, was different. He could read four tongues well: English, Latin, Greek, and bardic runes. It was said his room was full of books. He could recite the "Conception of Pyrderi," a tale Artos loved for the sheer sound of it, and the stories about the children of Llyr and the Cauldron and the Iron house and the horse made for Bran. Or at least Linn used to be able to tell them all. Before he had been taken ill so suddenly and dramatically, his best piece had always been the "Battle of the Trees." Artos could not remember a time when dinners of great importance at the castle had not ended with Linn's declaiming of it. In fact, Lord Ector's Irish retainers called Linn *shanachie* which, as far as Artos could tell from their garbled and endless explanations, simply meant "storyteller." But they said the word with awe when coupling it to Old Linn's name.

The problem, Artos thought, was that the old man hated him. Well, perhapss *hate* was too strong a word, but he seemed to prefer the young gentlemen of the house, not the impoverished fosterling. Linn especially lavished attention on Sir Cai who, as far as Artos was concerned, long ago let his muscles o'ertake his head. And Sir Bedvere, slack jawed and hardhanded. And Sir Lancot, the pretty boy. Once Artos, too, had tried to curry favor with the trio of lordlings, fetching and carrying and helping them with their schoolwork. But then they all grew up, and the three grew up faster and taller and louder. And once Sir Lancot as a joke had pulled Artos' pants down around his ankles in the courtyard and the other two called out the serving maids to gawk. And that led to Mag's getting sweet on him, which was why he had grown to despise Mag and pity the boys, even though they were older and bigger and better placed than he.

Still, there was a time for putting aside such feelings, thought Artos. The getting of wisdom was surely such a time. He would need help in reading the dragon's book. None of the others, Cai or Bedvere or Lancot, could read half as well as he. They could only just make out the prayers in their psalters. Sir Ector could not read at all. So it would have to be Old Linn.

But to his despair, the apothecary could not be found after dinner. In desperation, he went to talk to the old man's best friend, the smith.

"Come now, young Art," called out Magnus Pieter as Artos approached the smithy. "Did we not have words just yesterday? Something about a sword and a stone?"

Artos tried to think of a way to get the conversation around to Linn's whereabouts, but the conversation would not move at his direction. The smith willed it where he would. At last there was nothing left to do but remove the leathern bag around his neck and take out the jewel. He dropped it onto the anvil. It made a funny little pinging sound.

Magnus sucked on his lower lip and snorted through his nose. "By God, boy, and where'd you get that stone?"

To tell the truth meant getting swat for a liar. He suddenly realized it would be the same if he showed the book to Linn. So he lied. "I was left it by . . .Father Bertram," he said. "And I've. . . ." the lies came slowly. He was, by inclination, an honest boy. He preferred silence to an untruth.

"Kept it till now, have you?" asked the smith. "Well, well, and of course you have. After all, there's not much in that village of ours to spend such a jewel on."

Artos nodded silently, thankful to have Magnus Pieter do the lying for him.

"And what would you be wanting for such a jewel?" asked the smith with the heavy-handed jocularity he always confused with cunning.

Knowing that he must play the innocent in order to get the better bargain, Artos said simply, "Why, a sword, of course."

"Of course!" Magnus Pieter laughed, hands on hips, throwing his head way back.

Since the other smiths he had known laughed in just that way, Artos assumed it was something taught.

The smith stopped laughing and cocked his head to one side. "Well?"

"I am old enough to have a sword of my own," said Artos. "And now I can pay for a good one."

"How good?" asked the smith in his heavy manner.

Artos knelt before the anvil and the red jewel was at the level of his eyes. As if he were addressing the stone and not the smith, he chanted a bit from a song Old Linn used to sing:

> *"And aye their swordes soe sore can byte,*
> *Throughe help of gramarye. . ."*

From behind him the smith sighed. "Aye," the old man said, "and a good sword it shall be. A fine blade, a steel of power. And while I make it for you, young poet, you must think of a good name for your sword from this stone." He reached across Artos' shoulder and plucked up the jewel, holding it high over both their heads.

Artos stood slowly, never once taking his eyes from the jewel. For a moment he thought he saw dragon fire leaping and crackling there. Then he remembered the glowing coals of the forge. The stone reflected that, nothing more.

"Perhaps," he said, thinking out loud, "perhaps I shall call it Inter Linea."

The smith smiled. "Fine name, that. Makes me think of foreign

climes." He pocketed the stone and began to work. Artos turned
and left, for he had chores to do in the mews.

Each day that followed meant another slobbery kiss from
Mag and another pot of stew. It seemed to Artos a rather
messy prelude to wisdom. But after a week of it, he found the
conversations with the dragon worth the mess.

The dragon spoke knowingly of other lands where men walked
on their heads instead of feet. Of lands down beneath the sea
where the bells rang in underwater churches with each passing
wave. It taught Artos riddles and their answers, like

> "As round as an apple, as deep as a cup,
> And all the king's horses can't pull it up,

which was "a well," of course.

And it sang him ballads from the prickly, gorse-covered land
of the Scots who ran naked and screaming into battle. And songs
from the cold, icy Norsemen who prowled in their dragon ships.
And love songs from the silk-and-honey lands of Araby.

And once the dragon taught him a trick with pots and jewels,
clanking and creaking noisily all the while, its huge foot mixing
up the pots till Artos' head fair ached to know under which one
lay the emerald as big as an egg. And that game he had used later
with Lancot and Bedvere and Cai and won from them a number
of gold coins till they threatened him. With his promised new
sword he might have beaten them, but not with his bare hands.
So he used a small man's wiles to trick them once again, picked
up the winnings, and left them grumbling over the cups and peas
he had used for the game.

And so day by day, week by week, month by month, Artos
gained wisdom.

It took three tries and seven months before Artos had his
sword. Each new steel had something unacceptable about it.
The first had a hilt that did not sit comfortably in his hand.
Bedvere claimed it instead, and Magnus Pieter was so pleased
with the coins Sir Bedvere paid it was weeks before he was ready
to work another. Instead he shoed horses, made latches and a
gigantic candelabrum for the dining room to Lady Marion's
specifications.

The second sword had a strange crossbar that the smith swore
would help protect the hand. Artos thought the sword unbal-
anced but Cai, who prized newness over all things, insisted

that he wanted that blade. Again Magnus Pieter was pleased enough to spend the weeks following making farm implements like plowshares and hoes.

The third sword was still bright with its tempering when Lancot claimed it.

"Cai and Bedvere have new swords," Lancot said, his handsome face drawn down with longing. He reached his hand out.

Artos, who had been standing in the shadows of the smithy, was about to say something when Old Linn hobbled in. His mouth and hair spoke of a lingering illness, both being yellowed and lifeless. But his voice was strong.

"You were always a man true to his word," he reminded the smith.

"And true to my swords," said Magnus Pieter, pleased with the play.

Artos stepped from the shadows then and held out his hand. The smith put the sword in it and Artos turned it this way and that to catch the light. The watering on the blade made a strange pattern that looked like the flame from a dragon's mouth. It sat well and balanced in his hand.

"He likes the blade," said Old Linn.

Magnus Pieter shrugged, smiling.

Artos turned to thank the apothecary but he was gone and so was Lancot. When he peered out the smithy door, there were the two of them walking arm and arm up the winding path toward the castle.

"So you've got your Inter Linea now," said the smith. "And about time you took one. Nothing wrong with the other two."

"*And* you got a fine price for them," Artos said.

The smith returned to his anvil and the clang of hammer on new steel ended their conversation.

Artos ran out of the castle grounds, hallooing so loudly even the tortoise dozing on the rusted helm lifted its sleepy head. He fairly leapt over the two rocks in the path. They seemed to have gotten smaller with each trip to the dragon's lair. He was calling still when he approached the entrance to the cave.

"Ho, old flame-tongue," he cried out, the sword allowing him his first attempt at familiarity. "Furnace-lung, look what I have. My sword. From the stone you gave me. It is a rare beauty."

There was no answer.

Suddenly afraid that he had overstepped the bounds and that
the dragon lay sulking within, Artos peered inside.

The cave was dark, cold, silent.

Slowly Artos walked in and stopped about halfway. He felt
surrounded by the icy silence. But that was all. There was no
sense of dragon there. No presence.

"Sir? Father dragon? Are you home?" He put a hand up to one
of the hanging stones to steady himself. In the complete dark he
had little sense of what was up and what was down.

Then he laughed. "Oh, I know, you have gone out on a flight."
It was the only answer that come to him, though the dragon had
never once mentioned flying. But everyone knows dragons have
wings. And wings mean flight. Artos laughed again, a hollow
little chuckle. Then he turned toward the small light of the
cave entrance. "I'll come back tomorrow. At my regular time,"
he called over his shoulder. He said it out loud just in case the
dragon's magic extended to retrieving words left in the still cave
air. "Tomorrow," Artos promised.

But the pattern had been altered subtly and, like a weaving
gone awry, could not be changed back to the way it had been
without a weakness in the cloth.

The next day Artos did not go to the cave. Instead he practiced
swordplay with willow wands in the main courtyard, beating Cai
soundly and being beaten in turn by both Bedvere and Lancot.

The following morn, he and the three older boys were sent by
Lady Marion on a fortnight's journey to gather gifts of jewels and
silks from the market towns for the coming holy days. Some at
Ector's castle celebrated the solstice with the Druids, some kept
the holy day for the Christ child's birth, and a few of the old
soldiers still drank bull's blood and spoke of Mithras in secret
meetings under the castle, for there was a vast warren of halls
and rooms there. But they all gave gifts to one another at the
year's turning, whichever gods they knelt to.

It was Artos' first such trip. The other boys had gone the year
before under Linn's guidance. This year the four of them were
given leave to go alone. Cai was so pleased he forgave Artos
for the beating. Suddenly, they were the best of friends. And
Bedvere and Lancot, who had beaten him, loved Artos now as
well, for even when he had been on the ground with the wand
at his throat and his face and arms red from the lashings, he had
not cried "hold." There had been not even the hint of tears in his
eyes. They admired him for that.

With his bright new sword belted at his side, brand-new leggings from the castle stores, and the new-sworn friends riding next to him, it was no wonder Artos forgot the dragon and the dark cave. Or, if he did not exactly forget, what he remembered was that the dragon hadn't been there when he wanted it the most. So, for a few days, for a fortnight, Artos felt he could, like Cai, glory in the new.

He did not glory in the dragon. It was old, old past counting the years, old past helping him, old and forgetful.

They came home with red rosy cheeks polished by the winter wind and bags packed with treasure. An extra two horses carried the overflow.

Cai, who had lain with his first girl, a serving wench of little beauty and great reputation, was full of new boasts. Bedvere and Lancot had won a junior tourney for boys under sixteen, Bedvere with his sword and Lancot the lance. And though Artos had been a favorite on the outbound trip, full of wonderful stories, riddles, and songs, as they turned toward home he had lapsed into long silences. By the time they were but a day's hard ride away, it was as if his mouth were bewitched.

The boys teased him, thinking it was Mag who worried him.

"Afraid of Old Garlic, then?" asked Cai. "At least Rosemary's breath was sweet." (Rosemary being the serving wench's name.)

"Or are you afraid of my sword?" said Bedvere.

"Or my lance?" Lancot added brightly.

When he kept silent, they tried to wheedle the cause of his set lips by reciting castle gossip. Every maiden, every alewife, every false nurse was named. Then they turned their attention to the men. They never mentioned dragons, though, for they did not know one lived by the castle walls. Artos had never told them of it.

But it was the dragon, of course, that concerned him. With each mile he remembered the darkness, the complete silence of the cave. At night he dreamed of it, the cave opening staring down from the hill like the empty eye socket of a long-dead beast.

They unpacked the presents carefully and carried them up to the Lady Marion's quarters. She, in turn, fed them wine and cakes in her apartments, a rare treat. Her minstrel, a handsome boy except for his wandering left eye, sang a number of songs while they ate, even one in a Norman dialect. Artos drank only a single mouthful of the sweet wine. He ate nothing. He had heard all the songs before.

Thus it was well past sundown before Lady Marion let them go.

Artos would not join the others who were going to report to Lord Ector. He pushed past Cai and ran down the stairs. The other boys called after him, but he ignored them. Only the startled ends of their voices followed him.

He hammered on the gate until the guards lifted the iron portcullis, then he ran across the moat bridge. Dark muddy lumps in the mushy ice were the only signs of life.

As he ran, he held his hand over his heart, cradling the two pieces of cake he had slipped into his tunic. Since he had had no time to beg stew from Mag, he hoped seed cakes would do instead. He did not, for a moment, believe the dragon had starved to death without his poor offering of stew. The dragon had existed many years before Artos had found the cave. It was not the *size* of the stew, but the *fact* of it.

He stubbed his toe on the second outcropping hard enough to force a small mewing sound between his lips. The tor was icy and that made climbing it difficult. Foolishly he'd forgotten his gloves with his saddle gear. And he'd neglected to bring a light.

When he got to the mouth of the cave and stepped in, he was relieved to hear heavy breathing echoing off the cave wall, until he realized it was the sound of his own ragged breath.

"*Dragon!*" he cried out, his voice a misery.

Suddenly there was a small moan and an even smaller glow, like dying embers that have been breathed upon one last time.

"Is that you, my son?" The voice was scarcely a whisper, so quiet the walls could not find enough to echo.

"Yes, dragon," said Artos. "It is I."

"Did you bring me any stew?"

"Only two seed cakes."

"I like seed cakes."

"Then I'll bring them to you."

"Noooooooo." The sound held only the faintest memory of the powerful voice of before.

But Artos had already started toward the back of the cave, one hand in front to guide himself around the over-hanging rocks. He was halfway there when he stumbled against something and fell heavily to his knees. Feeling around, he touched a long, metallic curved blade.

"Has someone been here? Has someone tried to slay you?" he

cried. Then, before the dragon could answer, Artos' hand traveled farther along the blade to its strange metallic base.

His hands told him what his eyes could not; his mouth spoke what his heart did not want to hear. "It is the dragon's foot."

He leaped over the metal construct and scrambled over a small rocky wall. Behind it, in the dying glow of a small fire, lay an old man on a straw bed. Near him were tables containing beakers full of colored liquids—amber, rose, green, and gold. On the wall were strange toothed wheels with handles.

The old man raised himself on one arm. "Pendragon," he said and tried to set his lips into a welcoming smile. "Son."

"Old Linn," replied Artos angrily, "I am no son of yours."

"There was once," the old man began quickly, settling into a story before Artos' anger had time to gel, "a man who would know Truth. And he traveled all over the land looking."

Without willing it, Artos was pulled into the tale.

"He looked along the seacoasts and in the quiet farm dales. He went into the country of lakes and across vast deserts seeking Truth. At last, one dark night in a small cave atop a hill, he found her. Truth was a wizened old woman with but a single tooth left in her head. Her eyes were rheumy. Her hair greasy strands. But when she called him into her cave, her voice was low and lyric and pure and that was how he knew he had found Truth."

Artos stirred uneasily.

The old man went on. "He stayed a year and a day by her side and learned all she had to teach. And when his time was done, he said, 'My Lady Truth, I must go back to my own home now. But I would do something for you in exchange.'" Linn stopped. The silence between them grew until it was almost a wall.

"Well, what did she say?" Artos asked at last.

"She told him, 'When you speak of me, tell your people that I am young and beautiful.'"

For a moment Artos said nothing. Then he barked out a short, quick laugh. "So much for Truth."

Linn sat up and patted the mattress beside him, an invitation which Artos ignored. "Would you have listened these seven months to an old apothecary who had a tendency to fits?"

"You did not tell me the truth."

"I did not lie. You *are* the dragon's son."

Artos set his mouth and turned his back on the old man. His

voice came out low and strained. *"I. . .am. . .not. . .your. . .-son."*

"It is true that you did not spring from my loins," said the old man. "But I carried you here to Ector's castle and waited and hoped you would seek out my wisdom. But you longed for the truth of lance and sword. I did not have that to give." His voice was weak and seemed to end in a terrible sigh.

Artos did not turn around. "I believed in the dragon."

Linn did not answer.

"I *loved* the dragon."

The silence behind him was so loud that at last Artos turned around. The old man had fallen onto his side and lay still. Artos felt something warm on his cheeks and realized they were tears. He ran to Linn and knelt down, pulling the old man onto his lap. As he cradled him, Linn opened his eyes.

"Did you bring me any stew?" he asked.

"I. . ." the tears were falling unchecked now. "I brought you seed cakes."

"I like seed cakes," Linn said. "But couldn't you get any stew from Old Garlic?"

Artos felt his mouth drop open. "How did you know about her?"

The old man smiled, showing terrible teeth. He whispered: "I am the Great Riddler. I am the Master of Wisdom. I am the Word and I am the Light. I Was and Am and Will Be." He hesitated. "I am the Dragon."

Artos smiled back and then carefully stood with the old man in his arms. He was amazed at how frail Linn was. His bones, Artos thought, must be as hollow as the wing bones of a bird.

There was a door in the cave wall and Linn signaled him toward it. Carrying the old apothecary through the doorway, Artos marveled at the runes carved in the lintel. Past the door was a warren of hallways and rooms. From somewhere ahead he hear the chanting of many men.

Artos looked down at the old man and whispered to him. "Yes. I understand. You *are* the dragon, indeed. And I am the dragon's boy. But I will not let you die just yet. I have not finished getting my wisdom."

Smiling broadly, the old man turned toward him like a baby rooting at its mother's breast, found the seed cakes, ate one of them and then, with a gesture both imperious and fond, stuffed the other in Artos' mouth.

THE KNIGHT WITH THE TWO SWORDS
by John Steinbeck

The author of The Grapes of Wrath *is scarcely in need of much introduction though, at first glance, he may seem out of place in this volume. Malory's* Morte d'Arthur *was special to John Steinbeck (1902–1968). It was the first book he ever read and it captivated him. "Perhaps a passionate love for the English language opened to me from this one book," he later wrote. Arthurian images heavily influenced his first successful novel* Tortilla Flat *(1935). In 1958, after two years of reading and research, Steinbeck began a modern 'translation' of Malory's book. "I wanted to set them down in plain present-day speech for my own youngs sons, and for other sons not so young. . . If I can do this and keep the wonder and magic, I shall be pleased and gratified." Steinbeck never completed the task for he became intoxicated with the project and as he progressed so it grew from a basic modern rendition to a major revision and enlargement. As a result the project became too great. The completed portions were published in 1976 as* The Acts of King Arthur and His Noble Knights *from which I have selected this early episode of 'The Knight With the Two Swords'.*

49

In the long and lawless time after Uther Pendragon's death and before his son Arthur became king, in England and Wales, in Cornwall and Scotland and the Outer Isles, many lords took lawless power to themselves, and some of them refused to give it up, so that Arthur's first kingly years were given to restoring his realm by law, by order, and by force of arms.

One of his most persistent enemies was the Lord Royns of Wales whose growing strength in the west and north was a constant threat to the kingdom.

When Arthur held court at London, a faithful Knight rode in with the news that Royns in his arrogance had raised a large army and invaded the land, burning crops and houses and killing Arthur's subjects as he came.

"If this is true, I must protect my people," Arthur said.

"It is true enough," said the Knight. "I myself saw the invaders and their destructive work."

"Then I must fight this Royns and destroy him," said the king. And he sent out an order to all loyal lords and knights and gentlemen of arms to meet in general council at Camelot, where plans would be made to defend the kingdom.

And when the barons and the knights had gathered and sat in the great hall below the king, a damsel came before them saying she was sent by the great lady Lyle of Avalon.

"What message do you bring?" asked Arthur.

Then the damsel opened her richly furred cloak and it was seen that from her belt there hung a noble sword.

The king said, "It is not seemly for a maiden to go armed. Why do you wear a sword?"

"I wear it because I have no choice," the damsel said. "And I must wear it until it is taken from me by a knight who is brave and honorable, of good repute and without stain. Only such a knight may draw this sword from his scabbard. I have been to the camp of Lord Royns where I was told were good knights, but neither he nor any of his followers could draw the blade."

Arthur said, "Here are good men, and I myself will try to draw it, not that I am the best, but because if I try first my barons and knights will feel free to follow me."

Then Arthur grasped sheath and girdle and pulled eagerly at the sword, but it did not move.

"Sir," said the damsel, "You need not use strength. It will come out easily in the hands of the knight for whom it is destined."

Arthur turned to his men and said, "Now all of you try it one by one."

The damsel said, "Be sure, you who try, that you have no shame or guile or treachery before you try. Only a clean and unstained knight may draw it and he must be of noble blood on both his mother's and his father's side."

Then most of the gathered knights attempted to draw the sword and none succeeded. Then the maiden said sadly, "I believed that here I would find blameless men and the best knights in the world."

Arthur was displeased and he said, "These are as good or better knights than you will find anywhere. I am unhappy that it is not their fortune to help you."

A knight named Sir Balin of Northumberland had remained apart. It had been his misfortune in fair fight to kill a cousin of the king, and the quarrel being misrepresented, he had been a prisoner for half a year. Only recently had some of his friends explained the matter and had him released. He watched the trial anxiously, but because he had been in prison and because he was poor and his clothing worn and dirty, he did not come forward until all had tried and the damsel was ready to depart. Only then did Sir Balin call to her, saying, "Lady, I beg you out of your courtesy to let me try. I know I am poorly dressed, but I feel in my heart that I may succeed."

The damsel looked at his ragged cloak and she could not believe him a man of honor and of noble blood. She said, "Sir, why do you wish to put me to more pain when all of these noble knights have failed?"

Sir Balin said, "Fair lady, a man's worth is not in his clothing. Manhood and honor are hidden inside. And sometimes virtues are not known to everyone."

"That is the truth," said the damsel, "and I thank you for reminding me. Here, grasp the sword and see what you can do."

Then Balin went to her and drew the sword easily, and he looked at the shining blade and it pleased him very much. Then the king and many others applauded Sir Balin, but some of the knights were filled with jealous spite.

The damsel said, "You must be the best and most blameless knight I have found or you could not have done it. Now, gentle and courteous knight, please give me the sword again."

"No," said Balin, "I like this sword, and I will keep it until someone is able to take it from me by force."

"Do not keep it," the damsel cried. "It is not wise to keep it. If you do, you will use it to kill the best friend and the man you love best in the world. That sword will destroy you."

Balin said, "I will accept any adventure God sends me, Lady, but I will not return the sword to you."

"Then in a short time you will be sorry for it," the lady said. "I do not want the sword for myself. If you take it, the sword will destroy you and I pity you."

Then Sir Balin sent for his horse and armor and he begged the king's permission to depart.

Arthur said, "Do not leave us now. I know you are angered by your unjust imprisonment, but false evidence was brought against you. If I had known your honor and your bravery, I would have acted differently. Now, if you will stay in my court and in this fellowship, I will advance you and make amends."

"I thank Your Highness," said Balin. "Your bounty is well known. I have no resentment toward you, but I must go away and I beg that your grace may go with me."

"I am not glad of your departure," said the king. "I ask you, good sir, not to be long away from us. We shall welcome your return and I will repay you for the injustice done against you."

"God thank your good grace," replied the knight, and he made ready to depart. And there were some jealous men in the court who whispered that witchcraft rather than knightly virtue was responsible for his good fortune.

While Balin armed himself and his horse, the lady of the Lake rode into Arthur's court, and she was richly dressed and well mounted. She saluted the king and then reminded him of the gift he had promised her when she gave him the sword of the lake.

"I remember my promise," said Arthur, "but I have forgotten the name of the sword, if you ever told it to me."

"It is called Excalibur," the lady said, "and that means Cut Steel."

"Thank you, lady," said the king. "And now, what gift do you ask? I will give you anything in my power."

Then the lady said savagely, "I want two heads—that of the knight who drew the sword and the head of the damsel who brought it here. I will not be content until I have both heads. That knight killed my brother and the damsel caused my father's death. This is my demand."

The king was taken aback at the ferocity. He said, "I cannot in honor kill these two for your vengeance. Ask for anything else and I will give it."

"I ask for nothing else," said the lady.

Now Balin was ready to depart and he saw the Lady of the Lake and knew her for the one who by secret craft had brought death to his mother three years before. And when he was told that she had demanded his head, he strode near to her and cried, "You are an evil thing. You want my head? I shall have yours." And he drew his sword and slashed her head from her body with one stroke.

"What have you done?" Arthur cried. "You have brought shame to me and to my court. I was in this lady's debt, and moreover she was under my protection. I can never forgive this outrage."

"My Lord," said Balin, "I am sorry for your displeasure, but not for my deed. This was an evil witch. By enchantment and sorcery she killed many good knights, and by craft and false-hood she caused my mother to be burned to death."

The king said, "No matter what your reason, you had no right to do this and in my presence. It was an ugly deed and an insult to me. Now leave my court. You are no longer welcome here."

Then Balin took up the head of the Lady of the Lake by the hair and carried it to his lodging, where his squire awaited him, and they mounted their horses and rode out of the town.

And Balin said, "I want you to take this head to my friends and relatives in Northumberland. Tell them my most dangerous enemy is dead Tell them that I am free from prison and how I got this second sword."

"I am sad that you have done this," said the squire. "You are greatly to blame for losing the friendship of the king. No one doubts your courage, but you are a headstrong knight and when you choose a way you cannot change your course even if it lead to your destruction. That is your fault and your destiny."

Then Balin said, "I have thought of a way to win the king's affection. I will ride to the camp of his enemy Lord Royns and I will kill him or be killed. If it should happen that I win, King Arthur will be my friend again."

The squire shook his head at such a desperate plan, but he said, "Sir, where shall I meet you?"

"In King Arthur's court," said Balin confidently, and he sent his squire away.

Meanwhile, the king and all his followers were sad and shamed at Balin's deed and they buried the Lady of the Lake richly and with all ceremony.

In the court at that time there was a knight who was most jealous of Balin for his success in drawing the magic sword. He was Sir Launceor, son of the King of Ireland, a proud and ambitious man who believed himself to be one of the best knights in the world. He asked the king's permission to ride after Sir Balin to avenge the insult to Arthur's dignity.

The king said, "Go—and do your best. I am angry with Balin. Wipe out the outrage to my court."

And when Sir Launceor had gone to his quarters, to make ready for the field, Merlin came before King Arthur, and he heard how the sword was drawn and how the Lady of the Lake was slaughtered.

The Merlin looked at the damsel of the sword who had remained in the court. And Merlin said, "Look at this damsel standing here. She is a false and evil woman and she cannot deny it. She has a brother, a brave knight and a good and true man. This damsel loved a knight and became his paramour. And her brother, to wipe away the shame, challenged her lover and killed him in fair fight. Then in her rage, this damsel took his sword to the lady Lyle of Avalon and asked help to be revenged on her own brother."

And Merlin said, "The lady Lyle took the sword and cast a spell on it and laid a curse on it. Only the best and the bravest of knights would be able to draw it from its sheath, and he who drew it would kill his brother with it." And Merlin turned again on the damsel. "This was your spiteful reason for coming here," he said. "Don't deny it. I know it as well as you do. I wish to God you had not come, for wherever you go you carry harm and death.

"The knight who drew the sword is the best and bravest, and the sword he drew will destroy him. For everything he does will turn to bitterness and death through no fault of his own. The curse of the sword has become his fate. My Lord," Merlin said to the king, "that good knight has little time to live, but before he dies he will do you a service you will long remember." And King Arthur listened in sad wonder.

By now Sir Launceor of Ireland had armed himself at all points. He dressed his shield on his shoulder and took a spear in his hand and he urged his horse at utmost speed along the path Sir Balin had taken. It was not long before he overtook his enemy on the top of a mountain. And Sir Launceor shouted, "Stop where you are or I will make you stop. Your shield will not protect you now."

Balin answered lightly, "You might better have remained at home. A man who threatens his enemy often finds his promise turns back on himself. From what court do you come?"

"From king Arthur's court," said the Irish knight. "And I come to avenge the insult you have put on the king this day."

Sir Balin said, "If I must fight you, I must. But believe me, sir,

I am grieved that I have injured the king or any of his court. I know your duty is plain, but before we fight, know that I had no choice. The Lady of the Lake not only did me mortal injury but demanded my life as well."

Sir Launceor said, "Enough of talking. Make ready, for only one of us will leave this field."

Then they couched their spears and thundered together, and Launceor's spear splintered, but Balin's lanced through shield and armor and chest and the Irish knight went crashing to the ground. When Balin had turned his horse and drawn his sword, he saw his enemy lying dead on the grass. And then he heard galloping hooves and he saw a damsel ride toward them as fast as she could. When she drew up and saw Sir Launceor dead, she burst into wild sorrow.

"Balin!" she cried. "Two bodies you have killed in one heart and two hearts in one body and two souls you have released." Then she dismounted and took up her lover's sword and fell fainting to the ground. And when her senses returned she screamed her sorrow and Balin was filled with pain. He went to her and tried to take the sword from her, but she clung to it so desperately that for fear he might hurt her he released his hold. Then suddenly she reversed the sword and placed the pommel on the ground and drove her body on the point, and the blade pierced her and she died.

Balin stood with heavy heart and he was ashamed that he had caused her death. And he cried aloud, "What love there must have been between these two, and I have destroyed them!" Her could not bear the sight of them, and he mounted and rode sadly away toward the forest.

In the distance he saw a knight approaching, and when he could see the device on the shield, Balin knew it was his brother, Balan. And when they met they tore off their helmets and kissed each other and wept for joy.

Balan said, "My brother, I could not have hoped to meet you so soon. I came upon a man at the castle of the four catapults and he told me that you were released from prison and that he had seen you in King Arthur's court and I rode from Northumberland to look for you."

The Balin told his brother about the damsel and the sword and how he had killed the Lady of the Lake and so angered the king, and he said, "Yonder a knight lies dead who was sent after me, and beside him his love who destroyed herself, and I am heavy-hearted and grieved."

"It is a sad thing," Balan said, "but you are a knight and you know you must accept whatever God ordains for you."

"I know that," said Balin, "but I am sorrowful that King Arthur is displeased with me. He is the best and greatest king who reigns on earth. And I will get back his love or leave my life."

"How will you do that, my brother?"

"I will tell you," said Balin. "King Arthur's enemy, Lord Royns, has laid siege to the castle Terrabil in Cornwall. I will ride there and prove my honor and courage against him."

"I hope it may be," Balan said. "I will go with you and venture my life with yours as a brother should."

"How good it is that you are here, dear brother," Balin said. "Let us ride on together."

As they talked a dwarf came riding from the direction of Camelot, and when he saw the bodies of the knight and his beloved damsel he tore his hair and cried out to the brothers, "Which of you has done this deed?"

"What right have you to ask?" said Balan.

"Because I want to know."

And Balin answered him, "It was I. I killed the knight in fair combat in self-defense and the damsel destroyed herself in sorrow, and I am grieved. For her sake I will serve all women while I live."

The dwarf said, "You have done great damage to yourself. This dead knight was the son of the King of Ireland. His kin will take vengeance on you. They will follow you all over the world until they have killed you."

"That does not frighten me," said Balin. "My pain is that I have doubly displeased my lord King Arthur by killing his knight."

Then King Mark of Cornwall came riding by and saw the bodies, and when he was told the story of the death, he said, "They must have loved each other truly. And I will see that they have a tomb in their memory." Then he ordered his men to pitch their tents and he searched the country for a place to bury the lovers. In a church nearby he had a great stone raised from the floor in front of the high altar and he buried the knight and his damsel together, and when the stone was lowered back, King Mark had words carved on it saying, "Here lies Sir Launceor, son of Ireland's king, slain in combat with Sir Balin and beside him his love the lady Colombe, who in sorrow slew herself with her lover's sword."

Merlin entered the church and he said to Balin, "Why did you not save this lady's life?"

"I swear I could not," said Balin, "I tried to save her but she was too quick."

"I am sorry for you," Merlin said. "In punishment for the death you are destined to strike the saddest blow since the lance pierced the side of our Lord Jesus Christ. With your stroke you will wound the best knight living and you will bring poverty and misery and despair to three kingdoms."

And Balin cried out, "This can't be true. If I believed it I would kill myself now and make you a liar."

"But you will not," said Merlin.

"What is my sin?" Balin demanded.

"Ill fortune," said Merlin. "Some call it fate." And suddenly he vanished.

And after a time the brothers took leave of King Mark.

"First, tell me your names," he asked.

And Balan answered, "You see that he wears two swords. Call him the Knight with the Two Swords."

Then the two brothers took their way towards the camp of Royns. And on a broad and windswept moor they came upon a stranger muffled in a cloak who asked them where they were going.

"Why should we tell you?" they replied, and Balin said, "Tell us your name, stranger."

"Why should I, when you are secret?" said the man.

"It's and evil sign when a man will not tell his name," said Balan.

"Think what you wish," the stranger said. "What would you think if I told you that you ride to find Lord Royns and that you will fail without my help?"

"I would think that you are Merlin, and if you are, I would ask your help."

"You must be brave, for you will need courage," said Merlin.

Sir Balin said, "Don't worry about courage. We will do what we can."

They came to the edge of a forest and dismounted in a dim and leafy hollow, and they unsaddled their horses and put them to graze. And the knights lay under the sheltering branches of the trees and fell asleep.

When it was midnight Merlin awakened them quietly. "Make ready quickly," he said. "Your chance is coming. Royns has stolen from his camp with only a bodyguard to pay a midnight visit of love to Lady de Vance."

From cover of the trees they saw horsemen coming.

"Which is Royns?" Balin asked.

"The tall one in the middle," Merlin said. "Hold back until they come abreast."

And when the cavalcade was passing in the starlit dark, the brothers charged out from their concealment and struck Royns from his saddle, and they turned on his startled men, striking right and left with their swords, and some went down and the rest turned tail and fled.

Then the brothers returned to the felled Royns to kill him, but he yielded and asked mercy. "Brave knights, do not murder me," he said. "My life is valuable to you and my death worth nothing."

"That is true," the brothers said, and they raised up the wounded Royns and helped him to his horse. And when they looked for Merlin he was gone, for he by his magic arts had flown ahead to Camelot. And he told Arthur that his worst enemy, Lord Royns, was overthrown and captured.

"By whom?" the king demanded.

"By two knights who wish your friendship and your grace more than anything in the world. They will be here in the morning and you will see who they are," Merlin said and he would not speak further.

Very early the two brothers brought their wounded prisoner, Royns, to the gates of Camelot and delivered him into the safe-keeping of the warders and they rode away into the dawning day.

When it was reported, King Arthur went to his wounded enemy and he said, "Sir, you are a welcome sight to me. By what adventure have you come?"

"By a bitter adventure, my lord."

"Who took you?" the king asked.

"One who is called the Knight with the Two Swords and his brother. They overturned me and swept away my bodyguard."

Merlin broke in, "Now I can tell you, sir. It was that Balin who drew the cursed sword and his brother, Balan. Two better knights you will never find. The pity is that their fate is closing in and they have not long to live."

"He has put me in debt to him," said the king. "And I do not deserve kindness from Balin."

"He will do much more for you than this, my lord," said Merlin. "But I bring you news. You must prepare your knights for battle. Tomorrow before noon the forces of Royns's brother Nero will attack you. You have much to do now and I will leave you."

Then King Arthur mustered his knights quickly and rode toward the castle Terrabil. Nero was ready for him in the field with forces that outnumbered those of the king. Nero led the vanguard and he waited only for the arrival of King Lot with his army. But he waited in vain, for Merlin had gone to King Lot and held him enthralled with tales of wonder and of prophecy, while Arthur launched his attack on Nero. Sir Kay fought so well that day that the memory of his deeds has lived forever. And Sir Hervis de Revel of the line of Sir Thomas Malory distinguished himself as did Sir Tobinus Streat de Montroy. Into the battle Sir Balin and his brother raged so fiercely that it was said of them that they were either angels from heaven or devils from hell, depending on which side you held. And Arthur in the vanguard saw the brother's actions and praised them above all his knights. And the king's forces prevailed and drove the enemy from the field and destroyed Nero's power.

A messenger rode to King Lot and reported the battle lost and Nero killed while Lot had listened to Merlin's tales. King Lot said, "I have bewitched by this Merlin. If I had been there Arthur could not have won the day. This magician has fooled me and held me like a child listening to stories."

Merlin said, "I know that today one king must die, and much as I regret it, I would rather it were you than King Arthur," and Merlin vanished in the air.

Then King Lot gathered his leaders. "What should I do?" he asked. "Is it better to sue for peace or to fight? If Nero is defeated, half our army is gone."

A knight said, "King Arthur's men are weary with battle and their horses exhausted, while we are fresh. If we attack him now we have the advantage."

"If you all agree, we will fight," said King Lot. "I hope that you will do as well as I will try to do."

Then King Lot galloped to the field and charged Arthur's men, but they held firm and did not give ground.

King Lot, out of shame for his failure, held the forefront of his knights and fought like a devil raging, for he hated Arthur above all men. Once he had been the king's friend wedded to Arthur's half-sister. But when Arthur in ignorance seduced his friend's wife and got her with the child Mordred, King Lot's loyalty turned to hatred and he strove desperately to overcome his once friend.

As Merlin had foretold, Sir Pellinore, who once overthrew Arthur at the Fountain in the Forest, had become the king's loyal friend and fought in the first line of his knights. Sir Pellinore forced his horse through the press around King Lot and aimed a great swinging sword stroke at him. The blade glanced off and killed Lot's horse, and as he went down Pellinore struck him on the helm and drove him to the ground.

When King Lot's men saw him fallen, they gave up the fight and tried to flee, and many were taken and more were killed in flight.

When the bodies of the dead were gathered together, twelve great lords were found who had died serving Nero and King Lot. These were carried to St. Stephen's Church in Camelot for burial, while the lesser knights were interred nearby under a huge stone.

King Arthur buried Lot in a rich tomb separately, but the twelve great lords he placed together and raised a triumphal monument over them. Merlin by his arts made figures of the twelve lords in gilded copper and brass, in attitudes of defeat, and each figure held a candle which burned night and day. Above these effigies, Merlin placed a statue of King Arthur with a drawn sword held over his enemies' heads. And Merlin prophesied that the candles would burn until Arthur's death and at that moment would go out; and he made other prophecies that day of things to come.

Soon after this, Arthur, wearied with campaigns and governing and sick of the dark, deep-walled rooms of castles, ordered his pavilion set up in a green meadow outside the walls where he might rest and recover his strength in the quiet and the sweet air. He laid himself down on a camp bed to sleep, but he had not closed his eyes when he heard a horse approaching and saw a knight riding near who spoke words of complaint and sorrow to himself.

As he passed the pavilion, the king called out to him, saying, "Come to me, good knight, and tell me the reason for your sadness."

The knight answered, "What good could that do? You cannot help me." And he rode on toward the castle of Meliot.

Then the king tried to sleep again but his curiosity had risen to keep him awake, and as he pondered, Sir Balin rode near, and when he saw King Arthur he dismounted and saluted his lord.

"You are always welcome," said the king. "But particularly now. A short time ago a knight went past and he was crying out in sorrow, and he would not answer when I asked the cause. If you wish to serve me, ride after this knight and bring him to me whether he wishes to come or not, for I am curious."

"I will bring him to you, my lord," Sir Balin said, "or else he will be more sad than he is."

And Balin mounted and cantered after the knight, and after a time he found him sitting under a tree with a damsel beside him. Sir Balin said, "Sir Knight, you come with me to King Arthur and tell him the cause of your sorrow."

"That I will not do," said the knight. "I would be in great danger if I did and you would gain nothing."

"Please come with me, sir," said Balin. "If you refuse I must fight you and I don't want to."

"I have told you my life is in danger. Will you promise to protect me?"

"I will protect you or die in the attempt," said Balin. And with that the knight mounted his horse and they rode away, leaving the damsel under the tree. As they came to King Arthur's tent, they heard the sound of a charging war horse but saw nothing, and suddenly the knight was hurled from his saddle by an invisible force, and he lay dying on the ground with a great spear through his body. And he gasped, "That was my danger—a knight named Garlon who has the art of invisibility. I was under your protection and you have failed me. Take my horse. He is better than yours. And go back to the damsel—she will lead you to my enemy and perhaps you may avenge me."

Balin cried, "On my honor and my knighthood I will. I swear it before God."

And with that the knight, Sir Harleus le Berbeus, died, and Balin pulled the truncheon of the spear from his body and rode sadly away, for he was grieved that he had not protected the knight as he had promised, and he understood at last why Arthur had been enraged at the death of the Lady of the Lake under his protection. And Balin felt a darkness of misfortune hanging over him. He found the damsel in the forest and gave her the truncheon of the spear that had killed her lover, and she carried it always, as a sign and a remembrance. She led Sir Balin on the quest he had accepted from the dying knight.

In the forest they came upon a knight fresh from hunting, who, seeing Balin's sorrow-clouded face, asked the reason for his pain and Balin curtly answered that he did not wish to speak of it.

The knight resented the discourtesy, saying, "If I were armed against men instead of stags, you would answer me."

Balin answered wearily, "I have no reason not to tell you," and he recounted his strange and fatal history. The knight was so moved by the tale that he begged leave to join him in the quest of vengeance. His name was Sir Peryne de Monte Belyarde, and he went to his house nearby and armed himself and joined them on their way. And as they rode past a little lonely hermitage and chapel in the forest, there came again the sound of charging hoofs and Sir Peryne fell with a spear through his body.

"Your story was true," he said. "The invisible enemy has slain me. You are a man fated to cause the destruction of your loved friends." And Sir Peryne died of his wounds.

Balin said in sorrow, "My enemy is something I cannot see. How can I challenge the invisible?"

Then the hermit helped him to carry the dead into the chapel and they buried him in pity and honor.

And afterward Balin and the damsel rode on until they came to a castle with strong defenses. Balin crossed the draw-bridge and entered first, and as he did the portcullis rattled down and held him prisoner, with the damsel outside, where many men attacked her with knives to kill her. Then Balin ran up to the top of the wall and he leaped into the moat far below, and the water broke his fall and saved him from injury. He crawled from the moat and drew his sword, but the attackers drew away and told him that they only followed the custom of the castle. They explained that the lady of the castle had long suffered a dreadful wasting sickness and the only cure for it was a silver dish of blood from the virgin daughter of a king and so it was their custom to take blood from every damsel who passed that way.

Balin said, "I am sure she will give you some of her blood, but you need not kill her to get it." Then he helped to lance her vein and they caught it in a silver dish, but it did not cure the lady wherefore it was thought that the damsel did not fulfill one or the other or both of the requirements. But because of the offering they were made welcome and given good cheer, and they rested for the night and in the morning took their way again. Four days they continued without adventure, and at last lodged in the house of a gentleman. And as they sat at their supper, they heard moans of pain from a chamber nearby and Balin asked about it.

'I will tell you about it," the gentleman said. "Recently at a jousting I rode against the brother of King Pelham. Twice I struck him from his horse and he was angry and threatened revenge against someone near to me. Then he made himself invisible and wounded my son, whom you hear crying out in pain. He will not be well until I have killed that evil knight and taken his blood."

"I know him well, but I have never seen him," Balin said. "He has killed two of my knights in the same way, and I would rather meet him in combat than have all gold in the realm."

"I will tell you how to meet him," said the host." His brother, King Pelham, has proclaimed a great feast within twenty days. And no knight may attend unless he brings his wife or his mistress. The king's brother, Garlon, is sure to be there."

"Then I will be there also," Balin said.

And in the morning the three started their journey and they rode for fifteen days until they came to Pelham's country, and they came to his castle on the day the feast began, and they stabled their horses and went to the great hall, but Balin's host was refused because he had brought neither wife nor paramour. But Balin was welcomed and taken to a chamber where he unarmed and bathed himself and servants brought him a rich robe to wear to the feasting. But then they asked him to leave his sword with his armor; Balin refused. He said, "In my county a knight must keep his sword with him always. If I cannot take it, I may not feast." Reluctantly they let him take his weapon, and he went into the great hall and sat among the knights, with his lady beside him.

Then Balin asked, "Is there a knight in this court named Garlon, brother of the king?"

"There he is now," said a man nearby. "Look, he is the one with the dark skin. He is strange man and he has killed many knights because he has the secret of invisibility."

Balin stared at Garlon and considered what he should do, and he thought, "If I kill him now, I will not be able to escape, but if I do not I may never see him again, because he will not be visible."

Garlon had noticed Balin staring at him and it angered him. He rose from his place and came to Balin and slapped him in the face with the back of his hand and said, "I do not like you staring at me. Eat your meat, or do anything else you came to do."

"I will do what I came to do," Balin said and he drew his sword and cut off Garlon's head. Then he said to his lady, "Give me the truncheon that killed your love," and he took it from her and drove it through Garlon's body, crying, "You killed a good knight with that. Now it sticks in you," and he called to his friend outside the hall, "Here is blood enough to cure your son."

The assembled knights had sat astonished, but now they leaped to their feet to set on Balin. King Pelham stood up from the high table, saying, "You have killed my brother. You must die."

And Balin taunted him, "Very well—do it yourself if you are brave enough."

"You are right," Pelham said. "Stand back, you knights. I will kill him myself for my brother's sake."

Pelham took a huge battle ax from the wall and advanced and aimed a blow and Balin parried with his sword, but the heavy ax broke his sword in two so that he was weaponless. Then Balin ran from the hall with Pelham following. He went from chamber to chamber looking for a weapon but he could not find one and always he could hear King Pelham following.

At last Balin came to a chamber and saw a wonder. The room was hung with cloth of gold figured with mystic holy symbols and a bed was curtained with marvelous curtains. On the bed under a cover woven of golden thread lay the perfect body of an ancient and venerable man, while on a golden table beside the bed there stood a strangely wrought spear, a haft of wood, a lean iron shank, and a small, pointed head.

Balin heard Pelham's pursuing steps and he seized the spear and drove it into the side of his enemy. And at that moment an earthquake rumbled and the walls of the castle cracked outward and the roof feel in and Balin and King Pelham rolled in the tumbling rubble to the ground and they lay unconscious, pinned under stones and pieces of timber. Inside the castle most of the gathered knights were killed by the falling roof.

After a time Merlin appeared and cleared the stones from Balin and brought him to his senses. And he brought him a horse and told him to leave the country as quickly as he could.

But Balin said, "Where is my damsel?"

"She lies dead under the fallen castle," Merlin said.

"What caused this ruin?" Balin asked.

"You have fallen on a mystery," Merlin said. "Not long after Jesus Christ was crucified, Joseph, a merchant of Arimathea who gave our Lord his sepulcher, came sailing to this land bringing the sacred cup of the Last Supper filled with the holy blood and also that spear with Longinus the Roman pierced the side of Jesus on the Cross. And Joseph brought these holy things to the Island of Glass in Avalon and there he built a church, the first in all this land. That was Joseph's body on the bed and that Longinus's spear, and with it you wounded Pelham, Joseph's descendant, and it was the dolorous stroke I spoke of long ago. And because you have done this, a blight of sickness and hunger and despair will spread over the land."

Balin cried, "It is not fair. It is not just."

"Misfortune is not fair, fate is not just, but they exist just the same," said Merlin, and he bade Balin farewell. "For," he said, "we will not meet again in this world."

Then Balin rode away through the blighted land and he saw

people dead and dying on every side, and the living cried after him, "Balin, you are the cause of this destruction. You will be punished for it." And Balin in anguish pushed his horse to leave the destroyed country. He rode eight days, fleeing from the evil, and he was glad when he passed out of the blighted land and into a fair, untroubled forest. His spirit awakened and threw off his gloomy garments. Above the tops of the trees in a fair valley he saw the battlements of a slender tower and turned his horse toward it. Beside the tower a great horse was tied to a tree and on the ground a handsome, well-made knight sat mourning aloud to himself.

And because he had given death and suffering to so many, Balin wished to make amends. He said to the knight, "God save you. Why are you sad? Tell me and I will try my best to help you."

The knight said, "Telling you would give me more pain that I have already."

Then Balin walked a little apart and looked at the tethered horse and its equipment, and he heard the knight say, "Oh, my lady, why have you broken your promise to meet me here at noon. You gave me my sword, a deadly gift, for I may kill myself with it for love of you." And the knight drew his shining sword from its sheath.

Then Balin moved quickly and grasped his wrist.

"Let me go or I will kill you," cried the knight.

"There is no good in that. I know now about your lady and I promise to bring her to you if you will tell me where she is."

"Who are you?" the knight demanded.

"Sir Balin."

"I know your fame," said the knight. "You are the Knight with the Two Swords, and you are said to be one of the bravest of knights."

"What is your name?"

"I am Sir Garnish of the Mountain. I am a poor man's son, but because I served well in battle, Duke Harmel took me under his protection and knighted me and gave me lands. It is his daughter I love and I thought she loved me."

"How far away is she?" Balin asked.

"Only six miles."

"Then why do you sit here mourning? Let us go to her and find the reason for her failure."

Then they rode together until they came to a well-built castle with high walls and a moat. And Balin said, "Remain here and wait for me. I will go into the castle and try to find her."

Balin went into the castle and found no one about. He searched through the halls and the rooms and at last came to a lady's chamber, but her bed was empty. He looked from her window to a lovely little garden within the walls and on the grass under a laurel tree he saw the lady and a knight lying on a green silken cloth, and they had fallen asleep in a close embrace, their heads on a pillow of grass and sweet herbs. The lady was fair but her lover was an ugly man, hairy and heavy and uncouth.

Then Balin went quietly out through chambers and halls and at the castle gate he told Sir Garnish what he had seen and led him softly to the garden. And when the knight saw his lady in the arms of another, his heart drummed with passion and his veins burst and blood streamed from his nose and mouth. In his blinding rage he drew his sword and cut off the heads of the sleeping lovers. And suddenly the rage was gone and he was sick and weak. And he blamed Balin bitterly, saying, "You have brought sorrow to me on sorrow. If you had not brought me here, I would not have known."

Balin replied angrily, "Was it not better to know her for what she was and so be cured of loving her? I only did what I would want done for me."

"You have doubled my pain," Sir Garnish said. "You have caused me to kill what I loved most in the world and I cannot live," and suddenly he plunged his own bloody sword through his heart and fell dead beside the headless lovers.

The castle was quiet, and Balin knew that if he were found there he would be charged with murdering all three. He went quickly out of the castle and rode away among the forest trees and the thick darkness of his fate was on him and he felt the curtains of his life closing in on him so that he seemed to be riding in a mist of hopelessness.

After a time he came to a stone cross in the path and on it in letters of gold was written, LET NO KNIGHT RIDE ALONE ON THIS WAY. An old and white-haired man approached him as he read the words and he said, "Sir Balin, this is the boundary of your life. Turn back and you may save yourself." And the old man vanished.

Then Balin heard a hunting horn blowing the call that announces the death of a stag. And Balin said somberly, "That death call is for me. I am the quarry and I am not dead yet."

And suddenly a crowd of people clustered around him, a hundred lovely ladies and many knights in rich and glinting armor, and they welcomed him sweetly and petted and soothed him and led him to a castle nearby where they unarmed him and gave him a rich soft robe and led him to sit in the great hall where there was music and dancing and gaiety and brittle joy.

And when Balin was comforted the Lady of the Castle came to him and said, "Sir Knight with the Two Swords, it is the custom here that any passing stranger must joust with a knight who guards an island nearby."

Balin said, "It is an unhappy custom to force a knight to joust whether he wants to or not."

"It is only one knight. Is the great Balin afraid of one knight?"

"I don't think I am afraid, my lady," Balin said. "But a man who has traveled far can be weary and his horse worn out. My body is weary but my heart is fresh." And he said hopelessly, "If I must, I must, and I would be glad to find here my death and rest and peace."

Then a knight who stood nearby said, "I have looked at your armor. Your shield is small and the handles are loose. Take my shield. It is large and well made." And when Balin protested, the knight insisted, saying, "I beg you to take it for your safety."

Then Balin wearily armed himself and the knight brought his new and well-painted shield and forced it on him, and Balin was too weary and confused to argue, and he thought how his squire had said he was a headstrong knight and therein lay his trouble, and so he accepted the shield and mounted and rode slowly to a lake in which there was a small island so near to the castle that it was overlooked by the battlements. And ladies and knights were gathered on the walls to see the combat.

A boat big enough for horse and man was waiting at the waterside and Balin entered it and was rowed to the island, where a damsel stood waiting for him, and she said, "Sir Balin, why have you left your shield with your own device?"

"I don't know why," said Balin. "I am ground down with misfortune and my judgment all askew. I am sorry I ever came to this place, but since I am here I may as well go on. I would be ashamed to turn back. No. I will accept what comes to me, my death or my life."

Then from long habit in the field he rested his weapons and tightened the girth of his saddle. Then he mounted and said a prayer for himself and closed the visor of his helmet and rode toward a little habitation on the island, and the knights and ladies watched him from the tower.

Then a knight in red armor and red horse trappings rode toward him. It was Sir Balan, and when he saw that his opponent wore two swords, he thought it was his brother, but when he saw the device on the shield, he knew it could not be.

In dreadful silence the two knights couched their spears and crashed together, and both spears struck true and did not shatter, and both knights were flung to the ground and lay stunned. Balin was sorely bruised by the fall and his body ached with weariness. And Balan was the first to recover. He rose to his feet and came toward Balin and Balin staggered up to face him.

Balan aimed the first stroke but Balin raised his shield and warded it, and striking underneath he pierced helmet, and he struck again with that unhappy sword and staggered Balan, and then they drew apart and fought warily, cutting and parrying until they were breathless.

Balin looked up at the towers and saw the ladies in bright dresses looking down on them and closed with his opponent again. Then both drew new strength from battle rage and they slashed and cut ferociously and blades chopped through armor and blood poured from each one. A moment they rested and then returned to the deadly fight, each trying to kill quickly before their strength bled away; each cut mortal wounds in the body of the other until Balan staggered away and lay down, too weak to raise his hand.

Then Balin, leaning on his sword, said, "Who are you? I have never found anywhere a knight who could stand up to me."

And the fallen man said, "My name is Balan, and I am a brother of the famous knight Sir Balin."

When Balin heard this his head whirled and he fainted and fell to the ground. And when he came to his senses he crawled on hands and knees and took off Balan's helmet and saw his face so cut to pieces and covered with blood that he did not know that face. And Balin laid his head on his brother's breast and wept, and he cried, "Oh, my brother, my dear brother. I have killed you and you have wounded me to death."

Balin said weakly, "I saw the two swords, but your shield had a device unknown to me."

"It was a knight of that castle who made me take his shield because he knew you would have recognized mine. If I could live I would destroy that castle and its evil customs."

"I wish that might be done," Balan said. "They made me fight here on the island, and when I killed the defender they forced me to be the champion and would not let me go. If you should live, my brother, they would keep you here to fight for their pleasure, and you could not escape over the water."

Then the boat brought the Lady of the Castle and her retainers to the island, and the brothers begged her to bury them together. "We came out of one womb," they said, "and we go to one grave."

And the lady promised that it would be done.

"Now send for a priest," Balin said. "We want the sacrament and to receive the blessed body of our Lord Jesus Christ." And it was done, and Balin said, "Write on our tomb how through ill fortune two brothers killed each other so that passing knights may pray for us."

Then Balan died, but Balin's life lingered with him till midnight, and in the darkness the brothers were buried together.

In the morning Merlin appeared and by his arts he raised a tomb over the brothers and on it in letters of gold he wrote their story.

And then Merlin prophesied many things that were to come: how Lancelot would come, and Galahad. And he fore-told tragic matters: how Lancelot would kill his best friend Gawain.

And after Merlin had done many strange prophetic things, he went to King Arthur and told him the story of the brothers, and the king was saddened. "In all the world," he said, "I never knew two such knights."

MORTE D'ALAIN
by Maxey Brooke

The next two stories concentrate on different aspects of Merlin. Merlin the Enchanter we know, but what about Merlin the Detective? It was an idea that appealed to American industrial chemist Maxey Brooke who had never sold a story before and the result, 'Morte d'Alain' was his first published story. He wrote another in the same vein, 'Morte d'Espier' but unfortunately did not continue the series. He retired as chief chemist at a petroleum company twelve years ago and is now a part-time consultant and journalist. Whilst in the US army he witnessed the Bikini atom bomb tests.

It came to pass in those days a great calm descended on Merrie England. For five years and more the Danes had not molested the North. The head of Black Mored of Northumberland dried in the sun, impaled on a pike in the courtyard. Nowhere was there oppression or injustice or hunger or want, and the Knights of the Round Table lolled around the Court and waxed fat.

A few very young Knights fared forth to seek adventure and found none save gaming in the taverns. Indeed, it seemed that the day of great deeds was past and the winning of golden spurs was only a dream.

Night after night they gathered at the Round Table for feasting and drinking and telling of tales. The Great Hall rang with the lay of a wandering ministrel or the rafters echoed with hearty laughter at the antics of a group of dwarfs or of a feather-brained buffoon. Other times, they would sit open-mouthed at the feats of my Master Merlin. For the most part, my Master performed

70

what he called "small tricks," whose lore he had entrusted to me. Already I knew the secret of coating one's mouth with storax and secreting therein a small ball of wool soaked in the spirit called *al-kohl*, which is the essence of wines and meads. When this was done, one had but to blow one's breath on a lighted taper and a great rush of flame would issue from one's mouth. Already I had done this in the stables and such was the fear of the stable-lads that even now they turned pale at my approach. But when my Master Merlin heard of this he trounced me soundly and threatened to teach me no more of his art.

"For a magician must never perform cheaply," he had said, "and the awe of stable-lads is not worth the risk of exposing one's secrets." I recognized words of wisdom and promised never to perform again until he pronounced me ready.

Now, in my seventeenth year, I was allowed to participate in some of the "small tricks"—such as seeming to change water to wine with the aid of oak gall and fool's gold. And once, King Arthur himself commended me on my bravery in entering a large basket and allowing my Master to pierce it with many swords and pikes. I thanked him gravely, although I knew that at no time had I been in danger. It was after that that Merlin decided my apprenticeship was over and that I should be initiated into the deeper mysteries of sorcery.

No one was more surprised than I to find that sorcery was performed without the aid of spirits and demons, but followed the laws of nature.

"We magicians mask these things with incantations and rituals," explained Merlin, "not to protect ourselves but to prevent the knowledge from falling into evil hands. For if every man were a magician, no man's life would be safe. Knowledge begets knowledge, and each new knowledge is dangerous."

"And our King," I asked, "Does he know this?"

"He is well aware of it. And so long as we use this knowledge to amuse and to further good works he suffers us to continue our deceptions."

And so by day we studied the writings of the ancients and experimented with our vials and powders and alembics, hoping to add a grain to the sands of knowledge. By night we performed our "small tricks" for the Knights of the Round Table assembled, to amuse them and to help hold them together against the time of England's need.

But these were brawny men and full-blooded, given much to boasting and coarse jokes. They were also men of honor, high of temper and quick to take offense. And in these easy times of inaction many were the quarrels which flared up and which were deemed settled only with blood.

Time and again our good King forestalled bloodshed with decisions befitting a Solomon. When words would not suffice he allowed the Knights to settle their quarrel on the jousting field, but only with blunted lances. Yet all could feel the tension growing and growing. All knew that soon even the King's wisdom would not maintain the uneasy peace.

"Were I but King," I once said to my Master, "I would disband the court and do away with these quarrels once and for all."

"Aye," answered Merlin quietly, "and when the Knights returned to their holdings, there would be half a hundred trouble spots instead of one."

'Twas then I recognized that much of the King's wisdom was in reality my Master Merlin's. And 'twas then I knew why our King closeted himself with my Master before and after each gathering on the Round Table.

But even as a pig's bladder must burst when a jester belabors himself with it overmuch, so must strong men's violence burst when kept pent up overlong. And so it was that one evening, in a small room adjoining the Great Hall, a servant found the body of Sir Alain sprawled face down in a pool of blood.

Now let it be said that the servant, unlike many a baseborn man, did not lose his wits and spread abroad a hue and cry. Rather, as though he were answering a summons, he entered my Master's apartment and announced his discovery.

Merlin, albeit annoyed at having his studies interrupted, said to me, "Go, my son, and stand guard over the body. Let none enter the room until I arrive with the King."

I hurried posthaste to the small room. There, even as the servant had said, lay Sir Alain's body. And one could easily see that his death had come of no misadventure nor was it the result of a fair fight. He had been struck down from behind, murdered most foully. The gaping wound between his shoulder blades was from the blow of a wide Danish dagger, such as many of the Knights of the Round Table affected. A brutal crime and a callous one, as could be seen by the black footprint on Sir Alain's white talbard where the murderer had placed his foot in order to withdraw the dagger. And by the streaks of blood where he had coolly cleaned his weapon before returning it to the scabbard.

I arrived none too soon. Scarce had I time to note the condition of the corpse when a serving lad entered the room on some mission. On seeing the quantity of blood, the lad drew up and stood, mouth agape, for the space of six heartbeats. He turned and ran from the room, screaming at the top of his voice, "'Tis blood, 'tis blood, 'tis blood!"

Hard on his outcry came the Knights, the squires, the serving men, the court rabble. They stopped at my raised hand and all but the Knights disbanded at my word, for my fame as a sorcerer was waxing. The Knights continued to press around the door, held back only by fear of the magic pentagram I was enscribing in the air with my finger.

Their anger was only outdone by their disbelief that such a deed could have been done. To them it was readily evident that this was murder. And to them it was equally evident that one of their own company was the murderer, none but a Knight who had warred with the Danes and had won in fair combat such a weapon as had struck down fair Sir Alain.

As the first shock wore off, I could see the Knights drawing back and eyeing one another with distrust and suspicion. 'Twas an ugly thing to see—the breakdown of the feeling of brotherhood amongst them. Full glad was I at the appearance of the King, followed closely by my Master.

The King's face was white and drawn behind his huge red beard, and his brows were drawn together in anger. And only I knew the effort of my Master in keeping his face calm and reposed. The King turned to the Knights assembled and well did they draw back at his anger, though they were strong men and brave.

I expected a great roar, for the King had a full voice; but the King spoke softly, which was all the more frightening for his softness.

"Let him that did this step forth."

There was no movement.

"Let him that did this step forth and I will slay him honorably with my own hands."

There was no movement.

And the King's voice then rose to a roar that could be heard to the utmost parts of the castle. "Then I will seek you out, strip you of your Knighthood, and see you hanged from the highest battlements." Even Sir Lancelot could not conceal a quaking at the King's intensity.

He turned to my Master. "What will you need to reveal this foul varlet who calls himself a Knight?"

My Master stood a full minute, his head bent in contemplation.

"His blood will tell. I will need Sir Alain's blood-soaked talbard and the bloodstained stones whereon he lies. At moonrise let the Knights be assembled in the Great Hall—barefoot, to prove their humbleness, and clad only in singlets. Let each man be seated at his regular appointed place at the Round Table. Let no squires nor serving men nor other baseborn be present, for there is to be revealed a great mystery. And let none touch aught that he sees on the Great Table."

Without hesitation, although these were strange requests, the King said quietly, "So be it."

He turned on his heel and marched away toward the chapel. One by one the Knights followed to offer up prayers for Sir Alain's soul. My Master looked me full in the eyes, then he too departed, leaving me strangely aware of what I was to do.

Not for long was I alone with the corpse. Soon came two black-robed friars. They removed Sir Alain's befouled talbard and handed it to me with many an open sign of the cross and covert sign of the horns to ward off the evil eye. They then bore him away to prepare Sir Alain for burial.

Hard on the friars came workmen with bars and mauls to remove the bloody stones. Only my presence and the fear of some meaningless but strange hand passes I made overcame their lesser fear of the death chamber.

The stones I had carried to the Great Hall. Then closing the door, I chalked a few Arabic symbols thereon, knowing full well that none but my Master would enter.

Thereon I retired to our chambers where Merlin awaited me. Wordlessly he held out his hand for the talbard, and having spread it on a table, studied it full long. Though I wished mightily to talk of the day's happenings, I knew to hold my peace until my Master finished his meditations. I pretended to study an ancient scroll. At last my Master looked up from the table.

"My son, an hour before moonrise, take yonder casket to the Great Hall. Then station yourself at the door to see that all the Knights are garbed as I directed. When the Knights are assembled, enter with them and await my coming." He took the scroll from my hand, glanced at it, and smiled, "When you read Hebrew, hold the scroll thus." He reversed the scroll and returned it to me.

I spent the remainder of the day studying the Mysteries of Pythagoras to atone for the error in the manner of my reading of the Hebrew scroll. When at last the glass showed it to be an hour till moonrise, I put aside the Mysteries without being much wiser. The casket my Master had indicated I now took to the Great Hall and set it therein. I removed the signs from the door and awaited the Knights.

One by one they came, each looking darkly at the others. Each paused beneath where his shield was hung, removed his outer garments and shoes, and entered the Great Hall. Not a word was said.

On the dais, where the King was accustomed to sit, lay the bier of Sir Alain, lit at head and toe with tall tapers. In the dim light sat the Knights, even the King, shorn of their trappings, each in his place at the Round Table.

All eyes turned ever and anon to the eastern casement. As the silver edge of the moon appeared over the horizon, all turned toward the door. There in a great rush of flame and smoke appeared my Master Merlin, clad in his magician's robes and wearing a great coned cap.

He advanced to the foot of the Round Table, eyed each Knight in turn, and intoned solemnly, "Does the murderer wish to confess now or shall I call upon the powers of darkness to seek him out?"

There was a stir around the table as each Knight shuddered, but none spoke.

"Then so be it." He nodded to me.

I lifted the basket of stones torn from the floor of the murder room and stained with the blood of the dead man. I carried them around the table and my Master placed one stone in front of each Knight.

"The blood of the stones seeks the blood on the murderer's hands!"

Each Knight sat far back in his chair, eyes fixed on the stone in front of him. Fear was on every face.

Next I brought forward the casket. From it my Master removed a device most cunningly contrived; an arrow with an iron head mounted on a pivot, so that it could swing freely. This he set in the middle of the Round Table.

"Now I call on the greatest forces known: blood and iron! The blood of the murdered man cries for vengence. The iron is thirsty for that blood. I shall swing the arrow around and it shall come to rest pointing to that bloody stone before the murderer."

He gave the arrow a twirl. Around and around it went, slower and slower. And at last it came to a stop, pointing to the stone before Sir Warfield.

His face was white behind his black beard. He cried in a mighty voice, "'Tis chance! 'Tis but chance!" As well condemn a man on the throw of the dice."

"Nay, 'tis not chance," said Merlin quietly, "'tis the power of darkness. 'Tis the attraction of a murdered man's blood for iron."

He gave the arrow another twirl. Again it made its ever-slowing rounds and again it stopped and again it pointed to the stone before Sir Warfield.

He stood up, his mouth working for a moment; then once more he cried out, "'Tis trickery! Yon Merlin spun the arrow in such a manner as to make it stop here!"

With those words he gave the arrow a mighty buffet. And for the third time it stopped directly before him.

Sir Warfield stood looking at the arrow for a time one could count to ten slowly. Then he sat back in his chair, collapsing even as a jester's bladder when pierced with a bodkin.

"'Tis sorcery," he gasped, in a strangled voice, "'Tis sorcery. Aye, I killed him. I did him in even as that cursed arrow says. I killed him."

There was a silence in the Great Hall—a silence in part of relief and in part of revulsion. And King Arthur said slowly, "Take him away."

He was taken away and given over to the hangman. Even as the King had ordered, he was hanged from the highest battlements at dawn.

'Twould be a fitting end to this tale to say that the murder shocked the Knights back into a sense of duty, but such was not the case. Ere the week was up they were again boasting and brawling.

Back in our chambers, I awaited my Master's pleasure, but when he saw fit to say nothing, I asked, "Sir, riddle me this mystery. Did you truly call on the powers of darkness?"

"Nay, my son. There are no powers of darkness save in the minds of men."

He reached into his wallet. "Do you recognize this stone?"

"'Tis one of the cobbles from the floor whereon Sir Alain died."

"Nay. 'Tis a stone from the shores of a far land, and it is ofttimes called a lodestone. It has the strange power of attracting iron unto itself. I simply put this stone before Sir Warfield, knowing full well that the arrow, with its iron head, would always stop pointing toward it."

I tried to resume my studies, but another thought occurred.

"How did you know to put the stone before Sir Warfield, sir?"

"I had the Knights remove their shoes—not to humble themselves, as I said, but rather to enable me to examine each shoe. The stitching on the sole of Sir Warfield's right shoe matched the print on Sir Alain's talbard. Remember, no cobbler, however clever, can ever sew two shoes so that the stitching on them is exactly the same."

KING'S MAN
by Sasha Miller

Now we'll return to Merlin the Enchanter. In the legend, he falls in love with the sorceress Niniane who subsequently imprisons him in an underground cave. Before his imprisonment Merlin predicted the coming of Sir Lancelot, but the two characters do not meet in the Malory version (although we will meet Merlin again in this book). Sasha Miller picked on this point and developed it into an original story, which appears here for the first time.

The old man sat amid the odds and ends of his craft—the beakers, the retorts, the mortar and pestle. He shook his head in disbelief.

To commit such a folly as falling in love, he thought. It's appalling, it's unheard of, it can't be done—and yet, I've gone and done it. The others in my order will titter among themselves and wonder if the Myrdyn is losing his touch. I can hear them now. The old fool, they'll say. I've never relished being ridiculed. And by my own at that.

The pygmy owl that lived with him shuffled out of its hiding-place, shook its feathers, and stared at the mage.

"Go ahead, disapprove," he said irritably. "Not that it's any of your business. What do you know of men?" The owl merely gazed at him without blinking, and the Myrdyn looked aside first. "You're right. I am not a man,' he said. "Haven't been for ages." He had given it up to be what he was—the Myrdyn, head of the ancient Order of Myrdynni. He had been the Myrdyn so long that his real name had long been forgotten by all but him.

And yet it seemed like yesterday when he had stood around the fire with other young men and women ready to take their final oaths, listening as their teacher intoned the awful words.

"If you will be great," the Master said, "you must give up sexual capacity and put that drive into the wizardly arts. Then you will receive to your capability, and to the degree of natural function you are willing to relinquish. Who will be first?"

Like all things in magic, it was a balanced rule, stern but fair. Some of his companions had wavered then, unwilling to give up fleshly pleasures for power. But he had stepped forward eagerly, relinquishing everything without hesitation. And through the years he had progressed, becoming first a mage, then a lesser Myrdyn, then finally *the* Myrdyn. Now, indisputably, he was the oldest and greatest of his kind, greater even than the Master of his youth. And for the sake of a woman and what he thought he had given up for all time, he regretted it.

He fumbled inside his robe, searching the flaccid, wrinkled bags of scrotum and penis for the least sign of stirring. There was none, nor had he really expected it. He had not touched himself in a sexual way in years. His genitals were so lifeless that even when he piddled he squatted like a woman.

Sighing, he settled back in his chair and the pygmy owl, the old man's closest companion, waddled over to climb up his sleeve and nestle on his shoulder. Without realizing what he was doing, he laid his wrinkled cheek against the bird's warm feathers and, very tired, closed his eyes.

Art-Tyr habitually kept court at Isca. It was his favorite fortress, sturdily constructed in the way the old Roman invaders always built, and he spent so much time there that the Myrdyn, wanting to be as far away as possible from the barracks, had dug a cave for himself beneath the man-made hill. The well-preserved commander's quarters that housed Art-Tyr had been built with a hypercaust—a hot-air heating system that kept the dwelling warm even in the hardest winter. But the Myrdyn, snug in his cave, didn't envy him. Also, there was a bath—seldom used—in the town. An amphitheater stood near the walls and it was there that the king liked to gather with his warriors. When he had first begun his fight against those invaders who came swarming into the lands of Albion in the wake of the departing Romans, there were barely enough warriors to ring the bottom tier. Now, when they gathered, they filled it quarter-way up. The arena was perfect as a practice-yard, and it saw daily use as Art-Tyr's warriors honed their skills.

One day a summons came from the king. Unhurriedly, the Myrdyn made his way to the king's house. Art-Tyr received him alone, a mark of favor.

"You took your time," he said, scowling.

"But I am here."

Art-Tyr's expression lightened. "Yes. Well. The war goes slowly. I am minded to marry now, and get sons. You can chose the right one, better than me. Go now, find me a wife."

Find you a wife, the wizard thought. A wife who will strengthen your ambitions and turn your pretensions into true kingship. What Art-Tyr had always wanted—what the Myrdyn had carefully taught him to want—was power. That had all been part of the Myrdyn's great scheme. But that the woman need not be more than a warm breeding-hole between her legs so long as she brought power and soldiers and wealth, was from Art-Tyr alone.

"Yes, Sire," the old man answered, and then braced himself for the king's reaction.

"'Sire!'" Art-Tyr raised one weapons-calloused hand and cuffed him sharply on the shoulder, knocking him off-balance. "Thou, my uncle? Thou callest me 'sire'? How many times have I forbade thee to do so?"

"More times than I can count, good nephew," the old man answered. He rubbed his shoulder, pleased with himself. When Art-Tyr lapsed into familiar usage, he was in rare good humor.

"Take two gold marks," the king said, "and a mule. If that tight-fisted seneschal of mine objects, send him to me."

Two marks in gold was a fortune. But it wasn't the king's generosity that surprised the Myrdyn. It was the pompous way Art-Tyr talked about his foster brother—bad manners that would bring worse luck. He was glad Art-Tyr was no real nephew, just some warrior's by-blow the wizard had rescued from the dirt and had reared to assume the role he now played. Nevertheless, he thanked the king and left at once.

Ha, he thought, Art-Tyr would be suspicious and distrustful of a match made as quickly as I anticipate it will. He's quite stupid enough to reject it out of hand even though it is the one match that would unite the various factions of the Weallech. Imagine being called "foreigners" by those hairy northerners who've shoved us into this corner of Albion. But they have been quiet of late. So I'll go roaming where I please, enjoying my freedom until the money is spent and the mule footsore.

Of course he knew where to go, which woman to choose. He had been planning for this moment for years. In the old days, before the Romans had come, the yearly kings were chosen by the Queen in the proper fashion, not like these jumped-up quarreling puppies, squabbling among themselves for domination.

Rumor among the common folk had it that Lleogran of Trevena secretly followed the old ways. And furthermore, one of his kinswomen, descended from the most ancient Queens presently lived with him, unmarried. If the Myrdyn found this rumor reliable, he knew he would be able to conclude all negotiations briskly. All Art-Tyr wanted was to be king, and to fight. With this marriage, he'd have his wish; but the Queen would rule, and she would bring back the old religion that, the people feared, had been lost forever. The people, and the Myrdynni.

Power? Art-Tyr would never realize the power residing in the lady who sat at his side. Wealth? Soldiers? The arena at Isca would overflow with warriors, once the word had gone out surreptitiously that the old ways were coming back.

Occupied with these pleasant thoughts, the Myrdyn made his way quickly to Trevena, an earthen fortress perched on a headland with an access so narrow a couple of striplings armed with shepherds' crooks could have held off an army. No Roman had set foot in Trevena, nor any northern barbarian; Trevena was as it had always been—pure, the bastion of the ancient ways.

The news of his coming had gone before him, and many of Lleogran's people hurried out to welcome him and to escort him over the causeway and into the earthen-walled citadel where Lleogran and his kinswoman waited to greet him.

Then he saw her, and only her. The shock of recognition shattered every plan he had ever made. His presence in the here and now fell away like a worn-out garment and he took a step forward, arms extended. He *knew* this woman! He had known her intimately through untold past lifetimes, would know her again and again through the swirls of lifetimes yet to come. . . .

She was fire and earth and water, the holly, the rowan and the mistletoe, pale and vivid at once. Wander they called her, in the old tongue. Gwenhyvhar in the new. She lifted cool eyes to him and he realized she had felt nothing of what he had. And yet, she had the power. He could sense it sleeping in her. It was waiting for him to awaken it.

Fair she was, but mere beauty could not answer the riddle of her fascination. She had the kind of self-command that could hold a man at arm's length for eternity or invite him to her bedside with nothing more than a glance. And unless he were a fool he would go gladly, forgetting honor, other loyalties, all else.

For the first time in decades the old man wished that he could rise and throb and quiver with life.

With a tremendous effort, he turned the lover's gesture of greeting into a bow. "Lady," he said.

"I have heard of you," she said. "And I know why you have come." She made a gesture with her hand in the air, tracing a symbol the Myrdyn thought never to see again. He made the answering gesture, and she smiled for the first time. "Yes, Myrdyn of the Myrdynni, I accept gladly and will marry Art-Tyr at Isca. You can return and tell your king."

Her voice was warm and sweet, as warm and sweet as the secret place between her legs must be. With sudden bitterness, the Myrdyn wished his nephew were sterile, or a eunuch, and had never dreamt of taking a wife.

He needed the time alone before returning, to exorcise the memory of her. He avoided people, spending his time in the wild. Try as he would, she haunted his waking and sleeping hours, floating naked and tantalizing just out of his reach. For the Myrdyn, intense sexual desire affecting only his mind was thoroughly disagreeable. Some nights, when the thwarted rutting urge was strongest, he pawed the flabby, shriveled tag of flesh between his legs until it was nearly raw, trying to force the appropriate sensation into it. But it was to no avail.

When, during those days of wandering, he realized that he was not entirely sane, he knew he could trust himself enough to face the king again. Only the true madman has no doubts.

Before returning to Isca, he sewed his unspent money into the seams of his garments rather than have to answer questions. He went straight to the king and, by dint of heroic effort, presented the proposed marriage without a tremor in his voice. He needn't have worried. Art-Tyr, in the midst of a dicing game with his current mistress, accepted the old man's choice, asking only what the lady looked like.

She swam into the wizard's vision, as tempting as in the worst days of his madness and desire. Her skin shone with a weird pearly light and her hair floated around her, enhancing rather than hiding her nakedness. He swayed, near fainting.

"Beautiful," he said, looking at her. "Wondrous fair—" The foretelling came on him then, and he was unable to bite back the warning that rose unbidden. "She will bring you joy and pain, and your best friend will betray you."

Art-Tyr laughed loudly. "But Uncle, thou'rt my best friend until

I find a better," he said. "Thou betray me? Never in this life." He dismissed the old man's pronouncement of doom with a snap of his fingers. "Does she have a big mouth? You know, big mouth on top, bigger mouth on bottom. Not so good for—"he made an obscene gesture, pushing his middle finger in and out of a circle made with forefinger and thumb of the other hand—"but the babies fall out easier, eh, Nymia?" He grinned at the woman who had been a camp harlot before she attracted the king's eye.

Nymia had a very small mouth, which she emphasized by painting it only in the center and by seldom opening it very widely, even when she ate or drank. She shrugged and sniffed audibly. "It depends on what you like,' she said.

Art-Tyr laughed even louder. "The queen for heirs, you for tumbling." He pulled her close and began to paw at her breasts.

"There are, ah, certain marriage customs the Queen must insist on," the Myrdyn said. "It is her religion." He couldn't keep the tremor out of his voice, but the king didn't notice. He had freed one of Nymia's breasts from her bodice and was staring at it hungrily. His other hand was busy under her skirt.

"Tell Cai," he said. "Leave me now. I'm busy."

The old man fled gratefully. His tongue would have blackened and dropped out before he could bring himself to tell this creature, his nephew, how his and Wander's wedding must be consummated in the full view of everyone. It was an absolute necessity in the old religion, so all would know the king was strong and potent. If Art-Tyr objected he would be told that it was so any son begotten on that occasion would undeniably be the king's own.

Only sensible, of course. Necessary for everything the Myrdyn and the Queen believed in. His nephew, smothering the beautiful Wander in his embrace, her body exposed, her modesty violated— No matter that if everything worked as anticipated, Art-Tyr would die with the year's end as the old religion demanded. If the Myrdyn had to stand by and watch his beloved Wander given into the great calloused hands of his royal nephew, he would not be able to keep himself from doing someone great harm. A single well-placed thunderbolt. . . .

Grimly, he forced that picture from his mind. Let Wander torment him as she would; it was still preferable to the thought of her impaled by the barbarian he himself had chosen to be king.

With his last ounce of control he arranged the rite with the king's foster-brother. Cai barely raised an eyebrow; he was well known to be a lover of men so if it mattered to him, it was just a way to humiliate one of the women he hated so vehemently. Then the Myrdyn, released and fearing again for his sanity, fled to the shelter and safety of his cave.

Even from there the old man could not help being aware of the wedding plans; fifty warriors would escort the king, and fifty ladies would attend the Queen, all gifts from Lleogran. The royal couple would wear garments of new wool, embroidered with purple and scarlet threads. They would tread a path lined on either side with sword-blades, tokens of their owners' submission to Art-Tyr's rule. The Queen. . . .

The Myrdyn sat up abruptly, on fire with a decision that some part of his mind must have been contemplating all along.

I will work a truly monstrous magic, he thought. I will shed this impotent flesh and become young again, and fresh, and capable. The choice I made many years ago will be undone. I was mere Emrys once; I'll be mere Emrys once more. I'll leave this place, never see either of them again, make a new life, have a new direction, a new goal. I'll give up arcane power, and magic, and wizardly lore, and uncountable years in which to practice my craft, for the mortal life I once had. I'll do more than that. I'll find a new place, a new time in this world, where kings are just and heroes are brave, where all is cleanness and honor and a man will love his friends. I wonder if she'll ever think of me.

If only I could stay, could allow myself the possibility of following her beckoning glance and being allowed to bury my glorious living manhood in her sweetest, most secret recess— A giddy rush of sexual passion swept over him, so intense that his withered old penis almost stirred.

He shook himself wider awake, pulled a sheet of foolscap to him, and dipped a quill into the inkwell. Good thing he had kept the king's gold. The materials he would need were bound to be very expensive. The pygmy owl shook itself and flew out the door. The Myrdyn knew it would never return. He began to write.

Item. A future. That was easy. He could see that so clearly in his mind's eye he didn't need to make notes.

Item. A new past. He would have to alter the memories of certain men and women in this new time and place so that they would believe that he had been born of thus-and-such parentage, and had already lived thus-and-so-many years. Complicated, but merely a matter of attending to detail.

Item. He would have to find an explanation of his disappearance from his present. A new idea came to the Myrdyn, causing him to smile. Nymia. Of course. Despite the king's passion for her, the old man knew she must be banished. She had already moved to her own house close by the king's dwelling. Some cynics were already suggesting that should Wander fail to live up to Art-Tyr's anticipations, Nymia was making certain she would be convenient.

Usually Nymia ignored or belittled him. But she had also, on occasion, expressed a mild interest in his activities. It would be easy enough for him to create the notion that in idle moments she had learnt his craft, surpassed her teacher, and then set him under an enchantment herself. Her name would bear a reek that would make her an outcast forevermore, but he found himself untroubled by the prospect. He scribbled on the paper.

Item. He would even give her a few small magics for her own use thereafter. Water-witching, perhaps. Fire. But then, any fool could do fire if he had the least natural talent. Minor prophecy. Perhaps all three. He could afford to be generous.

Detail upon detail. It called for the most minute attention, the most careful craftsmanship. Nothing like it had ever been attempted before, to his certain knowledge. Nobody had held enough power to try it. But if he, the Myrdyn of the Myrdynni and at the absolute height of his abilities, could not do it, then there would never be anybody who could.

Item. He might retain no memory, or perhaps just a little, of his present existence.

Item. He might not survive the experiment.

He knew he must hurry his preparations and do it before Wander came to Isca. Otherwise, his resolve would fail him. As the time grew shorter he worked more quickly, taking shortcuts whenever he dared. Too soon, he would have to act, regardless, and be prepared to live or die by the results. If he succeeded, his torment would end; if he died, well, that would end it, too.

He built devices of foreign sweet-wood and spider's silk, transcribed in his own blood themes of dark, forbidden song, constructed intricate mechanisms sparkling with wild silver and globes of water-filled crystal. When he was done, he loaded everything on his back and left his cave on a moonless night. Sunrise found him standing on a hill out of sight of the citadel. The various themes, mechanisms and devices lay properly distributed around him. He looked around for the last time. The grass had never been so green, the world so lovely. He shrugged himself free of his earthly clothing and the chill of the morning raised goosebumps on his withered old flanks. He took up his staff, breathed deeply, and began to speak the Words of Power.

The crystal globes blazed with concentrated dawnlight, all focused cunningly upon the themes. They caught fire at once with a smell of scorched blood. The music, released, danced on its own smoke, chanting in antiphonal harmony with the crackling of the flames. The ground began to tremble and he realized too late that *something* was subtly wrong, something his traitorous desires had made him do or not do without his realizing it, that twisted what was even now taking place—

"No!" he cried despairingly. But before he could move to correct his error the wildwind swept him up and he was gone.

He awoke reluctantly. A savage ache filled his head and the last thing he wanted to do was to open his eyes. Cautiously, he rolled over. His eyelids felt glued together. Nevertheless, he forced one eye open long enough to get his bearings. And the pain came stabbing in with the afternoon sunlight, as he had known it would. He lay back into the softness of the grass, one arm over his face. A memory nibbled at the back of his brain, something immediate and yet nearly forgotten—

Did I drink too much? I don't think so. He scratched absently at his crotch and his penis stirred slightly. At least that part of him didn't feel as destroyed as the rest did.

Sometimes, he thought, I am a little mad. Imagine falling asleep in the open, under a single tree out in the middle of a clearing. More stupidity; my mail shirt is unbelted. I might just as well have hung up a flag, here I am, alone and helpless, waiting for an ambush. The nagging memory dug at him again. Something concerning a woman—

His nape hairs rose. There was a horse nearby. He could smell it. He heard metal clink on metal. Something brushed his chest.

"Who are you and why do you dare sleep under my tree?"

The knight felt groggy, sick. He wanted to stretch, fill his lungs to capacity, try to clear his head. Now he didn't dare; it would be a suicidal move. He groaned, silently cursing himself, and bit his lip. Very carefully, he moved his arm and opened his eyes.

A man sat on the horse, towering over him. He wore rich scale mail. His helm, dazzling in the late afternoon sunlight, covered most of his face. His shield was yellow with a black bear, silver-crowned. Most important, the horseman held a spear, and it was pointed unswervingly at the knight's heart.

Aha, so that's how it is, he thought. "If you will let me up I will arm myself and fight you if you wish," he said. His head throbbed until he thought it would burst the brain-pan.

The horseman sat still, considering. Then he backed the horse, brought the spear up, and socketed the butt. "We'll fight as we are, right now. I'll let you draw your sword," he added magnanimously.

I shall never drink too much again or whatever it was that I did do, not if it happens I live through this, the knight thought. What an unpleasant fellow this man is, a perfect example of what's wrong with the world these days. . . . Stiffly, he got up on his knees and pulled himself erect by holding onto the tree trunk. Do I dare fasten my vestment? No. He pulled his sword from the scabbard.

The stranger lowered his spear, spurring his horse forward. Unsurprised and with the ease of long practice, the knight executed a gliding side-step and let the spear-point slide past harmlessly. In the same movement he swung a two-handed blow that fractured the shaft of the spear and disabled the horse. While the stranger fought to jump away from the horse before it could cripple him in turn, the knight clasped the buckle on the belt that held his shirt together in the front. He just had time to grab his helm and slap it on his aching head before the other man finished drawing his sword.

Despite his vile mood and anger, the knight did not attack until his opponent had rid himself of the small wooden shield and got both hands fairly on his sword-hilt. Then he rushed forward to deliver the first stroke. His code of honor did not encompass stupidity.

After the first few blows he settled down and began methodically punishing the richly-clad oaf who had disturbed him. Gradually, with the exercise, he found his mood improving and his headache beginning to lift.

It ended as he knew it would, as it always did, with his opponent flat on his back, and himself straddling the body. He fumbled with the fastenings on the other man's helm, got it off, and held his enemy by the throat as he reached for the dagger strapped to his leg.

"I yield, by God!" the other man cried. He was dirty, bloody, and sweat-soaked; incongruously, he was grinning. "I haven't had such sport in months!"

Surprised, the victor delayed the death-stroke. "Who are you?" he asked.

"I am Arthur!" The man laughed hugely, unafraid. The two of them might have been playing on the practice field, rather than engaged in a deadly serious fight.

Only now did he recognize the dazzling bright thing on his opponent's helm. It was a crown. "Oh, God's mercy." He threw away the dagger, scrambled off Arthur's body, and pulled him to his feet. Then he dropped to his knees before him. "You are the king! I have come many weary miles across land and water so that I might be your man, if it please you. And I was on the verge of killing you! Forgive me, sire, I beg of you."

"And who are you, then?"

He bowed his head. "I am King Ban's son of Benwick," he said humbly. "I am Lancelot."

SIR PERCIVALE OF WALES

by Roger Lancelyn Green

Roger Lancelyn Green (1918–1987) was long a friend of the fantasy field. He compiled several anthologies of fantasy and supernatural fiction, wrote a number of studies of authors of fantasy fiction, and penned a few fantasies himself, most notably From the World's End *(1948). But he is most likely to be remembered for his retellings of myths and legends which covered* The Adventures of Robin Hood, The Tale of Troy *and, of course,* King Arthur and His Knights of the Round Table *(1953). Green spared no research in his background to* King Arthur *and his volume drew not only on Malory but on many of the lesser known medieval romances and ballads. For the following story he used a Middle English poem as his source plus incidents from the French* Conte du Graal.

In the wild forests of Wales there lived once a boy called Percivale, with his mother. Never another living soul did he meet for the first fifteen years of his life, nor did he learn anything of the ways of men and women in the world. But Percivale grew strong and hardy in the wild wood, of deadly aim with the dart, and simple of heart, honest and upright.

Now, one day as he wandered alone, discontented suddenly and longing for he knew not what, a sound fell upon his ears—not the voice of any bird, nor the music of wind or water, yet music

89

it was, of a kind that set his heart leaping, he knew not why. He paused listening in a leafy glade, and as he waited there five knights came riding towards him, their armour jingling and the bridles of their horses ringing like silver bells.

"Greetings, fair youth!" cried the first knight, reining in his steed and smiling down at Percivale. "Nay, look not so stricken with wonder: surely you have seen our like before?"

"Indeed not," said Percivale. "And, truth to tell, I know not what you are, unless you be angels straight out of Heaven, such as those of whom my mother teaches me. Come tell me, noble sirs, do you not serve the King of Heaven?"

"Him do we serve indeed," said the knight, crossing himself reverently. "And so also do all men who live truly in this the realm of Logres. But on earth we serve His appointed Emperor—the noble King Arthur, at whose Round Table we sit. It is he who made us knights—for that is all we are: and you too he will make a knight if you but prove yourself worthy of that great honour."

"How may I do that?" asked Percivale.

"Come to King Arthur at Caerleon," answered the knight. "Tell him that I sent you thither—I, Sir Launcelot of the Lake who, under King Arthur, rule this land of Pant, which is also called North Wales. Then he will set you such deeds to do, such quests to accomplish, as we of his Court follow after all our days: and, if you prove worthy, he will make you a knight. But not in great deeds of arms lies the true worth of knighthood—rather in the heart of the doer of such deeds: if he be pure and humble, doing all things to the glory of God and to bring that glory and that peace throughout all our holy kingdom of Logres."

Then Sir Launcelot bowed his head to Percivale, and rode on his way, followed by the four other knights, leaving him wrapped in wonder—but with a great longing and a great humility stirring dimly within him.

"Mother! cried Percivale excitedly as he came striding up the path to the little cave where they lived. "Mother, oh mother—I have indeed met with wonders this day! They said they were not angels, but knights—yet to me they seemed fairer than all the hosts of Heaven! And one of them—the leader—Sir Launcelot was his name—said that I too could be a knight. . . Mother, I shall set out to-morrow morning and seek for King Arthur who dwells in Caerleon!"

Then Percivale's mother sighed deeply, and she wept for a little while, knowing that the appointed time had come when she must lose her son. Indeed, at first she tried to persuade Percivale to remain with her in the peace and safety of the forest, telling him of the dangers and sufferings that a knight must undergo. But all that she said only made Percivale the more eager to set out on his quest; and at length she bowed her head quietly and gave him his way.

Early on the following morning Percivale clad himself in his simple garments of skins, took a long sharp dart in his hand, and prepared to bid his mother good-bye.

"Go bravely forward, my son," she said as she kissed and blessed him. "Your father was the bravest and best of knights: be worthy of him and of me. And if you live all your days in honour and purity, you too shall be numbered among the chosen few whose names will live for ever among the true Knights of Logres. . . Go on your way now, and remember that if dame or damsel ask your aid, give it freely and before all else, seeking no reward. Yet you may kiss the maiden who is willing, but take no more than a kiss, unless it be a ring—but be that only when you place your own ring upon her finger. Beware in whose company you travel on your quest, and see to it that only worthy men come near to your heart: but above all, pray to God each day that He may be with you in all your deeds—and pass not by church nor chapel without pausing awhile in His honour."

Very gravely Percivale kissed his mother good-bye, and set out through the forest, walking swiftly, yet with his head bowed as he thought of the solemn things which she had said to him. But in a little while the spring came back into his step and he went on his way singing joyfully and tossing his long dart up into the air until the keen blade flashed like silver in the sunlight as he caught it and whirled it up again and again.

The shadows were falling in long black folds between the trees and the sun drew near to the western hills when Percivale came suddenly to an open glade in the forest where the daisies clustered the green grass like snowflakes, and saw a pavilion of silk pitched beside a tinkling stream.

"Be this church or chapel," thought Percivale, "it is wondrous fair—and I will go into it!"

Stepping softly over the threshold, he passed into the shadowy bower, and there stood in wonder looking down upon a damsel who lay sleeping on a couch of rich silk and samite, with one arm stretched out, more white than the coverlet and her hair lighting up the pillowlike sun shine. Very gently Percivale bent down over her and took from her finger the one ring that she wore—a plain gold band set with a single red ruby: in its place he put his own gold ring from which shone one white diamond, and the maiden's ring he set on his own finger. Then, still without waking her, he kissed her gently on the lips and stole once more from the tent, his heart singing with a new wonder and a new longing.

Deep into the forest went Percivale, slept, when darkness fell, among the roots of a great oak tree, and with the first light was on his way again, striding through the wood until he came to the wide road which led to Caerleon.

At noon he reached the city gates, passed them without stopping, and in time found himself within the very castle.

King Arthur with many of his knights sat feasting there that day, for the time was Easter and they had ceased from their labours for a little while. Percivale stood by the door, marvelling at all he saw and envying even the serving-men who waited upon the King and his company.

And suddenly as he stood there unobserved, all eyes turned towards the door as a great man in golden-red armour strode unannounced into the hall. Now at that moment Sir Kay was standing beside the King holding in his hands the golden goblet from which it was Arthur's custom to pledge all his company ere the cup was passed round from hand to hand that each might drink to him and to the glory of the realm of Logres.

"Stay, you pack of wine-bibbing hinds!" roared the great red stranger. "Here is one better than all of you!" And with that he snatched the goblet from Sir Kay, drained it at a draught, and, with a great roar of laughter, strode from the hall with it still in his hand, leapt upon his horse and galloped swiftly away.

"Now, by my faith!" cried King Arthur springing to his feet, "this insult shall not go unpunished. Who will bring me back my cup?"

Then every knight rose as one man and cried: "Let this quest be mine!"

"Not so," said King Arthur, motioning them to sit once more. "Yonder red braggart is not worthy to fall at a knight's hands. Let some humble squire follow and overthrow him—one who seeks to be made a knight. Such a one who returns to my Court wearing the Red Knight's armour and carrying my golden goblet, will I knight forthwith!"

Then Percivale sprang forward from his place by the doorway and stood in the midst, clad as he was in the skins of wild goats and with the long dart held in his hand:

"King Arthur!" he cried, "I'll fetch your cup! I want some armour, and that golden suit will do me very well!"

"Bah!" exclaimed Sir Kay rudely. "What can this miserable goat-herd do against so great a knight?"

"Who are you, fair sir?" asked King Arthur, courteous as always to all men.

"My name is Percivale," was the answer. "I do not know who my father was, for I never saw him nor heard my mother speak of him. But she has brought me up in the forests of Wales—and I come now to ask you to make me a knight!"

"Make you a knight, indeed!" scoffed Sir Kay. "Go and tend sheep on the mountains before yonder ram in the golden armour makes you run away in terror!"

"A knight shall you be," said King Arthur, "if you bring back my cup and return wearing the armour of the robber who has taken it. Lo now, this quest is yours! Follow it only and no other!"

"I have no horse," said Percivale.

"One shall be ready for you at the door," answered Arthur. "Eat now swiftly, and get you gone. . . But you need arms and weapons. . ."

"I have my dart," interrupted Percivale. "As for armour, I'll wait until I can put on that golden suit which you all saw not long ago!"

When he had eaten Percivale rose to go: but as he passed down the hall, a damse stood before him and cried aloud: "The King of Heaven bless you, Sir Percivale, the best of knights!"

"Be silent, witless wench!" cried Sir Kay angrily, and he struck the damsel across the face.

"Beware of me when I return in my golden armour!" said Percivale looking scornfully at Sir Kay. "That unknightly stroke will I revenge with a blow that you will not lightly forget!"

Then he hastened from the hall, sprang upon the waiting horse, and rode away into the forest.

Percivale went much faster than the Red Knight so that before sunset he overtook him as he rode quietly up a mountain path towards a lone grey tower outlined against the pale pink of the clouds.

"Turn, thief!" shouted Percivale as soon as he was near enough. "Turn and defend yourself!"

A little way behind him three of King Arthur's knights reined in their horses to watch: they had followed all the way from Caerleon to see what should befall but not even now did Percivale know that they were there.

"Ha!" cried the Red Knight, wheeling his steed. "What insolent boy are you? And why do you bid me stand?"

"I come from King Arthur," answered Percivale. "Give me back the golden goblet which you stole this day at his feast! Moreover, you must go yourself to the Court and do homage there—but first of all you must yield to me and give me that fine suit of armour which you wear so proudly!"

"And if I do not?" asked the Red Knight, speaking quietly but his eyes flashing with fury like the lightning in the quiet sky before a mighty storm.

"Why then I will kill you—and help myself to cup and armour!" exclaimed Percivale.

"Insolent child!" roared the Red Knight in a voice of thunder. "You have asked for death—now take it!"

With that he set his spear in rest and came down the hillside like a mighty avalanche, expecting to transfix his enemy as if he were a butterfly on a pin. But Percivale leapt suddenly from his horse so that the spear passed harmlessly over its head, and stood in the middle of the path, shouting taunts:

"You great coward!" he jeered. "First you try to spear an unarmed man, and then you run away down the hillside!"

With horrible oaths the Red Knight wheeled his horse once more and came charging up the path, his spear aimed at Percivale. But this time Percivale drew back his dart and threw it suddenly—so suddenly that it sped like a flash of light over the Red Knight's shield and caught him in the throat just above the rim of his armour, so that he fell backwards from his horse and lay there dead.

Percivale knelt down triumphantly beside his fallen foe and drew out King Arthur's golden cup from the wallet at his waist. But when he tried to loosen the golden armour from the body he found himself defeated: for he did not know how it was fastened on, and thought indeed that it was all made in one piece.

After many vain attempts to pull the Red Knight through the gorget or neck-piece of the armour, Percivale changed his tactics. Swiftly he gathered together a pile of dry wood, and was busily striking a flint from the road against the point of his dart when suddenly he heard the sound of a horse's hooves, and looking up saw an old man on horseback dressed in dark armour, whose helmet hung at his saddle-bow, and whose grey hair fell to his shoulders.

"Greetings, young sir," said the old knight smiling kindly upon Percivale. "What do you with this dead robber whom you have slain so valiantly?"

"Out of the iron burn the tree," said Percivale, quoting a woodman's saying which his mother had taught him. "I want to get this man out of the armour and wear it myself."

The old knight's smile grew broader still, but he dismounted from his horse and showed Percivale how to unlace the armour and draw it off and on piece by piece.

"My name is Gonemans," said the knight presently, "and I dwell near by in an ancient manor-house. Come you thither with me, young sir, and I will teach you all things that you should know before you can become a worthy knight, for not alone by such a deed as this may you win to the true honour."

So Percivale went with Sir Gonemans and dwelt all that summer in his house, learning to fight with sword and spear, to wear his armour and sit his horse as a knight should. And he learnt also of the high order of knighthood which was so much more noble than the mere doing of mighty deeds: he learnt of right and wrong, of a knight's duty ever to defend the weak and punish the cruel and evil.

And at last he rode forth on his way once more, clad in shining armour, with a tall spear in his hand, after bidding a courteous farewell to Sir Gonemans. It was late autumn by now, and as he rode beneath the trees in the deep woods and forests the leaves gleamed red and gold like his armour which seemed almost to be part of the foliage and bracken through which he passed.

Many days rode Percivale in quest of adventure, and often as he went his eyes fell upon the ruby ring on his finger, and he thought more and more of the lovely damsel whom he had found sleeping in the pavilion.

At length on a dark, sombre evening when the clouds lowered threateningly above him, he came by a winding way among great bare rocks through a sad and desolate land, until suddenly he saw a dark castle in front of him.

The walls were shattered and overthrown, the towers were cracked down the sides as if by lightning: yet no weeds grew among the stones or even between the cobbles under the yawning gateway; and in the centre stood the great keep firm and solid in the midst of that desolation.

Beneath the sharp teeth of the portcullis rode Percivale, his horse's hooves ringing hollowly on the stone and on through dark arches and deserted courtyards until he came to the entrance of the great hall. Here he could see a light burning and so, having tied his horse to a ring in the wall, he walked up the steps and into a mighty room with a high roof of black beams. There was no one to be seen, and yet a fire burned merrily in the great fireplace, torches shone brightly from rings in the walls, and dinner was set at a table on the dais. Percivale walked slowly up the hall and stood looking about him: on a little table not far from the fire he saw laid out a set of great ivory chessmen, with a chair drawn up on one side as if ready for a game. While still wondering what all this might mean, Percivale sat down in the chair, and presently he reached out idly and moved a white pawn forward two squares on the board. At once a red pawn moved forward by itself: Percivale was alert in an instant, but all was quiet, there was not even the sound of any breath but his own. So he moved another piece, and immediately a red piece was moved also. Percivale moved again as if playing—and behold! the red pieces moved in turn, so cunningly that in a very few minutes he saw that he was checkmated.

Swiftly he re-arranged the pieces, and this time the red moved first and a second game was played, which Percivale lost also. A third time this happened, and Percivale rose in a sudden fury, drawing his sword to crush the pieces and hack the board.

But as he did so a damsel ran suddenly into the room: "Hold your hand, Sir knight!" she cried. "If you strike at these magic chesspieces a terrible evil will befall you!"

"Who are you, lady?" asked Percivale.

"I am Blanchefleur," she answered, and as she spoke she came forward into the light of the candles which stood near to the chess-table, and with a sudden gasp of wonder and joy Percivale knew her for the maiden in the pavilion. And even as he recognized her he saw his diamond ring shining on her finger.

He held out his hand to her, and saw her suddenly pause as she recognized her own ring which he still wore.

"Lady Blanchefleur," he said gently, "I have sought for you long. My name is Percivale—and I beg you to pardon me for the wrong I did you, meaning no wrong, when I took this ring from you as you slept, and took also one kiss from your lips."

"Percivale," she answered gently, "I have seen you only in dreams: each night you have come to me, wearing my ring, and have kissed me once on the lips—and my heart has gone out to you across the darkness. . . But in this magic castle I have waited for you: the time to speak of love is not yet. Come sit down to supper, for you shall see a more wondrous thing than yonder enchanted chess-board."

They took their places at the table: but there was no food nor wine upon it, nor did any man or woman come to wait upon them.

Yet Percivale sat silent, looking at Blanchefleur.

"Lady," he said at length, "all times are the true time for such a love as mine: lady, will you be my wife? I swear to you that no other in all the world shall come near me, nor shall my lips touch those of any save you alone."

Blanchefleur laid her hand in his with never a word, and as she touched him suddenly a roar of thunder shook the castle, the great door of the hall flew open, and a strange damsel, dressed and veiled in white, walked slowly into the hall, holding aloft a great goblet or grail covered in a cloth. A light shone from within the Grail, so bright that no man might look upon it: yet it was with another and a holy awe that Percivale sank to his knees and bowed his head in his hands.

A second veiled woman followed the first, bearing a golden platter, and a third followed her, carrying a spear with a point of white light from which dripped blood that vanished ere it touched the floor. As they passed up the hall and round the table where Percivale and Blanchefleur knelt, the whole room seemed to be filled with sweet scents as of roses and spices, and when the Procession of the Grail had passed down the hall once more and out of the door, which closed again behind them, there fell upon Percivale a peace of heart that passed all understanding, and a great joy.

"The Holy Grail draws near to Logres," said Blanchefleur. "Ask me no more concerning what you have seen, for the time has not yet come. One other must enter this castle and see it—and that is Sir Launcelot of the Lake. But, Percivale, you are more blessed than he: for through him shall come the ending of the glory of Logres, though in Logres there has so far been none so glorious as he, save only Gawain. Go you now to Camelot and wait for the coming of Galahad: on the day when he sits in the Siege Perilous you shall see the Holy Grail once more."

"Lady," said Percivale, rising to his feet, but standing with bowed head, "I would seek for it now! It seems to me that there is no quest in all the world so worthy."

"No quest indeed," answered Blanchefleur, "but not yet may you seek it. On the day when the glory of Logres is at its full, the Grail shall come to Camelot: then all shall seek, but only the most worthy shall find it."

"I would be one of those!" cried Percivale. "None but I shall achieve the Quest of the Grail!" And forgetting all else he ran down the hall, never heeding Blanchefleur's cry, leapt upon his horse and galloped away into the forest.

When morning came the madness seemed to leave him suddenly, and turning round, he tried to ride back in search of Blanchefleur. But though he wandered for many, many days he could never again find any trace of the desolate land or of the mysterious Castle of Carbonek.

Sad and wretched, Percivale turned at length and rode towards Caerleon. It was winter by now and the snow lay thick on the high road as Percivale came out from the mountains and forests of Central Wales and drew near to the city. One night he slept at Tintern on the Wye, and early next day rode slowly and sadly down the valley by the bright river.

Suddenly as he went he saw a hawk swoop from above like a shining bolt of brown and strike a dove. For a moment the two birds fluttered together in mid-air, and then the hawk flew triumphant up once more bearing his victim in his claws. But from the dove's breast fell three drops of blood which lay and glistened in the white snow at Percivale's feet. As he looked he thought of the blood that fell from the spear at Castle Carbonek; he thought of the ruby ring on his finger; but most of all he thought of Blanchefleur, of her red lips, red as blood, and of her skin like the white snow.

As he sat there on his horse four knights came riding towards him: and these were Sir Kay, Sir Ywain, Sir Gawain and King Arthur himself.

"Ride forward now," said King Arthur to Sir Kay, "and ask yonder knight his name, whither he journeys and why he sits thus lost in thought."

"Ho, Sir knight!" shouted Kay as he drew near. "Tell me your name and business!"

But Percivale was lost so deeply in his thoughts that he neither saw or heard.

"Answer, if you be not a dumb man!" shouted Kay, and then, losing his temper somewhat, he struck at Percivale with his iron gauntlet.

Then Percivale sat upright on his horse, reined backwards a little way, set his spear in rest, and cried:

"No man shall strike me thus and go unpunished! Defend yourself, you cowardly, craven knight!"

Sir Kay drew back also, levelled his spear, and they galloped together with all their strength. Sir Kay's spear struck Percivale's shield and broke into pieces; but Percivale smote so hard and truly that he pierced Kay's shield, wounding him deeply in the side and hurling him to the ground.

Then he sat with his spear ready, in case one of the other knights should attack him.

"I will joust with all or any of you!" he cried, "I will defend my right to sit my horse by the roadside without having to suffer the blows and insults of such a shameful knight as this!"

"It is Percivale!" exclaimed Sir Gawain suddenly. "He who slew the Red Knight—whose armour now he wears! Truly he must have been lost in deep thought of love to sit as he did while Sir Kay struck him!"

"Ask him to speak with us, fair nephew," said King Arthur, and Gawain rode forward towards Percivale.

"Gentle sir," said he with all courtesy, "yonder is King Arthur, our sovereign lord, and he desires you to speak with him. As for Sir Kay, whom you have smitten down, well he deserves this punishment for his lack of knightly gentleness!"

When Percivale heard this he was glad.

"Then are both mine oaths fulfilled," he cried. "I have punished Sir Kay for the evil blow he gave the damsel on the day when I came first to Caerleon; and I come before King Arthur wearing the armour of the Red Knight whom I have slain and carrying in my wallet the golden goblet which was stolen from his board!"

Percivale rode forward, dismounted from his horse, and knelt before King Arthur.

"Lord King," he said, "make me a knight, I pray you. And here I swear to spend all my days in your service, striving to bring glory to the realm of Logres."

"Arise, Sir Percivale of Wales," said King Arthur. "Your place awaits you at the Round Table—between Sir Gawain and the Siege Perilous. In the days long past Merlin the good enchanter told me that you would come when the highest moment of the realm of Logres drew near."

Then Sir Percivale rode to Caerleon between King Arthur and Sir Gawain, while Sir Ywain followed after them, leading Sir Kay's horse while Sir Kay lay groaning across its saddle.

Many deeds did Sir Percivale after this, but there is no space to tell of his adventures with Rosette the Loathly Damsel, how he fought with the Knight of the Tomb who lived in a great cromlech on a mountain in Wales, how he overcame Partiniaus

and Arides, King Margon and the Witch of the Waste City.
But always he sought for the Lady Blanchefleur, always he
was true to her alone: but he could not find her—until the
years were accomplished, and he found his way once to the
Castle of Carbonek not long after the Holy Grail came to
Camelot.

FOR TO ACHIEVE YOUR ADVENTURE
by Theodore Goodridge Roberts

There's little humour in Malory's Morte d'Arthur. Much of it is grim and, as we shall see, tragic. One of the few moments of levity is provided by Sir Dinadan, the court wit, who plays a number of pranks on his fellow knights at a tournament and includes Sir Launcelot dressed as a woman. Sir Dinadan has been ignored by most writers but not by Theodore Goodridge Roberts (1877–1953) who used him as the central character in a series of stories published in the American Blue Book magazine in the early fifties. A Canadian, who wrote a number of novels set in Newfoundland and Labrador, Roberts earned a minor reputation as a poet. Some of his best works are his historical adventures written early in his long career, such as The Red Feathers (1907) and The Cavalier of Virginia (1910), and his tales of the backwoods such as The Golden Highlander (1910). It is a shame that his Dinadan stories, which were amongst his last work, were not issued in bookform and have never been reprinted. In this story Roberts used as his base the Malory episode of Sir—, no, let him be revealed at the right time.

O ne of King Arthur's amiable if eccentric customs was, upon certain feast days, to delay his dinner until he had witnessed or received word of some fresh marvel or curious new adventure. Now it was on a White Sunday, and the hour of noon (which was dinner-time), that a hungry gentleman of the court looked from a window and beheld the approach of three men on big horses and a little dwarf on foot. He saw the riders dismount at the front door and observed that one of them topped the others by a head and a half, though all were taller than ordinary.

"This promises well!" he exclaimed; and so he hastened to the King and said with assurance, "Sir, you may sit down to dinner with an easy conscience, for an extraordinary adventure is nigh to hand or I have lost my erstwhile keen sense of such matters."

"I'll take your word for it my friend," said the King, who was peckish himself, having breakfasted early; and with that he let the company to the Hall of the Round Table, this being one of the days especially ordained for the assembly of the knights of that high fellowship.

Of the one hundred and fifty chairs at the table, all but a third were quickly occupied. Of the fifty absentees, some were questing private adventures which brooked no respite, some skirmishing with the king's enemies far afield, some in prison, some abed of wounds or fevers; and probably some occupied new graves or lay dead at the mercy of foxes and crows.

Now the three strange horsemen and the yet stranger dwarf entered the hall. Two supported the third between them and the dwarf strutted behind. The supporters were in silk and fine half-armour, but the one between them was garbed all in country wool and leather, as a herd-or ploughman. But in his garments alone did his appearance suggest a low fellow. In the words of an ancient chronicler, "He was large and long and abroad at the shoulders, and nobly visaged, and the fairest and largest-handed ever was seen." Yet he leaned and hung upon the squires as if his length and weight were too much for his own strength. But when he halted with only the table between himself and the King, he straightened his back and knees to his full height, bowed low and then stood upright again.

"What will you?" said Arthur, with a gracious gesture of the right hand. "Speak up and fear nought."

"God bless Your Majesty and all your noble fellowship," said the stranger.

"Gramercy," said the King. "Say on."

"I am come, puissant prince, to ask three favours," said the stranger.

Arthur nodded.

"But I promise there shall be no shrewd nor unreasonable asking," the other continued, "but only of such favours as may be granted easily in royal charity and knightly honour."

"Fair enough," said the King. "Name them."

"First, Your Grace, I humbly crave of your bounty sufficient meat and drink daily for my needs throughout the coming year."

"Granted. Any lost dog is welcome to as much. What next, young man? Speak up now and ask for something worthy a Christian prince's bestowal."

The stranger thanked the King warmly, then humbly begged to be excused for making further requests until another Whit Sunday a year hence.

"So be it," said Arthur kindly. "And in the meantime you shall have meat and drink enough, no matter how great your appetite. Now tell me your name."

"Ah, gracious and puissant prince, that I may not honourably do at this time!" cried the other apologetically.

"Quite," said the King; but he looked disappointed. Then he turned to Sir Kay, who was High Seneschal of all his castles and strongholds, and bade him supply the young man generously with all he might require daily throughout the next twelve-month. Whereupon the stranger followed Sir Kay from the hall; and those who had come with him, including the little dwarf, retired to their horses and galloped off.

This Sir Kay was a lord of great authority, but of no popularity with either his peers or his inferiors. His temper and manners were such as did not endear him to any honest person, gentle or simple. Now he mocked and insulted the young stranger.

"The King is as romantic and gullible as any old wife or skyraking knight errant, but I am of different stuff," he sneered. "He may think you of worshipful blood, but I can see that you are a low fellow by birth, even as you have proved yourself a lout in spirit. Any gentleman would have asked for a horse and arms and a perilous adventure: but such as a beggar is, so he begs. So, since marrowbones, dumplings and ale aplenty are the height of your ambition, you shall have your fill of them till you bulge with fat like the pig you are. And since you lack a name, I give you one now—'Beaumains'—in derision of your monstrous uncouth hands. Ha-ha!"

The youth listened to all this in silence, but with a balanced

face and a strained look about his beardless lips; and still he made
no protest even when he was set down at meat with potscrapers
and turnspits and the like in the greasy scullery. But Sir Kay's
behaviour toward the uncomplaining stranger displeased, and
was protested by certain good knights who chanced to get wind
of it; and one day the great Sir Launcelot himself rebuked Sir
Kay for it.

"If the youth is in truth what you say, then you are taking
an ungentle advantage of his lowly station," quoth the peerless
knight, but in his habitual mild voice. "And should he prove himself, or accident prove him, a person of high merit in himself or
of high blood then you will have a red face for your bullying and
bad manners. You call him Beaumains, and with cause—but you
bestow the name in petty derision, like a jealous scullion. Have
done, I pray you, for the credit of the order of knighthood."

Hard words, though softly spoken: but Sir Kay made to smile
them off, though with nothing of mirth in his grimace, for he
would sooner have jumped into the moat in full armour than
come to blows with Sir Launcelot.

"Just so," said Sir Dinadan, who happened to be of the company, in a cheerful tone of voice. "And your memory is equally
at fault with your manners, Sir Seneschal, if you have forgotten
that other young man upon whom you once exercised your spleen
in the bestowal of a name. You dubbed that one 'La Cote Mal
Taile', because he was rustically attired and you believed him
poor and friendless. And who did he turn out to be but an honest
gentleman's seventh son, who is now Sir Brewnor of the Round
Table, and would as lief demean his quality by tilting at the chief
cook in a contest of skewers as by breaking a spear on the chief
seneschal."

That was a nasty dose for the important foster-brother of King
Arthur to swallow, but he downed it in two wry-faced gulps, for
Sir Dinadan, though young and even a better poet than a knight-
at-arms, was no pushover. So Sir Kay went about his business of
stewardship, which was safer than disputing a question of chivalrous behaviour with such forthright and heavy-handed arguers
as Sir Launcelot and Sir Dinadan.

Now these two knights and several others would have welcomed Beaumains to their own tables and society, like a young
kinsman or friend, but he refused their courtesy with the same
meekness as he accepted the discourtesies of Sir Kay. And thus he
served out that humiliating apprenticeship a full twelve-month.

So the Feast of Whitsuntide came again, and with it as many of the Knights of the Round Table as could keep their rendezvous, and again King Arthur refused to go into the dining-hall without a promise, or at least a hint, of some imminent marvel or adventure. But the delay was short, for the word came soon of the arrival of a damosel urgently demanding audience with the king. So Arthur and all the knightly company entered the Hall of the Round Table and took their appointed seats; and then the damosel was brought before the King with due ceremony, and a little gilt chair was brought to her, upon which she sait with a high air.

"Now what is your petition, young lady?" the King asked kindly.

"I am here in behalf of a noble dame who is so besieged by a vile tyrant that she cannot win forth from her castle but in peril of her life or her honour; and because it is known that many of the best knights in the world are with you, I have come a long and hazardous way to pray Your Grace to deliver this noble lady from this ignoble duress," said the damosel, but with a voice and an air more suggestive of a demand than a petition.

But she was as comely a damosel, and as richly bedight, as any at any court in Christendom; so, Arthur, being only human, refrained from telling her to mind her manners. Instead, he requested the noble lady's name and that of her besieger, but in a somewhat constrained tone of voice.

"My lady's name you shall not know at this time, but as for her tormentor, he is called the Red Boar," replied the damosel.

"Just so," said Arthur, glancing to his right and left. "The Red Boar? Never heard of him. But he sounds a common scurvy fellow to me. And to say sooth, this whole affair rings shrewdly and uncouthly in my ears, and saucily too; and I tell you honestly, young lady, that were I a private knight instead of a responsible king I'd liefer seek honour championing the League of Swineherds against the Guild of Charcoal Burners than in this ambiguous knightly adventure of yours."

"Do I hear right?" cried the damosel, in a high voice and with a red face. "Is this the vaunted chivalry of King Arthur and his fellowship of the Round Table?"

And she shot a defiant and scornful glance at the King, who avoided it, then around at the knights who, taking their cue from their liege lord, followed his example of detachment. Even Sir Dinadan, though again in need of a profitable adventure, sat mum.

"Fie upon you, one and all!" she cried. "And you call this table of yours the seat and centre of chivalry! Bah and pah to you! I've seen your equals in valour and courtesy—and belike your betters—chomping bacon and guzzling cider round the buttery-hatches of beggar-beset monasteries!"

The shocked stillness and silence which followed upon the tirade was broken by a disturbance at the door which drew all eyes, including the king's; and all saw the youth nicknamed Beaumains pushing to enter the hall and two porters pushing and whacking to keep him out.

"What now?" cried Arthur, grateful for a diversion. "It is our petitioner of a year ago. Admit him, varlets!"

But Beaumains was already in, having cracked the porters' heads together, and was kneeling, cap in hand.

"Sir, grant me speech now!" he cried eagerly.

"Right civilly asked," said Arthur. "Speak, young man."

"Gramercy, lord! 'Tis the full year now since Your Grace granted me one request and permission to make two more."

"I remember it well. what would you now?"

"Sir, I would essay this adventure of the distressed lady and the Red Boar."

At this, some smiled and a few frowned, and Sir Kay whispered "Good riddance!" and the damosel cried in sneering derision that the poor oaf must be as mad as insolent, for the Red Boar was a match for fifty such base-born louts.

"Peace!" said Arthur to the damosel; and to Beaumains he said, in a different voice, "Think again, young man. Would you have me grant you certain death?"

Beaumains stood up then and said, earnestly yet humbly, "Sir, I have received nought but gracious favour at your hands, and so now pray your further kindness in all good faith. . . Sir, that with God's help and your permission I shall prove a match for the ruffian Red Boar, I do not doubt."

Now, Sir Kay leaned to the King and whispered, "The lout may be right, at that, for he has shown monstrous strength in the handling of cauldrons in the kitchen, and he has been fed like a prize porker."

Arthur scratched an ear reflectively.

"Be it on your own head then," he said. "The adventure is yours, my young friend. And so I must find your arms and a horse."

"Gramercy, generous prince!" cried Beaumains joyously. "But as to arms and horse, these are in the forecourt even now—my humble thanks to Your Grace just the same. I saw them from a window."

At that moment a squire came in and announced a dwarf on a horse much too big for him, and another great charger hung all about with arms and armour, at the front door. At that, Arthur and most of the Knights present quit their seats and hastened from the hall of the Round Table to see this marvel at first hand; and in the consequent jostle Sir Launcelot and Sir Kay were jammed cheek by jowl.

"What of your base-born scullion now?" asked Launcelot, in a soft voice but with a hard elbow at the seneschal's ribs.

"That was my little joke," gasped Sir Kay. "I knew it all the whole—or why did I recommend him for this adventure? If you doubt it ask the King."

Every champion present was eager to take part in the buckling and latching of Beaumains into his bright harness, which was of as fine plate and chain as any they had ever seen; but in this case, what with arguments and the snatching back and forth of this piece and that, many hands made hard work. But Beaumains was all rightly and tightly harnessed at last, and up in his high saddle, with a great shield before him and a great spear in his right hand. And so he and his dwarf rode forth and over the drawbridge.

In the meantime, the damosel had ridden off on her jennet. But the dwarf had observed her going and what way she went; and so he followed, and Beaumains with him. And Arthur and his noble company returned to their dinner; and on the way between courtyard and hall, the King exclaimed, "But what of his third request? He must have forgotten it in the excitement."

"Yes, Sire," said Dinadan, who happened to be at the royal elbow. "And by your leave I will follow him and learn of him."

"Well thought on," said Authur. "And I should like to hear also how he fares with the saucy damosel and the outcome of this encounter with the Red Boar."

So Dinadan withdrew on an empty stomache and, as soon as might be, took the road in pursuit of Beaumains and the dwarf, even as they pursued the damosel. The damosel went a league swiftly, then another at a softer pace, and thereafter let her jennet amble or even stop now and then to pluck a tidbit of tender herbage.

"He will overtake me at his peril," she said. "I'll put him in his place, the froward varlet!"

It was midafternoon when Beaumains and all his weight of horses and iron came heavily abreast of the jennet, with a thumping of great hoofs and a clanking of arms, and saluted the damosel with a toss of his spear.

"Who is this?" she cried in mock surprise.

"Your appointed champion, fair damosel, at your service—to the death even," replied Beaumains, stammering in his eagerness.

"Champion?" she jeered. "Fie upon you, fellow! D'ye think I have no eyes and cannot see your greasy kitchen rags behind that false show of steel? And to the death, d'ye say? You may die in the service you were born to, at the hands of a master-cook or mayhap of tumbling into a cauldron of soup, but never will you die like a gentleman nor in my service; and were I bigger, I'd whip you for your insolence."

He said nothing to that, but only showed abashed eyes and a red face in his open helmet.

"Champion, quotha!" she railed on. "Back to your pots an' pans, rogue!—before some errant knight happens by and drubs you with the flat of his sword, at my bidding."

"Nay, that I may not do, for I was given this adventure, and charged with it, by my liege lord King Arthur!" he protested.

"Is it his adventure or mine then?" cried the damosel. "A fig for your liege lord! But since I must suffer your company until some happy chance rids me of it (I'm praying that you'll tumble from your unaccustomed seat and break your neck) ride at my other side, I beg you, for I've a nose as well as eyes and would as lief have a kitchen midden as you 'twixt it and the wind."

So he drew rein till she had passed ahead, then rode up on her other side, and the dwarf with him.

"Fall back, scullion!" she cried. "Your place is twice the length of your spavined ploughhorse behind me—but you'd be all the way back to where you started from if I had my wish, Heaven knows!"

Again Beaumains and his attendant checked their charges and let the damosel pass ahead.

"Sir," said the dwarf, "I beg you to take the flat of your hand to her, for she is the veriest shrew I ever had the misfortune to meet, and but for fear of your displeasure, I'd tell her so myself."

"Peace, good Gligger," said Beaumains.

"Peace? Dear Sir, that's something we'll know little of in this company!"

"We must bear with it, however, in the way of duty," sighed Beaumains.

So they went forward another league without haste, and in silence save for the mutterings of the dwarf Gligger. Anon, a shout in their rear caused all three to look back; and there was a full-armed knight on a tall dapple-gray approaching at a gallop that shook the ground; and he came to a jouncing stop only when he was fairly knee-to-knee with Beaumains.

"Well met, my young friend!" he cried. "The King sent me after you with a question."

Now Beaumains knew him by voice and shield for Sir Dinadan, and so replied warmly, "I am His Majesty's beholden humble servant, sir, and Your Honour's too. What is the question?"

"Why, my friend, you told the King you would ask three favours of him, one at that time a year ago and the others today. The first was for a year's board and bed which was granted and has been honestly discharged; and the second was asked and granted this very day; but what of the third request? You rode off without naming it. Name it now, I pray you, that His Majesty's curiosity may be set at rest."

"The third request? It clean slipt my mind. . . . It is important, too, by my halidom! But in the excitement of arming and spurring on this adventure my wits flew away in every direction like a covey of partridges."

"I can understand that, my friend," said Dinadan kindly, with a shoot of an eye at the damosel, who had urged her jennet close to the war horses and was listening with a glint in her fine eyes and curl of soft bright lips that was more a sneer than a pout. "But name it even now, I beg you."

"Why sir, it was to have been for the company of a good knight to witness my behaviour in this adventure, and possibly to dub me knight at the end of it, should I prove myself worthy of that high honour by overcoming all obstacles in the achievemt of it."

"Fair enough! King Arthur would grant you that reasonable request blithely, I doubt not. What Knight had you in mind to observe and pass judgement on you?"

"Why, sir, any one of the first fifteen would have contented me: but now, alas, 'tis too late to obtain the King's consent," sighed Beaumains.

"Not so fast!" exclaimed Dinadan. "Of the first fifteen, d'ye say? Why not seventeen? For the heralds have raised me from the nineteenth to the seventeenth place on their list in the past month."

"Seventeenth? They be fools then, or knaves; for, of all the champions in this realm, there be only ten too able for you with horse and spear, and no more than fifteen to match you afoot and slashing, maugre my head!" Beaumains protested, with spirit.

"D'ye tell me so? cried Dinadan. "Gramercy! Gramercy! I fear you overrate my powers; but I'll not dispute your rating, for by it I qualify to serve you: and as I am as sure of the King's approval as if I had heard him grant your third request, and in the mood for a change of scene and occupation, I pray you to press forward to your adventure."

Beaumains was delighted, but not so the damosel.

"Do you call yourself a Knight, yet pray to serve a scullion?" she sneered.

"Even so," said Dinadan.

"Fie upon you then!" she railed. "You are a disgrace to your goldy spurs, else you would take this adventure of mine upon yourself and order this greasy lout back to the scouring of his skillets."

"Which God forbid!" cried the Knight. "I have risked limits and life for many damosels, only to be made a fool of in every case for my pains."

She looked him up and down and up again at that, and then straight in the eyes, and said coldly and with a horrid curl of her red lips, "That I can well believe."

"Even so," replied Dinadan, outwardly calm but sadly pricked in his vanity, "let me tell you, young lady, that never have I met with a damosel, nor any dame either, of so shrewish a tongue and such villanous manners as yourself."

At that the damosel stared at him with round eyes and a round mouth while the colour drained from her cheeks and brow; then her eyes filled with tears and she set whip to her jennet and rode off at a gallop. Gligger, the dwarf, chuckled gleefully and doffed his cap to the knight, but Beaumains looked distressed.

"A dose of her own medicine," said Dinadan, but with a note of uncertainly in his voice and a flicker of it in his eyes. "But 'twil do her no harm, and mayhap some good even. Let us hope so, anyway,"

Beaumains sighed and murmured, "It hurt her, I fear."

"God shield your tender heart!" laughed Gligger. "Hurt her, d'ye say? Ay, in her vanity, maybe. But the medicine I'd give her, were I bigger, and a cavalier instead of a humble servant, would hurt her more—and not in her vanity only!"

"Peace, good Gligger! And God defend us all from such humility as yours!" chided Beaumains.

So they pressed on after the damosel. The hoofprints of the jennet were plain enough on the soft earth and tender herbage of the forest track. And they soon came upon a wider track, and by sunset upon a wayside tavern; and there they drew rein and the taverner came out to them.

"Has a damosel passed this way?" asked Dinadan.

"Nay, she has not passed," said the taverner, in a low yet desperate voice. "She is here, sir—here again, even as she was last night. Then she was for Camelot, to get Sir Launcelot or maybe even King Arthur himself for a champion—and now she's back in a higher temper than before, and bids me look out for two rogues in stolen arms and an ugly jackanapes with a feather in his cap, and all upon stolen horses—craving Your Nobility's pardon! And she bids me refuse Your Honours the front door an' keep Your Lordships to the stables an' the scullery. God help me—for I can discern Your Worships' high stations at a glance, and the small master's gentility too—but so high and hot is her temper, I'd liefer cross King Arthur himself than her, as I hope for salvation!"

"I believe you, my good fellow," said Dinadan, and thereupon dismounted.

"Think nothing of it, good taverner," said Beaumains. "It is the damosel's humour. She plays a part, on a wager, that's all."

And he too got down from his high saddle.

"Then 'tis a pity her humour doesn't match her person," gibed the dwarf.

So they went to the stables, where they found the jennet in the best stall; but, with the help of a man in a sheepskin jerkin, they housed the three charges well enough and watered and fed all four beasts, but without any help from the taverner, who had excused himself apologetically and hurried back to his post within easy earshot of the unpredicatable demands of the damosel. Then Sir Dinadan and Beaumains got out of their harness. A wench brought them a great jack of ale, from which the knight drank first, Beaumains next, then Gligger and, last, the man in the sheepskin all that remained. Then the taverner reappeared, carrying a lanthorn, and led them back across the yard to the scullery, walking softly and with finger on lip.

"She supped right yeomanly and now sleeps," he whispered.

So they entered the scullery and from there stole on tiptoe to the kitchen, where the mistress and the wench went about the business of the hearth furtively and three or four children sat mum and motionless, all as if in terror of their lives. With whispers and guiding shoves, the three travellers were set at a narrow table and served each with a bowl of rich broth and a horn spoon.

"Not so loud, dear good lords!" beseeched the taverner

fearfully. "Quieter splashing an' sucking, I humbly beg ye!"

The dwarf cast aside his spoon, lifted the bowl to his lips with both hands and gulped down the contents to the last drop; and all the others could hear of the process was the convulsive labouring of his gullet. Dinadan and Beaumains made to follow his example—but the knight's esophagus proved unequal to it and he choked on a gobbet of fat and might have strangled of it but for the mighty back-thump dealth him by Beaumains. So Dinadan was saved, but at the price of peace; for the offending morsel was ejected with an explosion like the snort of a wild bull and great bowl was knocked from his hands to shatter on the stone-flagged floor. The stunned silence which followed was almost instantly broken by indignant shrill screams from an inner room, ordering the taverner to clear his house of rogues and scullions on pain of having it pulled down about his ears.

"Now who would do that pulling for her?" jeered Gligger.

"Her father's archers," gibbered the taverner. "She's a duke's daughter. She told me so. Back to the stable, dear lords, or I'm utterly done."

The three travellers returned to the stable and, in a little while, they were served there with bread and bacon and more ale. And there they slept in their cloaks, on clean straw. They slept soundly. Dinadan was the first to wake; he sat up instantly and looked about him sharply, like the good campaigner he was. He saw Beaumains and Gligger in the straw beside him, and his Garry and the other two chargers in their stalls. Then at the sight of an empty stall, he leaped to his feet with a shout. His companions sprang up, dazed but with knives in their hands.

"The jennet's gone—saddle and all!" Dinadan cried.

Beaumains uttered a stricken moan, but Gligger grinned and sheathed his knife. Now the taverner came cringing in at the open door.

"Lords, dear lords, be merciful!" he whined. "The lady would have it so, and I be a poor man with but the one life—not a noble knight an' adventurous—an' a poor wife an' five poor children. And she left a script for Your Nobilities."

He extended a scrap of parchment which Dinadan snatched and from which he read aloud, but haltingly, for it was unclerkly penned, as follows:

Fools don't ye know when ye be not wanted. I don't need

*yer company nor like it God wot. Go seek sum damosel in
sorer stress than Me an of stronger stummick. If ye be good
knights or only honest simple men let be I pray ye in Christ
Hys name for I crave a Champion no more than a beard.
Follow me not.*

Dinadan repeated it, then asked, "What d'ye make of it?"

The taverner wagged his head and knocked on it with knuckle.
Beaumains sighed. Only Gligger found his tongue.

"She'd liefer our room than our company, seemingly," he said,
and took the script from the knight's hand and bent his brows
upon it. "Here she says we're not wanted nor loved—which I've
suspected from the first. She charges us to let be for she desires
a champion no more than a beard on her chin. Is she mad then?
Nay, like a fox! If she has no need of a champion, why did she
come bawling to King Arthur demanding the best knight in the
world to rid a castle of a red boar?"

Beaumains shook his head and sighed. "Nay, methinks she
plays a part."

"Ha—a part?" exclaimed Dinadan. "Maybe you have something there. A part, quotha! Play-acting! She requests a champion,
but belike against her will, so she asks in so villanous a voice and
manner that Arthur and all his knights are offended and only
you, my friend—a youth unknown and unarmed—accepts her
adventure; and she flees away even from you. She does not desire
a champion, that's certain!"

"Nay, sir, she prayed you do drive me off and take the adventure
upon yourself," Beaumains protested.

"Ha, so she did! but come to think of it, that's no proof she
truly craves a champion. She was for choosing the less of two
inconveniences then—the would-be champion she could most
easily rid herself of at pleasure—and so she chose me."

"But why, sir? She knows you for a proven knight."

"The terrible intuition of her kind. She had but to look in my
eyes to know me for fair game, even as every other damosel I've
ever had ado with has known and proved me to be. But this one
will find herself mistaken, maugre my head! We shall follow her
and solve the mystery, but softly and secretly."

So they baited their horses, broke their fast hastily with cold
victuals and drink, armed and saddled and then went after the
damosel as fast as they could follow the jennet's tracks, which
were plain enough in the soft ground. After riding an hour and
more at a round pace, they issued from the forest into the valley

of a little river; and here were meadows level though narrow, and a stone bridge of two arches, and a big knight on a big horse at the hither end of the bridge. So they rode his way softly, but were no nearer than five lengths of a horse of him when he laid his spear in rest and bade them halt; whereupon they drew rein.

"Sir, did you see a damosel on a white jennet pass this way?" inquired Dinadan politely.

"I did, and spoke with her too," answered the stranger in a jeering voice. And then he asked, and even more jeeringly, "Which one of you is the scullion?"

"I am the one she dubs scullion," said Beaumains. "Why do you ask, sir?"

"That you will be glad to hear, for she bade me spare the poor pot-walloper."

"That you may not do, sir, if you be an honest cavalier, for this adventure is mine, of King Arthur's granting."

"Fiddle-de-dee, knave! Not for your Arthur nor any other prince does Sir Brun of the Bridge have ado with low fellows, save with stick or whip or the toe of his boot."

At that Dinadan whispered aside to Beaumains: "Are you a match for him, lad - on your word of honour?"

"Ay, sir, horse or afoot, by my halidom!" Beaumains whispered back.

"So bet it," said Dinadan; and he turned back to Sir Brun and said: "This gentleman is of high blood and great prowess at arms, and he has passed a year in King Arthur's scullery on a wager, and has taken on that damosel's adventure on a wager also, and is now impatient to deal with you and get forward to something nearer his match than a blubbery rustic bridgekeeper."

"What's that?" screamed Sir Brun. "*Blubbery*? You lie! You fear to meet me yourself!"

Dinadan sighed and said to Beaumains, "You see how it is lad. I have no choice in the matter. But the next shall be yours, I promise."

And he laid his spear and dressed his shield and rode at Sir Brun, who was already in motion to meet him: but the ride was so short that there was not enough force in the clash to break either spear or jounce either knight from his saddle. Then Dinadan lost his spear and let it go and so came pushing knee-to-knee with his antagonist; he leaned and gripped him by the top of the casque with his right hand and spoke a quick word, whereupon his dapple-grey Garry swung and backed with a skip and a twist and Sir Brun came out or his saddle like a hooked carp out of a pond and thudded to earth. Dinadan followed and set a mailed foot on Sir Brun's breast plate quicker than the telling.

The bridgekeeper begged for mercy with what breath was left in him after that thump. "Take my arms and horse—but spare my life!"

So Dinadan and Gligger disarmed him from top to toe, and hung all the pieces, along with his sword and spear and shield, to the saddle of his big horse; then the three went their way, leaving Sir Brun in a low state of mind and little else.

"Sir, that was something I have never seen done before," said Beaumains, in an awed voice.

"What was that?" asked Dinadan.

"Your method of unhorsing that big knight, sir."

"Oh, that! Effective I grant you, but not quite the sort of feat of arms for commemmoration in song and story. A trick, in fact; and to succeed in it your horse must be as tricky as you. But it has saved both Garry and me from a lot of unnecessary effort and bumps and slashes."

At noon they came up with the damosel, where she sat on a mossy stone with a plum tart in her hand and a little basket of more such kick-shaws on her knee. At sight of them she sprang to her feet with an inarticulate cry, overturning the basket.

"Sorry to upset you," said Dinadan smoothly, with a glance at the spilled pastries. "We received your penned admonitions and charges, but ventured to follow our line of duty nevertheless."

She cried "God defend me!" And then, "How did you cross the river?"

"Even by the bridge," said Dinadan; and with a gesture he called her attention to the fourth charger and its burden of arms and harness which she had overlooked in her excitement. She looked and understood.

"Oh! The rogue!" she gasped. "The big vile braggart! He swore that Launcelot nor Tristram was no match for him; and he would stop you for a month or forever if you pressed him; and as for the scullion and the manikin, he would chase them halfway back to Camelot. So I gave him a purse of gold—the villanous fat liar!"

"So?" queried the knight, slanting an eye at the dwarf.

"Bless my soul!" exclaimed Gligger. "I slipt it into my wallet for safe keeping, sir, and it clean slipt my mind."

"You should have mentioned it," reproved Dinadan mildly. "Had I known of a full purse, I'd have left the rogue his horse and arms. But no, on second thoughts you did well, my boy! Now, return the purse to the damosel; and let us hope this will show her the unwisdom of paying in advance for that sort of service."

The dwarf got down from his high horse, pulled the fat purse from his wallet and, louting and smirking innocently, proferred it to the damosel.

"Nay, not that!" she cried and struck it from his fingers, then clapt both hands to her face and wept and sobbed.

So Dinadan and Beaumains dismounted, the knight muttering the while, but Beaumains hardly breathing; and when Dinadan stopped to pick up and pouch the purse, Beaumains went near to the weeping damosel and down on one iron knee before her.

"I'll act as your ladyship's treasurer," said Dinadan.

She heeded him not, though her sobs subsided, but turned a disdainful glance upon Beaumains.

"Why kneel you there?" she cried. "D'ye think I'll dub you a knight? Out upon you for a fool!"

"I kneel to beg a boon of you," he answered humbly. "I pray you to charge your hirelings to set upon me instead of upon Sir Dinadan in future, for how else am I to perform a feat of arms for his judgement?"

"To horse! Here's treachery!" screamed Gligger, climbing to his own high saddle even as he screamed.

"An ambush!" bawled Dinadan; and he was no more than up and spear in hand when three knights came hurtling from cover and at him, and two more close on their heels. First, he picked the nearest of the leading three out of the saddle like a winkle out of its shell; then, discarding his spear, he crowded in between the remaining two of the van and knocked on their helmets with a short war-hammer that was his favourite weapon for mounted in-fighting. He drew his sword then, ready to apply other tactics to his next opponent or opponents. But now there were none; the other two lay sodded.

"Sir, you left but two for me," complained Beaumains, who stood nearby on his own feet, leaning lightly on his sword.

"Your own fault, my dear lad," said Dinadan, in a voice of mild reproof. "If you hadn't been down on your knees you'd been the sooner mounted and spurring."

"I admit that, Sir Dinadan. The fact is, I hadn't time to mount, let alone to spur."

"Not mounted, d'ye say. And yet you brought 'em both to earth! How did you do it? For no proved champion could do better, by my halidom!"

"Why, Sir, I slashed an' grabbed an' pulled an' slashed again to right an' left, for all I was able."

"Able enough!" cried Dinadan, dropped his sword and dismounting, and embracing Beaumains, with a clanging of breastplates. "I'll bestow the accolade even now, and right gladly; then back to Camelot to show your goldy spurs and change our winnings—four horses and sets of arms are mine and two are yours, but I'll call it fifty-fifty—for coin of the realm, before that deadly damosel leads us into another and fatal trap,"

"Gramercy, sir," said Beaumains; and he sank to one knee and bowed his plumed head.

Then Sir Dinadan took Beaumains' own sword and struck him on the left shoulder and the right and the left again with the flat of it, and chanted in a reverent voice, "In the names of the Holy Trinity I do hereby dub you knight. Arise Sir—, Sir—"

"Gareth," murmured Beaumains.

"Gareth, d'ye say?"

"Gareth of Orkney, sir,"

"Arise, Sir Gareth!"

And the new knight obeyed, and thanked Dinadan again, and glanced about him.

"I know the King of Orkney," said Dinadan. "That's to say I've met him three times, in the very best company—at royal joustings, in fact—for two tumbles and one draw. Truly a doughty jouster."

Gareth murmured modestly, "My own father, sir."

"Ha!" cried Dinadan. "Will Kay have a red face when he hears that!"

"Where is the damosel?" asked Gareth.

"Sir, at the first clash she went head first into that thicket, like a fox to earth," said Gligger, pointing a finger. "But here she comes out."

The damosel issued from the tangled hawthorns on her hands and knees. Her tall headdress now was crooked, her tear-smudged face was scratched and her fine gown was ripped and bedraggled. Still on all fours she stared blankly at the two knights and then at the motionless figures on the greensward.

"All sped," said Dinadan harshly.

"Dead?" she gasped incredulously.

The knights exchanged significant glances.

"It was not an occasion for chivalrous courtesies," said Dinadan sternly.

She stood up then and pointed a trembling finger at the most richly armed of the corpses.

"That was my father," she said; and though her voice was low and clear it chilled her hearers to the marrow. "A false knight, forsworn and outlawed—leader of robbers and murderers. He sent me to bring some great and rich knight of King Arthur's court to him—Arthur himself even, or else Launcelot or Tristram or Lamorak or another of great fame and wealth—to be held for ransom. He forced me to swear on my dead mother's rosary to make my plea to Arthur, and to bring the victim to the trysting-place, maugre my immortal soul! I made my plea, but in so unmannerly a fashion that no great champion, but only this youth, would undertake my adventure. And then you came, and would not stop or be driven off—neither of you. So I gave all my gold to the braggart at the bridge to stop you both: for without any champion I'd be free of my vow to keep that tryst. He didn't stop you. But I would have turned you somehow—even warned you at the price of eternal damnation—but they shifted the ambush full two leagues this side of the trysting-place."

And then she laughed; and the two knights stared at her in amazement and even Gligger looked dazed. And her laughter grew higher and wilder, and she pointed again and screamed exultantly, "And look at them now!" Then she swayed and fell and lay twitching.

The knights brought her out of that fit, or swoon, or whatever it was, with splashes of cold water from a nearby spring and sips of liquor from a leather bottle. She sat up at last, a pitiful figure, and hid her face with her hands.

"An astounding tale, if true," said Dinadan. "I am inclined to believe it, and doubtless Sir Gareth is too, but we must take you back to king Arthur, that he may hear it from your own lips."

She bowed her head yet lower in meek acquiescence. Then Dinadan took the purse of gold from his wallet and gave it to Sir Gareth.

"It is your adventure," he said. "I'm but an onlooker."

So Gareth helped the bedraggled damosel to her feet, and to where her jennet stood patiently, and up into the saddle. She looked down at him and whispered. "Will the King punish me."

"Nay, for what?" Gareth answered. "He is a just but merciful prince. At the very worst he may place you in a convent, for the good of your immortal soul."

"Shall I need money in a convent?" she whispered.

"Nay, you would lack nothing. But you have money. Here,

take back your purse now, for fear I might lose it on the way."

Dinadan then called Gareth for help in rounding up the newly acquired horses from the surrounding thickets. The knights and Gligger worked afoot, and the knights right heavily and hotly in their suits of mail; but the task was accomplished at last.

"We'll leave the five dead rogues as they are," said Dinadan. "We have enough hardware now without adding that junk to it. But the damosel! Where is she?"

She wasn't there: neither she, nor the jennet. They shouted, but got no answer. They shouted again and yet again, but all to no purpose.

"Stolen away," said Dinadan. "A guilty conscience, I fear. Ay, guilty indeed, to go without her purse!"

"She—had her purse," stammered Gareth. "I—she—I didn't think she'd run away."

Dinadan smiled cynically, but his hand on the new knight's shoulder was kind.

"Live and learn, dear lad," he said. "Even I am still learning!"

THE KING'S DAMOSEL
by Vera Chapman

Vera Chapman (1898–) is surely the grande-dame of British fantasy, though she did not turn to writing until she was well into her seventies. Formerly the wife of a country vicar, and later a Druid, she founded the British Tolkien Society in 1969 and published her first book, The Green Knight, *in 1976. That became the first part of a trilogy of Arthurian novels later collected as one volume as* The Three Damosels *(1978). From that I have selected the central story which remains one of the best full-length Arthurian fantasies. We are introduced again to Sir Gareth and to the shrew unnamed in the last story, but now revealed as Lynett: 'The King's Damosel'.*

How Two Brothers Married Two Sisters

The flags on the great towers of Camelot fluttered, the roof-tiles glittered in the sun—every window was garlanded with flowers or spread with carpets and gay draperies—bells pealed, and the shrill note of trumpets wafted up towards the blue skies. For this was a wedding day, a double wedding, two brothers marrying two sisters, as was meet and right, the brides being given by King Arthur himself.

In their tower bedroom the two brides were dressing. The elder

120

sister, whom one might have thought was the younger, all pink and white and golden—in tissue of gold, with her hair loose and flowing to signify her virginity, spread like fine gold thread over her shoulders, crowned only with a circlet of pink roses worked into a light diadem of goldsmiths' work. The other bride, in silver, was less happy. Her hair, black as night and straight as rain, was spread out, like her sister's, over the silver dress, and crowned with white roses—but it only made her face seem the browner and plainer (for she disdained to plaster it with red and white paint) and her figure the more gaunt and angular. Her great brown eyes were hidden under her eyelids, and her lips were pressed together.

Leonie, the fair bride, stepped across to her sister with a rustle of silk, and clasped a jewel round her neck.

"Be happy, Lynett darling," she said, and kissed her. Lynett drew a long breath, clenched her fists at her sides, and returned the kiss.

"Oh yes, I'm happy, Leonie dear—of course," she said.

The attendant maidens gathered round them—it was time to start the procession. Oh God, thought Lynett, now it begins.

Down the small twisting stair in single file, because you couldn't go any other way, her train-bearer fussing behind her and gathering her train in a bundle. Then into a room large enough to spread themselves and form up, two by two—Lynett and Leonie hand in hand, their trainbearers behind, the rest of the ladies following, all with posies and garlands—and so down the great double staircase, to the thrum of the lute-player behind them—out into the courtyard, and there the procession of the two bridegrooms met them.

This was the moment Lynett had dreaded—or the first of many moments to come. There they stood, the two brothers, side by side—Gareth and Gaheris. Gareth—her heart turned over as she looked at him. The man of all men. Gareth, the gentlest of the Orkney brothers—his tall figure, moving with the grace of strength, his blue eyes that stole her heart—Gareth, the adorable, and her sister's bridegroom. And beside him, Gaheris, to whom she had been given instead. Gaheris, tall enough, strong enough, fair like Gareth and blue-eyed—but his blue eyes were dull protu-berant pebbles, his skin coarse, his mouth drooping—as brutal as his brothers Gawain and Agravaine, and stupider. This one—for her! And Gareth whom she had brought through miles of forest to rescue her sister—she not liking him at first, and then drawn to him by a love she had tried hard to deny—now, after all this, taking her sister as the reward of his exertions, as one would choose the prize for a game—the first prize, and she the second prize to be kindly bestowed on his brother.

The two processions met, a rainbow of colour between the grey walls, and the two couples were brought face to face. Leonie, dimpling, mincing, from her small stature looking up confidently at Gareth, placing her hand in his with an altogether womanly smile; he taking it, proud and happy. Lynett and Gaheris confronting each other, stiff and hostile, drawing back—then, as was required of them, joining cold hands. And so, Sir Kay the Seneschal in his black velvet and silver lace marshalling them, they turned together and went up the steps into the chapel. Lynett was dimly conscious of all the company there—King Arthur himself, the young king, not so much older than herself—Lynett was eighteen and her sister nineteen. Arthur was about twenty, and had already being king some five years, since he pulled the Sword from the Stone, and already he was a renowned fighter and leader of men. By his side the Queen, the pale, moonlight-haired Guinevere, not long married to him. There was Merlin, white-bearded and eerie—Merlin knew too much, and at the sight of his frosty blue eyes Lynett's heart missed a beat—but there was not betrayal in those eyes. Merlin showed no uneasiness in a holy building—he had a kind of holiness of his own; but there were three women, withdrawn into the back of the church, who looked too much like witches to be there—the three sisters, Morgan le Fay, Vivian called Nimuë, and the Queen of Orkney. Surely the Queen of Orkney looked too young to be the mother of those four young men? But then witches could make themselves look what age they pleased. . . The Queen of Orkney was coming forward now, florid, red-haired, overdressed—as of course she must come forward as mother of the two bridegrooms.

Now, Lynett, you must remember where you are and what you are doing to do—and oh, my God! Lynett replied to herself, would it were otherwise.

The solemn pageantry of the wedding went forward.

"Wilt thou, Lynett, take Gaheris—"

No, no, no! she was shrieking inwardly. Not Gaheris—not Gaheris, but Gareth, Gareth, Gareth. But Gareth had taken Leonie, and Leonie had taken Gareth—*taken* him, taken him away, carried him off from Lynett forever. And now Gaheris had taken Lynett, for better or worse, and God knew what that might mean.

The jubilant voices of the choristers shattered the silence, with the flutes and viols and tabors, and the clouds of incense rose against the blue and gold painted ceiling. The priest was joining their hands, winding his stole around them. Now the procession led out. This was the end—or the beginning.

The endless tedium of the wedding feast had at last come to an end. From the gallery that ran around the great hall of the castle, two large rooms opened out, and these had been prepared as the two nuptial chambers. In each one was a vast bed, enveloped in curtains, with a pile of feather mattresses one could drown in—all garlanded with flowers and green leaves, strown with rose petals and scented herbs. Now for it. . .

The two processions led their two brides to their respective chambers, and undressed the victims with a mixture of ceremony and play. Lynett was at least free from Leonie's embarrassing presence for the moment. Though she could not see Leonie, Lynett was sure that she was reacting with giggles and dimples. She for her own part tried her best not to wince and shrink too perceptibly from the bridesmaids' playfully rough fingers, not to mind when they pinched her cheeks and pulled her hair.

They were all so nice to her, after all, kissing her and patting her head, and singing just the same songs as were being sung to Leonie in the next room. She roused herself to take part with a good grace in their games, threw the garter for them to scramble for, laughed and applauded when some girl, whom she didn't know from Eve and didn't care to know, caught it and held it up. At least they didn't make her get into bed naked, like so many brides; both she and Leonie had insisted on bedgowns, silken and fur-edged, so she wrapped hers round her and lay tense and tight, like a worm in a cocoon, while the girls withdrew to Leonie's room to bring in the first bridegroom.

And now Lynett could lie and think. Gaheris was coming now, and she would have to endure him, and the first thing he would discover would be that she was not a virgin.

Of the Wrong that was Done to Lynett

Five years back it was, when Leonie and she were carefree girls living in their father's great rambling house in Lyonesse. Lynett had never known her mother, and when her father had found himself with two daughters and no wife, he had put his younger daughter into the place of a son he would never have, and brought her up like a boy. He might have done the same with Leonie, the elder, but she had nothing boyish in her temperament—small and dainty, she was all feminine, not at all physically brave, sensitive rather than bold; you couldn't make a tomboy of her. Leave her in the nursery with her dolls and Madam Juliana, her governess; she would be happy trying on trinkets and gaudies. But Lynett was always ready to ride out on a horse too big for her, or shoot arrows at a wildcat, or tickle trout in the stream. Her father was Sir Lionel of Lyonesse—the lion was the emblem of the family and of the land, so the elder daughter was Leonie, the lioness, and the younger was Leonet, the lion's cub, which became Lynett—though some called her Linnet, the name of a silly little bird, which annoyed her very much. Nobody ever called her pretty—her hair was nothing but black wires, and her eyes two burnt holes in a blanket, so she made best or the worst of it, and grew as brown as a vagabond, her arms and legs scarred with briars and branches, her hair streaming like a witch's, till when she was eleven she had it cut short like a boy's so that she would wear a helmet. Ugly, they said—but she also, as her muscles developed tough and smooth, and her arms and legs moved without constraint, grew up with the grace of a young wild animal. But there were very few to notice it.

It was when she was just turned thirteen, at the beginning of a fine hot summer, that their father came to tell the girls they were to have a guest. "A very powerful knight," he said, "oh yes, very brave. His name is Sir Bagdemagus."

The girls laughed, with their arms round each other's necks, once their father had gone out of the room. "Bag-de-magus! What a name—Baggy–de–maggy. Old Baggy. . . . Wonder what he'll be like. Wonder if he'll be as baggy as he sounds—"

"I'll bet he will be," said Leonie. "Baggy and fat and flabby and toothless. Why can't Father ever bring home a nice *young* knight?"

"Father says he's brave," said Lynett. "He can't be all that baggy."

But when he arrived he surprised them. He leapt off his horse, all in a rush, and came striding and clanking into their hall in full armour, not shining but dull from travelling and hard wear. A tall man, tough and lean, his face marked with the lines of long jaw-muscles, broad in the shoulders, narrow in the hips; his hair, his bristling brows, his moustache, his small trimmed beard, all a lively tawny blond; his eyes boldly grey. He and Sir Lionel met with hearty back-slapping greetings; then the daughters were presented. Up to now, when their father's friends had visited, it had been a matter of a courtly exercise, under Dame Juliana's eye; deep curtseys, kissing of hands: "You are welcome, good sir," "Your servant, gracious lady," . . .and after that, to be seen and not heard. Not so now.

"So these are the wenches, Leo? Come on, give us a kiss—come on. Oh yes, this one's a little lady, no less. This one isn't—are you?"

Lynett looked up at him, ran her eyes over him. This man wanted to make her afraid, but she wouldn't be.

"No," she answered, and looked him in the eye.

"And you don't want to be a lady?"

"No, I don't."

"That's the spirit! I'll bet you'd rather be a boy, wouldn't you?"

"Yes, I would!"

He turned to Lionel.

"You've got a brave little tomboy there, Leo. Give her to me for six months and I'll make a man of her!"

"Oh, come away and don't talk nonsense," laughed Lionel, and led him off. From the background, Dame Juliana pounced upon Lynett.

"How *could* you, my lady—answering him back, and looking him in the face as bold as a beggar, and you never even curtsied—oh, you've disgraced us all . . .

Leonie pursed her lips and rounded her eyes, but Lynett tossed her head and laughed within herself at silly old Juliana. "Give her to me for six months and I'll make a man of her!" Oh, if it could be so. . .

All the evening she watched him, at supper and when they sat afterwards by the fire in the great hall. He told stories, wonderful stories, of adventures and wars and daring deeds; of marvels he had seen, and desperate perils he had been through. Always he himself had been there, had seen and known and done. He must have travelled all over the world, and he must be brave and clever, and certainly he cared for no man, and nothing in earth, heaven or hell could daunt him. She listened, and said nothing, and he took no notice of her, and she for her part asked nothing better, at the moment, than to listen.

She saw him next morning in the mews, that great, light, dusty room next to the stables, where the hawks were kept. He found her there, dressed in leather hose and a woollen doublet like one of the serving men, caressing the great peregrine falcon.

"Hello, boy!" he greeted her. She grinned back at him.

"Do you know anything about falconry?" he asked, sarcastic.

"Yes, do you?" she retorted.

"Impudence!—I suppose you know that's a highly dangerous beast you've got there?"

"What, Jeanne?" She rumpled the great bird's breast-feathers. "Now, fancy that. I think Jeanne forgets it when she's with me." The peregrine ruffled up and started to "bate", or beat the air with its wings, at the sound and smell of a stranger. "But you'd better keep away—she doesn't like strangers."

He laughed, shrugging his shoulders.

"Well, let's hear what you *do* know," he said, and proceeded to put her through a falconer's catechism. He couldn't fault her.

"Oh come on, then, enough of this. Can you ride?"

"Certainly I can. Come, I'll show you."

"Oh yes," he said as he followed her into the stables, "side-saddle on an ambling pad, like an abbess."

"Abbess indeed! You get your mount and I'll get mine." And presently she reappeared sitting astride on her father's big Brutus, whom she was forbidden to ride. But Dagobert the dwarf, who was her groom, came with her. He had protested against her taking Brutus, but he couldn't stop her; however, she couldn't prevent him following her on his little shaggy donkey, as he had orders to do whenever she went riding.

That was a thrilling ride. Some of the time she was terrified, galloping so furiously on big Brutus, but she wouldn't let this man know it. Dagobert's scanty white hair stood on end, as he laboured along behind. Bagdemagus led her over jumps, where Dagobert had to go a long way round, and through all sorts of dangerous places. It was terrible, it was wonderful—she had not known she could do it. At first she wished for it to be safely over—and then when they rounded and came back to the castle, and trotted soberly enough into the stableyard, she wished it could have gone on for ever.

She swung to the ground without waiting to be helped.

"I'll call you Robin," he said. "Linnet is no kind of bird for you to be named for."

"Not a bird," she said frowning. "It's Leonet really—the lion's cub."

"And so you are," and he clapped her on the shoulders as if

she had been any stable-boy. "But I like Robin best. You'll be my friend Robin?"

"For certain I'll be your friend Robin."

She worshipped and adored him, but it never occurred to her that there was anything of sex in her adoration. She looked to him as her father, or as to the brother she had never had. She was his page, his squire, his soldier. He was her captain. Day after day they rode together, and he taught her forest lore, and to shoot with the bow, and all the tricks of horsemanship; and told her stories, wonderful stories about his own adventures. Day by day she felt herself growing into a kind of manhood. This was life—not ninnying in parlours and gardens like Leonie and precious Dame Juliana.

"My lady Lynett," said Dame Juliana, "I think it not prudent that you should pass so much of your time with Sir Bagdemagus."

"Oh nonsense, Dame!" retorted Lynett. "He's my father's guest, and I can't slight him. My father says I may ride with him every day for my health," and she tossed her head and swept out of the door. Leonie followed her into their bedchamber.

"She's right, you know, Lynett," said Leonie. "Don't you see? You two stick together like lovers, and people will talk."

"Like lovers?" Lynett turned on her, not blushing, but in a royal rage. "Why, but that's ridiculous—how you dare to say such a thing! He—I—oh,—it's quite, quite different. Can't you *see*? It's nothing of that kind at all. I'm—I'm like a *boy* to him—he teaches me things—I'm his page—"

She stopped, looking at Leonie's smirking face.

"You've got a horrible mind, Leonie! Oh, it's not that sort of thing at all. I shouldn't like him if it was. Why, he's not a bit like those silly young fellows that come running after you—like Father's page that had to be sent away—or that horrible old priest—oh yes, I know—*not* like that at all. And anyhow nobody runs after me that way. I'm ugly. Everyone says so. *He* knows I'm ugly, so that's all right, you see?"

Leonie sighed.

"All very well, Lynett dear, but I still think you're wrong."

"And I still know you don't understand."

. . . Lynett and Bagdemagus rode companionably together and he discoursed to her of woodcraft and of fighting.

"If we could go on knight errantry together, boy Robin!" he said. "Just you and I, without your dwarf—riding for days through the forest—"

"Oh, if we could!" she agreed. "And camp at night around a fire in the forest, in the very heart of the forest—I'd cook for you, and fetch water from the spring in my helmet—"

"What if it rained, eh?"

"Oh, if it rained I wouldn't mind—we'd sit in a cave or a hollow tree, and sing songs—"

"But there wouldn't be room for Dagobert," he said, casting a glance at the dwarf behind them only just out of hearing.

"No, there wouldn't be room for Dagobert."

So at last, in the heat of the summer, they contrived it. Sir Lionel was away from home, as he often was. Lynett managed to send Dagobert away on an errand to an acquaintance of hers many miles distant—with an adequate bribe to hold his tongue. They could not make it more than a long day—they would have to be back before sun-down—but they would have a long, long day together, quite alone.

She stole out in the dewy sunrise, in her doublet and hose to meet him; this time on Mayflower, her cream-coloured mare, for she meant to enjoy this day without worries. They rode, and savoured the fresh morning, and laughed; they took their luncheon of bread and ale under a tree. Far and far they rode, into deep woods. As the afternoon went on, he shot a small deer, and skinned and gralloched it with his hunting knife; she set her teeth and took her part in the operation, not daring to admit that it made her feel slightly sick. Then, having built a fire, he showed her how to skewer the gobbets of venison on sharpened sticks and cook them over the fire. They feasted royally, in a warm nest of beech leaves at the foot of a big beech tree, their horses tethered behind them, shaking their bridles with a quiet sleepy noise. He produced a flask of wine, sweet, pleasant and quite surprisingly strong. Everything was quiet, warm and pleasant; they relaxed with their backs against the tree. Then he turned to her and said,

"You're my good comrade, aren't you?"

"Oh yes, I'm your good comrade," and she leaned against his shoulder.

"Well now, you'll do what a good comrade always does."

"What do you mean?"

He told her.

"No—no—no." Wide-eyed with horror, she shrank back against the tree, trying to get away from him.

The shock to her was beyond description.

"Come now, don't be silly. Don't waste time. You know you've been inviting me ever since I set eyes on you."

"I don't know what you mean."

"Oh, yes, you do. Come on."

"No—no—get away from me—don't touch me. . . I never thought . . ."

"Oh, yes, you did. You're one of that kind, are you? I know—tease a man, lead him on, drive him mad, just for sport, and then—'oh no, don't touch me!' By God's nails, my girl, I'll make you pay for this!"

"Let me go—" She tried to get away, but his hands were each side of her, pinning her against the tree. She managed to get her hand on the little dagger she had been using to eat with—but with a quick movement he snatched it out of her hand.

"None of that, now. There's nothing you can do, my beauty, so make up your mind to it." With that, he seized her and took what he wanted, roughly and brutally.

And there was indeed nothing she could do but to suffer the shameful violation of her body and the bitter disillusion of her mind. With his hot and sweating face close to hers, he was saying.

"And if you tell anyone of this—anyone at all—I'll come to your bedroom at night and slit your throat from ear to ear. Understand?"

Later, he stood up and and threw her like a limp doll against the roots of the tree.

"You can go home now if you want to. I must say you've disappointed me. Not much sport after all."

"How can I go home?" she said from the ground.

"How? Oh, your horse is there and you can follow my track. It isn't far really, and you can be back before dark. But I tell you again," and he bent over her, "if you breathe a word to anyone—your sister, or your father—especially your father—I will, I really will come into your room at night, whatever you do—and first I'll do the same thing to you again, and then I'll cut your throat. The blood will run all down in great gouts all over your shoulders and soak your sheets, and your soul will go right down into hell. I mean it, so remember."

And without another word he turned away, mounted his horse and rode off into the green.

She lay for a long time in a stupor of shock and misery. Then suddenly she was aware of a strange man standing by her. An old man with a white beard, dressed in a long white robe, with a white linen coif over his head—not a pointed cowl like a monk's but laid flat over his forehead and on it a strange jewel. Round his neck hung a small crystal globe, and in his hands was a long carven staff.

She struggled to her feet, clutching at her disordered garments.

"Do not be afraid of me," said the old man in a gentle voice. "I know what has happened."

"Who are you?—What do you want?"

"I? —Oh, I'm Merlin. As to what I want—why should I want anything? I am here to help you."

"To help me?" she looked up at him, unwelcoming. "How will you do that? Will you show me a cliff I can leap over, or a river I can jump into? Or perhaps you have a poison on you? My dagger's gone, he took it."

"No, child." He spoke firmly. "You have got to live."

"To live? What for?"

"For one thing, you might care to live to carry this Bagdemagus's head on your saddlebow."

"Ah." A touch of colour returned to her cheeks. "I could bear to live for that."

"And then to forgive him."

"Forgive him? Not I. Not in the ages of ages—not if the saints and angels begged me. I'll curse him, not forgive him. Look and listen now." She stood erect and stretched her hand before her, her fingers in a forked shape. "For the first time, Bagdemagus, I curse you."

"Don't do that," said Merlin, his voice deep and quiet. "Not only because it's against holy charity—"

"I don't care for holy charity. For the second time, Bagdemagus, I curse you."

"But not the third time! Oh my child, not the third time!"

She paused. "Why not?"

"Because they come back to you. Look!" He laid his hand lightly upon her head, and suddenly all the lights and shadows in the wood were changed, and through the strange flashing lights she saw two things running away from her—like spiky, bristling black globes, with thin black legs and padding feet like claws, that ran with a smooth and relentless movement—they turned for a moment, and she saw they had eyes and grinding teeth. The first that went was small and ugly, the second, that had just left her, was larger and much uglier.

"They will come back, you see," Merlin was patiently explaining. "Do you want the third to come back to you?"

"Oh no!" she exclaimed, and at once the sight vanished. She stood trembling. "No, I won't curse him the third time. But—what am I to do now?"

"What are you to do? Why, go home, of course, and go on living."

"I've lost all that a girl lives for."

He directed a thoughtful look at her. "I don't believe it, nor do you. If you really do believe that that particular thing is a woman's whole life, why, yes, I suppose so. Some women—yes, for some women, virginity is the only treasure they have to bargain with, and a place in a man's house the only thing they want to use it to buy. But not you, I think. Am I right?"

She nodded.

"Yes, I knew it," he said. "There's things you can do, and things you want to be. Go home and grow to your full stature."

She stood hesitating, her face crimson now.

"Oh, I know what you're afraid of. No, you won't conceive a child. Stop worrying. How do I know? I just know. —No, I don't think you'd better tell your father, or anyone else. We don't want a war just now. Say nothing, but wait. Your time will come. Now tie up your hair, get on your horse, and go home."

Under his quiet voice she did so. He guided her till she was within sight of the castle, and then turned aside into the woods. She slipped in unobserved. Bagdemagus had arrived back an hour before, they told her, but had received some sort of message, and was gone. She never saw him again . . .

. . . And so she had lost her maidenhead, and now Gaheris would find it out. Gaheris, coarse and stupid and violent. Gareth would have understood, and been patient and sympathetic. She could have told Gareth the whole story. But there *he* was, away in the next room with the bridesmaids and groomsmen singing round him and Leonie—No, they had finished singing, and were bringing her bridegroom to her. She shrank deeper into the bed and clutched the bedgown tightly round her. Here they came, Gaheris also in a long furred gown (thank God he wasn't naked either) supported by two groomsmen, probably more than a little drunk. They thrust him into bed beside her, with plenty of coarse jokes. The maidens tossed flowers at them, and sang:

> *Now you're married we wish you joy,*
> *First a girl and then a boy,*
> *Each year after, son or daughter,*
> *Now, young couple, go kiss together.*

Then they drew the curtains and left them. Both lay rigid, wrapped in their bedgowns, till the last of the crowd had gone and taken the torches and tapers with them, leaving them in the dark. Then without turning, he said to her over his shoulder,

"I think, madam, this arrangement is as little to your liking as it is to mine."

How Sir Ruber Laid Siege to the Lady Leonie

So once again she was left with time to remember, through that long, tense, sleepless night.

Cruel and violent were the changes that life had had for her, before she was seventeen years old. Leonie, she remembered, was just turned eighteen, when suddenly their father was brought back dying after a hunting accident. And hardly was he buried before the Knight of the Red Laundes moved in and took possession.

The Knight of the Red Laundes was horrible. At least Bagdemagus had had a pleasing appearance. This man. . . The Red Laundes, or plains, from which he took his name, were a dismal tract of swamp at a sluggish river's mouth, where trickling rusty water stained the mud and the roots of the reeds, all that would grow there. It flowed out of caves, red with iron, where it was said a tribe of dwarfs worked for him, making swords and armour—but not free dwarfs, as most of them were, working as good craftsmen for their own honour, but miserable slaves of the Red Knight. And he was like his land, a red man—they called him Ruber, the Red Knight—not Rufus, for his hair, short, bristly and scabby, was jet black; but his face was red, flushed, swollen and coarse. His teeth were decayed, and his breath was loathsome.

He came, with a company of twenty men, ostensibly to pay his condolences on the loss of the ladies' father, and so courtesy obliged them to receive him, although they were in mourning. Leonie and Lynett roused themselves from their grief, and gathered such household as they had—Dame Juliana, the old steward, the dwarf Dagobert, the cook and his boy, the two waiting maids, three housecarles—that was about all; and between them they did their best to organize a dinner for this unexpected guest and his twenty followers. Leonie, Lynett and Dame Juliana sat at the high table with him, in their black dresses, and tried to be as polite to him as possible. His conversation was far from polite.

At the end of the dinner, when Sir Ruber had made short work of the best wine they had left, he pushed his chair back and stood up, and rapped on the table with his knife handle for silence.

"Madam Leonie of Lyonesse," he said, "without more ado—I'm here to offer for your hand in marriage. You need a man to protect you, now that your father's gone—er—God rest his soul, of course—a man to take charge of you and your lands and your castle. Here I am, and I hope you'll say yes and we'll be married tomorrow. Eh?"

The three women gasped simultaneously, and shrank together; then they all got to their feet, and Leonie faced him. He and his twenty men waited for her reply.

"My lord Sir Ruber," Leonie said in her high clear voice, "thank you very much, but—no."

"No?" he shouted, his face suddenly convulsed. "You say no?—You *dare* to say no to my good offer?"

"That is so, my lord. I say no."

"But, God's blood and bones! This won't do—I won't have it. Madam, I say you *must*—"

"There's no *must* about it. Come Lynett, Juliana, quick—" for she saw him about to grab at her. The high arms of her chair checked him for a moment, as she and the other two women quickly dodged out of the door at the back of the dais, the household servants following them.

"Dagobert, push that big bench in front of the door—see that all the bolts are home—now—" and she led them all upstairs to the gallery that overlooked the hall. There, just as the Red Knight began to hammer on the door below, she opened a window above his head. He looked up and growled like an animal at her.

"Do you defy me, madam?"

"Yes, I do. And I am come to bid you good night and goodbye, thank you for visiting us, and please leave quietly."

"Oh no, we don't. We're stopping here, my lady, till I get yes for an answer."

"Then you will stop in the hall, for the door below is strong enough for a siege, *and*—the kitchen and larder and all the food and drink are on my side of the door." With that she slammed the gallery window and left him.

Later, Leonie called the household together—the steward, Dagobert, the cook, and all the others, and told them her plan, which was simply to sit tight in her own quarters, the soler chamber and the best bedroom, below which were the kitchen and larders, and leave Ruber and his gang in the great hall with nothing to eat or drink until they went away. Their defences were reasonably good—Dagobert and the housecarles piled so much stuff against the door that it could never be broken through, short of using fire.

"He won't set fire to it," Leonie reassured them, "for he doesn't want to damage the house. He covets it, even more than he wants me, so he won't burn it. Listen to the noise he's making, out there with his friends! But we'll starve him out."

And so they thought till next morning they peeped through the gallery window, and saw a large fire roaring up the wide chimney, and an ox roasting over it—an ox certainly stolen from the castle's own herd. There were hogsheads of wine, too, plundered from somewhere.

"I'm afraid we're not going to starve them out," said Lynett.

"My lady," said Dame Juliana, "do you not think, perhaps—as you have no man to protect you, and a woman alone needs a protector—after all, he has made you an honourable offer—"

"Honourable offer?" Leonie exclaimed, her blue eyes flashing. "Are you really suggesting, Juliana, that I should yield to that robber? I will not, not, not—and I'm grieved that you should think of it. Come now, we're well provisioned for a siege. What do you say?" She looked round at the servants. The maids just looked frightened; the steward stood on his dignity; but Dagobert, the housecarles and the cook applauded.

"Don't you give in to that brute, my lady. We'll beat him yet."

"We shall," she smiled at them. "No surrender."

How Lynett Became a Damosel Errant

So they dug themselves in, and endured the siege.

The days began to pass wearily—and hungrily. The servants managed to clamber over roofs and along ruinous galleries, and bring them news from time to time.

"They've taken all the horses, ladies. Taken and ridden them away somewhere—Brutus, and Mayflower, and all."

And next day:

"They've let all the hawks loose," said Dagobert.

"What, Jeanne too?"

"Yes, Jeanne too, I fear."

"Oh, damn and blast them!" cried Lynett. "I spent months on that hawk, and she had come to understand me, and—I'd got fond of her. All my work gone for nothing."

"At least they haven't eaten them," said Dame Juliana with a grimace. She had her gravest suspicions about the last dish which the cook, most apologetically, had served up to them.

—"If only we could get a message to King Arthur," said Lynett. "The young King Arthur. They say his knights go all about the country rescuing women from brutes like these. If somebody, somehow, could get to Camelot and tell him—"

"Somebody!" said Leonie. "But just who? Which of the servants could you send?"

Lynett frowned, and leaned her chin on her fist.

Leonie continued, "We can't spare any of the housecarles—there's only three of them anyway. Dagobert is too well known, they'd spot him at once. Barbon—could you go?"

Barbon the steward spread his hands.

"Pardon, my lady—my old limbs—"

"No, of course not. The cook—we couldn't do without him, and anyway King Arthur wouldn't listen to a cook—and the scullion boys wouldn't even know what message to take. That leaves—"

"Not me, my lady," said Dame Juliana.

"Well—"

Lynett got up, shaking her head as if coming out of water. "Of course. It has to be me. Who else could possibly go?"

"But Lady Lynett!" wailed Dame Juliana. "How can you go? How will you go? How will you get past the watchmen?"

"I'll go on my feet, since they've left us no horses, and I'll go dressed like one of the scullions. They don't trouble much about them, and I'll either slip out unseen or play some sort of trick on them. I'll do it."

"Oh, but Lady Lynett—the unseemliness of it!"

"It'll be more unseemly if Sir Ruber gets us," she retorted grimly. "Oh, I'll go, God help me, I'll find my way to Camelot somehow. It may take me a month, but if you can all—just keep alive till I come back?" Her resolute tone faltered and died away.

So, in a rough suit of hairy wool, none too clean, with her hair cut and her face smeared, she slipped out of the little back gate. It was heavily barricaded, but the housecarles unbuilt the barricade for her, and with prayers and God-speed opened the door and sent her on her way. The door closed behind her, she heard the crashing and rumbling as they rebuilt the barricade, and then she was alone, outside the walls. Alone—not even a horse to lend her courage.

It was pitch black, and she was down in the dry fosse that surrounded the castle. She shut her eyes for a second to adjust them to the dark; it seemed a little clearer when she opened them, but she felt more vulnerable too. On the high edge of the fosse there was a man pacing to and fro. She waited till he had gone by, and then scrambled up. The man was waiting for her—his arm shot out—she stepped quickly back, dodging his grasp.

"Please, master, let me by. I'm not doing no harm." She managed a reasonable simulation of one of the vagabond children who used to infest the courtyard. "I've just been in to get a bite from where the knights are cooking in the hall. You—wouldn't want to buy a couple of silver spoons now?"

"Oh, be off with you, devil's brat!" said the man, and lunged at her with his pike. Lynett gave a lamentable howl and ran off down the path into the forest.

So far so good. When she was far enough away from all human sounds, she stopped running and stood still. And now the excitement of the moment was spent, and it was very quiet indeed. Very quiet and dark, and the trees were overhead and the bushes close round her, and she was deadly afraid.

Nobody went into the forest at night. Nobody hunted at night, save a few desperate bad men. Even when she had been hoydenishly ranging round with Bagdemagus, she had never been in the forest after dark. And now she was alone, alone and on foot, and hardly even knowing her way, except that she must follow the path and keep going away from the castle. If only she could turn about and run back! But this she could not do, no matter how much she wishes. Go on—that was the only way.

So, trotting pathetically on the dusty path, looking to left and right, her hand clutching the dagger that was her only means of defence, she set out.

Dark and rustling, the forest closed round her. There was no moon, and the wind came in gusts, and between the gusts everything creaked and cracked. Noises—noises—She ought to know, she told herself, angrily, that that horrible shriek was a hunting owl, and that long wailing cry another owl, and the things in the bushes could only be small birds, or voles, or—or—She couldn't follow up the thought—what did it matter what they might be, when, Oh God, oh God, her heart was hammering so she could hardly breathe—She kept trotting along, not allowing herself to break into a run. She looked behind her, and the path was glimmering and empty. Again she looked back, and the moon was rising. Then against the rising moon, as she stood still for a moment, a thing came rolling. Like a rough black ball, it seemed to come rolling out of the moon and towards her, with a whirling, growling, worrying noise. Then it unrolled itself and rose up, a tall black shape, upright, surmounted by a head like a fox's, and came on towards her. She shrieked, but could not move. Within a few yards of her the thing turned suddenly and plunged into the bushes at the side of the path. But it was not gone. She heard it rustling along in the dark foliage at her side, as she turned and ran. And then as she ran she heard something else rustling on the other side of the path. They, whatever they were, were pacing her on both sides, running as she ran.

Then the moon came up behind her, and shone on the path ahead, and there they were—two of them—the tall, black, fox-headed things with gleaming eyes and teeth. They were standing each side of the path and waiting for her.

She gave a pitiful cry like a forsaken child, and crouched in the middle of the path. But in that instant came a whistling and a thin angry shriek from above—like a hawk's, but how could a hawk be there at night? And out of the sky dropped a furious flurry of claws and beak and thrashing wings, launching itself violently against those black bogies, dodging and dashing from one to the other—They cringed and shrank and fled—perhaps they fell to pieces, Lynett could hardly tell—but they vanished, as if the wind had blown them away, and the falcon, with a soft whirr of feathers, flew to Lynett's outstretched arm.

"Jeanne!" she exclaimed. "Oh, Jeanne! You came to help me—oh, my darling Jeanne!" and she caressed the hawk's soft downy neck. Jeanne paced up and down on her wrist, and put her beak to Lynett's ear. To Lynett's surprise, she heard Jeanne speaking in a soft throaty voice.

"Of course I came. Now you needn't be afraid of anything. I'm with you. When it comes daylight I'll catch a rabbit for you. Let me sit on your shoulder and then you won't have to hold your arm out." So they went on through the forest, and now indeed Lynett had no fear.

How Lynett was Affronted with a Kitchen Boy

So in three days she came, with her hawk, to the outskirts of great Camelot, where the young King Arthur's banners were flying.

"I must leave you here," Jeanne whispered, "for if I go in with you they'll put me in their mews, with all sorts and kinds of birds. But I'll come back again, sometime." And she lifted off from Lynett's arm and lost herself in the sky, and Lynett went on into the citadel.

She was brown enough and dusty enough, and looked the very picture of a ragamuffin boy.

"Hi, not that way!" a man said, as she reached the great main entrance. "Round to the back for such as you."

Bewildered in the crowd of strangers all pushing, jostling and shouting, she followed docilely enough, and found herself at the door of the great kitchen.

Here another rough man pushed her to one side.

"Kitchen boys sit on that bench there," he shouted above the noise.

"But I'm *not* a kitchen boy," she protested.

"I know you're not, yet. And you'll have no chance to be, unless you behave yourself till Sir Kay comes along—and *then* you'd better behave yourself."

There was nothing for it. Lynett was thrust on to a bench, the last in a line of equally ragged boys. At least there was some warmth in the great kitchen, and shelter from the rain outside, and there was an encouraging smell of food—encouraging but tormenting, she was so hungry.

Over by the big fireplace she saw him—Gareth. Tall, but with the softness of youth still about him; two-haired, and with startling blue eyes, that looked acrosss to her and seemed as if they would speak. He left the fire place and came to her side.

"Don't be afraid," he said. "It's always like this when you start." He put a bowl of savoury pottage into her cold hands. "There, eat it up before anyone comes along."

He stood by her while she ate the pottage, which was excellent and made her feel very much bolder. He was just concealing the empty bowl, when the man who had first spoken to Lynett came bustling by.

"Now then, you Pretty-Hands," he said, "look lively there—Sir Kay's just on his rounds now. You boys, stand up when he comes in, and be sure to call him Sir."

There was a stir at the door, and Sir Kay, a thickset, black-bearded man, impressively robed, entered with a retinue of cooks and kitchen clerks. He approached the boys on the bench, who all stood up obediently. Not so Lynett.

He halted opposite her.

"What's this, eh? Not another Pretty-Hands? Stand up, boy, when I speak to you."

Lynett remained sitting, but drew herself up to her full height, and spoke on a high note.

"*Master* Kay—for I will not dignify you with the honourable name of Sir—for if you are a Knight of the Round Table, their famous courtesy is a long way to seek."

Everyone around stopped talking, stopped whatever they were doing, and listened.

"*Master* Kay—I am no kitchen boy. I am a lady. I am a damosel in distress, come to ask a boon of King Arthur, and you and your minions have treated me like a scullion. Like a vagabond. Like a common kitchen knave. Because I have come among you dressed as I am—because I have escaped barely with my life from my castle, and journeyed on foot through perils that would daunt any one of your fat hangers-on—and therefore I come in my necessary disguise, and travel-stained—therefore you have let me be thrust into your kitchen, and let your kitchen-officer here treat me as if I were the wretchedest vagabond churl seeking employment—seek employment? I'd sooner seek it on the hobs of hell—"

She drew breath for a moment, and realized with a pleasurable shock that these men were afraid of her. She went on,

"I am a noble lady, the daughter of a great house, and I have come a long and perilous journey to ask King Arthur's help for my noble sister, shut up by a churl in her castle—through it seems there are churls elsewhere. I had heard that the Knights of the Round Table were courteous and ready to help ladies in distress. It seems they are no better than other mannerless churls. . . .'

She warmed to her theme. She tongue-lashed them, in a royal rage. Words came to her, red-hot. Sir Kay and his retinue stood fidgeting. At last,

"Lady, lady, enough!" he cried. "Lady, lady, lady—oh, I beg you—I ask your pardon—but enough, enough. Come with me and all shall be put right. King Arthur shall see you at once."

"Not so," she said. "Is the churlish fool going to thrust me into King Arthur's presence as I am, foul and travel-stained? No—you shall find me decent apparel, and a bath—"

"Oh, certainly. Only come this way, madam."

And he led her out of the kitchen, with all the crowd gawping. Pretty-Hands was lost and forgotten among the rest.

So the greatly chastened Sir Kay took her up many flights of steps, into a luxuriously furnished ladies' bower, where some very surprised court ladies bathed her, and combed her hair, and dressed her becomingly, with gasps and cries of astonishment for her adventures and her bravery. And at last she was led before King Arthur.

He was young, was King Arthur, not much older than herself, but full of power and dignity, as he sat dominating his Round Table. It was a simpler thing than it later became—as Lynett saw it that day it was just a vast, bare, circular board, with neither carving nor painting—all that came later. The knights sat round it in their appointed places, each with his shield behind him, over the back of his chair, showing his device. At the King's right sat his newly-wedded Queen, Guinevere the White Spectre; and at his left was Merlin, and at the sight of Merlin, Lynett's heart missed a beat. She had not expected to see him there.

Briefly she told her tale, and the King answered her courteously.

"Fair damosel, you are welcomed, and your wrong shall be righted. We have heard of this Knight of the Red Laundes. We will send a knight with you to rescue your lady sister. Now who—"

He broke off, for behind Lynett there was a commotion at the door, and someone had entered. She heard a fresh young voice say.

"My lord King, I claim this adventure for my own. This is the second boon I was to claim from you, of three you swore to grant me; and the third is that you make me a knight forthwith, that I may go with this damosel."

"Who is it?" asked the King, and Merlin whispered to him. Then he said,

"So be it. Young man, this adventure is yours. You shall be made a knight in due form as soon as may be. Lady, behold your champion."

And she turned and saw the kitchen-boy Pretty-Hands.

It was like a blow over the heart to her—she reeled with the shock, and grew pale and then furiously red.

"My lord King," she said in a choked voice, "is this a jest? If so, it is a sorry jest at my expense. . . . What? Cannot I come among you disguised as a kitchen-knave for safety on my perilous journey, but you must cast the same in my teeth, by giving me a kitchen-knave instead of a champion? My lord King, this was unmannerly done." And she broke into tears, and turned and fled from the hall.

She ran away down long stairways and corridors, alone and bewildered. She did not know where she should run, only that she must get away. And at last she sank down on the stone seat of a quiet cloister; and there Merlin found her.

"It's you again," she said. "What do you want?"

"As before," he said, sitting down by her, "I don't want anything. I've come to turn you into the right road again. Don't despise your champion."

"Champion! They gave me a kitchen-boy—just because I had to get here in disguise, and that upstart Kay had to take me for what I looked like—they mock me, they mock me—their Round Table, their flower of chivalry, pah!—I spit on them. . . . By the Mass, I think their kitchen-boy might be more courteous than they are,"

"Listen, my child," said Merlin very patiently, "there was no thought of discourtesy in the King's mind when he alloted young Beaumains as your champion—I swear he did not know of your disguise. No discourtesy was intended. As for the boy, don't despise him—as Sir Kay despised you. Don't you know that you can't judge the man by the apparel? You should know."

"Who is he then—this Beaumains?"

"No, I'm not telling you that. Try him and prove him for yourself. I'll only tell you that he is fated to be your champion, and the adventure is his. So go back now, and beg the King's pardon—"

"Beg his pardon—I?"

"He is the King. And take your champion and go. Your sister is waiting."

So she went back, saying very little, and the next day, horsed and accoutred as was fitting, she and Gareth set out on their journey together, as has often enough been told.

. . . And so now as she lay by Gaheris' side, she tormented herself by recalling the tauts, the snubs, the bitter insults she had heaped on Gareth as they journeyed, and how patiently and bravely he had borne it all, and how her growing love had fought with her pride, and overcome it—and all to this end, that she should hand him over to her sister—to live, as they would say, happily ever after.

How Lynett Became the King's Damosel

She must have dropped off to sleep, for she woke to hear Gaheris getting out of bed. It was still dark. She heard him putting on his clothes outside the curtains. Then he parted the curtains and looked in.

"Madam," he said, "I think it best we should part here and now. I am going, and I bid God-be-wi'-you. I hope we shall not meet again."

And he dropped the curtain—she heard the door creak and bump as he swung it to, and his footstep echoed down the stone passage. He was gone.

For a moment she lay stunned, then angry tears flooded her eyes. A slap in the face, nothing less. Granted she did not love him, that she had dreaded her bridal night with him, that she had felt relief when he had not touched her—yes, but to be left like this! The humiliation, the ignominy. With a sinking heart she thought of the next day, and many days after—the honeymoon of feasting and revelry. First would come the aubade, with the crowd of young men and girls waking them, as if the couple hadn't had enough songs, with songs of the dawn—with ribald cheerful enquiries as to how the night had passed—with ritual assurance that the bride had been found a virgin, and was so no longer—with the spicy caudle to restore their strength after the exertions of the night—

Leonie would enjoy it all, niminy-piminy though she might be, she was eager enough for her bridegroom, and she would enjoy blushing at the rude jokes. But she, Lynett—no bridegroom beside her. Alone, neglected, rejected. Tongues would clack like the great castle bell. He had found her too loathsome. He had found her not a maid—dear heavens, too true if he had known it. For whatever reason, he wouldn't have her. And there was left like an unsavoury morsel, chewed and spat out. . . . Then there would be the feasts and revels to follow. Must she sit at table with her sister and Gareth, unpartnered, the odd one out, with all around her singing of joy and love, and pledging them in loving-cups of hydromel? Neither maid, wife nor widow, not even an honourable old maid.

The burning words came tumbling to her mind, words she would say if there were anyone to say them to. Bitterly, she talked to an absent Gaheris in her head, on and on and on, till she felt herself bursting with unuttered anger, and her eyes were burning and her mouth dry and her stomach tied in a knot. . . .

At last she rose from the bed, and lit a candle—in a chest by her bedside were some of her clothes, with her money and jewels. She found the riding-clothes in which she, with Leonie, had ridden up from Lyonesse. Leonie had ridden side-saddle in a richly quilted kirtle, but Lynett had refused to go so long a journey in such inefficient equipment, and had worn breeches and ridden like a man. Here were her breeches, and a sufficiently rich doublet, and a useful cloak and hood. She put them on.

Then quietly stepping over the trampled flower-strewings with almost a shudder, she went down through the stony corridor and out. The summer dawn was colouring the sky, and she crossed a courtyard, breathing deeply of the fresh air. She slipped into the stables, and passed through into the mews. This was very like the mews in the Castle of Lyonesse, and she felt more at home here—its peculiar smell was right, and spoke to her of comfort. And there, on a spare perch, was Jeanne.

Jeanne must have slipped in somehow during the night, and was standing, unhooded and without jesses or bells, between two hooded goshawks. Jeanne had been gone into the wild for more than a year, and a hawk who does that is spoilt beyond redemption—it never comes back. But Jeanne had come back. She made a soft whirring noise and flew from her perch to Lynett's out-stretched arm.

Lynett gave a little cry of delight, and then, sinking her cheek against the bird's soft feathered breast, gave way to a flood of tears.

She wondered if Jeanne could still talk. Jeanne said nothing, but deep down under the feathers Lynett thought she could hear, as she sobbed, a kind of remote ticking, clicking noise as of something saying, "There—there—there—there—"

A small sound made her look up, and there was Merlin standing over her.

"You!" she exclaimed. "You again—you're always there when —when I hate—"

"Yes," he said calmly. "You do not often cry."

"No, I *don't* often cry."

"Then don't cry now. You're a woman grown, and a step nearer your destiny."

"How you do talk!" she said crossly.

"Now—there's no need to be discourteous, or petulant, or childish. You are of full age now. You should know that a man's need—or a woman's—is not for happiness, but to fulfil his destiny."

"My destiny!" She mocked, lifting her red wet face. "What destiny have I—neither wife, maid nor widow? What destiny?"

"That needs thought," he said. He paced away from her, the length of mews, and back again. Then he said, "To be, I think, a carrier—a bearer."

"A bearer of what? Of children?" she cried bitterly.

"No, not I think, of children. Not your wish—you have very little of the mother's milk in your humours. No, there are other things to bear and carry."

"Such as Bagdemagus's head?" she burst out.

He turned and looked at her rather sadly.

"So you still think of that?"

"You promised me!" she cried.

"I never promised. I held the hope before you, once, to stand between you and self-destruction. But there are better things to carry than a burden of vengeance. Things that you might indeed bear—"

"Such as what?"

"I will try to show you," he said. "I think you will be able to see."

He guided her to a low stool and made her sit, quietly taking Jeanne from her shoulder and replacing her on the perch—the big hawk submitting to his handling as if she knew him. Then he took from his neck the jewel that hung there. It was a glass globe about the size of a pullet's egg, full of strange cloudy threads of many colours, writhing through the crystal. He placed it in the palm of her hand and told her to look at it steadily; then he laid his right hand lightly on her head.

At first she only saw the reflections of the windows on the crystal; then for a long time, nothing at all. Then at last a picture began to form. A curtain, a dim curtain with a light behind it, and outlined against the folds the shadow of something. A cup, a large chalice like the cup of the Holy Mass. Behind the curtain were many people—she could hear the sound of their voices and their movements, but confusedly—and there was singing too. But something seemed to come to her from the dimly-seen shape of that cup—some great, great holiness. The holiness of the blessed

Mass, that she knew—but this was even more. The Chalice of Chalices. In the Holy Mass, she must struggle and aspire, and try hard to attain the grace and blessedness of the Presence—but if she could be near This, without a veil, all would be clear, all would be granted—without striving, without doubt, without distraction. It would all be there, the presence of All Goodness, All Holiness, All Compassion, All Beauty. And those that were within the veil with that holy thing sang softly, day and night for ever and ever, moving sweetly in their bliss as the stars move. . . .

Then the picture changed, and she saw the figure of a woman coming out of a door, as in some other place, and she carried in her hands that holy cup, but covered with a white cloth. She came pacing slowly forward, her eyes on the thing she carried, and then she lifted her face for a moment, and Lynett saw it was her own face.

She cried out in surprise, and the vision vanished; Merlin put his hand over the crystal ball and gently took it from her. He seemed to know what she had seen.

"Not for me," she said, her voice shaking. "It's too holy for me."

"But you are not too unholy for It," he replied quietly.

"That is a work for—a virgin—a woman of virtue." She looked up at him, angrily again. "I've lost my virtue and you know it."

"Child," he said, very calmly putting the jewel back on his neck, "some people seem to have taught you that there is only one virtue, at least for a woman, and that is chastity. Or virginity, which is not always the same. Believe me, there are other virtues. There is charity—and charity is forgiveness."

"Forgiveness!" she cried. "You're always talking about forgiveness."

"Well, yes," he agreed, "Perhaps I am. But everyone who prays the Christian man's prayer is always talking about forgiveness. Many people say I am not a Christian man—there are those who say I am the son of the Devil. None the less, I know that prayer, and I know what it means. And so should you."

She sat with downcast head, still looking at her empty hands.

"Then I'm afraid I do not have that virtue of charity."

"Then you must learn it."

"But how?"

"That is to be seen. But this is plan: there is work for you to do."

She thought of that veiled figure.

"Does it mean that I have to become a nun? Oh no—not—*not*

to cover up my head for the rest of my life!" and she ran her fingers through her long black hair.

He laughed. "A very sound reason to know you have no vocation to a convent! No, my girl; you'll not have to cover up your head for the rest of your life. You might have to wear a hood or a leather casque or even a helmet. You are to be King Arthur's Messenger to his knights. Come now, the King is on his way here. I'll present you to him."

Suddenly she thought with longing of the road, over the downs or through the woods, a-horseback or afoot—as she had gone, carefree and bold, on her quest to fetch Gareth—yes, for the moment she could think of Gareth without a pang. She was eager to be gone.

"I'll save your face too," said Merlin. "You can be away before the castle is astir, and you won't be found alone. They'll suppose you've gone with your bridegroom."

She pulled a comic face at the word—she could even smile now. Life was better already.

There was a footstep at the end of the mews, and the King entered. Merlin went down to meet him, and they talked together for some time; and then they came back slowly to where Lynett stood.

He was—the King. No other word for it. Young though he was, the air of command sat upon him, and the magnetism of his power could be felt. He moved with easy grace that gave him dignity beyond his years; his grey eyes and his firm lips had strength and authority, and sweetness also. Lynett felt something pluck at her heart. Her father, in the days when he had taught her skill and courage—all those heros of her romantic imaginings—even that wicked Bagdemagus as she had first thought him to be—something of the beloved Gareth—the leader who could call out her powers, make her grow, liberate her to be more than a woman, a complete being, a "man"—this was the King to follow. She sank on her knees before him.

"My lord King," she said, "make me your messenger. Send me forth."

He laid a hand on her shoulder, and a tremor ran through her at the touch.

"What do you say, Merlin—I cannot dub her a knight? No—but I'll do this. Lady—" and again the hand on her shoulder was raised a little and lowered—"I here create and dub you the King's Damosel."

Speechless, she held up her hands joined, to place between his. Merlin dictated the words:

. . . "I do become thy vassal of life and limb, to live and die in thy service, and in God's service, so help me God the Father, God the Son and God the Holy Ghost."

. . . They walked slowly behind the King through the corridors to a small retired room, where the light shone through horn windows on rich hangings and carven wood.

"My messenger must eat and drink," said the King, and saw that she did. . . . "And now, Merlin," he said, "the *mappa*."

Merlin took from a chest, and unfolded on the table, such a thing as Lynett had never seen before— As she had understood the word, a "*mappa*" was a linen napkin or tablecloth, such as the very rich and fine sometimes used. This was a large tablecloth, but painted on its surface, in coloured dyes, was a sort of picture, so it seemed to her, of the King's dominions, with rivers, woods, hill, roads, castle. Here and there little men were pictured going to and fro, and wild animals peeped out of the forests, or strange and terrible beasts hovered over hilltops. And each place had its name written beside it. She gasped at the wonder of it, and would have liked to spend a long time examining and admiring it; but the King recalled her to the business in hand.

"See—here is the Great Road, that the Romans made. All along it, look, are castles, and in each of those castles are knights who owe allegiance to me. I want you to go to each one, and bid them meet me here in two years' time, at the Feast of Whitsun. Oh yes, we'll have a tournament, a very grand tournament—but I want them here, and I want them to pledge their allegiance. I have messages for certain ones, also—some deserve praise, and some I must question, and rebuke some. I'll tell you each one in turn, presently—each one's name and what you are to say to him. But you are to go as a messenger of peace in every case. That is why I send a damosel—you will go, first, attended only by your father's dwarf, Dagobert, who is here with me."

He turned from the *mappa*, rather suddenly.

"Have you a horse?"

"I—yes, my lord King. I have—just the palfrey that brought me here, a lady's little palfrey—but—" She drew a breath, and spoke on an impulse. "My lord King—I'd like one of *your* horses. One of your great horses, such as your knights ride."

The king gave a shout of laughter, throwing back his head.

"Oh, Merlin, didn't you tell me she was a bold lady?— My dear Damosel, do you know what you are asking? My great horses, that my knights ride—my black horses—why, they're monsters! Four hands higher than your British horses. They are bred from the kind the Romans left in Britain—coal black, and as fierce as the devil. Do you really ask me for one like that? Four hands higher than a common horse?"

She looked up at him, not abashed.

"My father's Brutus was no smaller, and I mastered him. Let me try, my lord King!"

He laughed again. "Oh, bold lady—we shall see. Now—this castle, and this, and this, to be visited. And so you go northward. And the last I want you to visit, up here, almost by the Wall—is King Bagdemagus."

She started and turned pale—her eyes met Merlin's then she snatched her gaze away, and fought to recover her composure.

"*King* Bagdemagus?" she queried, carefully keeping her voice from shaking. "But how comes it that you call him King?"

"Oh, he calls himself King now! He's set himself up as a sort of king in defiance of me, and keeps his state there with his warriors—making a kingdom of violence and cruelty, where the only right is brute force. You will take him my demand for submission to my rule and the rule of God and the law."

"My lord King," she said, and her voice was still not quite under her control, "forgive me, but is this not a matter for an armed band of knights—"

"No, my lady, it is not. At least not this time. I am sending him an embassage of peace, for a first step. True, the armed band may come later— But first, I do not offer him war but peace, if he will take it. Besides, there are men among his band who are of a better kind than he, and who were my vassals once—I should to win them back. Make it known to them that I will welcome and forgive any such. The embassage of peace must be by a damosel. Are you afraid of this man?"

God knows, she thought, I *am* afraid. But I mustn't show it. Aloud she said,

"No, my lord King, I'm not afraid."

"Good, good. My knights will follow hard behind you in case of trouble, but they must not be within sight of you. You'll deal with this Bagdemagus for me, I know. You'll bring me either his submission, or"—he turned to Merlin with a smile, as if he did not really mean it,—"or his head."

How Lynett Came to Castle Hardy

She came in sight of the looming, ugly battlements of Castle Hardy, and stopped for a moment to gaze at it, sitting on her tall black horse. Above the winding road towered the castle, on a spur of the bare threatening hills—she had seen many castle on her travels, but nearly all shining, beflagged, with a welcoming look—none like this.

Dagobert, on his trotting donkey, drew rein behind her, and handed her an odd-looking thing he carried at his saddlebow, which proved to be a lady's tall conical headdress, a "hennin", in black satin with a floating veil of white, and a white scarf to go under the chin and hold it. Lynett took off the leather cap she was wearing, and carefully put on the hennin. She was wearing leather breeches and doublet, but over them was a coat of rich black velvet, trim in the waist and spreading in the skirts. Her long black hair hung loose over her shoulders, whether under the leather cap or the hennin. It had been by the King's instructions that she wore the coat, and her hair long, and put on the hennin when she neared a castle. She would have preferred her boyish attire, but he was anxious that she should always be recognized as a woman. She still insisted to herself that she was ugly, and made no attempt to be otherwise—her hair scraped back from her face, her sombre choice of colour, with nothing to adorn it. Often the ladies in the castles which she had visited had offered her prettier things to wear, and tried to make her alter her hairstyle, but she would have none of it. Yet anyone with eyes to see could have perceived a strange intense kind of beauty in her ivory-brown face, the clear skin warmed with sunburning, and her deep-set brown eyes.

She had a company that rode with her—four knights, four squires, and four men-at-arms, making twelve in all—thirteen with herself, which was a sacred number and well omened as long as the thirteenth was a woman. There was also old Dagobert, who made it fourteen, but he didn't count, any more than did Jeanne, who always rode on her lady's wrist. The four knights—Sir Percival, Sir Gwalchmei, Sir Lancelot, and Sir Bors—all knew "the Falcon", which was the name they gave Lynett no less than Jeanne, and swore by her, regarding her as their luck.

More than two years they had now spent on the road together, going along the length of Britain from south to north. When they came to castles that were known to be friendly to Arthur's rule, they would advance in a body; but when it was doubt-ful—this was by Arthur's express command—Lynett would advance alone, followed only by Dagobert on his donkey, and would make herself known as a solitary damosel, travelling in peace and asking a peaceful reception. If the reception were not peaceful the knights would follow her shortly. All were in possession of King Authur's secret password, and their camp was always closely guarded against any not having this.

They had met with innumerable adventures. Once they had been forced to take shelter in the cottage of a witch, who had tried to poison them—but Lynett's keen sense of smell had detected the poison in the broth the witch had offered them. Lynett had prevented the knights and their men from stringing up the witch on the spot, or forcing her to drink her own poisoned broth—but she had then tongue-lashed the witch till the men almost felt sorry for her.

Another time a band of forest robbers swooped down on them and carried her off. After a week, her distracted escort tracked her down to the robbers' hideout, a log cabin within a maze of thorn hedges—and burst in upon them to find her treating the robber chief for a broken arm and a fever. This time it was her own people who got the rough edge of her tongue, for she was just in the act of persuading the robber chief to take the medicine she had prepared for him. Of course she was glad to see her own knights again, and to be rescued by them—all the same, she had to tell them—

She was beginning to be known for a particular kind of elo-quence. She found it paid.

How Lynett Met Bagdemagus Again

So now at last she was within sight of Castle Hardy—she was about to meet that man Bagdemagus. The man who had taken her maidenhead. The man who had disillusioned her, disenchanted her, struck the cruellest blow to her ideals, her dreams and her pride— The only man who knew she was not a virgin.

All these months she had gradually travelled towards him in a fine flame of indignation and vengeance; now she suddenly felt, not so much afraid, as embarrassed. No, she would not meet him first in the presence of these her four knights, who respected her.

As by her usual custom, she would approach him alone, as a messenger of peace, and then the knights would follow; but this time not too speedily. She must have time to make her own impression on him in her own way. So she gave the knights orders not to follow her till she sent Dagobert back for them. They protested, saying it would be too dangerous for her, but she overruled them.

And now she stood before the drawbridge, and Dagobert blew on the horn that he carried.

"Who comes here?"

"A damosel bearing a message."

This was usual, and as a rule the next was, "Enter and welcome, fair damosel—" But instead she heard a rude shout of laughter.

"We'll not go in," she said aside to Dagobert, but it was too late. Men—at—arms, roughly dressed, hairy and untidy, pulled them forcibly inside the great door of creaking logs, and impelled them, in the centre of a crowd, up the sloping, turning pathway between the high earth wails, to the door of a log-built hall; here they pulled Lynett from her horse and dragged her inside the door.

The place was indescribably squalid—Lynett was by this time used to all the hardships and austerities of the less fortunate castles, as well as the splendour and state of the better ones—but never had she met with a castle quite like this. The smell of it rose up and affronted her. Everywhere was neglect, carelessness, waste and riot. Everything was dirty, casual, slovenly. The great hall bore evidence of riotous feasts, night after night, never cleaned up after. The hangings on the wall were rich, but torn and splashed with wine and grease—all the long tables had silver cups, but all were tarnished and battered. A smoke-hole over the central hearth took the smoke in a sort of fashion, instead of the newer fireplace and chimney. The smoke itself was heavy and polluted with the refuse flung into the fire. And the company was of the same kind. Among barbarous invading Saxons one might have expected such, but these men were Britons, and many of them wore the trappings of knighthood. But Lynett, as they pressed and hustled her, could call them nothing else but a gang of ruffians. There were no women present, not even serving-wenches; but at the high table there sat some three or four adolescent boys, with long hair painted faces, bedizened with satins and trinkets, giggling together in shrill voices.

There he was, at the head of his table—Bagdemagus himself, the man she had come to see. He had aged very quickly—he was fatter and flabbier, his skin was blotched and flushed, his cheeks were beginning to sag, his eyes were bloodshot, his fine spare frame was grown paunchy. Lynett looked at him and felt—no, not pity, but a kind of impersonal regret for a fine thing gone to ruin. Then, all her old resentment and indignation arose in her like a tidal wave, and filled her with courage to disregard her rude escort.

"Get away from me," she spat at them, and in some surprise they obeyed, leaving a clear space around her, with Dagobert two spaces behind, and Jeanne, unhooded as always, threatening on her wrist. She confronted Bagdemagus on the platform above her, and was quite certain he did not recognize her.

"My lord Bagdemagus," she began in her clear penetrating voice, "I come as a messenger of peace from King Arthur, the true overlord of all Britain, who bids me say thus—" and she unrolled the scroll she had taken from her scrip, and began to read.

Bagdemagus, bold and truculent as ever, loomed over her and listened, with an air of scorn, only waiting for her to have said enough; around her his rough and hostile men stood waiting in attitudes of menace, or of enmity, or of boredom. But she read steadily on, trying to disregard their muttering and spittings.

"The best thing about the woman," she heard one man say to another, "is that big hawk she carries. We'll have that."

"Yes, we'll have that," agreed his follow.

While she went on reading her scroll, Lynett quietly transferred it to her left hand, and with her right hand she loosened Jeanne's jesses, so that Jeanne could fly free. No, they would not have Jeanne.

The message from King Arthur called upon Bagdemagus to submit himself, as in duty bound, to King Arthur, and acknowledge his rule, and the rule of the Laws of Britain; and to that end, to appear and make obeisance before King Arthur at Camelot that coming Whitsun, on forfeit of his life and honour. It further called upon any of his knights who had aforetime been vassals of the King, to return to their old allegiance, without penalty or pain, and with assurance of the King's pardon.

"And to this end," it concluded, "that we might not seem to use force or coercion, we send in the first place these letters by our messenger of peace, our trusted damosel, whom receive with all honour. For be assured that, an ye do not, nor make due submission to us, our next messenger will not be so peaceable."

She concluded the reading, and as if held back till that moment, a thunderous shout of derision broke upon her. She stood compressing her lips, screwing up her eyes clenching her hands. And Bagdemagus gave words to the rest.

"Your King Arthur! We spit on your King Arthur! Submit myself? I'll see him frying in hell's flames. Boys, what'll we do with King Arthur?—and what'll we do with his charming messenger?"

A shout from the hall answered the question in the coarsest possible way. Lynett's face first reddened, then blanched bone-white with rage. She sprang up the steps to the platform.

"Hear me, you men!" she cried, making her voice heard across the tumult. "Hear me while I tell you what I know of this man, your leader. Oh yes, he doesn't know me yet, but he will—oh, he will. Knights, listen. This man deceived, betrayed and raped me, when I was a virgin, thirteen years old, and he a guest in my father's house. Cruelly and deceitfully—not by any persuasive seduction, look you, but practising on my innocence—I who trusted him as a father. Oh men and knights, the hardest of you would respect a child, below the age of consent, ignorant of all evil, trusting her father's guest. Not only the treasure of my body he took from me, but the innocence of my mind, the trust and confidence of my heart. As a father I trusted him, as a father, and lo what he did to me. . . ."

Bagdemagus stood aghast, recognizing her now, and his men drew a little away from him, muttering, swayed for the moment, moved with sympathy for her. If she had rested her case there, she might have had them on her side, but some devil of foolishness made her overplay her hand. She went on,

"Do I blush? It is he, whose brazen brows have never blushed, that should blush with shame now. Call this a knight, a noble, a paladin, a King to command your allegiance. . . .'

She went on and on. She warmed to her theme, and worked upon it. She harangued high and low. The mood turned again, and the crowd surged. Bagdemagus clapped his hands over his ears, and cried,

"Silence the scolding bitch!"

And another yelled,

"To the ducking-stool with her!"

"A common scold!" cried another.

"Put a bridle in her mouth!"

And the crowd rushed upon her.

Dagobert flung himself forward.

"Sirs, sirs," he cried, "respect my lady—"

To Lynett's horror, a hand in the crowd whirled up with a heavy mace, and brought it crashing down on the old man's head. He fell, and was trampled underfoot. Lynett stood for a moment stupefied. Then she gave Jeanne a quick and gentle shake from her wrist—the big bird took off, fluttering above the heads of the crowd, up into the smoke-hole. As she went, however, a bow twanged, and Lynett cried out again as a feather floated down. She could not see whether Jeanne had been hit. But she turned on her persecutors in a frenzy, and struggled while they pinioned her arms and dragged her away again—through corridors, stony and grim—up stairways—at last to a little bare cell, high up, cold, lonely and hopeless.

How Bagdemagus Dealt with Lynett

"So its you," said Bagdemagus, lounging in. "I might have known it."

A day had elapsed since Lynett's capture. Her prison was no dungeon—an attic, high up among the roofs of the castle, dry on the whole and not too cold, with a bed and various other provision for her comfort, and a window through which she could see how impossible escape would be. An old serving man, probably dumb, had brought her bread, meat and small ale. On the whole her captivity was not barbarous, but deadly tedious, and not without an ominous undercurrent of worse to come. There was poor old Dagobert, ruthlessly murdered, and Jeanne probably shot too. What better was she to expect?

She looked up as he entered, but did not move from the edge of the bed where she sat, upright and tense.

"Yes, it's me," she said. "And now your men have murdered my servant, and shut me up here, when you ought to have respected the King's messenger."

"King's messenger my foot!—Oh yes, it's you, boy Robin. Impudent enough for that or any job. Come here and kiss me." He dragged her to her feet, and clutched her to him—she struggled, fiery with hate. He held her a moment, and then threw her aside.

"No—on the whole, no. Not attractive. You've not worn well. Skin's gone coarse, hair's a mess, and your figure's gone bony and scraggy. I don't want you."

"Nobody asked you," she flung at him. "come to that, my lord, you've not worn so well yourself. Coarse skin—just look at you!

And red nose too—and as for figure, no one could call you scraggy—baggy, I'd say—"

He laughed, but with anger. "You dare! Impudent as ever. Bold Scold, that's what you are. Oh well, I don't want your ugly body now, don't fear. But I'll have a use for you all the same."

He turned to the door and whistled. A man came in with a leather apron and some metal things in a bag.

"You've got some useful knowledge I'd like to have. For instance—King Arthur's secret password?"

Grim terror struck her. This was it. This would be the test. Torture.

"No," she said, very pale.

"No? I think yes. There's things we could do to you. I and my friend here, not so pleasant, after all, as what I did under that beech tree. Things that would alter your mind quite a bit. I think you'll tell me."

"No."

"All right, the thumbscrews first. Begin with one hand. Just a first taste—"

The pain was atrocious. She screamed at the full stretch of her lungs, because she couldn't help it. The pain stopped—and then began again. At the third touch she fainted, but a strong aromatic smell jerked her back to consciousness, and she heard Bagdemagus saying, "You won't escape that way."

She would go out of her mind, she knew only too well. The pain would sent her mad, and she would tell them anything, anything— It came again. . . . Then a desperate plan formed itself. If she told him something—something he would think was the secret password—and his men would try to use it, but she could make it something that would warn them, that would bring them to her aid. . . .

She opened her eyes, and passed her tongue over her lips.

"I'll tell. All right, stop doing that and I'll tell."

"Why, good girl!" he said. "I knew you would. All right, Sarkos—take it off. Well?"

"It's this. 'The falcon's feather cries out.'"

"The falcon's feather cries out," he repeated. "Is this the true word? On your oath?"

"On my oath, yes."

"Look me in the eyes."

She did so, but the blaze of hatred in her eyes hid any trace of hesitation.

"Do you swear it on your eternal salvation?"

"I swear it," she said. (Oh God, oh God, she thought, You'll surely forgive this—it's under duress—oh, You know it's under duress.)

"Now think—say after me: if this is not the truth—"

"If this is not the truth—"

"May be the thing I fear most—"

"May be the thing I fear most—"

"Pursue me and overtake me—"

"Pursue me and overtake me—"

"And may the Black Ones that follow me—"

(Now how on earth did he know that? But she must go and say it—and if her voice faltered, it must seem only from the pain of the thumbscrew—)

"And may the Black Ones that follow me—"

"Overtake me and have my heart and my soul—"

"Overtake me and have my heart and my soul—"

"Amen."

"Amen."

She drew a long sigh, and collapsed on the floor with her face hidden.

"Will you let me to now?"

"Let you go? Oh no. My dear woman, what d'you think? No, you'll stay here, and if your password proves to be a deceit, we'll think of something to do to you. So, you see—?"

He left her, without lamp or candle, as the dusk crept over her chilly little room. Crouched on the small hard bed, she nursed her mangled thumb.

What had she done? The false password she had given would certainly bring her bodyguard to her rescue, if Bagdemagus or any of his men tried to use it to get into their camp—but would they come in time, when her enemies had discovered the deceit? Her deceit—oh yes, all was fair in war, but what, what had she done? Not only had she perjured herself, but what were those frightful words he had made her say! "May the Black Ones that follow me, overtake me and have my heart and my soul—"

How did *he* know about those Black Ones? Did he, perhaps, have Black Ones that followed him? And if so, what and how great must be the black devils that followed such a man. . . . Almost she felt—no, not pity but a sort of awestruck horror at the burden of his guilt. But this man had done her a fresh wrong now. He had made her forswear herself, so that her immortal soul was forfeit; and he had made her put herself in the power of those Black Ones— She shivered, drawn into herself with hatred, sucking her aching thumb. The corners of the room filled up with darkness. They were full of black bristling things—round spiny black balls with legs, that would presently roll out, and stretch into tall fox-headed figures— Also there were wings fluttering at the window.

When at last she dropped off to sleep, she was plagued with horrible dreams—plodding over miles of desert, clutching something—what was it? a sword, a pair of shoes, a basket, a book—whatever it was, she had to hold it tighter and tighter, though it turned red-hot and burned her. And behind her came the Black Ones. Once she stopped and turned on them, and said, "I know what you are. I made you. Go away!" but they grinned horribly at her, and would not go away. They came nearer, and grew larger and more hideous. . . . She awoke with a shriek.

The pale light of morning was coming faintly in—but something blocked the light of the window—wings fluttered—it was just and ultimate terror. . . . Then she looked again and the terror was turned to joy. It was Jeanne, clinging to the grating of the window.

"Oh, my darling!" she exclaimed. She thrust a finger through the grating—there was no glass—and ruffled the peregrine's breast feathers. Then she saw, tied to its foot like a jess, a strip of cloth—blue cloth, such as the young Lancelot wore. Oh yes, help was on the way. She sobbed with relief.

There was nothing she could do but wait. Jeanne seemed to have no speech now, though she clicked and chuckled and made whirring noises in her throat. The hours were long in passing. The mute serving-man brought in food—Jeanne, sensing a stranger, hovered away from the window while he was there. When he was gone, Lynett shared her meat with Jeanne. The day passed.

How Lynett Dealt with Bagdemagus

Then suddenly there was noise, and the smell and sound of burning. Not the encouraging smell of a household fire, but the panic smell of things that ought not to be burning. Voices shouting, heavy feet running, the grinding of metal on metal, the crash of objects falling. Lynett tried to lean out of her window and see what was going on, but her window was placed so that she could see nothing. Jeanne gave a hoarse cry, and soared out of sight.

Somewhere in the castle was burning, and Lynett would burn

with it. Was that the last malice of that man—to leave her to burn in a cage, so that her rescuers would find only her bones? She tried to pray—but how should she pray? Wasn't her soul damned already?

Then her door burst open, and there was Bagdemagus, struggling in the grasp of young Lancelot, who held him by the hair while two squires pinioned his arms.

"Have no fear, lady," said Lancelot. "Here is your enemy."

He held his sword over Bagdemagus's neck.

"Shall I cut off his head, lady?" he asked her.

Bagdemagus's face was yellowish-grey, and the sweat was tracing runnels in the dust from brow to chin. His hair fell forward over his eyes; he struggled, and fell limp, and then struggled again. Great dry sobs broke from him.

"Have mercy," he moaned. "Oh sweet lady, have mercy. Don't tell him to kill me. Don't tell him to kill me. Have mercy. I'm sorry for all I ever did to you. Oh lady, lady, spare me."

"No," she said.

"I implore you—I beg you—have pity, just a little pity—"

"All you ever did to me? You did more than anyone will ever know. You blemished my body and my soul. First you took my virginity, and then you made me forswear myself and damn my own soul. I do not forgive you."

He grovelled between his captors, sinking on the ground. He was beside himself with fear.

"You!" she said. "You taught me boldness—and now you haven't even the courage to face death decently."

"I am beaten, lady. I yield myself. Remember I loved you once—"

"Call that love? Your beastly appetite, that was all."

"Boy Robin—"

"Don't you dare to call me that. All right, kill him."

And Lancelot swung his bright sharp sword downward. It shore through everything—the man's head rolled on the ground, setting free a torrent of blood under Lynett's feet. She stood looking, spellbound. A horrible feeling came over her that she was going to be sick.

"Give me a drink of strong waters, quickly," she muttered. One of the squires handed her a flask of aqua-vitae—she gulped a mouthful of it. It scorched her throat but the one shock overcame the other, and the nausea passed; she drew a long breath, and leant back against the wall, white and shaking.

"How is it with you, lady?" said Lancelot. "You are not well—"

"I'm well enough," she said in a choked voice. "Just a fever I think; I'll carry his head to King Arthur."

"Come with me," he said, and gave her arm. He led her down through the castle, now strangely silent, only echoing here and there to slow footfalls, where they dragged the dead men away. The serving-men had made the best chamber ready for her, such as it was, and they left her quiet, on a warm soft bed—shaking, and unable to get any warmth into her body.

After three days the young Lancelot stood at her door. In his hand he held something round, black, hairy and bristling. She shrieked.

Always those round, black, hairy things—in all her dreams now. Rolling after her, or tracking her on their horrible thin legs—more of them and more of them—and now this. . . .

"Take it away," she screamed. "For God's sake take it away. . . . What is it?"

"The head of your enemy, lady," Lancelot said in gentle tones. "You said you would carry it to the King Arthur, as is your right and privilege. We have had it cunningly embalmed—it will not stink—and it is laid up in this goatskin bag—"

She forced herself to look at it.

"Oh, is that what it is? Well, put it in some other bag. Leather, or cloth, or basket, or what you will—only—not black and hairy." She shuddered.

"Why, with all good will, lady—nothing easier." He retired, shaking his head at her fancy, and went off to find a calfskin satchel.

So later they rode away together from that castle, and Lynett carried the head on her saddlebow, in a seemly smooth calfskin bag. And she wondered—should she not feel like Judith of old? She had avenged her virginity, and removed her King's enemy. The world was a better place without that Bagdemagus. His centre of lawlessness and crime was dispersed. King Arthur would be glad, and his dream of a better Britain, united, law-abiding, safe for honest men, was that much nearer. Her personal quest, her own long desired revenge, was accomplished, and she ought to find it sweet. And yet—and yet she looked at the thing that hung on her saddlebow, and felt not so much like Judith as like Salome. Oh, nonsense, she told herself. Just the disgust of seeing the thing done—no more than a squeamishness of the flesh. If these knights could kill men and sleep no worse, why should she shrink from it? And yet. . . .

Of a Vision in the Forest

They had a long journey before them, no less than the length of Britain from Northumberland to the Thames. Mostly they went from castle to castle, and claimed hospitality as they went; but sometimes it was an anxious and weary moment towards the end of the day, when they had to hope they had not missed the way to the next castle. . . . They were a smaller party now, only the knights and Lynett, for their work was accomplished for this time, and the squires and serving-men had remained behind to hold Castle Hardy till a castellan could be set there.

Yet, as the summer advanced, the boughs were leafy and they rode at ease, the bare moors soon giving way to pleasant green-woods. On warm nights they saw no reason to seek shelter under a roof, but camped in the greenwood; the knights raised a tent for Lynett ("pight a pavilion", the old romances would say). This was supported on their four lances, and the cloth of which it was made was carried in their saddlebags: in this tent they would make a narrow pallet for her, like any soldier's, and there she would sleep well enough, while they lay around the campfire outside, their heads resting on their saddles.

It was one of these calm and warm evenings, and they sat late round the camp-fire before sleeping. There were the four knights—Sir Bors, red-faced and slow, but infinitely reliable; Sir Gwalchmei, tall and dark and with a certain look of the great Gawain, for he was kin to the Orkney family; Sir Perceval, a strange man, straw-pale both in hair and skin, with great luminous blue eyes—it was said that his mother had brought him up in the seclusion of a forest till he was eighteen years old, without any knowledge of the world, and especially without any knowledge of women. He had been very reluctant to go on an adventure with Lynett because she was a woman, but the King had overruled his objections; and in their journeyings he had lost his fear of her, and accepted her as a sister, but he was never at his ease with the ladies in the castles. And the fourth was Lancelot, so young, so vulnerable, but always so ready with hand or sword. Long back in their journey he had ridden alone with Lynett, and from his overburdened heart told her of his unlucky love for Guinevere. Up to now it had been no more than distant worship, but he knew its force, and what must come of it in the end.

There they sat in the flickering firelight.

"Soon we shall be back in Camelot," said Lancelot, musing.

"And then, what shall we do?" said Gwalchmei.

"Have a good long rest, I hope," Bors pronounced so positively that they all laughed.

"Oh, agreed, agreed!" said Lynett. "But what after that?"

They sat silent for some time, and then Perceval spoke.

"We will go and find—It."

"Yes," they said one by one after him, "we will go and find—It."

Lynett looked from one to the other, with a sad feeling of being left out of a secret.

"What is—It?" she asked. "May I be told?"

The four looked from one to the other, dubiously.

"May a woman be told?" said Perceval, shaking his head.

"Well, why not?" said Bors.

"Yes, why not?" said Lancelot, and brushing aside the others, went on, "*It* is the Holy Grail."

"Ah!" sighed Lynett and bowed her head, and the rest sighed too.

"Lady," Lancelot continued, "we saw it once, but veiled, at Arthur's table. They say that once in seven years it is shown to men, but veiled, and then some must go in search of it to see it plainly. Once we saw it, we four. It was on Good Friday, in Camelot, as we sat round our fasting meal at the Round Table, in the Chamber of the Round Table. At noon—you remember?" He looked round at the others, who nodded as a chorus. "First the sky was darkened like midnight, and it thundered; then from the high window above, it came on a beam of light."

"How did it come? How did it seem?" whispered Lynett. Bors took up the tale.

"It was as if a cup or a chalice was covered with a veil—none carried it, it moved down of itself—"

"No," said Gwalchmei, "there was a hand that carried it. I saw the hand."

"Not so neither," broke in Perceval. "There was a damosel carried it, but veiled, heavily veiled from head to foot—not even her hands could be seen."

"But when it was amongst us, we were—how were we then, Perceval?"

"We were blessed," said Perceval simply, staring before with his pale eyes.

"We were—oh, it was like this," Bors went on, almost stammering in his eagerness. "It was as if the dry bread and salt fish and the water in our our cups was turned into the food we liked best in all the world. Oh, it wasn't that really, but the same pleasure as if it were. . . . Oh, long ago, when I was a child, and had had a fever, and had tasted no meat for days, when I was recovered my mother cooked me a dish, and it was the best thing I had ever eaten in my life—a roast chicken with herbs—it was like that. Was it not?" and he looked round at the others.

"For me," said Perceval, "it was like peaches warmed in the sun, that angels might eat in Paradise when man was not yet fallen."

"For me," said Gwalchmei, "Yes, it was like I remember once when I was hunting with my father, and we were starving hungry, and he cooked a deer over a camp-fire and we ate it in haste—so hungry we were. The food one had longed for. . . . And what to you, Lancelot?"

Lancelot's face was red in the firelight.

"I cannot say," he said. "I think the bread and fish were still bread and fish, but I tasted nothing, for—my lady was there." Then he sunk his head on his knees.

"They say", Bors went on, "that it can cure every sickness, and every grief, if a man seeks it truly and finds it. We all saw its veiled shape, for a moment, and felt its blessing; and then it was gone. We would have departed that moment to seek it—though God alone knows which ways we should have gone—but Arthur forbade it, saying the time was not yet come."

"But when we return," said Lynett, "might it be the time?"

"God only knows the time," said Perceval.

She thought deeply, staring into the cracking fire, and then said,

"Might a woman go in search of the Grail?"

They all looked up, startled at the idea.

"Surely," said Lancelot.

"A woman—!" exclaimed Perceval.

"Why not?" said Bors.

"Perhaps if she were a virgin—" said Gwalchmei, and then seeing Lynett's face redden, "Oh, pardon, lady. I only meant—you are, of course, a married lady, the wife of Sir Gaheris. I meant no disrespect."

—But he does't know, thought Lynett unhappily.

They sat in silence, then suddenly across the soft forest rustlings came the sound of a bell, struck once. A clear silver bell—it came again, not tinkling, but sounding slow and regular, sweet as crystal. And with it there came to their nostrils the smell of incense, true holy incense of myrrh and galbanum. And far away from where they sat, between the trees, along some unknown pathway, a light glowed.

They sprang to their feet and stood gazing out between the dark tree trunks. The light grew—and at last there came in sight an awesome procession, lit with its own strange gleam, and singing as it came.

First came slowly pacing a noble white hart—taller than a red deer, and spotless white, with his great spread of horns held proudly aloft and between the hours as it were a cavern crucifix, from which a white light radiated. Then behind the white hart came six maidens all in white, veiled so that their faces could not be seen, but with golden circlets over their veils—they moved with bowed heads, and sang softly. Then came thurifers and acolytes and priests, all in their due vestments, but with their faces hidden in white hoods. Then four tall men, walking side by side, each of which carried some sacred thing covered with a rich cloth, so that none could see what it was. And then behind them, guarded by four young boys, came slowly pacing a damosel, whose soft white veil fell over her, wrought with golden flowers, and coverd the thing she carried, preciously in both hands. The veil covered it as it covered her, but from that hidden thing a light rayed out, a light that was every colour, and whose colours were so pure that they carried bliss to the eyes and the heart.

The five watchers fell on their knees while the procession went by. The silver bell sounded, slow and sweet; the soft voices chanted; the incense drifted across in blue clouds. And then at last all was gone, and there was nothing but the quiet forest.

Of the five, not one could speak a word, nor look at one another. They turned away and with one accord lay down to sleep.

Of a Glamour and a Trial

They continued on their way, through the dense forests and then again through open downlands. There came a day when they had set out cheerfully enough in the morning—a fine day in the late summer—and yet about noon as they stopped, and dismounted, and sat on a green bank together to eat their luncheon, they looked up and found mist all round them. A gentle mist at first, and then a dense white fog—a white blindness, where all sense of direction was lost. They mounted their horses and rode slowly on, watching the edges of the road. But after a time this direction failed them. The dark came down.

"We can't go on in this," said Lancelot.

"If we've followed the road, we should be nearing a castle now," said Gwalchmei.

"There should be a light—yes, look—"

The fog seemed to lift a little, and far off a small point of light appeared.

"Could it be the castle? No, look, it's moving—"

"A man with a lantern!" cried Perceval. "Come on, he'll guide us—"

"No, no!" Lynett cried, and clutched his arm. "Not a man with a lantern! Don't you see—it's *the* Man with the Lantern—"

"The *ignis fatuus*, God shield us!" the knights muttered, and crossed themselves. Far off, three, four, five points of light danced and jumped in the dark distance.

"What can we do?" They gathered together. "We can't go on in this—God knows what sloughs and quagmires are round us. This is evil country."

In the end they could do nothing but stay where they were, crouched on the ground in the close circle made by their horses, all the cold, damp, miserable night. They drank what they had in their flasks, and ate hard bread—they had endured hardships together before this. But when the daylight came there was still no break in the fog, and they were perished with cold and had no more provisions. They tried to move on step by step, but every direction was unsafe, and no trace of road could be found.

Darkness fell again, and they were all exhausted, weary, famished. The horses cropped the scanty grass of the wasteland, but they shivered also. It was no summer mist—it was bleak, chilly, penetrating. And another night of this misery lay before them.

Then, strangely, as the light dimmed, the mist seemed to clear, and to their surprise they found they were not on the bare plain, but in a wood—a clear high wood of arching trees. It seemed they must have strayed into it as they moved in the fog. There was a wide, well-marked path before them through the wood, and walking along it, away from them, were three women.

"Why, this must be the way!" exclaimed Lynett, and they all mounted their horses and went on at a footpace into the wood, endeavouring to overtake the three women. But fast as they went (short of breaking into a trot, which they felt unwilling to do) the three still kept ahead of them.

There seemed to be more light between the trees; the fog had receded. Coming closer behind the three women now (who heeded no calls) they could see them a little more plainly. All were in undistinguishable black robes, but their heads were unveiled. The one on the left had jet-black hair flowing almost to her feet; she in the middle had florid yellow curls, dressed high and sumptously on her head; and she on the right had golden-red hair that floated around her. They seemed to come to a place where their ways divided—the black and the golden one went on towards the left, but the redhead parted from them and went to the right. And there, coming down to meet her with the light on his face, was Merlin.

Lynett cried out,

"Oh, there's Merlin! This *must* be the right road—come on!" and urged her horse that way. But somehow she could not pass. There seemed to be an invisible barrier that thrust her back to the other path, and ahead of her, Merlin and the red-haired woman were suddenly gone. She looked back, and the fair-haired one was gone also—there remained only the dark-haired one, and she had turned to face them, and behind her was a fair and stately house, with lights glowing in every window.

A grand place it seemed—no fortified castle, but a palace, with broad steps leading up to a wide open door. The dark-haired woman was smiling, with outstretched arms.

"Come in, come, all of you," she exclaimed. "Be welcome, weary travellers."

Serving-men were suddenly there to take their horses as they dismounted; they passed up the steps, and through the doors into the light and warmth. Music of harps came out to meet them, and perfume, and even more welcome, the smell of good meats roasting. A noble hall, its floor tiled in bright patterns and strewn with scented herbs; long tables laid, and bright cressets burning against burnished shields all along richly draped walls. All was welcome and comfort. Fair pages and gentle maids led them away to exchange their worn garments for rich and easy robes; then they found themselves seated at the table and feasting royally. One and all, the knights and Lynett too, gave themselves up unquestioning to the heavenly comfort, sank into it with nothing but thankfulness.

Then the handsome dark-haired lady took Lynett by the hand and led her away to her bower. From the stately style of the hall, Lynett expected a rich enough chamber—tapestries on the walls, perhaps, and a table covered with a carpet—but not this. Here

were carpets richly piled on the floor, so that one's feet made no
noise, and silken cushions lying in heaps. Above, from a carved
and painted ceiling, a lamp of many-coloured glass diffused a
soft light. From every corner of the little room, fantastic images
looked down, and jewelled pendants glittered. Lynett had heard
of such rooms, in palaces among the saracens and paynims, but
never thought to see one.

The black-haired lady sat down upon a pile of cushions, and
beckoned Lynett to do the same; then she poured her a cup of
sweet wine.

"My dear," she said, "we are not strangers. I met you at your
wedding, don't you remember? I and my two sisters—"

Lynett stammered some uncomprehending words.

"Yes," the lady went on. "I am your aunt by marriage. Queen
Morgause of Orkney, your bridegroom's mother, is my sis-
ter—the third of us is Vivian, who is betrothed to Merlin. But
King Arthur is also our mother's son. So we are all kinsfolk?"
She smiled and drew Lynett closer to her.

"Oh, I know, child, you have no joy of your marriage. There's
little I don't know. . . . And so you have become messenger to
my brother Arthur? —Oh, but he is making a great mistake, this
Arthur. He intends to make himself king over all this land. And
I do not intend that he should. . . . Oh, you may look surprised.
You will of course not understand why he should not. You think
him a great king and a good king—but there are things you don't
know, things you can't understand. . . . Listen now. What does
this Arthur give you for the hard service you do for him?"

"Give me?" said Lynett, staring rather stupidly.

"Yes—every servant deserves his wage. What do you get in his
service?"

"Get? Why, I had never thought. . . . Why, I'm like one of his
knights. What should we get? He gives us armour, and he gave
me clothing, and one of his own great horses—"

"Nothing more? Even knights must eat."

"Oh, we have *bouche de court* when we're there—and he gives
me enough gold pieces to pay for lodgings on the road when I
need them—oh, and he gave me this beautiful ring—"

"In other words, you serve him for bare board and lodging?
Why, child, that's a villein's fee! He should do better for you
than that!"

Lynett's face reddened. "We his knights—I—I mean, I don't
want for anything. Why should I desire anything more?"

"Oh, you're simple!" The lady smiled. "Why, child—those

other knights, each has his manor, his own house and his lands to which he can return when his errand is over. But what have you? Your house in Lyonesse is not your own, now your sister is married and dwells there with Gareth. Your Gaheris has made no provision for you since you left him. What home have you to return to, when your errantry is over? What has this Arthur given you? Had you thought of that?"

"I hadn't thought of that," said Lynett, her eyes downcast.

"Now I," said the lady, "I could do better for you than this. I also need a messenger. I would reward you well, with gold and houses and lands."

"I could not leave my service with the King."

"You need not. All I should ask is that you continue as you are, but carry a message from me also from time to time, and send word back to me of where you are, and where the king is going to send you."

Lynett looked up enquiringly, a long straight look.

"And that you change your mind a little about certain things."

"No," said Lynett.

"Ah, but think— Not, perhaps, a palace like this, though I could give you that if you really wanted it—but a comfortable moated grange, with orchards and beehives and dairies, and the rich fields around it, and a lovely little garden of herbs—like your old home in Lyonesse."

"No, no, no!" said Lynett, and thrust her fist into the soft cushion before her.

"No? Oh well, perhaps not. But another offer—why not go home? —oh yes, give Arthur due notice, that having done this errand, you work for him no more—say you have had enough of roaming. Go home to Lyonesse, where your sister lives with Gareth. She is with child, and—a man's fancy sometimes strays at such times. I will promise you, if you will pledge yourself to me, that he, Gareth, will turn to you—"

A sudden fierce longing gripped Lynett's heart, and she averted her face. The lady could hear the sharp intake of breath.

"Oh yes, I know, that would be your heart's desire. I will promise you this, without fail. You will have nothing to do but to be there, and remember me and what I shall tell you. And there will be his son, and you will teach him what I shall tell you as he grows up. It would be easy enough for you—why should you not go home?"

"No again," said Lynett, but this time her hands were gripped tightly together.

"I am sorry then," said the lady, frowning, "for I cannot be your friend as I should have wished. Promise me one thing, though—that you will never forgive this Bagdemagus, though he is dead."

"Oh, I can promise you that!" she exclaimed, looking up and meeting those hot dark eyes.

"That's right. Never, never for your own honour and the dignity of your womanhood. Never, never forgive him!"

"That I never will!"

"Then there is one point on which we can shake hands," and the dark woman stretched out her hand to take Lynett's. Lynett clasped her hand, and at once the dark woman seized her hand and pulled it, so that Lynett fell forward on the carpet—but it was no longer a carpet, but hard, gritty ground, and Lynett was being dragged forward over it, roughly, by someone gripping her hand—the rocks raked her body and her knees—another hand pulled her hair—

Gone was the coloured bower and the lady. There was only a barren plain, in a pale clouded light, and two rough men in the livery of Bagdemagus were dragging Lynett along the ground. She shrieked and struggled.

"Now we've got you," said one of the men. "A fine bodyguard you have, all fast asleep. We've not left much of them." As she twisted her head, struggling, she could glimpse dark forms, flung down—dead horses or dead men.

"You had your vengeance of Bagdemagus, our chief," said the other man, "and now we'll have our vengeance on you."

"And so will King Arthur avenge me," she spat back at them.

"So? And then we'll take vengeance on King Arthur, and so it goes merrily on."

She spoke no more while they hauled her up, flung her over a saddle, and carried her away. The prison where they left her at last was far underground and pitch dark.

Of the Terrible Head

As she lay in the darkness, on filthy straw, a man thrust open the heavy creaking door, and came in bearing a torch. It was one of Bagdemagus's followers, a rough, bearded, uncouth man as they all were, clad in the coarse russet that was his livery. He carried something with him.

"Here, you scolding hellcat," he said. "You can have some company. Here's our Chief's head, that your leman cut off at your orders—you can have it with you to think about. Scold it if you want to—*he* won't hear you." And holding the torch up with his left hand, he hung on a nail in the stony wall opposite her the calfskin bag whose contents she knew only too well. "There. Now you can contemplate that, my lady, while we take our time, and decide what we shall do with you. It won't be quick or easy, you can be sure." And he went out, clanking the great door to, and shutting out the light of even his smoky torch.

There in the dark she sat, knowing nothing, but that *that* horrible thing was there on the wall above her, to set the seal on all the other horrors of darkness. . . .

Then presently a faint and repulsive light began to glow from the bag where that head was—a pale glow like rotting fungus in a tree-stump, or decaying fish in a dark cellar. Her hair rose, and a deadly coldness gripped her. The horrible light grew and grew—and then she seemed to see the dead face through all the leather and wrappings—it was plain to see, and it grew and grew, larger and larger till it loomed over her, covered the vault above her, filled the whole cell— She shrieked, but there was none to hear her. For a moment her brain was numbed, almost in a swoon. Then slowly the terrible face receded, shrank again, down and down, till it was not much more than lifesize. And now it hovered on the wall before her, and was no longer a vast Sphinx, but Bagdemagus's face, dead and ghastly. But in its ghastliness there was a terrible grief. Not only the collapse of decay, but that the whole face drooped. The brows drooped, the eyelids were pressed together—the nostrils were pinched, the lips pressed together also, the corners of the mouth dragged down in a dolorous curve— It was like the face on a crucifix.

Then those compressed eyelids opened a glimmering crack, and the thin lips parted, and the head spoke, hoarsely and quavering.

"Forgive me."

She gave a cry, clasping her hands to her breast.

The head spoke again.

"Forgive me. . . For God's sake. . .Lynett. . .grant me pardon and let me go."

She answered, speaking in a whisper.

"How can you speak to me? Where are you? Are you in Hell?"

"I do not know," replied the spectral head. "I do not know if this is Hell. But I know that I suffer, and I know this is not Purgatory, for in Purgatory there is hope, and here there is none.

In Purgatory there is progress, and there is no progress, no going on for me. Oh, that I could enter into Purgatory and begin my purgation! But I cannot, till you forgive me."

"You pleaded with me before, and I said no," she replied. "Why do you think I should forgive you now?"

"I pleaded with you then, because I was in fear of death. But now I am dead, and things are different. I see now what I could not see before, and I ask your forgiveness because I am sorry for what I did."

She sat silent.

He went on,

"I understand so many things differently, after being dead for a few days—or is it a few months, or a few years? It's hard to tell.

"But now I know what I did. The thing that I never understood was your innocence. How could I, when I had never met that kind of innocence before? A plain touch-me-not chastity, like your sister's, I could understand—but your frank friendship, with no thought of evil—that was strange to me. I mistook it for bold wanton invitation. It never crossed my mind that you had no thought of lust. I had never met a girl like you before, and I truly thought that your desire was like my own. And so, in my stupidity, I destroyed that innocence. It's true that I loved you, in my way, but I did not know what it was I loved, and I trampled on it. And now I know what it was I did—and I weep for it."

"Is this true?" she said softly and breathlessly.

"In the name of God, before Whom I stand," he said, "it is true. We who are dead can no longer dissemble."

And tears, difficult reluctant tears, forced themselves between the tightened eyelids, and spilled slowly down the furrowed cheeks.

Answering tears sprang into Lynett's eyes, and something seemed to break from round her heart.

"Oh, you poor man," she whispered.

"Forgive me—now?"

"I forgive you," she said.

"Give me a sign. Kiss me on the brow. Come, do not be afraid of me. I have no body to harm you."

Quivering, and with her teeth clenched against the horror, she took two steps across the cell, and reached up, and kissed that livid, gleaming brow. It was colder than stone.

At once the ghastly face relaxed, and Lynett felt her whole body relax also. A strange kind of warmth came over her, and for a moment she felt an inexplicable sensation of light and relief.

"Thank you," the dead face said, and the eyes opened, and were lucid and mild. "And thank God—oh, thank God! Now I can go. Leave me here when you escape—"

"When I escape? But how, and when?"

"Quite soon—now. I will help you. Get ready—"

Footsteps were approaching along the stony corridor outside. The door creaked, as the guard unlocked it and pushed it open. He carried a pewter platter with food—but at the moment when he opened the door, the head shone out with a livid blue light, tinged with green, the lips drawn back in a gleaming grin. The man dropped the platter, and staggered—Lynett snatched the platter up, and brought the edge of it with a swinging blow against the man's head. He went down like a log. The door was open behind him.

Lynett could hear a totally unexpected sound—the head was laughing.

"Oh, well done, Boy Robin! Go on now, go on—"

And she slipped through the door, and was out into the inky-black tunnel beyond.

Of a Dweller in Darkness

She ran into the darkness. There were two ways only, up and down, and she ran down, with some dim feeling that her captors must be above, and therefore downwards must be away from them. There was no gleam of light—she just ran on blindly, feeling her way along the walls of the narrow passage. Yet somehow, in that terrifying darkness, for the moment she was upheld by a strange unreasoning euphoria. Not only that she was out of her prison, and had a chance to escape—but from the minute she had forgiven Bagdemagus, she had a sense of being set free. She knew that those black bogies were gone—the round bristling things with the running legs and the hidden teeth—gone, and never would return. Though she might be walking into death, she rejoiced. Neither would that dream come again, of trudging through the wilderness clutching a burden, clutching, clutching— Whatever it was, she had let it go. Now she had nothing in her hands at all, and walked with them outstretched, touching the sides of the passage. But the passage went on and on, down and down, and the glow of rejoicing died away. Now she was cold, and trembling in the dark. Deeper and deeper. Where would this dark way lead her? Should she turn back? But no, that way she would walk into the hands of the enemies. Death either way. No longer running, she groped her way along. She was afraid even to stand still.

Presently she began to hear the rushing of water. Carefully, now. She felt every step before her, holding to the sides of the passage, which was becoming more irregular and broken. Then suddenly there was no hand-hold either to right or left of her, and in front of her was the deep roar of a torrent. Left without her support, she lost her balance, fell, and plunged into icy, rapid water.

Drowning in the dark, she struggled helplessly. She came to the surface, gulped a breath of air, and felt something gash her head as she came up—not stunning her but cutting her cruelly. She went down again, the water tearing in through her gullet and her nose—death clutching her—

Then she was seized from beneath and carried upward—her mouth reached the surface and she could breathe, but a hand was over her head, covering her forehead, eyes and nose, keeping her from lifting her head further. A voice said close to her ear, above the rush of the water.

"Keep quite still. You are safe with me, but you are in more danger than you know. The roof of the cavern is scarcely a handsbreadth above your face."

A man was supporting her in the water—she was lying supine over his breast; his right arm was firmly round her, and his left hand was protecting her face. So much she could feel, also that he seemed to be naked in the water. She lay still, though trembling, and it seemed to her, very strangely, that she felt no revulsion or fear at so close a contact with this man's body. Rather did she feel confidence and safety, even in that terrifying dark water and under that menacing roof of cruel rocks.

He spoke again.

"Now take a deep breath and hold it while you count fifty. We are going under the water."

Obediently she did so, and they went down into the dark again. She could not count fifty—she had no wits to count at all. But suddenly they were up in the breathable air again, and she heard him say "Fifty". But still there was no light.

Then there was gravel under them, and he picked her up

and carried her, and laid her, as far as she could feel, on a sandy beach, But still all in pitch dark. She lay a long time just breathing, trying to gather a little strength. Perhaps she even slept. There was no difference between eyes open and eyes shut.

"Are you a little recovered?" the unknown man said. His voice was very gentle and musical. "That is a dangerous way—nobody knows it but I. How did you come to be there?"

"I was escaping from enemies," she said.

"Ah, yes, of course. What else?"

He was moving about in the dark.

"Rest here," he said. "I will go and get fire for you." She heard his steps go a little way off, and a sound of stone and pebbles being disturbed; then, to her astonishment, a spark of light, as the unknown man struck flint on steel, and brought up a little flame—a small fire of dry sticks grew up, and for the first time for a very long while, Lynett could see.

She was in a vast cavern, so vast that she could not make out its limits at all; she could only see that where she was lying was a beach of sand and stones, on the edge of a dark expanse of water. All the rest was lost in the darkness. Her rescuer, who was crouched over the little fire, was a tall young man, finely proportioned, but with a strange pale skin and a mane of ash-coloured hair. He was naked, except for a leather loincloth which he seemed to wear more as a shield than a garment. As he turned from the fire, she saw his face, and it was as beautiful a face as she had ever seen.

"Come to the fire," he said, without looking up.

There was something strange about the way he was handling the fire. He carefully felt each twig, and then pushed it forward by one end; then his hands hovered round and over the flames, always at a certain distance, as if they felt for an exact degree of heat. He ringed the fire carefully with a little bank of sand, so that it could not spread. He seemed to have a cache of firewood, flint and steel, and other things, in a corner under some rocks.

The fire burned up and made a comforting glow. Lynett was dreadfully cold, and her garments dripped and weighed her down.

"Now," said her rescuer, "You must take off your clothes, and dry them at the fire. Oh—" as he caught the sound of her protesting gasp, "don't be afraid of me. I am quite blind."

How Lynett was Brought Back to Light

The strange blind man had a flask of some rare cordial, which he fetched from a crevice in the rocks—moving unerringly there guided by his feet and hands, and some inexplicable sixth sense. The cordial was rich and creamy, and wonderfully reviving—food as well as drink; and Lynett, crouched naked over the fire, and still a little self-conscious in spite of the young man's assurance, began to feel a little better. He talked to her, in rather uneasy halting sentences, as if unused to talking much.

"I am called Lucius," he said.

"Lucius? —That means— Of the Light?"

"Yes, although I have long lived here in the dark. My mother named me Lucius when we first—came into the dark. She named me for the light she hoped we would both see again." He sighed and paused, and then went on. "I was not born in the dark. I think I once had another name. I can remember when I could see, and I can remember when we had light. I don't know how old I was. There was a wicked man, somewhere up there—" and he waved his hand uncertainly upwards, "who shut up my mother and myself, because she would not yield to him. A long, long time we were shut up in darkness."

"Was his name Bagdemagus?" asked Lynett.

"Oh no—this much I do remember. His name was Breuse Saunce Pitié."

Lynett sighed with relief. To have to un-forgive Bagdemagus again was a thing she could not have borne.

He continued.

"He proved himself without pity to myself and my beautiful mother. A long, long time we were there in the dark—until what with the dark and what with famine, my sight faded, and my mother died."

"Oh, dear God!" exclaimed Lynett. "And how long was this?"

"I do not know. We had no means of knowing, down here, how the days, weeks, months, years passed. I know my mother kept some kind of reckoning, scratched on the stones of our prison; but I did not know how to read it, even when they let us have a rushlight, as they did at first. I only know I grew. And when I found she was dead, I escaped down the dark passages, for the jailers left the door open thinking that I must be dead too—so I fled down the dark passages, being then completely blind as I am now, and found my way into a world of caves and tunnels and streams. I learnt to fend for myself and make my way in the dark. Here I have no need of eyes, for I can feel, and hear, and smell, and—well, I can feel without touching. I did not, of course, come by way of the rushing water, or I never would have lived. There are other ways. and I learnt that way later. I know all the way now. But in the end I found my way to the end of the caves, and there I found my nurse."

"Your—nurse?"

"Yes my nurse is a good woman. I will take you to her very soon, and she will look after you as she has looked after me. She lives between the dark and the light. She brought me out into the light, and let the sunshine strengthen me. I can feel it though I never see it—and I sit in my nurse's garden and smell the flowers, and hear the birds, and feel the butterflies alight on my hands. But I do not go much into the lighted world. It is—difficult for me. Here in the dark I know everything, and it is my own; but out in the light world, once I am beyond my nurse's garden, there are strange people, and dogs and other beasts, and I find them—difficult. But here—here's my kingdom."

He laughed, and stood upright, and launched himself into a leaping run, into the dark, at the same time giving a shrill whistle, and seeming to guide himself by the echo, like a bat. He vanished into the depths, and then came back and seated himself beside her.

"But come now—if you are rested and your clothes are a little dry, I will take you to my nurse."

"What is your nurse's name?"

"She says she has no name, but is just to be called the Servant of The White One; but some call her White, or Candida; others say she is the Witch of the Cave, but I know she is no witch. Others call her Sibylla. To me, she is my nurse."

Lynett got herself painfully into her partly-dried clothes— sticky leather and sodden wool—and followed the blind man.

"You had better have a torch," he said, giving her a stick dipped in tar, from a sheaf of them which he kept in his hoard. "I keep a few here, in case my nurse comes to visit me. She needs to see, just as you do." He lit the torch at the fire, then put away his things in marked places under stones, and carefully extinguished the fire with sand. Then he took up a long thin wand and swung it before him, but not gropingly—he was indeed, as he said, at home in his dark kingdom. Lynett's little torch showed her his fine, lithe figure stepping out before her, and dimly lit up the bewildering arches and tunnels through which he led her.

After many long wanderings, he stopped and held up his hand.

"We must stop here," he said. "Look where I shall point. There is the shrine of the White One, whom my nurse serves. There is her image. They say she has a strange beauty."

Lynett held up her torch in the direction where he pointed. Then she screamed—for what she saw was horrible and obscene.

A vast stalagmite had formed itself, perhaps aided by men's hands, into the shape of a woman—"naked like a beast" was the thought that occurred to Lynett. A naked woman, but with no beauty to clothe her nakedness. The breasts and genitals were grossly, crudely exaggerated. The woman was old, flesh-fallen, hideous. The face, if there were face at all, was turned away. The lewd, sagging shape gleamed ghostly in the torchlight.

"Oh, but it's hideous!" Lynett cried. The blind man turned to her, his pale sightless eyes reproachful.

"Do not say so. I have never felt her shape, for she may not be touched by anyone—but my nurse has told me. This is the Mother of All. She has many shapes, and this is how the people of old saw her. Her woman-parts are shown, that other women keep hidden, because it is for that we honor her. She gave birth to us all, and still gives birth, and she nourishes us all from her breasts. And she is old, because she *is* old—from the Beginning, next to the Father. She keeps us all in life, under the Father's power."

In the stillness it seemed that he could feel the shudder that Lynett gave.

"You must not be afraid of her. My nurse has told me much about her. She has many faces, they say, and I shall never see any of them—but they say that her voice and her touch, when she manifests herself, are sweet and gentle."

Round the foot of the figure was a ring of flat stones, and on those stones, Lynett saw, were little offerings—small bunches of flowers, some withered, some fresh; milk and honey in earthenware saucers, a few flat cakes of bread, a handful of sweet berries. The blind man, as he passed, raised his fingers to his lips, throwing a kiss to the image. But Lynett turned her head aside, and covertly crossed herself.

As he led her further, round an angle of rock, to Lynett's surprise she saw a gleam of light ahead of them. It seemed to come nearer, and she realized they were reaching the exit from the caves. They came out through an archway into a deep gully, with the sky far overhead. It was a long time since Lynett had seen the daylight. Blinking in the dazzle, she put out her torch;

the blind man went on, swinging his wand before him, making no difference.

A rough arch, possibly made by man out of huge stones, spanned the gully; they emerged from it into warm sunshine, birdsong and the humming of bees.

This was a deep gorge, but wide enough to let in the sun; the sides were thickly grown with brambles and ferns, and with small bushes and patches of grass. And here, built into the hillside with the rock for its back wall, was a small hut, part of stone, part of wood and thatch, with smoke going up through a smokehole. and a little garden round it. Vegetables stood in neat rows, an apple tree showed its early fruit, the flowers of summer glowed in the borders, and three straw-thatched beehives vibrated to the humming of the bees; somewhere behind the apple tree, hens clucked.

A woman came out of the cottage.

"Are you there, my son?" she called in a pleasant voice. "Oh, but who is this you have brought with you?"

She was a tall woman, and extraordinarily graceful; a long flowing robe of fine white linen clothed her from head to foot. It folded smoothly round the pure oval of her face, and fell to her brown bare feet. Her face was sunburnt brown, and worked all over with small wrinkles—but these wrinkles were a fine network, not marring the smooth lines of the face, but running over all like the crackles in some kinds of pottery. Her mouth was generous, wide lips opening over perfect teeth, and her eyes, deep-set, were large and light blue. Without doubt she had once been a beautiful woman, and was still a handsome one, but remote and withdrawn. She moved and spoke quietly and without haste.

The blind man answered,

"Nurse, I found her in the cave. She is a gentlewoman, and she is fleeing from an enemy, just as I was. Nurse, we must take her in."

"Why, of course we must," said the woman in the white robe. "Come, my dear."

Of the Sibyl, and That Which She Served

So Lynett found herself sheltered and tended in the little cottage of the Sibyl, that some called the Witch of the Cave. Quiet nights followed quiet days. There seemed to be no hurry. Indeed, Lynett was worn out with all she had gone through, and needed to be fed and warmed and rested.

Sitting at the door of the cottage, where the sunshine gathered between the high rock walls of the gorge, Lynett asked the Sibyl her history.

"I was a country wife like other country wives," the Sibyl said, "only perhaps that I knew a little more, and cared to learn a little more, than my neighbours, about plants and herbs, and the seasons, and the sun, moon and stars. Also sometimes I had glimpses of something—of that which men call the Sight. Not a comfortable gift, and let you pray that you never have it. I was married fifteen years ago, but never had a child; and then my husband died, and I was left alone. Soon after this, a woman came one day to my door, looked at me and said, "You are she." So then I had to leave everything, and come here. For I was she."

"I do not understand," said Lynett.

"I was the one chosen to be the Servant of the White One. There has always been a woman here who tends the shrine within the cave, and keeps the words and the secrets, and never lets the power of the White One be forgotten. She must guard the Old Wisdom, and remember it. People come here for help, in sickness or in perplexity, and the Servant of the White One must help them.

"The old Sibyl brought me here, and showed me the holy figure of the White Lady, and gave me the secret words, and the other secrets—and then she lay down in front of the holy image, and folded her hands, and died. I laid her to rest in the same little cave where the bones of her predecessors are laid, and built up the wall again. Some day I shall know the time, and I shall go in search of the next Sibyl, and then I shall do as she did."

There was silence between them for some minutes. Then Lynett broke the silence.

"And Lucius—?"

"Ah, Lucius. One day, just so suddenly, he crawled out of the cave like a lost wild animal—dirty, hairy, starved so that his bones nearly broke through his skin—running on all fours, staring with his great pale eyes, but never blinking, so I knew at once that he was blind. How old was he? God knows—possibly seven or eight—hard to tell. He told me how he and his mother had been imprisoned in the darkness by some accursed ruffian, till he had gone blind and she had died. To think a man could do such things, dear God. .... How long had they been imprisoned for? Again, hard to tell, for in the dark one loses count of days and nights. But she had taught him gentle ways—may the Mother cherish her soul! —he knew the manners of a Christian, and he remembered old hymns and prayers, and stories and songs wherewith she had beguiled the time. After he had found the poor lady dead, and escaped somehow—no one knows how—from his prison, into the world of the caves, he lived somehow in the dark—God alone knows how. Perhaps the gnomes of the caves helped him—there are such beings, and I have seen them. But he learnt to run about those caves like a bat, and swim in the dark waters too, and never feels the need of eyes when he is down there in the dark. He can walk in the sunlight with his staff, and I see to it that he does so, but it's strange to him. In the dark he is at home, and he feels his way, I think, as the bats do, by the echoes."

She broke off, as Lucius came up to the little garden, and put his arms round her.

"Here, Nurse," he said, "I've been walking in the lanes—see what I have found for you! How sweet they smell," and he put into her hand a sheaf of bluebells and pink campions. "And here's some for you," and he laid another bunch in Lynett's lap. "Blue and pink, they must be. I can remember blue and pink." He fingered the flowers delicately. Lynett felt the tears spring to her eyes.

So the days passed in the Sibyl's cottage. May ran on into June and July, and the little green apples grew big on the apple tree.

Sometimes people would come and consult the Sibyl—country people from the villages and farms, mostly women. They would whisper with her on the bench outside the cottage. Some would bring small gifts of farm produce, or little bunches of flowers, but many brought nothing, and Lynett never saw anyone bring money. The Sibyl would sometimes give a bunch of herbs, or a flask of cordial, or a box of salve, and always with a blessing. One day Lynett heard her voice raised.

"No," she was saying, "no and no again. If that is what you want, go elsewhere. I serve the Mother of life, not of death."

Lynett spent much time with Lucius. Sitting under the apple tree in the warm sunshine, she contemplated him, as he stretched out on the dry grass. He was a tall man and well shaped; his skin was sun tanned, for he seldom wore much clothes, but under the tan was the peculiar opaque pallor found in men who have been long in prison, so that he seemed as if made of old ivory. His big blank eyes were bright, and so clear that one could hardly believe there was no sight in them; they followed the direction of what he heard, as if indeed he could see.

A strange man, and she felt strangely towards him. Not like any other man she had met. All those knights, of whom she had met so many, and to whom she was a sister and a comrade-in-arms—they were for the most part thick-limbed, red-faced, hairy, muscle-bound in their carapaces of leather and metal. Apart from them there were priests, pale soft creatures as a rule, anaemic from much fasting, or dried up and acid. Or there were hermits, lean and ancient, remote and holy, not unlike the Sibyl. And there were farmers and villeins—but this man, this Lucius, was not like any of these. She thought of other men she had cared for—her father, and King Arthur, and yes, even Bagdemagus before he had wronged her, and as she had first imagined him to be, and could bear to think of him now. She had not felt for any of them as she felt for Lucius. They had been leaders; but Lucius was one whom she longed to protect. Gareth?—ah, the beloved gentle Gareth—but he had exasperated her by his persistent meekness—raised a devil of contradiction in her, that moved her to try him and bait him to see if she could get a reaction out of him—no, he was not like Gareth. Yet, although she desired to protect him, she could not forget how he had held her life in his hands, down there in the awesome underground torrent. He was no weakling, no child. He was the master in his own element.

Sometimes he would take her for walks on dark nights through the woods, striding on before her, swinging his wand when she could hardly grope her way through the dark coverts. He would stop and interpret for her every rustle, every scent in the darkness. "Moles at work there—they turn up the fresh soil. . . . Fox away out to the left—oh, a long way out—gone to meet his vixen. . .that's a robin on the branch. . .owl in the pasture, yes, he's caught something. . .the hay's been cut in the valley. . . ."

There was one night when, to her terror, a dark furry mass came rolling out of a hollow— "Stand still," he said, "it's only a bear." The creature rumbled throatily, and Lucius made its own rumbling sounds back at it. "All's well, old fellow. You know me. We're friends. Go your way, and good night to you." And the bear turned its back on them and lurched away into the bushes.

She thought of all this, as he lay stretched out at her feet. He got up and came closer to her.

"Will you let me feel your face?" he said.

"Why, yes," she said, and sat still while he ran his finger delicately over every inch of her face. A quite inexplicable thrill wakened in her body at that touch.

"Oh," he exclaimed, "I think you must be beautiful."

"I'm not," she said. "I'm ugly—I always have been ugly. My colour is pale and yellowish, my hair is black as night and straight as candles, my lips are thin and have no redness, there's no beauty about me at all."

"But my hands tell me you are beautiful," he persisted. "I know. I know. I wish I could see you. —But what's this? You're crying."

Sitting by the small fire in the cottage, on a rainy summer afternoon, the Sibyl drew the long thread from her spindle. Lucius was away by himself in the caves. Lynett sat by, with her hands idle; she had no skill in spinning.

"Child," said the Sibyl, "something troubles you."

Lynett hesitated, and then, breaking the silence with a rush, she said,

"Mother Sibyl—tell me this—why did you tell that poor boy that the—the White One in the Cave was beautiful? She's foul and frightful."

The Sibyl thought for a long time before replying—Lynett was afraid she had given her offence, but for her life she could not have said otherwise. Presently, after looking long into the fire, the Sibyl said,

"You must understand this. There are many ways of seeing the White One. Lucius must not ever see her with his eyes, because he is a man, and no man may see her and live. That is the law. But I have taught him to see her inwardly.

"Those who first found the White One, and perhaps fashioned her—they must have been women, or if any man helped them he must have been put to death afterwards. It is the Law. Those who first knew her, oh, far, far back—they recognized her for what she is. She is the Mother—oldest of all things except the Father of all. She brings us to conception and birth, she feeds us, she receives us back into her womb when we die, she sends us forth again. It is she that brings the female to the male, the hind to the hart, the ewe to the ram. Without her there is no life. They saw her thus—the breasts that nourish, the gates of birth through which we all must pass. Do you think they knew aught of comeliness or seemliness? I am told that in other countries and in later times, the people made images of her according to their sight and their thought, and some of them were beautiful. But this, my holy image in which her power dwells, is far, far older. To those who first knew it, there was neither beauty nor foulness, but only That Which Is. The parts of woman which mortal women hide, not from loathing, but from reverence. And old—indeed, how should she not be old? And yet some have seen her in visions, walking the hills in eternal youth.

"There are many who are afraid of her—there are men who have hated her, to their destruction. But women should not be afraid of her. *You* should not be afraid of her."

How Lynett Found Love Too Close to Death

"Come and see my kingdom," Lucius said.

"*See* it? she questioned gently.

"Yes—you can take torches, as my nurse sometimes does. She says it is a wonderful sight, and I know it is a wonderful place. Come and let me show you!"

So they went in, she carrying a satchel full of the little pine splinters, dipped in pitch, that were always kept ready by the Sibyl. Inside the first precinct of the caves, the lamps burned before the White One, but the Sibyl had covered the figure with a veil. Lynett said nothing to Lucius as they passed it, but he, sensing where it was, made his customary reverence.

It was a miraculous region he showed her. Some of it she had passed through before, but then she had been distressed, apprehensive and exhausted; now she was able to give heed to the eerie beauty of it. Grotto beyond grotto, cavern beyond cavern, gleaming with stalactites, golden and rosy, silver, black and white—like ivory and flesh and flowers, and sudden snow, and falls of black velvet. On and on he led her. They visited the edge of the torrent from which he had rescued her, and listened to its awesome noise.

"It's dangerous," he said, "but I know how to master it. I like it, because it's dangerous. I swim there for pleasure, and that was how I found you. But I can only go down it—no one can go up. There is another way round, you see, to the beginning—the place where it comes out of a narrow crack in the rock. I go up there and shoot all the way down. That was how I chanced to be there and felt you in the water—before I touched you. . . . No, we'll not swim here. I know a pleasanter place."

They passed a place where the water was hot, and steamed in the light of Lynett's torch. "Oh, heavens, sulphur!" she exclaimed. "This must be the gates of hell!"

"No, no," he laughed. "I know the sulphur vapors. There is a kingdom of fire down here, and fiery spirits, as my nurse has taught me, but they are not spirits of evil. There would be a different feeling if they were. No, it's no power of the Evil One. All this part is under the realm of the Mother. Have no fear."

He led her onward following the course of the warm stream; soon the passage opened into a large vaulted expanse, and Lynett's torch showed a clear lake, of a strange jewel-like blue, extending before them. "Feel the water now," he said. She stooped and dipped her hand in. It was just between warm and cool, a delightful temperature. All the edge of the lake was clean white sand, fine and soft, gleaming blue in the torchlight reflected off the water.

"See me now," he cried, and sprang from her side into the water, as confidently as an otter into the pool. There he swam and plunged, dived and surfaced like a fish. By the glimmering light of her torch she watched him in wonderment. The torch burnt down, and she lit another and yet another.

"There's a place in the wall where you can set the torch," he said, and found it with his fingers. "Place it there, and come and swim with me."

She fixed the torch where he showed her and then—reassuring herself that he could not see her—slipped off her clothes and plunged into the water to join him. She could swim a little, enough to enjoy it. There was hardly any current, and the mild, warm water caressed her skin. He swam towards her, laughing for pleasure, waking musical echoes, and caught her hands. Then his arms went round her in the water, and she felt with surprise that her body welcomed his touch.

Then later they lay side by side on the soft sand, and the torch glimmered down and left them in darkness. They spoke no word, but drew towards each other. And there at last Lynett knew the pleasure of a man's love.

Now began for Lynett a time of happiness such as she had never known before. She loved and was beloved, and there was nothing any more to be afraid of. With her perfect companion she wandered in a dream, whether in the warm September woods, or in his own glittering caverns, or sitting quietly by the Sibyl's fireside, or lying in his arms on beech leaves or on sand.

No longer need she fear bad dreams. All the terrors and tensions, all the hatreds and graspings and gripings, were smoothed away, and she was relaxed and washed as if by a new birth.

"You are happy, child," said the Sibyl, as they plucked the apples together under the apple tree. The walls of the gorge closed them round, and the far side was in deep shadow, but the sun gathered all its rays on the side where the cottage stood, and glowed back from the cliff behind them. The dry grass around them buzzed with insects, and the autumn flowers were bright; not a breath of wind disturbed the orchard. Lynett and the Sibyl were filling osier baskets with the apples, Lucius was away in the woods, walking with his staff—the Sibyl had told him he must store up the sunshine while he could.

"You are happy, child."

"Yes, I am happy."

"I know. Your happiness wraps you round like a garment. Child, I know that you and my Lucius are lovers."

"You—know?" Lynett put down her basket, and stood leaning against the tree, looking anxiously in the Sibyl's face.

"Yes, indeed I know. How could I not know? Oh, I'm glad for you, and glad for him—oh, glad, glad, glad!" She put her hands on Lynett's shoulders. "Now he has attained manhood, and you have attained womanhood. The Lady has blessed you." She sighed deeply.

"Then," said Lynett, "why do you sigh? Why are there tears in your tears?"

The Sibyl drew away gently from her, and turned her face, letting her white veil fall forward. For a long time she was silent, than at last she said,

"Why must I drop bitterness in your sweetness? But you must be told. Some day you must be told."

"Told what?" cried Lynett in an agony.

"This, dear child. He hasn't a year of life left in him."

"What?"

"It is so. No child could endure the years of darkness and privation and remain whole. He is a dying man."

"Oh, but surely, surely. . . ." Stricken, Lynett saw her happiness fall away to nothing before her. "I can't believe—his body is so strong, and so beautiful—"

"Yes—the Lady has done the best she could for him in the short time he has. I have often seen it. While he was growing, she built him in spite of all, but now that he is full grown, now his bones are crumbling within, and he begins to dry up and wither. Sometimes he coughs, and his cheeks are flushed. That is not the rose of health but the rose of death."

"Oh, could you not— You are a healer, and know leech-craft—could you not cure him?"

"Do you think I haven't tried? Every herb, every medicine, every magic—I've tried all. I have tried every saint, every hallow, every relic. Pilgrimages I cannot go on, for I cannot leave him, and to take him from here would hasten the end. But everything else I've tried. Some good I have done him, by wholesome food and sunshine and—and love—" Her voice was choked with tears. Lynett put her arms round her, caressing her thin bony shoulders beneath the linen.

"How long?" she asked her in a whisper.

"About a year, I think, with care."

"And there's nothing, nothing—"

A thought flashed into Lynett's mind.

"There is one Hallow that would surely heal him."

"Yes?" The old woman lifted her sad face.

"The Holy Grail."

"Ah—the Holy Grail. If one could find it—"

"The knights with whom I travelled—the knights of King Arthur—were resolved to go in quest of it. They had had a brief Sight of it at Camelot, once. Once in the woods, as we journeyed together, we saw its Procession in the distance, with the Holy Stag. Far, far off it was. But they spoke then of how they would some day seek it. I said then that I would like to seek it, but they said it was not for a woman—or at least not for a woman who was not a virgin."

"And you believed them?"

"Of course."

"Oh, child, there are things you do not know."

"Do you mean that I—I, a sinful woman—"

"Think less of being a sinful woman. Your great sin is absolved, don't you know that?"

"My great sin? But I'm—an unfaithful wife, and no virgin—"

"The man who had your virginity is dead, and your marriage was in name only—you've told me. No, your great sin was that of unforgiving, and that is repented, and absolved, and forgotten. You have felt that it is so. Let no man say that you are not fit to seek the Grail."

"But—" a dreadful recollection came back upon her. "You

remember I told you—he made me perjure myself. I had to damn my own soul."

"My dear, do you still believe in a God who would exact payment of such a debt? In fear of your life, in duress if ever there was duress? No. Forgive us our debts as we forgive our debtors. Think no more of it."

She picked up the basket of apples and turned towards the cottage.

"Yes," said Lynett. "I think I shall have to go in search of the Grail, for Lucius's sake. And now I remember, I am Arthur's Damosel. Oh, dear mother, I should not have stayed here so long. . . . In any case I must go. . . . Does he know his condition?"

"Yes, he knows. He lives much on the border of the other world, and I think the prospect of death means little to him—only of late, since he found you—"

"I will go. I will go, and I will find the Grail, and come back to him, with health and length of days in my hand."

She told him, lying on the warm sand of the cavern, which had become to them as dear and familiar as a conjugal bed.

"So I must go, my love. But I'll come back to you, and I'll bring you your certain cure."

"Perhaps you will also bring my sight?" he said. "I should so love to see you."

She suppressed a little gasp of dismay.

"Surely, my dear, if I can. But you—might not like me if you saw me. I tell you, I am not beautiful."

"I know you are," he persisted. "And I know how a beautiful woman should look. I remember my mother, before the trouble—yes, and all her lovely ladies. Oh yes, I know that you are beautiful. Oh, my dear, ask the Holy Thing for my sight!"

She gazed past him into the depths of the cavern, into the glitter of the stalactites in the dim torch which was all she now needed. To have him see her! No, it would be unbearable. To see the disappointment in his look, to have him turn away from her when he knew the truth—oh no. And yet, and yet, it was not only herself he should desire to see. Flowers and trees, sunrise and sunset, the whole wide sky—could she deny him those, because she dreaded what he would see in herself?

She kissed him on his closed eyelids. "I will go and bring back your eyesight if I can," she said.

Of the Setting Out of the Grail Company

They met her at the outskirts of Camelot, just where the road turns to give a distant view of the towers—Lancelot, Perceval and Bors, on their great horses; Lynett, plodding along the road barefoot in a brown smock, ran towards them. In a moment they were off their horses, surrounding her eagerly.

"Brothers, oh brothers—"

"Our Lynett—our Falcon's Feather—where have you been all this while?"

"We thought you were dead, and we mourned you," said Bors.

"Until this morning, and then we knew you were coming," said Lancelot.

"You knew I was coming? How did you know?"

"It was Jeanne," said Bors. "Ever since daybreak she was bating on her perch and crying out. We couldn't bring her, for none of us dare hold her, even hooded—she'd have broken away from us. But she's there awaiting you."

"Also I had a dream," said Perceval.

"And I knew," said Lancelot.

She looked from the one to the other. "But Gwalchmei—where is he?"

"Ah, poor Gwalchmei," said Bors. "He fell in the fight, when we lost you. We seemed to be seized by an enchantment—dreaming of a palace and a lady, and then suddenly we woke, and Bagdemagus's ruffians were upon us, and you were dragged away—we fought them, but they beat us off, and—Gwalchmei was slain."

The colour drained from Lynett's face.

"Oh, not Gwalchmei— Oh, Gwalchmei—" and she sank down by the roadside with her hands over her face.

Gwalchmei—he had given his life for her. And bitterest regret and remorse of all, she knew that for all of that time she had forgotten him. She had forgotten all of them, and one of them had died for her.

"Sister, no tears," said Perceval, with a hard look in his pale eyes.

"We are knights, sister, and death is our trade. You have looked on death before, and not wept. Gwalchmei died as a knight should die, and as he would have wished."

She looked up at him, her hair and her tears all over her cheeks.

"He was our brother in arms. He was—Gwalchmei, and we knew him. He gave his life trying to save me."

"I had thought you had more fortitude," said Perceval. "But a woman still—"

"Oh, enough, Perceval!" exclaimed Bors, with a look that silenced him. Lancelot said nothing, but stretched out his hands to Lynett and drew her gently to her feet; then he took her head on his shoulder, and let her cry as she wished. Presently he whispered to her,

"You are changed, lady."

"Yes, I am changed."

She looked round at them bleakly.

"You were four once, a complete square, the pillars of the house. Now you are only three, and the square is broken."

"No, we are still four," said Bors, "now that you have come back to us. As four we will go together on the Quest."

No need to ask what Quest.

"Oh, yes, brothers—I'll come with you on the Quest—if—*if* you will have me?"

"A woman?" said Perceval, and still his pale eyes were cold. "Our gallant sister, and dear to us, but still a woman?"

"Why not?" said Lancelot.

"We will ask Merlin," said Bors, "and as he decides so let it be."

Arthur gave his consent with reluctance. The quest of the Grail was a thing to which certain knights, from time to time, felt a call, rather like a holy vocation, and no man might or ought to hinder them. But few of them returned.

They stood outside the door of Merlin's chamber; he had a turret room in the castle, very high and private. The four of them stood together, and Lancelot knocked.

"Enter!" said Merlin's voice within, and solemnly as in a ritual, they opened the door and entered. Merlin, in his robes, stood to receive them; the room was dark, and lit by a large fire, and its light illumined him, but scarcely showed them the strange things the dark corners of the room contained.

"We are four," said Lancelot, speaking for the rest, "who have Arthur's leave to follow the quest of the Holy Grail."

"Four knights?" said Merlin, as they ranged themselves before him.

"Three knights, and—one is a damosel."

"Ha, a damosel?" exclaimed Merlin, startled. He peered at them in the uncertain firelight. "Come here, damosel. Oh yes, it's you. I might have known."

Putting out a long white-draped arm, he drew Lynett to him. She came unresisting. He laid his hand on her shoulder and looked searchingly into her face.

"Yes," he said at last, in a low voice for her alone. "You're ready. All is well. Go and have no fear. You understand now, do you not?"

She nodded. "Yes, I understand."

Perceval, close behind her, said, "Master Merlin—tell us— may a woman truly be numbered among us?"

Merlin lifted his eyes from his contemplation of Lynett's bowed head, and speaking across her, said,

"Yes, Sir Perceval. A woman may truly be numbered among you. As you know, knights in search of the Holy Grail must set out in a company of four, no more and no less. I name the Damosel Lynett here amongst you as the fourth of your company. So be it.

"Now listen to your road learning.

"From here you must travel all together, towards the West, the direction of those who seek. Then each will receive a sign according to his nature, and that sign he must follow. For you, Sir Perceval, the sign of water; for you, Sir Bors, the sign of fire; for you, Sir Lancelot, the sign of earth; and for you, Lady Lynett, the sign of air. These will lead you on your four several ways, and not one of these will be at all like another, for each has his way set out for him that only God and his heart know. But in the end you will all meet together, and the place where you meet will be Carbonek— Are you all shriven and houselled?"

"Yes," they all replied, and Lynett marvelled, having always thought of Merlin as no Christian at all, to hear him anxious that they should have received the Holy Sacrament.

"Then go, and the Lord be with you," he said.

So they went, and followed the road west from Camelot. And on the second day their road led them through a thin country of small dry bushes; and the light of midday shone upon something bright golden in colour—a great golden beast, prowling ahead of them through the bushes—a lion.

"I didn't know there were lions in this land," said Lynett in a startled whisper to Lancelot.

Lancelot and Perceval put hands to their lances. But Bors said, "This is my sign, the sign of Fire—" and he urged his unwilling horse forward towards the beast. The lion looked over its shoulder and walked on, as if inviting him to follow; and the horse seemed to lose its fear, and went forward; and they lost sight of Bors among the small trees.

"He follows his sign," said Perceval, sighing.

And the next day they came to the sea coast, and to a causeway made along the edge of the sea, and they rode along the causeway. And when the tide came up, and brimmed to the edge beside them, they saw two dolphins sporting and leaping in the waves. And Perceval threw off his armour, crying "This is my sign, the sign of Water," and plunged in after them. Lynett shrieked, and would have dived in after him, but Lancelot held her back with force.

"No, my dear," he said, holding her in spite of her struggles. "All is well with him. He's in no danger, he'll not drown. This is his sign, as the lion was Bors'. We shall see him again."

But Lynett wept and shook, and Perceval's horse trembled and for a long time would not leave the spot. That night, when they took shelter in a monastery, they left Perceval's horse behind with the monks.

So now it was Lynett and Lancelot who rode alone, and as they rode they opened their hearts to each other on many things. Lancelot told her of his heartbreaking love for Guinevere, and how his loyalty and duty to Arthur pulled him one way and his love pulled him another, till he was nigh tortured to death between them, and how he had chosen the adventure of the Grail so that he might put distance between him and his torment; but for all that, he feared he could never attain the Grail, because he knew the imperfection of his own heart. And Lynett told him her own story, and did not keep back even her love of Lucius.

"And who am I," she said, "who can claim no purity of heart or body, to seek the Holy Thing? And yet I must do it for love's sake. Oh, surely you, Lancelot, are no worse than I am? Let's take heart, both of us—"

"I will, surely," said he, "for I think that is my sign yonder." And they looked, and along the road, and leading away to the right, was a noble white bull. "The sign of Earth," he said. "But, Lady Lynett, must I leave you all alone?"

"I shall be well enough," she said. "Have no fear for me. For, after all, I must soon get my sign too. A bull for Earth, but what is the sign for Air?"

"Why, the Twins," he said, "or the Water-carrier. And so—are you sure you will be well?—and so good-bye, dear Lady Lynett—" and he rode away after the white bull.

Of the Finding of the Grail

So now Lynett went on alone. The road now led her away from the sea, and through sandhills, and it was high noon, and though it was winter, all seemed dry and hot, and the sun beat down. The belt of sand between the road and the sea widened, all bristling with coarse rough bent-grass. Nothing else was visible. The heat grew intolerable, and both Lynett and her horse drooped and could hardly stagger along. Then far off a small object, like some sort of statue, broke the monotonous roll of the sandhills. As she drew nearer, it showed itself to be no statue, but a young man, only lightly draped, holding a large earthenware vessel on his shoulder. As she came up to him he tipped the vessel forward and began to pour a stream of water out of it. Water! Both Lynett and her horse plunged desperately towards it—she jumped from the horse and ran to place herself in that cool stream, and then. . . .

Then a gust of wind, out of the windless sky, so violent that it wrenched her neck and shoulders, hit her and spun her round—water and sand whirled together—the horse's reins, over her arm, snapped, and she tried to look round for the horse, but there was nothing, nothing but that whirling— Away and away, the relentless wind howling through her very brain—driven before it, walking, running, flying—?

She lost all count of time—then, after what seemed an endless period, the wind slackened, and awareness came back to her, and she knew herself to be walking along a bare open road, still carried by the wind, but no longer whirled about, and able to look around her. Now it was no longer a waste of sandhills that surrounded her, but stony ground covered with trees, but such trees! White bleached skeletons, all stretched one way with the pressure of the wind, shining here and there with encrusted salt. Large trees and small, relics of little low shrubs and of what had once been fine spreading shade-trees—and yes, there were traces of walls, and now the ruins of houses—a town, but as desolate as the trees—in the deserted street, the skeleton of a horse, of a dog—yes, of a man. Of many men and women. And as she went on, there were those with flesh still on them—with clothes still on them—and oh heavens, some that still seemed to be alive. . . .

It was then that the wind increased again, and with it a mist that wrapped her round, and voices in the mist.

"You haven't forgiven him really—you still hate him—how could you forgive him?"

She was back in that wood under the beech tree, enduring what she had endured then—she heard his contemptuous laugh as he flung her from him. She was back in his hall of Castle Hardy, and he was saying, "Oh, a scold's bridle! To the ducking-stool with the bold scold!" and then in his prison-room under the roof, his look of disgust— "No, not attractive!"

Then he was putting the thumbscrew on her. Then he was making her swear that frightful oath—

And then those Black Things were rolling towards her, and uncoiling and rising towards up tall with foxes' heads—

Shrieking she ran before the howling wind, and the voices went on, "You've not forgiven him—you've not forgiven him—and you'll not be forgiven yourself, never, never, never—now's the time the Black Things will have you—"

Then in desperation her thought reached out to Lucius, and something of warmth and tenderness came through the driving wind. And then a great feeling of pity, a pity that covered her enemy also. An impulse of compassion like a sob burst from her.

"Oh, God forgive us all!" she cried, and then she turned and faced into the wind. "I'm done with you, Black Things!" she said steadily, speaking into the tempest. "I have forgiven him, and you will go and pursue me no longer. I am not afraid of you. All that is past, and I am free."

And suddenly the wind dropped, and all was still. The desolate land lay calm before her, in the light of sunset. And there across the stony plain rose a castle, pinnacle, black against the westering sun, and she knew it was the Castle Carbonek.

Long, long she walked across that dreary plain, and at last reached the gateway. A man, clothed in black and with his face hidden in a cowl, stood by the door.

"I bid you enter if you can," he said. "This is indeed the Castle Carbonek in the Waste Land. If you can read the riddle of what is within, and attain the healing of the Fisher King, then you may bring back life to the Waste Land and attain your heart's desire. But not if your heart's desire be unworthy.

"Earth and water have long ago proved you; air you have lately endured; but now fire."

And at that moment the castle portal, through which, Lynett was about to go, sprang all into a blazing fire.

"Go through the fire," said the hooded man.

But Lynett faltered and hung back.

"Go through the fire," he repeated. "Have no fear—if you have truly forgiven your enemy, and if you desire nothing for yourself, the fire will not hurt you."

"Then God be my helper!" cried Lynett, and strode straight into the fiery doorway. She shrieked with the pain, one moment only, and then she was through the fire, and into the castle.

Her hair still crackled where the flames had touched it, and her clothing smelt of fire, but she was through it. The great stony vaults of the Castle Carbonek stretched before her, and suddenly with a deep and heavy clang, the door swung shut behind her.

All was gloom and silence. A dim light came from somewhere, only enabling her to see the awesome dark arches, and another door, a strong oaken door, ahead of her. No human face or voice. No human thing at all—not a bench, nor a shelf, nor a weapon, nor a vessel, nor trace of a window, nor any sign of human occupation. She went towards the door, with her footsteps sounding loud on the stone floor. As she approached the door, it opened silently and let her through, closing equally silently behind her. Again her footsteps echoed, alone and dreadfully solitary, through another bare vault, and to another door—this also opened, but behind it was a dimmer light, and some sort of soft carpet under her feet, for now her footsteps made no noise. Quieter and quieter—no sound anywhere but her own breathing and the beating of her heart. Enough light, faint and greyish, to show her which way to walk, but no more. She wanted to scream aloud to break the terrifying silence, but she did not. She went on, gasping now because she was conscious of her breathing—and reached, not a door, but a heavy black curtain. It gave to her handling, and she was in a dimly lighted room.

Tapers burned, quietly in air that was not stirred by any breath. In the midst of the room a great bed, a bed of state, with curtains drawn back, and in that bed lay a dead man. His calm noble face was turned upward in peace, and his hands folded on his breast above a rich pall of black velvet embroidered with silver. An old man, but comely. His hair was white but thick and smooth, and his beard was white but trim; his neck and shoulders were bare above the velvet pall.

She stood looking at him, calming her thudding heart and entering into the solemn and sad peace that lay around the dead man; and then she screamed—for the fine marble face was dissolving before her eyes, dropping away, shrivelling—the neck and shoulders, the arms and hands, drying, perishing, becoming a tissue of sinews—the whole body was crumbling into bones and dust—there was the face, that a moment before had been so beautiful, now a hollow skull, crossed with a few stretched webs of skin and wisps of lanky hair—

In spite of all her self-control she screamed—and then people whom she could not see came up behind her and seized her fast, and laid her in the bed beside the dead man. She could feel his bony arm and shoulder touching her own. Someone drew the black cover over her face, and she thought to herself, "This must be death. . . Well, if it is death, let it be so. It is hardly as bad as I thought"—and she yielded herself to being dead.

And in a moment she was lifted up, and bright lights shone about her—she was carried away and set on her feet.

She was in a great room, or hall, like a brightly lighted church. Candles glowed against painted and gilded walls, and the smell of incense came wafting up. There she was standing behind something like an altar rail, and to her astonishment, her three companions were by her side—Perceval, Bors and Lancelot.

Before them a deep apse stretched away to the eastward, and above it a window glowed with such colours as were never seen on earth; but a rich parclose screen hid the apse from their view, and before the screen lay a narrow couch, and on that couch a man lay propped on pillows. He wore a crown, and a purple tunic, but from the waist downward he was swathed in linen bandages. And with awe and terror, Lynett recognized his face—it was the same face as the dead man's, that had crumbled into a skull. But this man was alive, though his face was fine drawn with pain, and his deep-set eyes held an awesome light.

He spoke courteously.

"Welcome, knights and damosel," he said. "You should know me—I am called the Fisher King. Long ago I was sore wounded in the thigh, and never can be healed but by that one who shall achieve the Grail. You four have passed through your probations, and now you are near the final step. Behold."

And as he spoke, they heard the single note of the silver bell, as long ago they had heard it in the forest. Then, from the far end of the great dim hall, came the procession. Not led by the white hart this time, but by a tall man, bareheaded, who carried high a crucifix of gold and ivory. For now all those whose faces had been hidden before were unhooded and unveiled—the chanting maidens, the thurifers, the solemn musicians, the white-robed men and boys—and each of the four Grail-seekers thought he (or she) saw among them at least one remembered face of one long dead. Solemnly and with great stateliness the procession moved on. The four men were there, and the four holy things they carried were unveiled now—a sword, a lance whose point dripped blood, a cup that received it, and a silver platter. And finally came the maiden who carried the Grail, but she alone was veiled. She carried the Holy Vessel high before her, and it was covered with a veil also, but it seemed to Lynett like a fine bowl or dish, closed with a curiously wrought cover, as if the very precious food of some great lord was being carried to him. The procession passed by the Fisher King, and she expected it would stop and serve him from the Holy Vessel; but no, it passed on, and none turned a head towards him. They went on, at their slow and steady pace, behind the parclose and into the apse, where none could see them; and the maiden carrying the Grail vanished with them. When long ago they had seen the procession in the forest, a light of bliss had radiated from the Grail and filled them with happiness; but nothing reached them now. It was there, the power and the loveliness, but not for them. And if not for the Fisher King, then for whom?

Silence fell, as the last of the procession disappeared. The Fisher King said nothing; the almost invisible attendants said nothing. They waited. The four waited, wondering what should come next. Something was required of them. Lynett looked at each one in turn—they were eager, enraptured, but had no words. The pressure of the silence deepened, and the Fisher King's head drooped, as if he lost hope. Then prompted by some strange impulse, Lynett spoke into the silence, terrified at her own voice.

"To whom do they serve of the Grail?"

And at once it was as if a great company sighed deeply; the Fisher King lifted his head, and stretched out his hand to her, beckoning.

"Well have you asked, daughter. Come, and your question shall be answered."

He drew her towards him, clasping her hand, and with his mouth to her ear, whispered a name.

But that name was so secret, so sacred and mysterious, that it may be spoken by none save those to whom it is given in the rightful way and at the rightful time; least of all may it be told here. For that name is Holy, and that name is Wonderful.

So then the unseen people behind her led her away with a gentle pressure, and she looked behind to see if her three companion knights were to follow her, but a barrier of crossed spears held them back. Bors had hidden his face; Perceval stood gazing anxiously; but Lancelot was stretching his arms out across the spears, as if he would struggle to follow her. But none of them might follow.

She was led through the parclose screen, into the apse, where the procession had gone; and there the Grail was revealed to her.

Afterwards—how long she could not say—she was taken back into the great hall, and saw her three comrades kneeling round the couch of the Fisher King. In her hands she held a bowl, which sometimes seemed to her like a plain bronze bowl, the size of her two cupped hands, unadorned save for the roundels at the rim—and sometimes seemed to be that rich and glorious thing she had seen behind the parclose screen. In it lay two wafers, like consecrated Hosts.

On bended knee she presented the holy vessel to the Fisher King. She saw him stretch out his emaciated hand and take one of the wafers—the three knights, kneeling, watched with awe. And, as the Fisher King put the wafer to his lips, suddenly the colour came into his face, and a softly glowing light radiated from him. With one smooth movement he rose from his couch, and the bandages dropped from his legs, showing him fully clothed and nobly armed. His face was hale and firm, and the hand that had been wasted and tremulous was well-fleshed and powerful. He lifted above his head the jewelled sceptre that had lain beside him, and cried with a great voice,

"Deo gratias!"

And the voices of unseen presences took up the chant.

The three knights had been led away—Lynett never knew how or where, nor had she any chance to bid them farewell. All she knew was that she now stood at the great gateway of Carbonek, and the Fisher King was beside her, and in her hands she still held the sacred bowl.

"Now you have your answer to prayer," he said, "and now you must go. Take the Holy Thing in your hands, and go on foot, with such speed as you may, back to where you are awaited."

She looked before her—it was the fall of evening; she had long lost all count of days and hours. It seemed to be about sunset, on an evening in spring. The bloom of the sunset was in the sky, and the bloom of growth on the hedgerows and coppices; the evening star hung like a jewel.

"Go straight before you," he said. "Look—over there, straight ahead, is a hill where burns a beacon. Keep that in sight. When you reach its summit, you will see a round mere below you, and beyond it another hill. Go on towards that hill, walking always so that the mere and the beacon are in a line—thus you will be on a straight track, with no quagmires or chasms. So on again, mere and hill, and hill and mere. And by daybreak you will reach the Cave of the Sibyl, and you will give that which is in the Holy Vessel to the man for whom you sought it."

"But am I so near, then?"

"Nearer than you thought. When you were led here, some of the way was through the Country of the Mind, and as you go back, some of it will be through the Country of the MInd again. But you will know when you come to the land of living men.

"Speak to none, salute no man by the way. You will not be tired, nor hungry nor thirsty, for the Holy Thing you carry will sustain you.

"But remember this: when you reach your beloved, and give the Holy Thing into his hands, he may have one boon granted to him, one boon and no more. Either his life, or his sight. He may not have both, and—you may not choose for him. He alone must choose, and as he makes his choice, so must it be."

"Is this—is this indeed the Holy Grail that I carry?" she asked, for now it seemed to her only the simple bowl of bronze.

"Have faith—have you not seen?" For suddenly it blazed again with gold and gems and a light beyond anything earthly—then the glory was gone. The Fisher King covered it with a dark cloth.

"Now go," he said, and kissed her on the brow. "In the Name of God!"

And she went steadily down the path and away from the Castle Carbonek—never looking behind her, for she knew it would no longer be visible to her if she did. Fixing her eyes on the beacon ahead of her, she began her long walk.

Of the Boon that was Granted

It was a serene evening as she set out—an evening that waited for something. No wind breathed—the soft misty bloom of the horizon seemed to hold a tension of waiting—for what? For moonrise, for spring, for Easter? Dimly she wondered what day it was. Could it be Good Friday?

How different from the time—how long ago?—when she had approached the castle. Then she had been driven by a tyrannous wind. Now, no wind. Only silence, and waiting. Something she remembered of the way she had come—it had been through a desolate land, a desert place, with skeleton trees, and beasts and men. . . . Now she began to recognize the waste places, but a change was coming over them. A soft light, greenish as the red afterglow of sunset faded, was raying out from the Holy Vessel she carried, and where its light fell, the green grass sprang up in the twilight, and the wave of life rippled outwards. The gaunt trees put on the soft colours of living bark, and buds were swelling on the twigs, ready to break at the first touch of sunlight. Buds of crocus and daffodil pierced the soil. A stir of sleepy birds was heard in the trees, and here and there some little furry beast looked out from its burrow with bright eyes. As the evening darkened, it was not sleep that came upon the countryside so much as a breathing readiness for waking. Life flowed into all the land, life that only waited for the morrow's sun. In cottages lights shone softly. A dog in a doorway (surely she had seen a white skeleton there?) sighed deeply and happily in its dream; and a horse stood relaxed in sleep in its pasture. By the roadside—where she had seen huddled corpses before—a man, a woman and a child lay embraced, and she saw the woman raise herself on her elbow, and touch the man's face, and heard her say softly to him, "Tomorrow. . .hope, hope, hope!" before she fell asleep again.

At the summit of the hill, where the beacon flared, she paused. Yes, there was the round mere, gleaming dully under the deepening sky, and there was the next hill, with a cairn of stones visible on it, and there, too, a beacon. Remembering what she had been told, she went on, keeping the mere and the beacon in line, walking fearlessly through the dark as the night fell, and never looking down at her feet. And over the next hill she knew she was in the world of earthly men.

But still it was a night of spring, and the full moon rose, and she saw the dormant leaves and flowers all around her. The virtue of the Grail still radiated forth, for sometimes she passed a cottage where a light shone in a window, and in some way she knew that some sick one within had received healing.

But now her own thoughts came back upon her. Soon she would be back—she would be with Lucius, and she would bring him the answer to prayer—but to his prayer, not hers. He might have one boon, and one only—life, or sight. She had gone to bring him life—what if he chose sight?

If he chose sight, how he would enjoy the world of light and colour around him—for a short time. And then he would die. But perhaps he would think it worth while to have a short time to enjoy the world's full beauty. Beauty! Oh, he would look at her, and see her, and know that she was not beautiful. No deceiving herself—no deceiving him. He would see her as she was—ugly. She had always known it. Oh, yes, he would not be deceived. He remembered his mother, and her lovely ladies. Lovely ladies! With a true woman's reaction, Lynett realized that she would not have time so much as to smooth her touselled hair or wash her dusty face, for she must go straight to him with the Holy Vessel. Oh, he would look at her, and turn away—he would not know how to dissemble his disappointment. He might try, afterwards—how pitiful that would be!—but she would have seen his first look. And that would be all she would have to remember—afterwards, when he was gone.

But if only he would choose life—just as he was, without sight! How glad she would devote the years of her life, as many as might remain, to caring for him, nursing him, being his eyes. Perhaps—oh, perhaps there might be children. . . . She would give him everything, everything but sight. . . .

But it was he who must choose.

Why, why had this thing come upon her? Could she not have left things as they were? Perhaps—perhaps if she did not tell him there was a choice? If she told him that she brought him life, but could not bring him sight? —The eyes of the Fisher King were suddenly before her, and the Holy Vessel shook in her hand. No, not that—but if it were not there at all? If she had achieved no Holy Grail? If she had never gone on the quest?—Then, of course, he would die, and soon, very soon. But at least he would die still loving her, still believing her to be beautiful. Supposing—down there in the valley she saw the spire of a little lonely church. Supposing she stole in there, and left the Holy Vessel on the altar, and went away back to him empty-handed—saying she had failed to achieve the Grail, as so many had failed before— Or if she dropped it into the depths of the last of those guiding meres? All would be a before—

The temptation was sharp, and she stood still, trembling all over, as her hands which held the bowl—now the simple bronze bowl—shook as with a palsy.

No—how could she tell herself that all would be as before?

Never as before. No—with a deep sigh, she cast her eyes up to the vault of stars above her—itself another great bowl—and went on. Love could do no less.

The path led her at last into a way that she knew. The day was breaking—the soft gradual light of an April dawn—surely it was Easter?—was all around her, and the colours of all things began to show, and the long shadows were all lying the wrong way. She was at the entrance to the long coombe that led into the cleft where lay the Sibyl's Cave. She hastened on.

There he was, coming to meet her—tall, pale, almost naked, glimmering against the dark shadows of the gorge. A ghostly beauty was his, as he walked from the cavern in the sunrise.

"My love," he said. "I felt you coming long before I heard you. In my dreams I felt every step of the way you took. And I know you have it with you—the Holy Thing Itself."

He fell on his knees before her. Trembling, she laid one hand on his head, the other hand holding the cup.

"Beloved," she said, "I have It here, and I have the answer to your prayer. But It will give you one boon only." She strove to keep her voice steady. "Either you may choose life, or—you may choose sight. You may not have both. And only you may choose. So—choose, my dear, and may God guide you to choose aright."

She knelt facing him now, with the Holy Cup between them; and to her eyes it seemed that it was once more the Great Grail, glowing with gold and sparkling with gems, and a soft light radiated out from it. Lucius put a hand on her shoulder, and fixed his sightless eyes intently upon her face. There was no escape for her now.

"I do not hesitate," he said. "I choose sight. Lord, let me receive my sight, though it were but for a day."

Under his steady gaze, she withdrew the veil from the Holy Cup, and took the single wafer it contained, and like a priest, placed it in his mouth.

A flash of light seemed to fall between them—and then as she saw clearly, Lucius's eyes, with a full light of perception in them, were looking into hers.

"Oh," he cried, "you are beautiful! You are beautiful! You are beautiful!"

Her hands were empty—but now he had clasped her in his arms, and was kissing her, and then drawing back to look at her face—then looking around at the brightening landscape of morning—and always coming back to look at her face, and her body, and her face again.

She moved her hands, seeking the Holy Cup. It was gone. "Where is—It?"

"I saw nothing. I see only you. You're beautiful—oh my love, you're beautiful!"

At the door of the cottage, the Sibyl watched silently. Tears were streaming down her face, but she lifted her arms in thanksgiving.

Of the End

The time of happiness lasted about the space of a month. From April into May—and all that time was sunshine and warm winds, days and nights of beauty. Together they enjoyed all the loveliness of the countryside, and each other most of all. They made love among the primroses, and among the bluebells, and in the beechwoods, and on the tops of high hills. He could never have enough of looking at her.

For she was beautiful, in very truth. She had, indeed, long been beautiful, for any who had eyes to see. Her face, once pale, was now brown and warm tinted as a gypsy's, with a bloom of health on her cheeks; her brown eyes were long-lashed and brilliant; her lips were red, and her teeth flashed between them when she smiled. Her long black hair, which she now brushed and combed carefully, or braided with flowers, was sometimes like a silken curtain, and sometimes gleamed with blue like a starling's back. And her body, which in that secret and secure place could often be naked, was brown and smooth and shapely as our mother Eve's. And over all was the glow of love and happiness.

Sometimes they went back into the cavern with torches, and explored it—she was the one, now, who could show him the underground river, and the warm bathing pool under the stalactites, and the white sand beside it. He had to shut his eyes to recapture his old skill, and he was less fond of his dark kingdom now than he had been. Neither could he enjoy swimming, even in the warm pool, as he used to. He was weaker, and often feverish. Passionately he craved for every moment of light above ground—discovering sunrise and sunset, moonlight and starlight, and his nurse's quiet and loving face, but always coming back to Lynett. And his nurse—if she sometimes wept quietly, she hid it from the happy lovers.

And after about a month, the end came, quickly and quietly and without pain.

They did not lay him in the grotto with the bones of the Sibyls but dug a grave for him under the apple tree. And there they stood, looking at the green turves and the flowers they had set above him.

"I took him from you," Lynett said to the Sibyl.

"No, my dear. I could not have kept him, nor could you. A man belongs to himself and to God."

They were silent for a time.

"There is a thing I don't understand," said Lynett. "What became of it—It—the Holy Grail that I carried?"

"It went back. It always goes back when its work is done. I never saw it, nor did he. Only you could see it. It has gone back to its own place, but it will be shown again to Arthur and his knights when the time comes for the last great quest. Perceval will go out when that time comes, and Gawain of Orkney, and Lancelot—and Lancelot's son, who will achieve the Quest."

"And I—what am I to do now?"

"Let me think, and I will tell you." The Sibyl left her side and paced away among the shadows of the gorge. A terrible foreboding fell upon Lynett. She thought of how a woman had come to the Sibyl's door as she sat mourning her husband, and had said to her, "You are she." Could she bear to be named as the Sibyl's successor? Cold sinking fear gripped her at the thought.

The Sibyl ceased her pacing and came back to her.

"No, my dear," she said. "I know what you are fearing. No, not that. I am not going to name you as the next Sibyl. Time is coming soon that I must go, and another come, but it will not be you." She smiled, she almost laughed. "I know you're relieved. No, that's not your destiny. Yours is another path, the one you least expect. First you must go back to King Arthur, and tell him all that has befallen. You must not forget that you are still his messenger. And then—you must go home."

"Home? What home have I?"

"You must go back to Lyonesse, where your sister Leonie lives with Sir Gareth."

"Ah—" Her heart seemed to contract suddenly.

"Yes. You are fit to go back now. You are cured of your love for Gareth—are you not?—and you will no more have any jealousy or craving. Your sister Leonie has borne Gareth a son, Gawain the younger, and you will have much to teach him, and maybe his son after him."

"To teach him!" she burst out, with something of her old bitterness. "Who am I to teach a man? An aunt, an old aunt! A nursemaid!"

"No, my dear. Not a nursemaid. Your father taught you the arts of chivalry, though you were a woman. And you, a woman, will teach his grandson the arts of chivalry. Perhaps before the end you will have a greater part to play than anyone knows."

So later, on a cold morning when the sunshine of May had turned to rain, Lynett, alone and on foot, set out again from the Sibyl's cave. And from a branch above her, with a soft whirr of wings, Jeanne flew down and settled on her wrist. And from the road ahead of her, Bors, Perceval and Lancelot, leading her tall black horse, came to meet her.

THE LADY OF THE FOUNTAIN

from the *Mabinogion*

The Arthurian tales are really a mongrel mixture of myths from a variety of sources and characters may appear in different guises and not necessarily in their "Malorised" form. This is true of Lynett whom we have already met in the last two stories. Here she reappears as Luned, the maiden of the Lady of the Fountain. The story comes from the collection of Welsh myths known as the Mabinogion *which had existed for centuries but were not written down until after the ninth century. Five of the stories included in the* Mabinogion *are Arthurian, although their origins span several centuries. "The Lady of the Fountain" was one of the later additions and betrays a Norman-French influence. The character of Owain appears as Yvain in the romance of that title by Chrétien de Troyes, who was writing his adventures at about the same time as "The Lady of the Fountain" was recorded in the twelfth century. The first full translation into English was made by Lady Charlotte Guest (1812–95) who worked on the project for almost twenty years until 1849.*

King Arthur was at Caerlleon-upon-Usk; and one day he sat in his chamber, and with him were Owain the son of Urien, and Kynon the son of Clydno, and Kai the son of Kyner, and

Gwenhwyvar and her hand-maidens at needle-work by the window. And if it should be said that there was a porter at Arthur's palace, there was none. Glewlwyd Gavaelvawr was there, acting as porter, to welcome guests and strangers, and to receive them with honour, and to inform them of the manners and customs of the court, and to direct those who came to the hall or to the presence-chamber, and those who came to take up their lodging.

In the centre of the chamber King Arthur sat upon a seat of green rushes, over which was spread a covering of flame-coloured satin, and a cushion of red satin was under his elbow.

Then Arthur spoke. "If I thought you would not disparage me," said he, "I would sleep while I wait for my repast; and you can entertain one another with relating tales, and can obtain a flagon of mead and some meat from Kai."

And the king went to sleep. So Kai went to the kitchen and to the mead-cellar, and returned bearing a flagon of mead, and a golden goblet, and a handful of skewers upon which were broiled collops of meat. Then they ate the collops, and began to drink the mead.

"Now," said Kai, "it is time for you to give me my story."

"Kynon," said Owain, "do thou pay to Kai the tale that is his due."

"Truly," said Kynon, "thou art older, and art a better teller of tales, and hast seen more marvellous things than I: do thou therefore pay Kai his tale."

"Begin thyself," quoth Owain, "with the best that thou knowest."

"I will do so," answered Kynon. "I was the only son of my mother and father, and I was exceedingly aspiring, and my daring was very great. I thought there was no enterprise in the world too mighty for me; and, after I had achieved all the adventures that were in my own country, I equipped myself, and set forth to journey through deserts and distant regions. And at length it chanced that I came to the fairest valley in the world, wherein were trees of equal growth; and a river ran through the valley, and a path was by the side of the river. And I followed the path until mid-day, and continued my journey along the remainder of the valley until the evening; and at the extremity of a plain I came to a large and lustrous castle, at the foot of which was a torrent. And I approached the castle; and there I beheld two youths with yellow, curling hair, each with a frontlet of gold upon his head, and clad in a garment of yellow satin, and they had gold clasps upon their insteps. In the hand of each of them was an ivory bow, strung with the sinews of the stag; and their arrows had shafts of the bone of the whale, and were winged with peacock's feathers; the shafts also had golden heads. And they had daggers with blades of gold, and with hilts of the bone of the whale. And they were shooting their daggers.

"And a little way from them I saw a man in the prime of life, with his beard newly shorn, clad in a robe and a mantle of yellow satin; and round the top of his mantle was a band of gold lace. On his feet were shoes of variegated leather, fastened by two bosses of gold. When I saw him, I went towards him and saluted him; and such was his courtesy that he no sooner received my greeting than he returned it. And he went with me towards the castle. Now, there were no dwellers in the castle, except those who were in one hall. And there I saw four and twenty damsels embroidering satin at a window. And this I tell thee, Kai, that the least fair of them was fairer than the fairest maid thou hast ever beheld in the Island of Britain; and the least lovely of them was more lovely than Gwenhwyvar, the wife of Arthur, when she has appeared loveliest at the Offering, on the day of the Nativity, or at the feast of Easter. They rose up at my coming, and six of them took my horse and divested me of my armour. And six others took my arms and washed them in a vessel until they were perfectly bright. And the third six spread cloths upon the tables and prepared meat. And the fourth six took off my soiled garments and placed others upon me; namely, an under-vest and a doublet of fine linen, and a robe, and a surcoat, and a mantle of yellow satin with a broad gold band upon the mantle. And they placed cushions, both beneath and around me, with coverings of red linen; and I sat down. Now, the six maidens who had taken my horse, unharnessed him as well as if they had been the best squires in the Island of Britain. Then, behold, they brought bowls of silver wherein was water to wash, and towels of linen, some green, and some white; and I washed. And in a little while the man sat down to the table. And I sat next to him; and below me sat all the maidens, except those who waited on us. And the table was of silver, and the cloths upon the table were of linen; and no vessel was served upon the table that was not either of gold, or of silver, or of buffalo-horn. And our meat was brought to us. And verily, Kai, I saw there every sort of meat and every sort of liquor that I have ever seen elsewhere; but the meat and the liquor were better served there than I have ever seen them in any other place.

"Until the repast was half over, neither the man nor any one of the damsels spoke a single word to me; but, when the man perceived that it would be more agreeable to me to converse than to eat any more, he began to inquire of me who I was. I said I was glad to find that there was some one who would discourse with me, and that it was not considered so great a crime at that court for people to hold converse together.

"'Chieftain,' said the man, "we would have talked to thee sooner, but we feared to disturb thee during thy repast now, however, we will discourse."

"Then I told the man who I was, and what was the cause of my journey, and said that I was seeking whether any one was superior to me, or whether I could gain the mastery over all. The man looked upon me; and he smiled, and said, "If I did not fear to distress thee too much, I would show thee that which thou seekest."

"Upon this I became anxious and sorrowful; and, when the man perceived it, he said, 'If thou wouldst rather that I should show thee thy disadvantage than thine advantage, I will do so. Sleep here to-night, and in the morning arise early, and take the road upwards through the valley until thou reachest the wood through which thou camest hither. A little way within the wood thou wilt meet with a road branching off to the right, by which thou must proceed until thou comest to a large sheltered glade with a mound in the centre. And thou wilt see a black man of great stature on the top of the mound. He is not smaller in size than two of the men of this world. He had but one foot, and one eye in the middle of his forehead. And he has a club of iron; and it is certain that there are no two men in the world who would not find their burden in that club. And he is not a comely man, but, on the contrary, he is exceedingly ill-favoured; and he is the woodward of that wood. And thou wilt see a thousand wild animals grazing around him. Inquire of him the way out of the glade; and he will reply to thee briefly, and will point out the road by which thou shalt find that which thou art in quest of.'

"And long seemed that night to me. And the next morning I arose and equipped myself, and mounted my horse, and pro- ceeded straight through the valley to the wood; and I followed the crossroad which the man had pointed out to me, till at length I arrived at the glade. And there was I three times more astonished at the number of wild animals that I beheld than the man had said I should be. And the black man was there, sitting upon the top of the mound. Huge of stature as the man had told me that he was, I found him to exceed by far the description he had given me of him. As for the iron club which the man had told me was a burden for two men, I am certain, Kai, that it would be a heavy weight for four warriors to lift; and this was in the black man's hand. And he only spoke to me in answer to my questions. Then I asked him what power he held over those animals.

"'I will show thee, little man,' said he.

"And he took his club in his hand, and with it he struck a stag a great blow, so that he brayed vehemently; and at his braying the animals came together, as numerous as the stars in the sky, so that it was difficult for me to find room in the glade to stand among them. There were serpents, and dragons, and divers sorts of animals. And he looked at them, and bade them go and feed; and they bowed their heads, and did him homage as vassals to their lord.

"Then the black man said to me, 'Seest thou now, little man, what power I hold over these animals?'

"Then I inquired of him the way, and he became very rough in his manner to me: however, he asked me whither I would go. And when I told him who I was, and what I sought, he directed me.

"'Take,' said he, 'that path that leads towards the head of the glade, and ascend the wooded steep until thou comest to its summit; and there thou wilt find an open space like to a large valley, and in the midst of it a tall tree, whose branches are greener than the greenest pine-trees. Under this tree is a fountain, and by the side of the fountain a marble slab, and on the marble slab a silver bowl attached by a chain of silver so that it may not be carried away. Take the bowl and throw a bowlful of water upon the slab, and thou wilt hear a mighty peal of thunder, so that thou wilt think that heaven and earth are trembling with its fury. With the thunder there will come a shower so severe, that it will be scarce possible for thee to endure it and live. And the shower will be of hailstones; and after the shower the weather will become fair, but every leaf that was upon the tree will have been carried away by the shower. Then a flight of birds will come and alight upon the tree; and in thine own country thou didst never hear a strain so sweet as that which they will sing. And, at the moment thou art most delighted with the song of the birds, thou wilt hear a murmuring and complaining coming towards thee along the valley. And thou wilt see a knight upon a coal-black horse, clothed in black velvet, and with a pennon of black linen upon his lance; and he will ride unto thee to encounter thee with the utmost speed. If thou fleest from him, he will overtake thee; and, if thou abidest there, as sure as thou art a mounted knight he will leave thee on foot. And if thou dost not find trouble in that adventure thou needest not seek it during the rest of thy life.'

"So I journeyed on until I reached the summit of the steep, and there I found every thing as the black man had described it to me. And I went up to the tree, and beneath it I saw the fountain, and by its side the marble slab, and the silver bowl fastened by the chain. Then I took the bowl, and cast a bowlful of water upon the slab; and thereupon, behold, the thunder came, much more violent than the black man had led me to expect. And after the thunder came the shower: and of a truth I tell thee, Kai, that there is neither man nor beast that could endure that shower and live; for not one of those hailstones would be stopped, either by the flesh or by the skin, until it had reached the bone. I turned my horse's flank towards the shower, and placed the beak of my shield over his head and neck, while I held the upper part of it over my own head. And thus I withstood the shower. When I looked on the tree, there was not a single leaf upon it; and then the sky became clear, and with that, behold the birds lighted upon the tree, and sang. And truly, Kai, I never heard any melody equal to that, either before or since. And, when I was most charmed with listening to the birds, lo, a murmuring voice was heard through the valley, approaching me, and saying, 'O knight! what has brought thee hither? What evil have I done to thee, that thou shouldst act towards me and my possessions as thou hast this day? Dost thou not know that the shower to-day has left in my dominions neither man nor beast alive that was exposed to it?'

"And thereupon, behold, a knight on a black horse appeared, clothed in jet-black velvet, and with a tabard of black linen about him. And we charged each other; and, as the onset was furious, it was not long before I was overthrown. Then the knight passed the shaft on his lance through the bridle-rein of my horse, and rode off with the two horses, leaving me where I was. And he did not even bestow so much notice upon me as to imprison me, nor did he despoil me of my arms. So I returned along the road by which I had come. And, when I reached the glade where the black man was, I confess to thee, Kai, it is a marvel that I did not melt down into a liquid pool, through the shame that I felt at the black man's derision. And that night I came to the same castle where I had spent the night preceding. And I was more agreeably entertained that night than I had been the night before; and I was better feasted, and I conversed freely with the inmates of the castle, and none of them alluded to my expedition to the fountain, neither did I mention it to any; and I remained there that night. When I arose on the morrow, I found ready saddled a dark-bay palfrey, with nostrils as red as scarlet; and, after putting on my armour and leaving there my blessing, I returned to my own court. And that horse I still possess, and he is in the stable yonder; and I declare that I would not part with him for the best palfrey in the Island of Britain."

"Now of a truth, Kai, no man ever before confessed to an adventure so much to his own discredit; and verily it seems strange to me that neither before nor since have I heard of any person besides myself who knew of this adventure, and that the subject of it should exist within King Arthur's dominions without any other person lighting upon it."

"Now," quoth Owain, "would it not be well to go and endeavour to discover that place?"

"By the hand of my friend," said Kai, "often dost thou utter that with thy tongue which thou wouldst not make good with thy deeds."

"In very truth," said Gwenhwyvar, "if were better thou wert hanged, Kai, than to use such uncourteous speech towards a man like Owain."

"By the hand of my friend, good lady," said Kai, "thy praise of Owain is not greater than mine."

With that Arthur awoke, and asked if he had not been sleeping a little.

"Yes, lord," answered Owain, "thou hast slept a while."

"Is it time for us to go to meat?"

"It is, lord," said Owain.

Then the horn for washing was sounded, and the king and all his household sat down to eat. And when the meal was ended Owain withdrew to his lodging and made ready his horse and his arms.

On the morrow, with the dawn of day, he put on his armour, and mounted his charger, and travelled through distant lands and over desert mountains. And at length he arrived at the valley which Kynon had described to him; and he was certain that it was the same that he sought. And, journeying along the valley by the side of the river, he followed its course till he came to the plain and within sight of the castle. When he approached the castle, he saw the youths shooting their daggers in the place where Kynon had seen them, and the yellow man, to whom the castle belonged, standing hard by. And no sooner had Owain saluted the yellow man than he was saluted by him in return.

And he went forward towards the castle, and there he saw the chamber; and when he had entered the chamber he beheld the maidens working at satin embroidery, in chairs of gold. And their beauty and their comeliness seemed to Owain far greater than Kynon had represented to him. And they arose to wait upon Owain, as they had done to Kynon; and the meal which they set before him gave more satisfaction to Owain than it had done to Kynon.

About the middle of the repast, the yellow man asked Owain the object of his journey. And Owain made it known to him, and said, "I am in quest of the knight who guards the fountain."

Upon this the yellow man smiled, and said that he was as loth to point out that adventure to Owain as he had been to Kynon. However, he described the whole to Owain, and they retired to rest.

The next morning Owain found his horse made ready for him by the damsels; and he set forward, and came to the glade where the black man was. And the stature of the black man seemed more wonderful to Owain than it had done to Kynon; and Owain asked of him his road, and he showed it to him. And Owain followed the road, as Kynon had done, till he came to the green tree; and he beheld the fountain, and the slab beside the fountain with the bowl upon it. And Owain took the bowl, and threw a bowlful of water upon the slab. And, lo, the thunder was heard; and after the thunder came the shower, much more violent than Kynon had described; and after the shower the sky became bright. And when Owain looked at the tree there was not one leaf upon it. And immediately the birds came, and settled upon the tree, and sang. And, when their song was most pleasing to Owain, he beheld a knight coming towards him through the valley; and he prepared to receive him and encountered him violently. Having broken both their lances, they drew their swords and fought blade to blade. Then Owain struck the knight a blow through his helmet, headpiece, and visor, and through the skin, and the flesh, and the bone, until it wounded the very brain. Then the black knight felt that he had received a mortal wound, upon which he turned his horse's head and fled. And Owain pursued him, and followed close upon him, although he was not near enough to strike him with his sword. Thereupon Owain descried a vast and resplendent castle. And they came to the castle-gate. And the black knight was allowed to enter, and the portcullis was let fall upon Owain; and it struck his horse behind the saddle, and cut him in two and carried away the rowels of the spurs that were upon Owain's heels. And the portcullis descended to the floor. And the rowels of the spurs and part of the horse were without; and Owain, with the other part of the horse, remained between the two gates, and the inner gate was closed, so that Owain could not go thence; and Owain was in a perplexing situation. And, while he was in this state, he could see through an aperture in the gate a street facing him, with a row of houses on each side. And he beheld a maiden, with yellow curling hair, and a frontlet of gold upon her head; and she was clad in a dress of yellow satin, and on her feet were shoes of variegated leather. And she approached the gate, and desired that it should be opened.

"Heaven knows, lady," said Owain, "it is no more possible for me to open to thee from hence than it is for thee to set me free."

"Truly," said the damsel, "it is very sad that thou canst not be released, and every woman ought to succour thee; for I never saw one more faithful in the service of ladies than thou. As a friend thou art the most sincere, and as a lover the most devoted. Therefore," quoth she, "whatever is in my power to do for thy release, I will do it. Take this ring, and put it on thy finger with the stone inside thy hand, and close thy hand upon the stone. And as long as thou concealest it will conceal thee. When they have consulted together, they will come forth to fetch thee in order to put thee to death; and they will be much grieved that they cannot find thee. And I will await thee on the horseblock yonder; and thou wilt be able to see me, though I cannot see thee: therefore come and place thy hand upon my shoulder, that I may know that thou art near me. And by the way that I go hence do thou accompany me."

Then she went away from Owain, and he did all that the maiden had told him. And the people of the castle came to seek Owain to put him to death; and, when they found nothing but the half of his horse, they were sorely grieved.

And Owain vanished from among them, and went to the maiden, and placed his hand upon her shoulder; whereupon she set off. And Owain followed her until they came to the door of a large and beautiful chamber; and the maiden opened it, and they went in and closed the door. And Owain looked around the chamber; and behold there was not even a single nail in it that was not painted with gorgeous colours; and there was not a single panel that had not sundry images in gold portrayed upon it.

The maiden kindled a fire, and took water in a silver bowl, and put a towel of white linen on her shoulder, and gave Owain water to wash. Then she placed before him a silver table inlaid with gold, upon which was a cloth of yellow linen, and she brought him food. And of a truth Owain had never seen any kind of meat that was not there in abundance; but it was better cooked there than he had ever found it in any other place. Nor did he ever see so excellent a display of meat and drink as there. And there was not one vessel from which he was served that was not of gold or of silver. And Owain ate and drank until late in the afternoon, when, lo, they heard a mighty clamour in the castle. And Owain asked the maiden what that outcry was.

"They are administering extreme unction," said she, "to the nobleman who owns the castle."

And Owain went to sleep.

And a little after daybreak they heard an exceeding loud clamour and wailing. And Owain asked the maiden what was the cause of it.

"They are bearing to the church the body of the nobleman who owned the castle."

And Owain rose up and clothed himself, and opened a window of the chamber, and looked towards the castle. And he could see neither the bounds nor the extent of the hosts that filled the streets. And they were fully armed. And a vast number of women were with them, both on horseback and on foot; and all the ecclesiastics in the city, singing. And it seemed to Owain that the sky resounded with the vehemence of their cries, and with the noise of the trumpets, and with the singing of the ecclesiastics. In the midst of the throng he beheld the bier, over which was a veil of white linen; and wax tapers were burning beside and around it, and none that supported the bier was lower in rank than a powerful baron.

Never did Owain see an assemblage so gorgeous with satin and silk and sendal. And following the train he beheld the lady, with yellow hair falling over her shoulders, and stained with blood, and about her a dress of yellow satin, which was torn. Upon her feet were shoes of variegated leather. And it was a marvel that the ends of her fingers were not bruised, from the violence with which she smote her hands together. Truly she would have been the fairest lady Owain ever saw, had she been in her usual guise. And her cry was louder than the shout of the men or the clamour of the trumpets. No sooner had he beheld the lady than he became inflamed with her love, so that it took entire possession of him.

Then he inquired of the maiden who the lady was.

"Heaven knows," replied the maiden, "she may be said to be the fairest, and the most chaste, and the most liberal, and the wisest, and the most noble, of women; and she is my mistress. And she is called the 'Countess of the Fountain,' the wife of him whom thou didst slay yesterday."

"Verily," said Owain, "she is the woman that I love best."

"Verily," said the maiden, "she shall also love thee not a little."

And with that the maid arose, and kindled a fire, and filled a pot with water and placed it to warm; and she brought a towel of white linen and placed it around Owain's neck; and she took a goblet of ivory and a silver basin, and filled them with warm water, wherewith she washed Owain's head. Then she opened a wooden casket and drew forth a razor whose haft was of ivory, and upon which were two rivets of gold. And she shaved his beard, and she dried his head and his throat with the towel. Then she rose up from before Owain, and brought him to eat. And truly Owain had never so good a meal, nor was he ever so well served.

When he had finished his repast, the maiden arranged his couch.

"Come here," said she, "and sleep, and I will go and woo for thee."

And Owain went to sleep; and the maiden shut the door of the chamber after her, and went towards the castle. When she came there, she found nothing but mourning and sorrow; and the countess in her chamber could not bear the sight of any one through grief. Luned came and saluted her; but the countess answered her not. And the maiden bent down towards her, and said, "What aileth thee, that thou answerest no one to-day?"

"Luned," said the countess, "what change hath befallen thee, that thou hast not come to visit me in my grief? It was wrong in thee, and I having made thee rich—it was wrong in these that thou didst not come to see me in my distress. That was wrong in thee. As it is, I will banish thee."

"I am glad," said Luned, "that thou hast no other cause to do so than that I would have been of service to thee where thou didst not know what was to thine advantage. And henceforth evil betide whichever of us shall make the first advance towards reconciliation to the other; whether I should seek an invitation from thee, or thou of thine own accord shouldst send to invite me."

With that Luned went forth. And the countess arose, and followed her to the door of the chamber, and began coughing loudly. And, when Luned looked back, the countess beckoned to her, and she returned to the countess.

"In truth," said the countess, "evil is thy disposition; but, if thou knowest what is to my advantage, declare it to me."

"I will do so," quoth she.

"Thou knowest that except by warfare and arms it is impossible for thee to preserve thy possessions. Delay not, therefore, to seek some one who can defend them."

"And how can I do that?" said the countess.

"I will tell thee," said Luned. "Unless thou canst defend the fountain, thou canst not maintain thy dominions; and no one can defend the fountain, except it be a knight of Arthur's household. And I will go to Arthur's court; and ill betide me if I return thence without a warrior who can guard the fountain as well as, or even better than, he who defended it formerly."

"That will be hard to perform," said the countess. "Go, however, and make proof of that which thou hast promised."

Luned set out, under the pretence of going to Arthur's court; but she went back to the chamber where she had left Owain. And she tarried there with him as long as it might have taken her to have travelled to the court of King Arthur. And at the end of that time she apparelled herself, and went to visit the countess. And the countess was much rejoiced when she saw her, and inquired what news she brought from the court.

"I bring thee the best of news," said Luned, "for I have compassed the object of my mission. When wilt thou that I should present to thee the chieftain who has come with me hither?"

"Bring him here to visit me to-morrow at mid-day," said the countess, "and I will cause the town to be assembled by that time."

And Luned returned home. And the next day, at noon, Owain arrayed himself in a coat and a surcoat and a mantle of yellow satin upon which was a broad band of gold lace; and on his feet were high shoes of variegated leather, which were fastened by golden clasps in the form of lions. And they proceeded to the chamber of the countess.

Right glad was the countess of their coming, and she gazed steadfastly upon Owain, and said, "Luned, this knight has not the look of a traveller."

"What harm is there in that, lady?" said Luned.

"I am certain," said the countess, "that no other man than this chased the soul from the body of my lord."

"So much the better for thee, lady," said Luned; "for, had he not been stronger than thy lord, he could not have deprived him of life. There is no remedy for that which is past, be it as it may."

"Go back to thine abode," said the countess, "and I will take counsel."

The next day the countess caused all her subjects to assemble, and showed them that her earldom was left defenceless, and that it could not be protected but with horse and arms, and military skill.

"Therefore," said she, "this is what I offer for your choice: either let one of you take me, or give your consent for me to take a husband from elsewhere to defend my dominions."

So they came to the determination that it was better that she should have permission to marry some one from elsewhere. And thereupon she sent for the bishops and archbishops to celebrate her nuptials with Owain. And the men of the earldom did Owain homage.

And Owain defended the fountain with lance and sword. And this is the manner in which he defended it: whensoever a knight came there, he overthrew him and sold him for his full worth, and what he thus gained he divided among his barons and his knights; and no man in the whole world could be more beloved than he was by his subjects. And it was thus for the space of three years.

It befell that as Gwalchmai went forth one day with King Arthur he perceived him to be very sad and sorrowful. And Gwalchmai was much grieved to see Arthur in this state, and he questioned him, saying, "Oh, my lord! what has befallen thee?"

"In sooth, Gwalchmai," said Arthur, "I am grieved concerning Owain, whom I have lost these three years; and I shall certainly die if the fourth year passes without my seeing him. Now I am sure that it is through the tale which Kynon, the son of Clydno, related, that I have lost Owain."

"There is no need for thee," said Gwalchmai, "to summon to arms thy whole dominions on this account; for thou thyself and the men of thy household will be able to avenge Owain if he be slain, or to set him free if he be in prison, and if alive to bring him back with thee." And it was settled according to what Gwalchmai had said.

Then Arthur and the men of his household prepared to go and seek Owain; and their number was three thousand, besides their attendants. And Kynon, the son of Clydno, acted as their guide. And Arthur came to the castle where Kynon had been before; and when he came there the youths were shooting in the same place, and the yellow man was standing hard by. When the yellow man saw Arthur, he greeted him and invited him to the castle. And Arthur accepted his invitation, and they entered the castle together. And, great as was the number of his retinue, their pres ence was scarcely observed in the castle, so vast was its extent. And the maidens rose up to wait on them; and the service of the maidens appeared to them all to excel any attendance they had ever met with; and even the pages who had charge of the horses were no worse served that night than Arthur himself would have been in his own palace.

The next morning, Arthur set out thence with Kynon for his guide, and came to the place where the black man was. And the stature of the black man was more surprising to Arthur than it had been represented to him. And they came to the top of the wooded steep, and traversed the valley till they reached the green tree, where they saw the fountain, and the bowl, and the slab. And upon that Kai came to Arthur, and spoke to him.

"My lord," said he, "I know the meaning of all this; and my request is that thou wilt permit me to throw the water on the slab, and to receive the first adventure that may befall."

And Arthur gave him leave.

Then Kai threw a bowlful of water upon the slab, and immediately there came the thunder, and after the thunder the shower. And such a thunderstorm they had never known before, and many of the attendants who were in Arthur's train were killed by the shower. After the shower had ceased the sky became clear, and on looking at the tree they beheld it completely leafless. Then the birds descended upon the tree; and the song of the birds was far sweeter than any strain they had ever heard before. Then they beheld a knight on a coal-black horse, clothed in black satin, coming rapidly towards them. And Kai met him and encountered him, and it was not long before Kai was overthrown. And the knight withdrew, and Arthur and his host encamped for the night.

And when they arose in the morning they perceived the signal of combat upon the lance of the knight. And Kai came to Arthur and spoke to him.

"My lord," said he, "though I was overthrown yesterday, if it seem good to thee I would gladly meet the knight again to-day."

"Thou mayst do so," said Arthur.

And Kai went towards the knight. And on the spot he overthrew Kai, and struck him with the head of his lance in the forehead, so that it broke his helmet and the headpiece, and pierced the skin and the flesh the breadth of the spear-head, even to the bone. And Kai returned to his companions.

After this, all the household of Arthur went forth one after the other to combat the knight, until there was not one that was not overthrown by him except Arthur and Gwalchmai. And Arthur armed himself to encounter the knight.

"Oh, my lord!" said Gwalchmai, "permit me to fight with him first."

And Arthur permitted him. And he went forth to meet the knight, having over himself and his horse a satin robe of honor which had been sent by the daughter of the Earl of Rhangyw; and in this dress he was not known by any of the host. And they charged each other, and fought all that day until the evening; and neither of them was able to unhorse the other.

The next day they fought with strong lances, and neither of them could obtain the mastery.

And the third day they fought with exceeding strong lances. And they were incensed with rage, and fought furiously, even until noon. And they gave each other such a shock that the girths of their horses were broken, so that they fell over their horses' cruppers to the ground. And they rose up speedily and drew their swords and resumed the combat. And the multitude that witnessed their encounter felt assured that they had never before seen two men so valiant or so powerful. And, that had it been midnight, it would have been light from the fire that flashed from their weapons. And the knight gave Gwalchmai a blow that turned his helmet from off his face, so that the knight knew that it was Gwalchmai. Then Owain said, "My lord Gwalchmai, I did not know thee for my cousin, owing to the robe of honour that enveloped thee. Take my sword and my arms."

Said Gwalchmai, "Thou, Owain, art the victor. Take thou my sword."

And with that Arthur saw that they were conversing, and advanced towards them.

"My lord Arthur," said Gwalchmai, "here is Owain, who has vanquished me and will not take my arms."

"My lord," said Owain, "it is he that has vanquished me and he will not take my sword."

"Give me your swords," said Arthur, "and then neither of you has vanquished the other."

Then Owain put his arms around Arthur's neck, and they embraced. And all the host hurried forward to see Owain, and to embrace him; and there was nigh being a loss of life, so great was the press.

And they retired that night, and the next day Arthur prepared to depart.

"My lord," said Owain, "this is not well of thee; for I have been absent from thee these three years, and during all that time, up to this very day, I have been preparing a banquet for thee, knowing that thou wouldst come to seek me. Tarry with me, therefore, until thou and thy attendants have recovered the fatigues of the journey and have been anointed."

And they all proceeded to the castle of the Countess of the Fountain. And the banquet which had been three years preparing was consumed in three months. Never had they a more delicious or agreeable banquet. And Arthur prepared to depart. Then he sent an embassy to the countess, beseeching her to permit Owain to go with him for the space of three months, that he might show him to the nobles and the fair dames of the Island of Britain. And the countess gave her consent, although it was very painful to her. So Owain came with Arthur to the Island of Britain. And, when he was once more amongst his kindred and friends, he remained three years, instead of three months, with them.

And, as Owain one day sat at meat in the city of Caerlleon-upon-Usk, behold a damsel entered, upon a bay horse with a curling mane and covered with foam; and the bridle and so much as was seen of the saddle were of gold. And the damsel was arrayed in a dress of yellow satin. And she came up to Owain, and took the ring from off his hand.

"Thus," said she, "shall be treated the deceiver, the traitor, the faithless, the disgraced, and the beardless."

And she turned her horse's head, and departed.

Then his adventure came to Owain's remembrance, and he was sorrowful; and, having finished eating, he went to his own abode and made preparations that night. And the next day he arose, yet did not go to the court, but wandered to the distant parts of the earth and to uncultivated mountains. And he remained there until all his apparel was worn out, and his body was wasted away, and his hair was grown long. And he went about with the wild beasts, and fed with them, until they became familiar with him. But at length he grew so weak that he could no longer bear them company. Then he descended from the mountains to the valley, and came to a park that was the fairest in the world and belonged to a widowed countess.

One day the countess and her maidens went forth to walk by a lake that was in the middle of the park; and they saw the form of a man. And they were terrified. Nevertheless, they went near him, and touched him, and looked at him. And they saw that there was life in him, though he was exhausted by the heat of the sun. And the countess returned to the castle, and took a flask full of precious ointment and gave it to one of her maidens.

"Go with this," said she, "and take with thee yonder horse and clothing, and place them near the man we saw just now. And anoint him with this balsam, near his heart; and if there is life in him he will arise through the efficacy of this balsam. Then watch what he will do."

And the maiden departed from her, and poured the whole of the balsam upon Owain, and left the horse and the garments hard by, and went a little way off and hid herself to watch him. In a short time she saw him begin to move his arms. And he rose up and looked at his person, and became ashamed of the unseemliness of his appearance. Then he perceived the horse and the garments that were near him. And he crept forward till he was able to draw the garments to him from off the saddle. And he clothed himself, and with difficulty mounted the horse. Then the damsel discovered herself to him, and saluted him. And he was rejoiced when he saw her, and inquired of her what land and what territory that was.

"Truly," said the maiden, "a widowed countess owns yonder castle. At the death of her husband he left her two earldoms; but at this day she has only this one dwelling that has not been wrested from her by a young earl who is her neighbour, because she refused to become his wife."

"That is pity," said Owain.

And he and the maiden proceeded to the castle. And he alighted there; and the maiden conducted him to a pleasant chamber, and kindled a fire, and left him.

And the maiden came to the countess, and gave the flask into her hand.

"Ha, maiden!" said the countess, "where is all the balsam?"

"Have I not used it all?" said she.

"Oh, maiden!" said the countess, "I cannot easily forgive thee this. It is sad for me to have wasted seven-score pounds' worth of precious ointment upon a stranger whom I know not. However, maiden, wait thou upon him until he is quite recovered."

And the maiden did so, and furnished him with meat and drink and fire and lodging and medicaments until he was well again. And in three months he was restored to his former guise, and became even more comely than he had ever been before.

One day Owain heard a great tumult and a sound of arms in the castle, and he inquired of the maiden the cause thereof.

"The earl," said she, "whom I mentioned to thee, has come before the castle with a numerous army, to subdue the countess."

And Owain inquired of her whether the countess had a horse and arms in her possession.

"She has the best in the world," said the maiden.

"Wilt thou go and request the loan of a horse and arms for me," said Owain, "that I may go and look at this army?"

"I will," said the maiden.

And she came to the countess, and told her what Owain had said. And the countess laughed.

"Truly," said she, "I will even give him a horse and arms forever—such a horse and such arms had he never yet. And I am glad that they should be taken by him to-day, lest my enemies should have them against my will to-morrow. Yet I know not what he would do with them."

The countess bade them bring out a beautiful black steed upon which was a beechen saddle, and a suit of armour for man and horse. And Owain armed himself, and mounted the horse and went forth, attended by two pages completely equipped with horses and arms. And, when they came near to the earl's army, they could see neither its extent nor its extremity. And Owain asked the pages in which troop the earl was.

"In yonder troop," said they, "in which are four yellow standards: two of them are before, and two behind him."

"Now," said Owain, "do you return, and await me near the portal of the castle."

So they returned; and Owain pressed forward until he met the earl. And Owain drew him completely out of his saddle and turned his horse's head towards the castle, and, though it was with difficulty, he brought the earl to the portal, where the pages awaited him. And in they came. And Owain presented the earl as a gift to the countess, and said to her, "Behold a requital to thee for thy blessed balsam."

The army encamped around the castle. And the earl restored to the countess the two earldoms he had taken from her, as a ransom for his life; and for his freedom he gave her the half of his own dominions, and all his gold and his silver and his jewels, besides hostages.

And Owain took his departure. And the countess and all her subjects besought him to remain; but Owain chose rather to wander through distant lands and deserts.

And as he journeyed he heard a loud yelling in a wood. And it was repeated a second and a third time. And Owain went towards the spot, and beheld a huge craggy mound in the middle of the wood, on the side of which was a gray rock. And there was a cleft in the rock, and a serpent was within the cleft. And near the rock stood a black lion; and every time the lion sought to go thence the serpent darted towards him to attack him. And Owain unsheathed his sword, and drew near to the rock; and, as the serpent sprang out, he struck him with his sword and cut him in two. And he dried his sword, and went on his way as before. But, behold, the lion followed him and played about him as though it had been a greyhound that he had reared.

They proceeded thus throughout the day until the evening. And when it was time for Owain to take his rest he dismounted, and turned his horse loose in a flat and wooded meadow. And he struck fire, and when the fire was kindled the lion brought him fuel enough to last for three nights. And the lion disappeared. And presently the lion returned, bearing a fine large roebuck. And he threw it down before Owain, who went towards the fire with it.

And Owain took the roebuck, and skinned it, and placed collops of its flesh upon skewers around the fire. The rest of the buck he gave to the lion to devour. While he was doing this, he heard a deep sigh near him, and a second, and a third. And Owain called out to know whether the sigh he heard proceeded from a mortal, and he received answer that it did.

"Who art thou?" said Owain.

"Truly," said the voice, "I am Luned, the handmaiden of the Countess of the Fountain."

"And what dost thou here?" said Owain.

"I am imprisoned," said she, "on account of a knight who came from Arthur's court and married the countess. And he staid a short time with her; but he afterwards departed for the court of Arthur, and has not returned since. And he was the friend I loved best in the world. And two of the pages in the countess' chamber traduced him, and called him a deceiver. And I told them that they were not a match for him alone. So they imprisoned me in the stone vault, and said that I should be put to death unless he came himself to deliver me by a certain day; and that is no further off than the day after to-morrow. And I have no one to send to seek him for me. And his name is Owain, the son of Urien."

"And art thou certain that if that knight knew all this he would come to thy rescue?"

"I am most certain of it," said she.

When the collops were cooked, Owain divided them into two parts, between himself and the maiden; and after they had eaten they talked together until the day dawned. And the next morning Owain inquired of the damsel if there was any place where he could get food and entertainment for that night.

"There is, lord," said she. "Cross over yonder and go along the side of the river, and in a short time thou wilt see a great castle in which are many towers; and the earl who owns that castle is the most hospitable man in the world. There thou mayst spend the night."

Never did sentinel keep stricter watch over his lord than the lion that night over Owain.

And Owain accoutred his horse, and passed across by the ford, and came in sight of the castle. And he entered it, and was honourably received. And his horse was well cared for, and plenty of fodder was placed before him. Then the lion went and laid down in the horse's manger; so that none of the people of the castle dared to approach him. The treatment which Owain met with there was such as he had never known elsewhere; for every one was as sorrowful as though death had been upon him. And they went to meat; and the earl sat upon one side of Owain, and on the other side his only daughter. And Owain had never seen any more lovely than she. Then the lion came and placed himself between Owain's feet, and he fed him with every kind of food that he took himself. And he never saw any thing equal to the sadness of the people.

In the middle of the repast the earl began to bid Owain welcome.

Then said Owain, "Behold, it is time for thee to be cheerful."

"Heaven knows," said the earl, that it is not thy coming that makes us sorrowful; but we have cause enough for sadness and care."

"What is that?" said Owain.

"I have two sons," replied the earl, "and yesterday they went to the mountains to hunt. Now, there is on the mountain a monster who kills men and devours them; and he seized my sons. And to-morrow is the time he has fixed to be here; and he threatens that he will then slay my sons before my eyes unless I will deliver into his hands this my daughter. He has the form of a man; but in stature he is no less than a giant."

"Truly," said Owain, "that is lamentable. And which wilt thou do?"

"Heaven knows," said the earl, "it will be better that my sons should be slain against my will than that I should voluntarily give up my daughter to him to ill-treat and destroy."

Then they talked about other things; and Owain staid there that night.

The next morning they heard an exceeding great clamour, which was caused by the coming of the giant with the two youths. And the earl was anxious both to protect his castle, and to release his two sons. Then Owain put on his armour, and went forth to encounter the giant. And the lion followed him. And, when the giant saw that Owain was armed, he rushed towards him and attacked him. And the lion fought with the giant much more fiercely than Owain did.

"Truly," said the giant, "I should find no difficulty in fighting with thee, were it not for the animal that is with thee."

Upon that, Owain took the lion back to the castle and shut the gate upon him; and then he returned to fight the giant as before. And the lion roared very loud, for he heard that it went hard with Owain. And he climbed up till he reached the top of the earl's hall, and thence he got to the top of the castle; and he sprang down from the walls, and went and joined Owain. And the lion gave the giant a stroke with his paw which tore him from his shoulder to his hip, and his heart was laid bare. And the giant fell down dead. Then Owain restored the two youths to their father.

The earl besought Owain to remain with him; and he would not, but set forward towards the meadow where Luned was. And when he came there he saw a great fire kindled, and two youths with beautiful curling auburn hair were leading the maiden to cast her into the fire. And Owain asked them what charge they had against her. And they told him of the compact that was between them, as the maiden had done the night before.

"And," said they, "Owain has failed her: therefore we are taking her to be burnt."

"Truly," said Owain, "he is a good knight; and if he knew that the maiden was in such peril I marvel that he came not to her rescue. But, if you will accept me in his stead, I will do battle with you."

"We will," said the youths.

And they attacked Owain, and he was hard beset by them. And with that the lion came to Owain's assistance, and they two got the better of the young men. And they said to him, "Chieftain, it was not agreed that we should fight, save with thyself alone; and it is harder for us to contend with yonder animal than with thee."

And Owain put the lion in the place where the maiden had been imprisoned, and blocked up the door with stones; and he went to fight with the young men as before. But Owain had not his usual strength, and the two youths pressed hard upon him. And the lion roared incessantly at seeing Owain in trouble. And he burst through the wall until he found a way out, and rushed upon the young men, and instantly slew them. So Luned was saved from being burned.

The Owain returned with Luned to the dominions of the Countess of the Fountain. And when he went thence he took the countess with him to Arthur's court, and she was his wife as long as she lived.

And then he took the road that led to the court of the savage black man, and Owain fought with him; and the lion did not quit Owain until he had vanquished him. And when he reached the court of the savage black man he entered the hall, and beheld four and twenty ladies, the fairest that could be seen. And the garments which they had on were not worth four and twenty pence, and they were as sorrowful as death. And Owain asked them the cause of their sadness. And they said, "We are the daughters of earls, and we all come here with our husbands, whom we dearly loved And we were received with honour and rejoicing. And we were thrown into a state of stupor; and, while we were thus, the demon who owns this castle slew all our husbands, and took from us our horses and our raiment and our gold and our silver. And the corpses of our husbands are still in this house, and many others with them. And this, chieftain, is the cause of our grief; and we are sorry that thou art come hither, lest harm should befall thee."

And Owain was grieved when he heard this. And he went forth from the castle, and he beheld a knight approaching him, who saluted him in a friendly and cheerful manner as if he had been a brother. And this was the savage black man.

"In very sooth," said Owain, "it is not to seek thy friendship that I am here."

"In sooth," said he, "thou shalt not find it then."

And with that they charged each other, and fought furiously. And Owain overcame him, and bound his hands behind his back. Then the black savage besought Owain to spare his life, and spoke thus: "My lord Owain," said he, "it was foretold that thou shouldst come hither and vanquish me; and thou hast done so. I was a robber here, and my house was a house of spoil; but grant me my life, and I will become the keeper of an hospice, and I will maintain this house as an hospice for weak and for strong as long as I live, for the good of thy soul."

And Owain accepted this proposal of him, and remained there that night.

And the next day he took the four and twenty ladies and their horses and their raiment and what they possessed of goods and jewels, and proceeded with them to Arthur's court. And, if Arthur was rejoiced when he saw him after he had lost him the first time, his joy was now much greater. And, of those ladies, such as wished to remain in Arthur's court remained there, and such as wished to depart departed.

And thenceforward Owain dwelt at Arthur's court, greatly beloved, as the head of his household, until he went away with his followers; and those were the army of three hundred ravens which Kenverchyn had left him. And wherever Owain went with these he was victorious.

And this is the tale of The Lady of the Fountain.

BURIED SILVER
by Keith Taylor

Keith Taylor is a young Australian writer fascinated by the Dark Ages of British history. During the mid-seventies he wrote a series of stories about an Irish harpist called Felimid mac Fal, a descendant of Druids and Faëries, who travels throughout the British Isles at the time of the Saxon incursions. He had fought on the side of Arthur at Mount Badon, but in the early stories he finds himself in Kent under the Jutish king Oisc. The stories are set in the historical Arthurian period not the traditional romantic age and thus when we encounter a band of Arthur's knights, led by Palamides, they are not quite as we have come to expect. The villa in the story actually exists. The tales of Felimid were collected in the volume Bard *(1981); two more books have since been added to the series.*

1

Anno Domini 418: In this year the Romans collected all the treasures which were in Britain, and hid some in the earth so that no-one afterwards could find them, and some they took with them into Gaul.

ANGLO-SAXON CHRONICLE

An enormous wolf padded through the dark, hunting. Its color was white as a thick frost. Hate and purpose filled its mind. It limped on the right forepaw.

Ten mounted men slept with feral lightness by their ponies, under the sky. Nine of them had taken oaths to serve the other with their lives. They would kill at his command, or on a whim of the moment if he did not restrain them. Mercy was not in their way of thinking.

By chance, another band of ten horsemen was camped some miles away. They too were hardened by battle and fighting, but native to Britain, unlike the others. Neither group knew the other existed.

That would change.

The man who would change it was happily ignorant of them all. Felimid had come as a stranger to the Kentish village in which he was staying, a welcome guest. Its people were British, not Saxon or Jutish; he'd satisfied himself of that before he entered the place.

The night was Beltaine Eve. All across Britain and Ireland the fires kindled, live orange glitters in the dark. With the blue dawn, the people drove their cattle out to pasture through the fires, waving leafy branches and yelling. The beasts lowed wildly, trailing a reek of singed hair from their legs, kicking and plunging, horns shedding sparks. The people cried praises to their Lord the Sun. They danced about the fires and washed ecstatically in the dew.

Felimid moved among them. He wore a soft brown doeskin kilt, and his body by contrast gleamed white as birch in its first exposure since the autumn. His harp's golden strings made a woof for finely loomed sound in their ancient frame; his fingers ran across them like live shuttles. He sang for the season.

> "*Life returns with my Lord the Sun as the tender
> May winds blow,
> As a thousand rills and mountain streams run white with
> melting snow,
> And the bear revives from his winter death with motions
> dazed and slow
> In a forest wild with odors of things beginning to grow—
> Of the trees reviving with him as pale saps quicken and
> flow—
> But he cannot see what the Druids see, or know what the
> Druids know.*
>
> "*The grim insatiable Romans, whose way was to crush and
> grind,*

*Who sucked the good from their conquests till nothing was
left but a rind,
Observed how the Druids fought them, and murdered all
they could find.
They said, 'The cult is finished,' in reports they sanded
and signed,
(Transfix the morning-mist with a spear—describe the
dawn to the blind!)
But the Eagles have flown from Britain and left the Druids
behind.*

*"Life returns with my Lord the Sun at the fairest time of
year,
Life returns and laughter, to banish a long-held fear,
As the blood runs hot, exulting, and passion is tenfold dear,
And through the nights of April the piles of kindling rear
In every village and steading as Beltaine Eve draws near.
The Druids wait for an ancient Word which only Druids
can hear."*

Baskets of oatcakes were carried among the dancers. The village women each took one, blindly. One cake had been charred black. Whoever received it was the carline, and the folk shunned her for three days, the watered form of a darker rite. Once, she would have been sacrificed to the Sun, but the Romans had come and gone since then, as the Cross-worshippers had come. . .and decidedly not gone, for their strength was growing. So the carline's part had been reduced to that of a kind of scapegoat, here in the east. Far in Britain's west and north, the old customs were still adhered to.

The carline this year was a young girl with a hand-sized purple blotch disfiguring her face. An accursed thing. When he saw it, Felimid guessed the lot had not been as fair as it looked; the black cake had been forced on her in some way.

She was driven counter-sunwise around a fire, and made to leap it, skirts whirling. The bard felt a pang of sympathy for the girl as she ran from the village in a hail of sticks, bones and clods. In three days, she might come back. How she lived in the meantime was up to her. She couldn't hear, but Felimid sang her encouragement none the less.

*"Freedom comes with my Lord the Sun to those who dare
be free,*

As the cold grey grip of winter slackens from earth and tree:
They must freeze or starve no longer, who lack for com-
pany!
The pack's constraint is broken, the wolf runs solitary,
No more to her sleepy cluster clings torpid the amber bee—
Must men continue to huddle? And must it be so for
thee?"

His mouth formed a wry shape. He recognised a certain fatuity
in the question. For most souls, its answer was yes. Himself
included. Although he had more choice than most about where
he huddled, and with whom, his trade was scarcely one that
went with a recluse's habits. Why did he linger here, if not for
company?

The moment's introspection blew away. He whirled into the
May Dance with the villagers, a couple of whom were women
quite pretty enough to interest him. They had eyes for the stranger
bard as well.

The dance took its course. It ended with a score or so of
couples delightedly paired, and scattering for privacy. Felimid
ran up the rolling slopes hand in hand with a jaunty brown girl
who reminded him of Regan. Her eyes darted about for the first
clovery hollow that looked dry. Having found one, they tumbled
into it with no coy looks or abashed mutterings.

Her name was Linnet, for the bird. Her skirt lay entangled with
his doeskin kilt, as if the garments sought to imitate the wearers.
The first pleasure over, she said dreamily, "You're far from home.
You haven't kith or kin. Can you stay?"

"I can, but I'd not wish that on you. An enemy of mine
may be somewhere about. He's a fell one, and if he finds
me he will spare nobody with me. That's the way of it, Linnet."

The pack's constraint is broken, the wolf runs solitary—
She did not believe him. She thought he was inventing lies to
excuse leaving her quickly. But she decided not to tell him so.
What was done at Beltaine had little to do with the rest of the
year.

"What's that?" She asked, suddenly.

Felimid's hand between her shoulder-blades pressed her to the
warm earth. "Stay down," he warned.

They squirmed on their bellies to the lip of the hollow. Ten
riders passed disconcertingly near, with the faint ring of harness
and thud of hooves on turf that Linnet had heard. She whitened

at the sight of then. Even Felimid, more experienced with strange-ness, was taken aback.

Their leader was ordinary enough. Bearded and olive-skinned he was, in baggy trousers, leather boots rich but worn, and a broidered tunic with the threads raveling out. Wealth and posi-tion gone sour in mounted epitome.

The nine on ponies who rode vigilantly behind him were fear-ful. The wind blew from them, Felimid's way; he caught a foul whiff of their short squat bodies. Dish-faced, narrow-eyed and saffron-skinned, they all wore tunics, hats and footgear of greasy leather or fur. One of them, he who rode next to the bearded leader, wore a bright silk kirtle under this leather. Their weapons were recurve bows, short sabres and long lances. The bard had never seen men like them before. He was glad of it.

"They are goblins!" Linnet said. "Goblins out of Annwn—I mean Hell—come to enslave us! Or eat us! Felimid, let's run!"

"Na, the'd see us and ride us down. And goblins they are not, or even half-goblins. I know how such do look. These are men of some kind."

"They look like a murdering kind to me, goblins or not."

"And there I'll never dispute you. Let's lie silent and watch."

She lay low. Not, however, silent. "The one who leads—is he that enemy you spoke of?"

"Na. That one travels unmounted, and unaccompanied. These are all strangers to me."

And if I'm granted my wish they will so remain. But my horse is in yon village, and if I lose him, Tosti's bound to run me down. This is unfair and the gods do not love me.

Linnet went on thinking of the strangers as goblins, no matter what Felimid had said. She tried to squirm into the ground, and prayed that they wouldn't find her.

Although her village was British, it lay in debatable country. Five years earlier, it had paid tribute to King Oisc and called him master, in exchange for peace. That state of affairs could never have lasted. As the incoming Jutes and Saxons moved westward, they'd have burned the village and made thralls of its people, but when a vast combined host under Aelle of the South Saxons had gone down to defeat at Badon, the barbarians' advance had been checked and even turned back. For the present, they were Jutish steadings that vomited fire and sparks at the stars through collapsing roofs. Linnet's village had some while yet to be free, which meant in effect that instead of fearing King Oisc's men solely, it must fear all.

The villagers were running like disturbed ants. Grinning blood-thirstily, one of the squat men reached for his quiver. His leader spoke a sharp command, and with ill grace the fellow let his hand fall—to rest on his sabre-hilt. The ten strangers rode on at the same unhurried pace.

The village gates thudded shut, trapping a few of Linnet's people outside. They tore screaming at the timbers until their hands were bloody, maddened by the conviction that slaughter was upon them. The gates remained shut. The trapped folk cowered from the riders, who ignored them, to their bewilderment but immense relief.

"Let the chief man of this manure heap come to the ramparts and speak!" cried the leader. "*Loquerisme Latine?* It's your honor to receive us as guests for the night! Open your gates and let us in, before I lose patience!"

Felimid had Latin. He didn't much like what he heard. Surely it sounded better than several might-have-beens, but he was not going to consign them to that particular tense just yet. They still ranked as might-bes. Words were cheap.

The village headman thought so too. "We receive no bandits," he quavered. "Go your way, or answer to the justice of Count Artorius!"

Five years before, he'd have said King Oisc. Now he must appeal to the Count of Britain, last symbol of Roman authority, who probably did not know this village existed, and in any case was not within a hundred miles of it.

The leader of the newcomers seemed to know. He leaned back in his grey mare's saddle and roared.

"Bandits? Fool! We're pilgrims, bound upon a holy mission! I am Sergius of Arles, and these men guard my person! Open your gates this instant! If you refuse, they will cut down these folk without, and then fire your roofs with burning arrows. They will scale your puny palisade and kill you all to the youngest child. You think nine men cannot do so much? Let me tell you, these are Bulgars—or, if you do not know that word, Huns! Do you hear? *Huns!* I tell you, they could wipe you out if they were but five! No more foolery. Open your gates at once, or have the truth of my words proved."

The villagers looked at the ten stark riders, istened to their people pleading at the gates, considered the inadequacy of their ramparts, and obeyed.

The ten rode in with a *clip-clop* and jingle. Those outside the walls waited to see if surrender would only bring carnage. It didn't, or not at once. Then they too crept fearfully back. Concealed on the nearby hillside, Felimid recommenced breathing and belted his soft doeskin kilt around him again.

"Come," he said. "We'd better go down."

Linnet hung back. "I'm afraid!"

"That's sense. I'm somewhat afraid myself. But I'd be more afraid to sleep out on these slopes tonight. My enemy may come, and I tell you I'd rather face all ten of yon beauties than he! Besides. . .if he enters your village to find me, they and he may kill each other, and that'd be too wonderful for words. If he doesn't, I've a charm in my harp that may settle them, do they grow restive. And leave them my horse I will not."

Then Linnet went with him, but she shuddered as they passed through the village gates, watched by the slit-eyed Bulgars. They looked even fouler when one was near them. Sparse drooping moustaches they had, and series of crescent-shaped scars along their jaws. Whether they lacked beards because of the scar tissue, or adorned themselves with scars to compensate for having no beards, Felimid didn't care to suppose. But there wasn't a test of eye, ear or nose by which they weren't abominable.

On the other hand, Sergius was handsome. Curling black hair, olive skin, straight nose and full firm mouth all helped make him so, and yet the effect was marred somewhere. To Felimid he looked like a man without imagination or sympathy. Force of character in plenty though. It wouldn't do to underestimate him.

He saw Felimid, and saw that he was armed. Not even to go love-making at Beltaine would Felimid put aside his weapon when he had cause to think Tosti Fenrir's-get might be about. Sergius's eyes narrowed.

"You, there! Surrender your weapon."

The bard turned his head, and looked at two Bulgar bows drawn to the ear. He surrendered his weapon. Sergius examined it thoughtfully, the silver pommel shapen for a cat's head snarlingly a-grin, the staghorn grips incised with a basket-weave pattern so that they would not slip in a sweaty hand, and the downcurved steel hilts adorned with intricate spirals of silver wire. He half drew the blade. Slenderer than most swords of the time (because Kincaid did not need so much weight behind a blow in order to bite), mirror-blue and mirror-shining, it bore inlaid words in strange heathen characters. So Sergius thought of them.

"Where did you steal this?"

As often before, Felimid's tongue betrayed his judgement. "Said the pot to the kettle, how battered and sooty you are."

Sergius backhanded him across the face. Felimid whitened and began to tremble. If Sergius thought about it, he must have believed he saw fear.

"I do not like insolence," Sergius said. "Remember it."

"Great lord," the village head whimpered, "of your mercy—"

"Be quiet, old fool, old satyr. Do you suppose I have no eyes, and didn't see what your rabble were about, as I approached? Pagan rites and ceremonies to the Devil's delight! On my estate in Aquitania, I hang peasants for participating in such things. If you'd have my mercy, speak when spoken to."

The headman louted, and backed away. Three hundred years of the *pax Romana*, and then a century of bloody chaos, had taken the heart to fight from these people the legions had once protected and taxed. The village men had almost thrice the number of Sergius's Bulgars, but could fight them no more than five-and-twenty sheep can battle nine wolves. The bard appreciated it. He knew better than to stand up and urge them to resist. He supposed he was fortunate not to lie pierced by arrows as it was.

One of the Bulgars had already gone looting. He shouted for glee, from the hut that had served to stable Felimid's dun gelding. It reared and stamped as the squat cutthroat led it forth. It didn't like him.

"Yours?" Sergius demanded. "Of course it is. Who in this collection of hovels could own such a beast? The thieving has been good in these parts of late. I can see that."

"Lord," Felimid said, biting back the retort that sprang, leaped, vaulted nigh-irresistibly to mind, "might I ask what brings you here?"

"A holy pilgrimage. Ancestors of mine had lived in Britain from its early days as a province. They were merchants and traders for the most part. Two, brother and sister, followed the Blessed Albanius as his disciples, and like him they became martyrs to the Faith. They were buried in decent fashion at a villa somewhere on these downs, clean against the law of their time, and they have now been recognised as saints of God themselves. It's a great honor for my family. It were a worthy deed to take their bones out of this remote island now perilled by heathens and devils. They can be enshrined with reverence at Arles. I have a little information, and hope that God will guide me."

Story-telling was Felimid's trade. He knew a tale rehearsed and conned by rote when he heard it. That did not necessarily make it a lie; perhaps it was just that Sergius had told it time and again, until it wore ruts in his tongue. But why tell it to the bard at all? Why not say curtly that the reasons were no concern of his? From a man so arbitrary, it seemed the more likely response. Unless it had become habit with him to tell the tale at every opportunity, to promote belief.

If he worked at it so hard, it was bound to be a lie. Felimid did believe he'd come to Britain in search of *something*. His nine killers were to help him guard it, once it was found. . .whatever it was. Not saintly bones, anyhow, and no shrine at Arles would ever receive it.

Nor did Felimid care, save as the quest gave grief to him.

2

Sergius did not trust the bard out of his sight. He judged him rightly for the single man of resource and initiative in the village, and one who might make trouble. He'd have slain him out of hand were the bard not a wanderer, a bringer of news, who had some familiarity with these parts. He might even have heard of the ruined villa Sergius was seeking.

"There are many on these downs," Felimid said. "Kent had more villae than any other part of Britain, once. Where are they now? All burnt or abandoned. Grass grows over the foundations, and Saxon yokels swill hogs nearby. Few traces are left of most of them. Have you no map, lord?"

"No map," the Greek answered tersely. "There used to be one, I believe, but it was lost before I was born. The information I have is written. I hired a rascal in London who was confident that on its basis he could lead me to the very place; over-confident, as it fell out. I became sure after fruitless days that he'd led me too far westward."

"And now it seems you lack a guide."

"I was angered," Sergius said. "I hope the crows get more joy of him than did I. Take notice and beware of lying to me, harper.

"Now. The villa in question was great and prosperous even for Kent, an investor's country estate. He left farming to his tenants. *He* was no British crofter, I'll have you know, but a Roman magnate. There must be more left of his mansion than you have described. Walls partly standing, cellars intact. . .and there was a mosaic pave showing Europa carried off by the bull.

That may have survived. My ancestor's writing shows that it was well laid. *Less than five miles from the road linking Londinium with Noviomagus*—those are his words."

"Then your guide misled you indeed, for it's nearly *ten* miles to the west of that road you are at this moment. Do the writings not give direction?"

"The parchment is old, it has suffered. Words and phrases are illegible."

"And the map is lost? A shame, that," Felimid said, as animatedly as if it mattered to him. "But wouldn't a magnate, a man of business, be choosing to live near London, that was the stomach of all Britain's trade? And is yet, by what I've heard? I'd try further east and north were I you, lord. In what did your ancestors deal?"

"In lead and in shut mouths," Sergius replied. "This is useful, but I had about supposed as much for myself. Is there no more you can tell me?"

Felimid knit his brows, thinking, he was well aware, for his life. If he claimed too little knowledge, Sergius would decide that he was useless; if too much, that he was lying.

Felimid said, "I did pass by such a villa, half a year since, while travelling to Thanet. There were fire-scorched stone walls, half fallen down, and a litter of broken roof-tiles covered the floors. I remember no pave that pictured a bull. By the divisions of the fields, and they still show though they have been fallow a long time, it must have been a great estate, as you say—but I'm thinking it lay too far over eastward."

"You will guide us there and we will look."

"Lord, let it be done. But Kent is held now by the Jutes under King Oisc. They do not love intruders. Even the common folk have spears and axes always ready to hand, and they are hard fighters. Their dogs are savage too."

"I've heard this. But they have had their reverses lately, and they are neither horsemen nor archers. My Bulgars were both from the time they were born—and as for hard fighters, ask them in Thrace! Ask those who man the forts along the Danube!"

A young girl screamed as she ran from behind a hut. A grinning Bulgar caught her, slapped her head back and forth several times with a stone-hard palm, and dragged her towards shadow. Her brother dared object. The Bulgar instantly slid a foot of curved blade up through his viscera, lungs and heart. The youth fell dead. His sister threw herself upon him, her screams rising to an appalling, grief-stricken pitch.

"If you dispute him, he will serve you the same," Sergius told the horrified bard.

"They are a—devout band of pilgrims you lead."

Sergius shrugged. "They are pagan, and the villagers half pagan at least. It matters not what they do to each other. I am come to take sanctity's bones to a proper resting place. Without the Bulgars, I could not have journeyed this far alive."

"Can you trust them not to slay you?" Felimid asked, with a certain hope in his mind.

"They are my sworn men, bound to me by oaths of blood. For a Bulgar, that is an unbreakable claim. I have tested them in other places than this. Nay, they numbered seventeen when we set out, and eight have fallen by the wayside in no idle sense. Those remaining have not wavered."

Loosing a sign, Felimid visibly relaxed. He was unarmed, after all. But in his mind he swore a bloody oath, as the child's screams echoed in the night.

The Bulgars sat around a great scorching fire, now fallen into red embers. It had devoured the village store of fuel, and parts of several huts. An ox the people could not spare had been roasted. The Bulgars' faces shone with grease and contentment. They were in a mood for song. They gave the bard to understand that if he did not please them, perhaps they would roast him too.

Felimid left the fire on the pretext of fetching his harp. It was the opportunity he'd waited for. In the friendly shadows, he gripped the village headman by the arms and said low, "Give the word to your people that they must move away from the fire and stop their ears when I play. As a bard of power, I tell you that if they fail it will be their destruction. But if they do this thing, I'll give them back their village."

He returned to the fire, cradling the harp Golden Singer in his arms. He felt her whispering, soul to soul, and there was a fey look in his green eyes. Yet the question he put to Sergius was commonplace as could be.

"Have they Latin?"

"None of them. Kugal there has foully mangled Greek, but he's the only one—and of their wolf-barking I've a few yelps only."

"Then you will have to give him the gist of it, and he them."

Felimid knew little that could appeal to a bloody-handed Hun, or even what one might call music, but he'd sung of Sigifrid Fafnir's-bane to the Jutes. He knew how the Burgund kingdom had been broken by the huns under Attila, eighty years before, and with that he hoped to tickle their pride. He expanded the story to the conquest of all Germanic tribes, and the breaking of Rome's northern frontiers. (He knew nothing of the Hunnic disasters at Chalons and the Nedao, nor would he have mentioned them.) Kugal unbent sufficiently to nod.

The villagers surreptitiously crept out of sight and hearing, a few at a time.

Now!

The enchanted harp could produce three strains; one for laughter, one for sorrow, and a third for sleep. None of the three could be resisted. He might have harped sleep upon these men, but that had been a gentle kindness he felt in no mood to give; nor was there much laughter in his soul, just then. He sat by the fire, and played sorrow.

It began gently, so gently. The harp-strings uttered a sigh, a melancholy breath of sound. It captivated with sadness, made a man think maudlin thoughts and cherish them. Then, without warning, it gripped hard and held hard, tormenting with anguish. Although Felimid never moved from where he sat, he had gone away somewhere distant and enclosed. He was immune to what he did.

The Bulgars shuddered and knew they were nothing. Their fathers had ridden across the world. From the Caspian to the Baltic the Huns had been absolute masters. What were they now? *Where* were they? That was the dread of it, the mighty and terrible brought down to the same dust as slaves.

Kugal's many victims sobbed and groaned in his head. He was they, they were he. Iron, constricting grief covered him, and despair like a shroud. Beyond thought, beneath manhood, he whimpered on his belly.

Felimid's smile was cruel. He paced around the fire, tearing pain from golden strings. As with Kugal, so it was with the others. Even Sergius ploughed his face through the dirt in slow writhings, and blubbered. His brain shook. His nerves were chilled.

The Bulgars were never out of reach of their weapons. As he walked, Felimid kicked their bows, their quivers, their lances into the shimmering coals. The weapons smoked briefly. Yellow flames sprang to life and began their meal.

The harp-strain never faltered. Sometimes it cried high and sometimes it wept low, and at last it ceased, but it never faltered.

Felimid made one more circuit of the fire. The Bulgars did not resist as he drew their sabres and flung those, too, on the burning pile. The wood and leather of the grips began to char.

away. The blades would be too hot to hold and their temper ruined by the time the Bulgars recovered from their trance of sorrow. Last of all, the bard unbuckled his own stolen weapon from around Sergius's waist. The Greek pawed feebly at him with tear-stained hands.

Sleep, laughter and sorrow. Let them sleep forever; let Arawn laugh when he welcomed them to the House of Cold; let their sorrow be lasting. The villagers would see to them, now that their teeth were drawn.

Felimid saddled and bridled the dun gelding. He no longer wished to stay. His waiting enemy was dreadful, but he was one creature, not a frenzied mob such as the villagers might become when their awe faded somewhat. Their bloodlust could well encompass *all* strangers among them, even—or perhaps especially—their saviour.

And perhaps, after all, Tosti was nowhere about. In three nine-nights there had been no sign of him. Still, the bard drew the sword Kincaid, and rested him across the dun gelding's withers as he rode forth in the empty exhaustion that was the price of magic. The villagers watched him go, the awe of what he'd done clinging to him like a mantle of shadow.

Then they recovered their wits.

Then it was time for hate to run free.

3

A ravening howl broke across the downs. Felimid, two or three miles east of the village by then, felt his skin turn cold and move in ripples on his flesh, despite the balmy night. That was not just any wolf.

Tosti Fenrir's-get was after him.

He did not even attempt to believe he'd heard some ordinary or even natural wolf. His dun gelding, the trained war-horse from King Agloval's stables, snorted with fear at the bare sound and lengthened its stride to run. Felimid drew rein sharply. No use to run. Nothing on four legs could distance a manwolf, or match its endurance.

Felimid tossed up the sword of Ogma in a wheeling flicker of starlight on metal. The weapon turned over, came down, and the staghorn grips fitted neatly into Felimid's palm as he caught it.

Here was their hope. No harp-strain could balk Tosti or stop him—but the silver in the blade made it a potent weapon. The cat's-head pommel was silver, as were the oghams running down the superlatively crafted blade. On one side they said, "*I was made by the hand of Goibniu for the hand of Ogma,*" and on the other, "*See that I slay those who need slaying, ye who wield me.*"

The wolf howled again, mindless eager and far closer. Nothing was left of the man but hate and purpose.

The dun gelding took the bit in its teeth and bolted. This time, Felimid did not try to hold it back. It would rebel, buck and roll in a frenzy to be rid of his constraint and run freely, far away. Like all animals, it could sense magic.

Points of cold fire above, coarse grass below. Thudding roll of hoofs and dim undulation of land eastward. Bunch and desperate stretch of muscle. Hand on sword and endless roving of eyes.

Then Tosti was there, rough-coated, white as bitterest frost, his eyes pale as water in a dish, lambent and hating. His lip wrinkled back from bone-cracking teeth in a mortal, mirthless grin. Loping he came, with a gait that lurched, touching his right fore-paw but lightly to the ground. He was huge; he seemed half as big as the horse. His lame foot did not perceptibly hinder him. He rushed in—

Felimid's bright blade flashed down in all its terror. The wolf slid aside, elusive as marshlights. *Slay! Bite off that hand! Bring down the horse!*

He darted in from behind for a hamstringing bite. Twisting about from the hips, Felimid cut backhand. Again the raw dazzle of metal, more savage to Tosti than any direct gaze of the Sun's eye. He was untouched, but the mere proximity of silver sent a fear through his beast-nerves that he couldn't defy. He melted in retreat for the second time.

And came back.

Again, and again, and again.

The gelding raced, blind in its abysmal terror. Felimid had no concern to spare for it. Nothing mattered but the wolf, the snarling, darting wolf that fell back from his agile weapon-hand time after time, and ever returned. It was the nightmare in which one constantly fends off a thing which cannot be stopped.

When Felimid tried to strike home, the wolf simply wasn't there. Untiring, unrelenting, he bounded in and out, like one of Arawn's annihilating white hounds. His color helped the bard to hold him at bay; he was easy to see—but he moved like a flame, like a shadow, like a ghost that couldn't be touched, and Felimid knew that if his fear-sticken horse fell, or he himself was thrown, it would be the end.

Felimid panted and shuddered with the strain of defence; the wolf was maddened by this endless frustrating of his attacks.

Tear out horse's throat! Thick hot salt blood! Bring down, screaming. . .dog with hurting bright wand of pain. Make him fall!

Craving never fulfilled; madness. The sword of Ogma sprang and whirled in an endless dance; Felimid's hand never slowed, though it was long after midnight, and the stars were paling for dawn. If the wolf did not bring down his enemy soon, sunlight would force him out of the skin. He'd be human then and naked, and unweaponed. *No!* The creature howled a raging protest at the sky.

It lunged for one of the dun's pounding forelegs, to crack it in massive jaws. Felimid's eyes and sword flickered down, but an iron-shod hoof struck first, by blindest chance. The wolf hurtled head over tail. Felimid glimpsed its broken skull. He could have sworn he saw it bound to its feet, shattered skull and all, the brains, bones and scalp mending in instants, flowing together. . .and he must have seen it, because almost immediately the wolf returned. No injury was visible.

When a werwolf is out of the skin, it can be killed by anything that would kill a normal man or woman. When it wears the skin in beastly form, nothing can kill it, except silver.

Felimid cut and stabbed incessantly. Pain was heavy and dull in the marrow, ablaze in every joint of weapon-hand, arm and shoulder. His lungs hurt; his legs ached. Gasping and foam-spattered, the poor brute he rode was near foundering. He'd ridden and swung a brand forever. To no gain at all. And the lightening sky was in front of him.

The monster was herding, driving them eastward; some remnant of human cunning must still inform the beast's brain. They were surely deep in King Oisc's undisputed lands. Felimid seldom hated, but he hated Tosti now, would have killed him at the cost of his own death immediately after.

Where is he? There! Here! Skewer him through! Na, he's out of reach and laughing, laughing, without sound. Have I died? Is this my torment in the House of Cold? Is this Tosti the manwolf, or a hound of Arawn's death-pack?

Because song and verse came almost as naturally to Felimid as breathing, and because he wanted to defy, to course, he rasped a chant against the ubiquitous white form.

> *"The wolf is a hunter deserving of meat;*
> *It fits a poor mongrel to snarl and retreat.*
> *Wolf! Cur! Come lick my feet!*
>
> *"Forage for offal in some broken town,*
> *Or walk as a man and pretend to renown.*
> *Wolf! Cur! Cringe belly down!*
>
> *"Sniff round the hut of some terrified slave,*
> *Bear off a child and think yourself brave!*
> *Wolf! Cur! Tear up a grave!"*

Tosti flashed out of the dark like an arrow, in fury too great for even silver to daunt him. Whether a beast's rage drove him, or the stung pride of King Oisc's warrior henchman, Felimid never knew. With a gasped, exultant cry, Felimid tensed his arm to drive steel down the gaping red throat—and the dun crashed forward, sobbing from broken lungs.

The bard flew over its head, gripping his sword fanatically. Far better to fall on the blade than meet Tosti's rush unarmed. No deliberate thought, but a night-long ferment of rage, fear and hate went into that determination.

The leather bag containing Golden Singer flew elsewhere, cast from his back as he'd been cast from the gelding's. Felimid hit the earth, drawn in on himself with the elasticity of a stoat. The jolt shook his guts and brain, but he rolled somehow, and found himself standing. Instinct had betrayed the wolf; he'd paused to rip out the gelding's throat. The nearest live flesh was the most tempting.

"Come!" Felimid panted. "Come on!"

The beast snarled. Time seemed to waver, to flow sluggish as congealing wax, and the moment in which they faced each other was very long in passing. Jaw dripping red, wrinkled muzzle, with jagged black scars twisting through the white fur, and ice-pale eyes, uncanny in the beast's head, mirrors of a ravening hate: These things the bard saw.

"Come on!" Felimid said again.

Behind him, the sky-rim was lightening. The first sun-ray would flash over it like a hurled spear, at any moment. The wolf paused, wanting in a frustration that maddened to accept the invitation, to spring and tear. But the changing was imminent, the silver shone too brightly. He fled.

Nothing made of natural flesh could have overtaken him. Felimid didn't try. Gone. The wolf had gone, like water vanishing into sea-sand as a wave ebbs. The glorious Sun lifted.

Felimid was unhurt. Bruises, a wrenched muscle in one leg, a sore heel and arm; trifles. As he'd flown out of the saddle, his sword, held point-first in front of him, had sheathed itself in turf at a shallow angle almost to the hilt, and as Felimid had rolled over to come to his feet, the blade had been torn out of the ground again. He'd had exceptional good luck not to sheathe it in his own body.

Limping, he looked for and found the harp, Golden Singer. She hadn't a mark on her. By rights there should have been nothing in the bag but smashed wood and a tangle of shining strings. He shuddered at the thought. Though the harp-bag was supposed to have the power to keep whatever it contained safe from damage, it was a power Felimid preferred not to test.

The horse was well out of any pain. Tosti Fenrir's-get had utterly destroyed its throat, now splintered white bone showing through a wreckage of torn meat. It was not the fall that had broken its neck. Felimid had heard the poor brute scream after it went down; yes, after. A wicked creature, but game; it had deserved better.

He'd been chivvied a long way. Now he stood deep in King Oisc's lands, and with no horse. Tosti was King Oisc's man. He could summon help if he lived to do so, for he'd shed the skin and resumed human form. He must have done. Shapeshifters couldn't run as beasts in daylight—Tosti Fenrir's-get was a man, naked and unarmed, who could not be far distant.

Felimid found the wolf's trail. Before long, the limping quad-rupedal tracks became a man's even stride. A huge man—even naked and unarmed, Tosti was a danger.

Felimid never paused. He remembered those other wolves in Oisc's pit, and the fight in Cerdic's barn. This long night's ride had been only the last of the terrors Tosti had made him endure; the very last, one way or another.

The downs rolled smoothly away, green-gold on the crests, grey-green with shadow in the wide dips between, like an ancient, fertile sea. Native Britons had farmed it for generations, and then it had been taken over for Roman estates. Lately, it had been the first choice of incoming Jutish yeomen. There were no patches of woodland where a man might lose himself, no running streams in sight to wash out his tracks.

A hill rose before him, little but abrupt. Coarse tussocks grew between stones, and boulders crowned it. Tosti's tracks ended at the bottom. He must have mounted the hill from stone to stone, leaping—no other means could fail to leave tracks the bard could see, save sprouting wings to fly.

The blood throbbed in Felimid's heart and brain as he climbed. His gaze roved back and forth after motion, or any color or shape that did not belong. A rabbit bounded away, showing the white under its tail.

Felimid saw something else white. Unlike the rabbit, it stayed motionless, long and wide as a finger on the hill's bouldery crown. A fragment of chalk? A spatter of bird dung? Something about its shade and texture made Felimid think not. A sudden eddy of wind tossed it up, revealing the tail-tip of a wolf's empty skin. Felimid climbed on. Sometimes, he was a very stubborn man.

From the corner of one eye he glimpsed an explosive spring and lift; Tosti, great and sinewy, hurled a heavy rock as a child throws a ball. Felimid jumped like a seared wildcat. The rock grazed his hip, taking away a hand-sized patch of hide and sending him sprawling.

Tosti ripped another sizeable boulder out of the hillside, as if it had been a turnip. Felimid rose, ignoring the pain. Tosti topped him by half a foot, with great lean muscles as hard as ships' cables; the rock he'd plucked up was a yard across, and maybe a foot through the middle. He handled it with terrifying ease. His dreadful face grinned.

Felimid swung his blade at the giant's left wrist, but Tosti turned his rock like a shield. Metal clanged, pale hot sparks jumped, and numbness ran up Felimid's arm to the elbow. Tiny things wriggled on the wet dark underside of the rock. Almost contemptuously, Tosti slung the rock into Felimid's arms. It carried him stumbling backwards and bore him down. Tosti ripped up another, and loomed above Felimid to crush him into the ground.

Felimid did not roll aside. The sword of Ogma whirred in a low scything sweep, and bit into Tosti's leg at the side of the knee. It severed the tendon like seamstress's knife cutting thread. The edge went on through muscle and cartilage, chopping into bone, and that leg collapsed. Tosti went down with the rock still in his hands.

The bard thrust once.

Kincaid's needle point entered Tosti from the right, below the floating rib. It led the way through Tosti's lung, and both edges widened the wound behind it. The windpipe split apart, and the great vessel that left the manwolf's heart. Felimid half turned the blade as he drew it back. Blood and air ran down its grooved channel.

Tosti heard the storm-sound of Wotan's daughters riding. He saw their cold eyes. With his life's blood bursting in his chest like the geysers of Helheim, he shouldn't have been able to speak, but, somehow, he did.

"I curse you," he whispered.

Then he settled and rolled heavily, like a log. A bursting scarlet river ran from his mouth. Felimid seized his drenched beard and cut off his head.

Felimid sat on the stone that had almost crushed him. His forearms rested on his knees, his hands hung slackly from his wrists, and he watched the dead man as he'd done for long minutes. He held his sword-hilt in loosely curled fingers; a sticky redness glued it to his hand. He felt strange, as if sitting some distance away from himself.

I'm alive, he thought. *I'm alive, and Tosti lies there. It's over between us. I can see, and breathe. . .I'll have this day that he would have taken from me. He's dead.*

He'd an odd difficulty believing it. Maybe the huge body would leap up, and replace its head on its shoulders, and fight again. It didn't seem plausible that anything mortal could have finished Tosti Fenrir's-get.

At last he dragged the huge corpse among the boulders, and placed its severed head under one bent knee to keep the ghost from walking. Then he worked hard for an hour to raise a cairn over Tosti's form, ignoring his own pain-racked body. When the stones were heaped high as Felimid's chin, he spread the wolfskin atop them to mark the grave, weighting it down so that the wind would not blow it away. No Jute of Kent who found the cairn could fail to know who and what, lay beneath it.

> *"The maker of corpses, the maker of verse;*
> *You might have done better, I might have fared worse.*
> *Wolf! Man! Sleep with your curse!"*

4

The bard was weary, and slept for some hours. He awoke ravenously hungry, and cut steaks from the dun gelding. Although they were tough, he chewed assiduously, gaining strength from the meat. Then he saw the riders.

For an icy fracturing of time, he thought they were Sergius and his Bulgars. Their number was the same, and they had a martial look. After watching a little longer he knew they were not the same men, and whistled in relief.

Sergius had ridden a grey mare, his greasy killers ponies. These riders bestrode tall powerful war-horses, bigger even than the dun gelding had been. Their casques and mail shirts glittered in the sun. There could not be two war-bands in Britain so mounted and armed. He hoped he was right. They appeared to be following the dead gelding's trail, and he couldn't outrun them.

Before long he faced them, a half circle of horsemen, some of whom he recognised. They were Count Artorius's men; marked by hard fighting and hard sleeping, shields battered, helmets dinted, cloaks rent and stained, smelling of sweat and smoke, they were still the hope of Britain. A kind of glory clung to them.

"Felimid!" Young Gareth of Dun Eiddyn exclaimed, and his elder brother Gaheris echoed him. "What do you here?"

"Yes," their leader agreed. "What do you here; and what in the name of all the saints has been happening to you?"

Him, too, Felimid knew: he'd been a cataphract of the Empire once, and served on the Danube against the Slavs and Huns. An expedition against them had resulted in his capture. Enslaved, he'd been traded down some great German river and become a Saxon thrall. His masters had crossed the Narrow Sea to Britain like many others of their kind, and once there, the thrall from the East had escaped. Now he was a horse-soldier again, fighting for what was left of Rome in this island.

Felimid said, "Good hail, Palamides! I promise you, I've passed such a day and night as you'd scarcely believe!"

Black eyes studied him. "Probably. I can see this; you require a meal in your belly and some rest before you think of talking."

"I've had some rest," Felimid answered, yawning. "I've had a meal, too. . .of sorts. . ." He swayed on his feet. "But true for you, I'd be none the worse for more."

"Then join us."

"I thank you. But tell me first, for the love of the gods, what *do* you here? Were you after searching for me?"

"No, Felimid. I had not thought you were in these parts. The lads and I have been harrying Saxons, and we're soon to rejoin the Count at Verulamium. When Gareth came upon prints of a horse almost as tall as ours, fleeing a wolf huger than it had any right to be—well, then my curiosity would not let me ignore the matter. I might have known the rider would be you!"

Later, over a meal and a fire, the bard told the ten of Sergius, and his evil looking troup. Palamides listened hard, his clean-shaven face pensive, and never interrupted. Nor did he ridicule the bard's claim to have sung ten fierce warriors helpless. He knew that bardic powers were real and had been even greater before the Cross, before the Romans.

"I can tell you the fellow lied to you," he said at last.

"I'd guessed that much." Felimid laughed. "Saints' bones! Garbage! If there ever were martyred saints in that one's family, the rest must have married badly ever since!"

"Oh, most irreverent one, that isn't what I meant. I was thinking of the tale he spun about coming from Arles. He never could have sworn Bulgars to his service so far west. In Thrace perhaps, or on some shore of the Euxine, perhaps in Constantinople itself, but not in Arles. Then why should he say so? Arles or Constantinople, it's all the same to a Briton; the other end of the world."

"Maybe he wasn't knowing that," Gareth suggested, nettled.

"And desired to make the journey he'd taken seem smaller, and so less important? It could be. Felimid. Did he give nothing away?"

"Hmm." Chin on his knees, arms wrapped about his legs, Felimid searched his memory, the trained memory of a bard. "There was one thing. It signified little to me, but the way he said it echoed of some private meaning. I asked him what his ancestors had traded in. He answered, 'In lead and a shut mouth.'"

"Lead and a shut mouth," Palamides repeated. His eyes gleamed suddenly. "By Peter! Did he so?"

"Can you riddle it?" asked the bard.

"I believe I can. More than lead comes out of lead mines. There is silver, too. Britain was a great source of both, mind you, before the legions marched away; I've heard that British silver once supplied the mints of Gaul—and that when the legions left, before it became terribly plain that they'd never come back, many citizens hid their treasure against pirates and rebels in hope of better times. More than one never had a chance to dig it up again, I'll wager. Perhaps some cache of the sort is what this Sergius is hunting for."

"A long journey he's made," Felimid said, "for a table service and maybe a casket of coins."

"Far too long a journey, for that," Palamides agreed. "It must be a greater hoard. Did this Sergius not say to you that his ancestors dealt in lead? He could not resist boasting that they were great magnates, either. What if his family had been lessees of a mine, or more than one? Why, Maximus had his own mint in London when he'd usurped the rule of Britain, not long before the end." Palamides grew excited. "Suppose this family I am hypothecating helped supply the silver, and for all we know, operated the mint! Much could have stuck to their fingers, and they might have amassed even more after the legions left. Suppose they were too greedy, and waited too long, and were forced to flee very quickly, leaving the bulk of their wealth behind? Well hidden, it goes without saying."

The cataphract's teeth glinted in the firelight. "I daresay there is nothing in it, but if it should be true, the Count of Britain can make better use of this treasure than any stranger whose family lived in Britain a hundred years ago."

He might have been a native Briton himself as he uttered the words—the war-band of Count Artorius was a group apart, each man in it sworn to the Count and to Britain, no matter what his origins.

"Sergius will not be needing it," Felimid said darkly. "He's almost surely dead."

The bard was mistaken. Sergius had lived; he'd escaped from Linnet's village with five of his Bulgars. And he was armed; having left his own sword by his horse after robbing Felimid of Kincaid, he regained it later. Kugal too was armed, with his short Hunnic sabre. He'd crawled a little way into the darkness before the bard's music had reduced him to whimpering meat—his other weapons had all been destroyed, but Kugal with a sword was formidable enough. There were no words in any tongue for the way he craved vengeance. The bard had shamed him.

Felimid lay in pleasant unawareness among the Count of Britain's war-men. Sleep beckoned. The bard was awake and thinking, none the less. His eyes shone dimly in the starlight, moving to watch three of the party as they went to stand sentry-go.

This was a strange business. There might be treasure; more likely there was none. Palamides claimed not to believe, but his barely suppressed excitement said differently. He wanted Felimid to take him to the ruined villa the bard had spoken of to Sergius. On the morrow, he'd do that. There was no difficulty, for the place did exist, and it even lay on the way to London, where Felimid wanted to go. It would be interesting, thought the bard, to look for this supposed hoard, and *these* men would not kill him out of hand when he was of no further use in their treasure hunt. Trouble was more likely if by chance some rich treasure *was* found.

Improbable. . .

A wolf's hellish howl echoed shockingly close. The eerie sense of a thing twice experienced, and the blind, terrifying conviction that Tosti had returned, sent shivers up Felimid's spine. A horse screamed in the dark somewhere.

"I curse you," Tosti had said.

The screaming horse galloped blindly into their camp, and four men halted it by main force, clinging to saddle and bridle, dragging its head down.

"Palamides!" yelled the bard. "That is Sergius's grey mare!"

"Come with me!" snapped Palamides. "You, Balin, Kehydi, come along—and bring firebrands! I'll know what's afoot here."

The mare plunged and kicked so wildly that all four men were tested to hold her. Her eyes had become orbs of blood rolling madly in her head. Her ears lay flat back, and foam spattered her from chest to flanks. Her terror was pitiful.

Felimid gripped the sword of Ogma, and ran after Palamides. He moved in a waking nightmare. By rights the nightmare should have been over, but seemingly it was not.

The wolf bayed exultantly to hear them coming. Then his wild lupine joy ceased, as if some sudden hand had forced him into a muzzle. Did he sense the nearness of silver that had slain him once?

Balin discovered something mangled and sodden on the grass, stumbling over it. Torches streaming uncertain red-gold light revealed what was left of a man, but the wolf had vanished. Its victim was Kugal, Sergius's henchman. Although not dead, he was dying quickly. He gurgled a few phrases that had no meaning for his hearers. Even in his death agony he saw that they did not understand, and tried again. Then he died.

"He spoke in Greek," Palamides said.

"Well, and said what?"

"It sounded like—*white wolf, demon!* Odd. The wolf you slew was white."

"It was, indeed," Felimid answered in a strange voice. "Let's return and build up the fire. You will not believe the things I have to tell you."

He was absolutely right.

"It's folly," Palamides said, with the certainty of common sense. "You did not *see* this madman Tosti become a wolf. You saw a wolf, any wolf, that harried you through the night but gave up the chase at dawn. Then you chanced upon Tosti again, wearing a wolfskin—as he's done all the time you have known him!—and slew him. That was well done." *If true.* He did not speak the words, but it was plain he thought them. "It's evident now that *your* wolf lives, and was not one and the same with Tosti. It must be rabid, foaming mad, or it would never behave as it does. We must keep careful watch."

"A white wolf, and it lame of the right fore-foot? A white wolf whose tracks turn to those of a man? That is stretching chance, Palamides. And Kugal named him demon.'

The Thracian's mailed shoulders lifted slightly. For superstition, there was not much to choose between a Hunnic warrior and a Celtic bard—so said his shrug.

Felimid slept not at all for the rest of that night. Snarling wolves with pale eyes prowled ever at the fringes of his vision. Time and again he heard a dying voice say, "I curse you."

With daybreak, they discovered the full carnage that had been done little more than a mile from their camping place. Five men, counting Kugal, lay torn and mangled on the turf. Five sturdy ponies were similarly scattered in grotesque death, the place like a butcher's yard. Something powerful and deadly had run mad there with the lust of slaughter. The stink of black clotted blood hung heavy in the air, and flies were busy.

"It played with them," Gareth muttered. "See? The horses scattered in terror, but it went out after them, herded them back one by one, and tore them apart in sight of their masters. Then it turned on the men. It's not canny.'

"Faugh! No ghost did this."

"True. No ghost that ever I heard of leaves tracks." Felimid pointed to wolf prints. "But these were not made by the same wolf I saw. That one was lame, this one is not. And big as this wolf must have been, the prints of the other were bigger yet. Tosti's dead, and no matter how you disbelieve, I *know* the lame wolf was he. This one has to be different, and yet. . .two wolves, both given to wanton slaughter, both cunning as no right wolf is." Felimid did not know what to think. The detached, insouciant wits that had served him well in other emergencies seemed useless now. "It's beyond me."

Palamides looked at him with irritation and a certain concern. "We're ten armed and armored men of Artorius's war-band. We have nothing to fear from any wolf, natural or demoniacal."

"I hope so," Felimid muttered, not sounding hopeful. "Ha, what's this?"

"Torn clothing."

"It belonged to Sergius. That's one of his boots yonder, I am thinking."

"Then he will be dead. The wolf dragged him off and ate him."

"His garments are shredded apart, but there's no blood upon them."

"Forget it, and all your misgivings," Palamides said decisively. "Think of taking us to the villa Sergius sought. By Peter! These men didn't come so close to us by chance. They must have been searching for the same place as we. Don't question events too closely, Felimid—now you have a horse to replace the one you lost. That ought to please you."

Felimid smile wryly, but he was sore troubled.

5

Long ago, the abandoned villa's roof had fallen in. Time had broken the stone walls almost to the ground; a century's wind and rain, scouring the floors, had sifted weed-grown earth into the corners. Nothing remained of the outbuildings but shallow dimples in the ground where post-holes had been. Stubs of broken pillars and two complete ones outlined three sides of a square, showing where a colonnaded walk around an open courtyard had formerly given shade. Grassy soil in a thin layer had sifted across the courtyard pave itself.

"And fools can say even now that the Empire stands in the West," Palamides muttered bleakly. "Huh! Whatever remains of the western Empire is here in Britain."

Felimid walked about the grassy courtyard, stamping with his heel. "I'm thinking there is laid stone under here," he said. "It's flat as a table, and has the feel. Sergius said something about a pave with a design of Europa and the Bull. Not but that he mayn't have meant the floor of some room, or another villa entirely."

"Spread out and search," Palamides ordered. "Little use to dig before we've some idea of whether this is the right villa."

No floor of the villa's interior rooms bore any such scene. "Let's have this earth spaded away," Palamides said, "and see what we find."

The warriors drew lots for the work. Yellow-haired Kehydi of Demetia lost, and grumbled as he plied the spade. It slid easily between earth and pave, the depthless soil peeling away in unresisting strips, so that the task went quickly.

The stones were cleared at last. They took shelter among the walls from a brief but heavy downpour of rain, and when it was over the courtyard pave had been washed clean. Despite fading and discoloring of the mosaic scene, and the approach of dusk, the outline of a great bull with a naked maiden clinging to his back was distinct.

Palamides's dark eyes gleamed. "I hadn't believed this could truly be the right place, on such meagre knowledge. But we've found it! The right place!"

"That is fine," growled Gaheris of Dun Eiddyn. "Now where do we dig for this wonderful treasure? We don't know where on the estate it was hidden. Are we to probe every foot of those unused fields out there?"

"No need, my unlettered friend," Palamides said amicably. "You forget we have this man Sergius's mare, and with her, her saddle and saddle-pouches. I thought these writings of his ancestor's which led him so far might be within, and so they were. I read some interesting things while the rest of you were watching Kehydi work. . .Hand me the crowbar. With any luck, you are about to see the value of being educated in Adrianople."

Palamides moved back and forth, thumping the bar on the pave. The hollow sound, when it came, was almost the same as the noises elsewhere—but not quite. A febrile anticipation gripped them.

"Is there a cellar below?" Gareth asked.

"Not a cellar," Palamides answered, smashing the bull's hind quarters to shards. "They ripped up the courtyard pave and excavated a makeshift vault beneath. Then they roofed it over with timber, spread new mortar and put down a new mosaic pave." Impatiently, he levered up a couple of the underlying flat stones. "It grows too dark! Make lights, some of you. Let others bring the mattocks and break me this hole wider. By the Passion! If nothing is down there but a cellar full of bones and broken wine-jars, then Satan's own amount of senseless death has gone into finding it!"

Despite his mordant words, he had the treasure-hunter's fever. His lean body had grown tense within his mail. Avidly, he watched the work progress. Even the bard—who, if asked, would have said he cared not if any treasure existed—grew absorbed in the drama. A need to *know* gripped him. Because of it, what happened was partly his own fault.

The werwolf came silently as a ghost, stalking among the ruined walls. The horses raised no panicked warning, for the wind blew from them to him as he advanced. He lusted for warm blood to wash his tongue, living meat to tear. But his vestiges of human cunning told him what must be done first. He rushed across the courtyard without even a snarl to alert the engrossed men.

He sprang. His rough-coated hurtling body slammed Felimid flat to the pave. The bard lifted an arm to ward his throat, but the wolf's fangs were not seeking there. He gripped Felimid's sword-belt, and jerked with preternatural strength. The buckle broke like a tinsel gaud. The belt snapped from around Felimid's body. Young Gareth of Eiddyn lunged with his sword; the werwolf scarcely noticed. With Felimid's scabbard crosswise in his mouth, the creature ran.

. . . Even through the leather-covered wooden sheath, the inlaid silver characters on the blade caused pain. Every tooth in the shapeshifter's jaw was a spike of raw discomfort. Every nerve in his beast-body twitched with horror. Still, he did not drop the thing as he longed to do. Racing through the dusk, he made one more bound, and one more, and still another. Men were contemptible, slow and confused. They could not follow him. Soon he would drop the sword, when he had run so far that none of the men could possibly find it in time. Then he would turn and go back. Soon!

"I ran him through," Gareth was saying, aghast. "I drove this blade from side to side, I swear it! He shook himself free as a dog shakes drops of water, and look! There is no blood!"

"You missed your stroke," Palamides told him, but his conviction was shaken.

"Never!"

"Never, indeed," the bard said sickly. He grabbed the crowbar. "Dig! The beast will return! He's taken Kincaid, the only weapon we had between us that could slay him. Unless we find silver beneath this pave, we are all dead men, I tell you plain. Dig!"

Flat stones and a layer of gravel had been cleared away, baring heavy timbers totted by damp and time. Felimid drove the crowbar into them. Palamides and the others watched as though he'd gone mad.

He levered a big shard of wood from the crack between two planks, rammed the crowbar down, wrenched, twisted, struck, hammered. One of the planks broke. Felimid rained blows on the one beside it. The timbers suddenly slid inward, taking a slippage of gravel and pavestones with them. Crashing sounds came from the hole beneath. The actual mosaic held together without support, a thin crust of delicately patterned fragments over blackness. A few blows of the crowbar smashed it apart, and Europa was legless below the thighs.

"Watch for the wolf," gasped Felimid. He dropped the crowbar clattering down the hole. Then, seizing a torch, he lowered himself after the tool one-handed. He had but a couple more feet to drop, and he released his hold and landed lightly, slipping a little on the fallen rubble.

For a treasure chamber, the place looked inglorious. There were beetles and spiders, a choking musty smell, and great pale curtains of cobweb. They withered away when Felimid touched them with his flaring brand.

Torch gleam rested on an iron pole-ladder. Muscles cracking, he wrestled it into position. Men yelled above him. Louder yet sounded the maddened neighing of war-horses, and over all a heart-freezing howl. Gareth clambered down the ladder. "It's come back," he said unnecessarily, lips pale.

Felimid broke the lid from an iron-bound casket, tucked it under one arm and climbed. His head and shoulders emerged into torchlit chaos. Mail-shirted men struck and hacked with useless swords at a snowy monster which laughed at their efforts. Two had fallen before him. Thick dark streams of blood wandered glistening across the slippery mosaic tiles. Horses stamped and shrieked. The wolf was elusive as running water, implacable as *geas*. He killed again while Felimid watched.

The bard swung the box about his head, spilling the contents widely. Coins rained everywhere, shining in the torchlight, bounding, ringing, rolling. Some struck the wolf's pelt. He spasmed as if stung by wasps. For an instant he stood very still among the detested pieces of silver, trapped and baffled. Then he made a desperate, deadly leap at the bard.

They tumbled into the rude vault together. The wolf voiced an improbably naive yelp of surprise as they fell. They hit bottom with a brutal jolt. Felimid landed atop the beast and heard lupine ribs crack. They knit, healing, even as he moved to clap a wrestling hug around them. Gareth let out a war-yell and swung the torch. Man and man-beast rolled over. Felimid clung madly to the shaggy back, inflicting daggerwounds that did not bleed and closed at once when the stabbing blade was withdrawn.

Gareth dropped his useless sword as the bard struggled, and groping about the floor, he touched a round flat object with its surface figured in relief; a silver table-plate, satisfying heavy. He threw it spinning with all his strength.

It stuck in the monster's hairy side, edge-on between two ribs. He raised a howl of agony that shook the vault. Felimid had lost his dagger; he clung to the wolf's snout with hooked fingers, while his other hand searched blindly for a weapon. His fingers caught a short, chunky ingot.

With desperate strength, he smashed it through the wolf's skull. Into the shallow brain-pan it drove and stuck there, spattering grey, pink and red up his arm. The wolf jerked epileptically, dislodging the thrown plate from his side, and lay feebly twisting like a beheaded snake.

Like a snake, too, he writhed out of his skin.

Dark-haired, olive-skinned, Sergius lay on the blood-stained hide. There was a gash between his ribs, and the chunky silver ingot was driven into the back of his head like a wedge. Felimid turned him over with a foot, breathing harshly, and felt of the wolfskin. It was the same. It had been Tosti's, while the huge Jute had been alive.

"Sergius found Tosti's cairn," the bard said, his eyes locked with Gareth's.

"If he wasn't above robbing graves," Gareth replied, "he got what he deserved."

The torch on the floor guttered out. When Palamides and Gaheris came down the ladder with new ones, they wasted little time assuring themselves the pair were unhurt, and even less marvelling over the transformation of Sergius, for the contents of the vault held them dumb-founded. Not Palamides at his most optimistic had come near the truth.

There was household silver in masses, including plates, trays, candelabra, bowls, wine-cups, sauce-boats and dishes. Tarnished black and draped in cobwebs though they were, the weight and feel of them spoke for their genuineness. There were other caskets of coins, and there had been leather bags, long since rotted away, their contents in piles on the floor, or scattered by the struggle just ended. There were *denarii* of fine and impure metal, worn clipped siliquae, Treviri coins from Gaul, and great numbers bearing the head and name of Magnus Maximus. There were stacks of flattish or chunky ingots, some stamped with marks of authority, others more crudely moulded and bearing no mark, doubtless cupellated on the sly and smuggled to this estate. Someone had thought to make a profit out of the final confusion in the province. It was not a king's ransom, because no king in Britain could have paid it.

"I was wrong to think you superstitious when you warned me of the manwolf," Palamides remarked later, "but it seems you were wrong to believe the manwolf was Tosti Fenrir's-get."

"Not so," the bard contradicted. "Until two nights since, the manwolf was Tosti. He came from his mother's womb as a wolf cub, they say, but he could shed the skin or assume it as he pleased, as long as he did it by night. Because I knew the story, I dared not bury the skin with him. I spread it atop his cairn instead, and then Sergius came by—and stole it." With a faint thickening of blood Felimid thought again of Tosti's curse. Such things are potent in the West. "I hazard he slept with it by him last night—no, the night before that—and the curse of the wolf descended on *him*. He became a beast and savaged his own men; then he trailed us, to gain the silver or to be sure it stayed hidden forever, who knows? He's dead now and cannot tell us. As for the skin—" Felimid built a fire and flung it in. "I ought to have done this when I first had the chance."

The wolfskin moved, squirmed, then flapped like a rag in a gale. Felimid pinned it down among the flames with the crowbar, and endured the stink while it burned.

In the morning, he found Kincaid where the wolf had dropped him, a dazzle of sunlight on pommel and belt-buckle signalling where he lay. The sword hadn't been carried far.

For his share of the treasure, Felimid clenched both his fists full of silver coins and was content. "I must travel light and fast," he told them, "and I'm bound homeward, to Ireland."

"Not immediately, I fear."

Mild though it was, the Thracian's tone halted Felimid in his tracks. "What's this?"

Palamides gestured at the courtyard pave, which his men had restored as best they could, to cover the vault again. They had even replaced the strips of turf Kehydi had removed.

"We cannot bear the tenth part of that treasure away with us. It must remain until Artorius is told, and can send a strong force to get it. We here are the only ones who know it exists—at present. We stay together until it is safe in the Count's war-chests. That means riding to Verulamium."

"Verulamium? Away north of the Thames, north of London?"

"It's no such cause for dismay," Palamides said, smiling faintly. "One can ride from Verulamium to the coast with ease in less than a day, and thence take ship'round to your own country."

"Palamides, please understand. I must leave Britain at once. There are friends of mine who will suffer greatly if it becomes known that I live. I've had setbacks and changes of plan enough now."

"Then I'm sorry to present you with another, but you need not fret. I'm as fixed upon keeping this business secret as you are. Ride with us hooded and cloaked so that none will recognise you, if you wish. I'd rather you did. You haven't been to Verulamium? It's a deserted, abandoned city like many another; the Count has made it his base for this summer's work. There'll be no difficulty finding you decent quarters, even luxurious ones, where you can bide unnoticed. You needn't so much as set foot outside them if you don't wish to."

"You'd prefer that, too," Felimid said slowly.

"Be reasonable! Felimid, you showed three years ago that you understand what the Count is doing. You know what this hoard will mean; money to pay armorers, to pasture the horses, to buy supplies, gifts to smooth over differences between bickering kings and princes who seem determined to let the sea-wolves have Britain! And it's here, in Kent! Do you wonder that I dare not take the slightest chance? King Oisc would have an army here within three days, if he knew!"

"I'm not likely to tell him. He'd kill me on sight."

"All right. Forgive me, but you might tell someone else, and seek to ransack this place before us. Once you were at large you'd find any number of greedy rascals eager to listen to a story of treasure. Why, now that I think of it, I hardly trust myself."

The bard said explosively, "Your brains have rotted! Tell anybody else, I? And be killed once I'd led them here, as Sergius would have killed me? I'm a bard, man! I shall go home to Ireland and I shall be wealthy there! *Come back to this loathly slaughteryard?* I'll never set foot in the kingdom of Kent again as long as free choice is mine!"

Palamides, the saturnine and aloof, burst into unfeigned laughter. "By Peter, what a flow of speech! My friend, you've convinced me and won me quite—but I must have your company on the road to Verulamium, none the less. My duty demands it." His laughter ended; iron rang in his voice. "And we will forgo the delights of your music on the way."

Swiftly, he caught the harp Golden Singer from where she lay among Felimid's gear. Handing her to Gareth, he said in the tone of a soldier giving orders to a soldier, "Hold this in safety for him."

For all his vehement protests, Felimid had known in his heart that he would let Palamides persuade him, that he would acquiesce in the end and ride to Verulamium. . .until now. He whitened with anger.

"Never touch the harp of a bard," he said with quiet menace.

"Easy, Felimid. You cannot fight seven seasoned war-men, all in mail. Even if we be all friends here."

Sighing, the bard relaxed. His hand had been at his sword-hilt, unwilled by him. "Do I look so foolish as to try?"

"For an instant there, you did."

The bard grew thoughtful. No. He couldn't fight seven men in mail and full battle-gear, and he in mere cloth—but his battle instincts had not assessed it that way. His instincts had cried that there was only Palamides to deal with. He saddled the grey mare and tied his few belongings in a neat bundle behind the saddle.

In a way, it was true. Palamides was no a Celt. Felimid and the others were. The Thracian's men came from the west and north of Britain, where Roman values were superficial at best; they did not think of themselves as soldiers in the Roman sense so much as warriors of one man's personal war-band. They valued personal honor and individual whim more than discipline. And of course they reverenced bards as the sons of Erin did. Maybe Palamides had never really understood that.

Over the grey mare's back, Felimid caught Gareth's eye, and held it—unconsciously assuming the almost regal pose his bardic powers entitled him to. They mounted to ride. Directly he was in the saddle, Felimid held out his hand confidently toward Gareth. Gareth handed him the harp, without hesitation. Felimid caught the harp-bag's broad strap and settled it in its accustomed place on his back.

"Farewell, Palamides!" he smiled, and kicked the grey mare to a gallop.

There was hot panting pursuit that breathed after him—

Palamides in a transport of fury, riding a war-horse bred for weight and power, not speed. Felimid had neither mail nor casque nor shield nor lance to cumber him; the bard rode lightly as thistledown, singing to the bright, clear sky.

Before very long, Palamides realised how useless it was to follow; seething, he turned for Verulamium instead. When he arrived, he would wax passionate, no doubt, in his denunciation of Gareth's irresponsibility, but Gareth would bear his punishment with a carefree heart, his honor untainted. When the Thracian returned with a strong force to bear the great cache of silver away, he would find it untouched. Felimid's claim that he wasn't interested in the wealth of kings had been the truth. The wealth of a bard was in the harp on his back, in the magic of his song, and in the honor that his own people held him in.

Felimid settled his horse to an easy walk on the road to the coast, free at last of nightmares of werwolves and Jutish halls, of dark forests and dark magics. The world lay before him, and he could think of nothing more he wanted than that. He was a bard after all, Felimid mac Fal of Erin, a poet and a wanderer—and he had never really wanted to be a warrior.

JAUFRY THE KNIGHT AND THE FAIR BRUNISSENDE
Rendered into English by Alfred Elwes

During the twelfth and thirteenth centuries minstrels and troubadours spread tales of Arthur and his knights throughout Europe. His exploits became merged with local folklore and a wild hotch-potch of adventures resulted. Most of the tales were perpetuated by chroniclers and romancers and found their way into Malory's Morte d'Arthur, but not all. The following tale of Sir Jaufry and Brunissende had lain forgotten for six hundred years until unearthed from the French Imperial Library by Jean-Bernard Lafon (1812–84). The original had been written down by an unknown Provençal troubadour when he heard the tale told at the court of King Pedro II of Aragon who reigned from 1196 to 1213. It was first translated into English by Alfred Elwes in 1856. There was a subsequent printing with engravings by Gustav Doré in 1868, but apart from a new translation in the United States in 1935 and a recent reprinting of the Elwes text in America in 1979 the work has been largely overlooked and has been unavailable in Britain for over a century. Jaufry, incidentally, does appear briefly in Malory as Sir Griflet in Book I, but

there he is a hotheaded youth. If you have ever
wondered what became of him, read on.

The Adventure of the Forest

'T was on the day of Pentecost, a feast which to Carlisle had
      drawn a host of knights, that Arthur, King of Briton's isle,
his crown placed on his brows, and to the old monastic church
proceeded to hear mass. And with him went a brilliant train, the
Knights of the Round Table. There were Sir Gawain, Lancelot du
Lac, Tristrem, and Ivan bold, Eric frank of heart, and Quex the
seneschal, Percival and Calogrant, Cliges the worthy, Coedis the
handsome knight, and Caravis short i' the arm; the whole of his
bright court, indeed, was there, and many more whose names I
have forgot.

When mass was done, they to the palace home returned 'mid
laughter and loud noise, the thoughts of each on pleasure only
bent. Each on arrival gave his humour play. Some spoke of love
and some of chivalry; and some of ventures they were going to
seek. Quex at this moment came into the hall, holding a branch of
apple in his hand. All made room for him; for there were few who
did not fear his tongue and the hard words which it was wont to
utter. This baron bold held nothing in respect. E'en of the best he
ever said the worst. But this apart, he was a brave stout knight, in
council sage, a valiant man of war, and lord of lineage high; but
this, his humour and his biting words, took from him much that
was of right his due.

He, going straightway to the king, thus said:

"Sire, an it please you, it is time to dine."

"Quex," replied Arthur, in an angry tone, "sure thou wast born
but to awake my wrath, and out of season ever to discourse. Have
I not told thee, ay, a thousand times, naught should induce me to
partake of food, when thus my court had met, till some adventure
had turned up, some knight were vanquished, or some maid set
free? Go sit thee down at bottom of the hall."

Quex went without a word among that joyous throng, where
men of all conditions, knights and lords, minstrels and moun-
tebanks, ceased not their tricks, their gay discourse, their laughter, till the hour of noon. At noon, King Arthur called Sir Gawain,
and thus spoke:

"Fair nephew, cause our chargers to be brought; for since

adventure cometh not to us, we must fain seek it in the open field; for should we longer stay, our knights, indeed, would have a right to think that it were time to dine."

"Your will, my lord," Sir Gawain said, "shall be obeyed."

And at the instant he the squires bade to saddle horses and their armour bring. Soon were the steeds prepared, the nobles armed. The king then girded on his famous sword, and at the head of his bold barons placed, set out for Bressiland, a gloomy wood. Having along its deep and shady paths awhile proceeded, the good king drew rein, and 'mid the greatest silence bent his ear. A distant voice was then distinctly heard, calling at intervals for human help, and turn by turn invoking God and saints!

"I will ride yonder," bold King Arthur cried; "but with no company save my good sword.'

"An it please you, my lord," Sir Gawain said, "I fain would ride with you."

"Not so, fair nephew," the king made reply; "I need no company."

"Since such your wish," said Gawain, "have your will."

Arthur called quickly for his shield and lance, and spurred right eagerly towards the spot whence came the plaintive voice. As he drew near, the cries the sharper grew. The king pricked on with greater speed, and stopped before a stream by which a mill was placed. Just at the door he saw a woman stand, who wept, and screamed, and wrung her trembling hands, while she her tresses tore in deep despair. The good king, moved to pity, asked her why she grieved.

"My lord," she weepingly replied, "oh! help me in God's name! a dreadful beast, come down from yonder mount, is there within devouring all my corn!"

Arthur approached, and saw the savage beast, which truly was most frightful to behold.

Larger than the largest bull, it had a coat of long and russet fur, a whitish neck and head, which bristled with a pile of horns. Its eyes were large and round, its teeth of monstrous size; its jaws were shapeless, legs of massive build; its feet were broad and square. A giant elk were not of greater bulk. Arthur observed it for a certain time with wonder in his mind; crossing himself, he then got off his horse, drew forth his sword, and, covered with his shield, went straight into the mill. The beast, however, far from being scared, did not so much as even raise its head, but from the hopper still devoured the corn. Seeing it motionless, the king believed the beast was lack of spirit, and, to excite it, struck it on the back: but still the creature moved not. He then advanced, and standing right in front, lunged at the beast as though to run it through. It did not even seem to note the act. Arthur then cautiously laid down his shield, replaced his sword, and, being stout and strong, he seized it by the horns, and shook it with great force; natheless he could not make it leave the grain.

In rage, he was about to raise his fist, so as to deal it on the head a blow; but lo! he could not then remove his hands—they were as riveted unto its horns.

Soon as the beast perceived its foe was caught, it raised its head, and issued from the mill, bearing, pendant from its horns, the king, aghast, distracted, and yet wild with rage. It then regained the wood at easy pace; when Gawain, who, by good fortune, happed to ride before his friends, beheld it thus his uncle carrying off—a sight which half-deprived him of his wits.

"Knights!" he exclaimed aloud, "hie hither! help to our good lord! and may the laggard never sit at his Round Table more! We should indeed deserve dishonoured names were the king lost for want of timely aid."

As thus he spoke, he flew towards the beast, not waiting for the rest, and couched his lance as though to strike at it.

But the king, fearing harm would come to him, addressed him thus:

"Fair nephew, thanks; but e'en for my sake halt. If thou do touch it, I am surely lost; and if thou spare it, saved. I might have slain it, and yet did not so; something now tells me I held not my hand in vain. Let it, then, go its course; and keep my men from coming on too near."

"My lord," Sir Gawain answered him with tears, "must I, then, let you perish without help?"

"The best of help," the king rejoined, "will be to do my bidding."

Sir Gawain was at this so much incensed, he cast down lance and shield, he tore his cloak and handfuls from his hair.

Just at this time Ivan and Tristrem came, with lances lowered, and at top of speed; Gawain threw up his hands, and loudly cried:

"Strike not, my lords, for his, King Arthur's sake; he's a dead man if you but touch the beast."

"What, then, are we to do?" inquired they.

"We'll follow it," quoth Gawain: "if the king be hurt, the beast shall die."

The monster still kept on its even way, not seeming to remark the knights, until a rock it reached, lofty and round and high. It scaled it, as a swallow, rapidly; and Gawain and his friends, who at a distance followed, sad and full of thought, saw it, when thus the summit was attained, crawl straight towards a peak which overhung. There, stretching out its head, it held the king suspended o'er the abyss. Judge the alarm of Gawain and his friends, who each beside was almost wild with rage! Hearing their cries, they who remained behind came up full spur, and reached the lofty rock, where at the summit, they beheld the king hanging thus helpless from the monster's horns. They then gave loose to the most doleful cries that ever had been heard. I cannot picture to you their despair. Brave knights and pages then you might have seen tearing their hair and rending their attire, that wood reviling and the strange adventure which they had come to seek. And Quex exclaimed, by way of final stroke:

"Alas! fair chivalry, how hard thy lot! this day to cause the death of our good king, and lose thy valour when 'twas needed most!"

Saying these words he sank upon the ground. The king, however, still remained suspended in mid air, the beast meanwhile not offering to stir. The monarch feared to drop in that abyss; and in low voice he prayed the saints and God to save him from this pass. Then Gawain, Tristrem, and I know not who beside, took counsel how they might heap up their robes, so as to break the brave King Arthur's fall. Gawain had scarce proposed it to the crowd than each one doffed his garments speedily.

In haste they brought their cloaks and mantles gay; stripped off with eagerness their doublets, hose; and in an instant every knight was bare: such was the heap of garments 'neath that rock, the king had fallen without deadly risk. When this the beast beheld, it stirred as though it would draw back, and slightly its head. The crowd below, alarmed, at once upraised a cry; and on their bended knees prayed Heaven to guard the king, and bear him safe and sound. The beast with mighty spring then leaped below; and setting Arthur free, itself it changed into a handsome knight, in scarlet richly clad from head to heel. This noble bent his knee before the king, and smiling said:

"My liege, command your men their garments to resume; they now may dine in peace; though somewhat late, the adventure has been found."

Arthur amazed, nay, half-distraught at this adventure strange, now recognised the knight,—a courtly guest, esteemed among the brave, the courteous and the sage.

Adroit in arms, gay, graceful, and beloved; among the first in strife, yet kind and modest, too—this lord was master of the seven arts, and in all spells was versed. For some time past, between him and the king a compact stood, whereby it was agreed, if he himself transformed when all the court was met, he should as guerdon three good gifts receive—a cup of gold, a charger of great price, and from the fairest damsel a sweet kiss.

Gawain at once ran up, fearing his uncle in his fall was crushed; and you may safely judge of his surprise—finding him thus in high good humour, stand loud laughing with the beast.

"In faith, fair friend," quoth he, "you can indeed enchant poor folks, and force even barons to throw off their clothes."

"You may resume them, good my lord," said the enchanter in the same gay tone; "for lo! the king no longer needs their use."

They did indeed soon put them on again, nor stayed to pick or choose; the court at once returned to fair Carlisle, the monarch and Sir Gawain riding on ahead. The palace-walls soon echoed with their joy. The pages brought them wherewithal to wash, and soon the knights were placed about the board. Grand was that court, and rich and brave and good; many a puissant name, full many a king, and many a duke and count, were seated there. Gawain the valiant knight, and Ivan the well-bred, each holding the queen's arm, then led her in, where, at the table, sat she 'neath the king. Gawain then placed himself the other side, and Ivan by the queen: at once with laughter they began to tell of the enchanter's skill; and when Queen Guenever, and they, the knights who were not in the wood, had learned the doings there, they were indeed surprised; and soon loud laughed and chatted with the rest. Meanwhile Sir Quex before the king and fair Queen Guenever the golden dishes placed; he then sat down to eat his own good meal, for he did boast a famous appetite, while ready pages served the other knights. Nothing was wanting at that banquet high: the roebuck, kid, and succulent wild-boar; the crane, the bustard, capons, swans, wild-geese; peacocks, and fine fat hens and partridges; white bread and purest wine—of all good things the best was there beheld. Served by a host of graceful youths beside, the guests did honour to the feast.

Eating and drinking then engaged each thought; when straight there entered, mounting a fleet horse, with spotted robe, a youthful squire, tall and of noble mien. Never, do I believe, was man more finely-shaped. His shoulders were at least two cubits broad, his features regular, his eyes were sparkling, full of love and mirth; his hair was shining as the brightest gold, his arms were large and square, his teeth as ivory white. His frame, which tapered at the waist, was well developed, and displayed his strength. His legs were long and straight, and feet high-arched. His violet and well-cut robe rested in graceful folds on hose of the same hue. A garland of fresh flowers crowned his brows, to which the sun had given a deeper tint, heightening the colour of his ruddy cheeks.

Entering the hall, he alighted from his horse, and came with quick and joyous step to kneel at the good monarch's feet. He then his purpose opened with these words:

"May He who made this world and all it holds— He who no suzerain hath—now save the king, and all that's his!"

"Friend," replied Arthur, "thank thee for those words; if thou dost seek a boon, it shall be thine."

"My liege, I am a squire, come from far unto your court, because I knew so doing I should meet the best of kings; and I conjure you for St. Mary's sake, if you so please, to arm me now a knight."

"Friend," said the king, "arise, and take thy seat; it shall be done thee even as thou wilt."

"Never, my liege, if you permit, will I uprise from hence till you have granted me the boon I ask."

"It is conceded," then exclaimed the king.

The squire arose as these fair words were said, and went to take his place at that rich board. But scarcely was this done, than lo! the guests beheld a knight, well armed, and on a charger fleet, come riding in. Crossing the hall, he with his lance did strike a lord upon the breast, and stretched him dying just before the queen. He then rode out, exclaiming as he went:

"This have I done to shame thee, wicked king. If it do grieve thee, and thy boasted knights should care to follow, I am Taulat Lord of Rugimon; and each passing year, on this same day, will I return to do thee the like scorn."

Good Arthur drooped his head, enraged, yet sad; but then the squire rose, and knelt before the king:

"Sire," he said, "now give me knightly arms, that I may follow up that haughty lord who casts dishonour on this royal court."

"Friend," exclaimed Quex at this, "your courage will be higher when you're drunk. Sit yourself down again, and drink another bout; the heart will be the merrier, and you can better floor a knight with wine than with a sharp-edged sword, however stout!"

The squire to this responded not a word, out of his duty for the worthy king; but for such cause, Quex had for his speech paid dear. Arthur, however, gave his anger vent, and thus exclaimed:

"Wilt thou, then, Quex, ne'er hold that biting tongue until I've driven thee from out my court? What has emboldened thee to speak thus vilely, and to a stranger who a suit prefers? Canst thou not keep within thee all the spite, the envy, wicked words, and slanderous thoughts with which thou art swelling o'er?"

"My lord," the squire said, "pray let him have his say; little heed I the flings of his forked tongue, for which I will a noble vengeance seek. Vile word ne'er sullieth honour. Let me rather have a suit of arms, to follow him who now has issued hence; for I do feel I shall not eat at ease till he and I have met in deadly fight."

The monarch courteously replied:

"My friend, I willingly will give thee steed, good arms, and knightly spurs; for thou dost ask these gifts as squire of gentle birth. But thou art all too young to fight with him who now has left this hall. Not four among the knights of my Round Table can dare to meet his blows, or touch him in the field. Leave, then, this care to others; I should grieve to lose at once so stout and brave a squire."

"Since, sire, you think me stout, and call me brave, 'tis wrongfully or but to jeer you wish to stay my fighting; but in that you'll not succeed save you refuse to grant the boon erewhile you promised me: and should a king forget his promise made, gone are his lustre and his courtesy."

The monarch answered:

"Friend, I yield me to thy ardent wish; thou shalt be armed a knight."

He then commanded two attendant squires at once go seek his armour, lance, a fine and tempered shield, the casque, the sharp-edged sword, the spurs, and horse of price in full caparison; then, when they brought the arms and horse, he caused the squire to put the hauberk on, he buckled his right spur, girded his sword upon the youth's left flank, and having kissed him gently on the mouth, he asked of him his name.

"Sire, in the land where I was born my name is Jaufry, son of Dovon."

The king, on hearing speak thus, sighed heavily, and said, while tears were in his eye:

"Ah! what a knight and lord of mark was this same Dovon! He was of my table and my court. A brave knight and a learned: never had he superior in arms. None were held stouter or more dread in fight. May God, if he so will it, grant him grace; since for my sake he died! An archer pierced his heart with a steel bolt, while he a keep held out on my domain in Normandy."

Meanwhile a squire brought Jaufry a bay steed. The young

knight placed his hand upon the bow, and leaped upon the horse, all armed as he then stood, without the use of stirrup; then called he for his shield and lance, consigned the king to God, and having taken leave of all the rest, he galloped from that hall.

Estout de Verfeil

The charger, which was fleet and fair to view, started off like an arrow from its bow. So that, as Jaufry left the castle-gates, he hoped he yet should overtake the knight; and therefore cried aloud to two men on the way:

"Good fellows, if you can, tell me the road just taken by the lord who left the castle yonder even now. If naught prevent you, point me out the way."

One of those men replied:

"Speak you of him whose armour was so bright?"

"The same," quoth Jaufry.

"He is on before; you start too late, sir knight, to catch him up."

"By Heaven!" murmured Jaufry, much aggrieved, "he cannot flee so far, or sink so deep, but I will reach him. I'll seek him the world through, where land and sea are found, and will discover his retreat even beneath the earth!"

This said, he held his course; and spurring, came to a broad causeway where fresh prints of horse's hoofs appeared upon the dust.

"Methinks," said Jaufry, "that a knight erewhile hath passed this way: so I will follow up this selfsame road while thus the trail is seen."

Putting his horse into an ambling pace, he rode on all that day without a town or castle being met. At eventide he still continued on, when a loud cry, followed by a din of arms and clash of steel on helm, suddenly rose from out the heavy shade.

Jaufry spurred readily towards the spot, and cried:

"Who are ye, lords, who at this hour do fight? Reply, since eyes of man cannot behold you."

But no one replied; and when, as fits a bold and venturous man, he reached the place whence came the clashing noise, the fight was over and the din had ceased. Whilst then he listened, seeing naught, and at the silence wondering, there rose from out the shade deep sighs and moans; when, stooping forward, he made out a knight so sadly hurt the soil was bathed in blood.

"Knight," he exclaimed, "speak, and inform me for what, and by whom, thou hast been so sorely used."

The wounded man could not e'en stir his lips or move a limb; his arms grew stiff; and, with two fearful groans, he yielded up the ghost.

"Knight," then cried Jaufry to the corpse, "it grieves me not to know thy slayer, or whether thou wert wrong or whether right: thou now art dead; but if I can, I even will learn why and by whose hand."

He then departed and resumed his way, now on the trot and now at ambling pace, stopping at intervals to bend his ear and give a look around. For some time, nothing met his ear or eye; but, after having ridden for a space, a noise of battle once again assailed him. Steel, wood, and iron met with such dread force, it seemed as though the thunder vexed the air, and that this din proclaimed the bursting storm. At once, then, to the side from whence it came Sir Jaufry turned his horse; and, with his shield about his neck, his lance in rest prepared, he spurred with ardour on, for, in his mood, it seemed as though he ne'er should learn who slew the knight and who were they that fought. On, then, to that affray he hotly came; but to behold, stretched stiff upon the ground, a knight all armed, whose casque and head beside had by a single blow been cloven to the teeth, while his steel hauberk was all red with gore. Jaufry his visor raised, and touched him with his lance; but, seeing no life was there, exclaimed with grief:

"Heaven! shall I, then, never know whose hand hath slain these knights?"

Full of impatience, he resumed his course; and when he far had ridden, lit upon another knight, whose body was so shattered with his hurts that blood and life were oozing fast away. Moved deeply at his cries and sad laments, Jaufry drew near, and kindly asked what hand had dealt such measure to himself and the two others slain, and which side was moreover in the wrong?

"Alas!" the wounded man made answer with a sigh, "I will explain to you the simple truth. It is Estout, the master of Verfeil, who has reduced us to the state you see, to feed his pride. This knight is known so quarrelsome and fierce, that without mercy and without a cause he doth assault all comers far and near."

"Tell me," said Jaufry, "was he wrong in this?"

"I will, my lord, with Heaven's help, and that without e'en lying by a word. I and my friends were going to our rest, when Estout to my castlegates hard by, rode up, and bade us high defiance. Had it been day, we should have tarried long ere venturing forth;

for we did know him master of such skill, that few as yet could e'er make head against him—so merciless beside, as never in his lifetime ever known to grant his foeman grace: seeing him not, the bridge was lowered, and at once was passed. He, having drawn us far upon the road—the better for the treacherous ends he had—suddenly stopped, and turning, with lance couched, on him who pressed him nearest, stretched him dead upon the earth.

"By this time we had recognised Estout, and turned our horses' heads; but he with threatening words pursued us close, and reaching my companion, slew him with a blow. He then his rage concentrated on me, and with such fierceness, thinking my end come, I missed my aim, the lance just glancing from his shield; but he with one stroke bore me from my horse, and three times struck me as I helpless lay, so that, good faith, he little life hath left. This, my good lord, is how the thing hath happed."

"Know you," asked Jaufry, full of thought, "the road he took, and where he may be met?"

"My lord, I cannot tell; but little do I doubt that you will find him earlier than you wish. Haste, then, to fly such presence; for believe, you cannot gain thereby aught else but iron: an you take my advice, you'll change your route."

"Change my route, say ye?" quoth Sir Jaufry; "no, by my troth; nay more, I will but follow him the closer up; and, should I catch this lord, we part not, he may rest assured, without a struggle; and without learning, too, which of us twain doth bear the stouter heart, the stronger arm, or wield the better sword."

He took his leave, with these words, of the knight; the latter prayed him to pass by his keep and send him aid from thence.

"I will not fail," said Jaufry.

Towards the manor of the dying man he took his way, and after some brief space he saw high towers and two squires well armed, who mounted guard before a raised drawbridge.

"Friends," he exclaimed to them, "God save you both!"

"And you, my lord, from every harm," they said.

"I have sad message for you," added Jaufry, "and bad news. Your lord is lying yonder sorely hurt; and his two comrades are both slain. Estout de Verfeil has misused them thus. So hasten to your lord, who wants your help."

He then commended them to God, and parted in all haste. Jaufry resumed his way, now trotting hard and now at ambling pace, until he reached a valley deep and dark. There he beheld the blaze of a great fire, round which were met a numerous company. Trusting he might get tidings there of Estout and of

Taulat—for truly counted he on fighting both—he straightway rode to where the fire was, and found there figures that awaked surprise. Lords in rich vestments roasted a wild-boar; meanwhile, by dwarfs, stunted and out of shape, the spit was turned.

"Good sirs," said Jaufry civilly, "could I but learn from some of you where I may meet a lord I have followed this night through?"

"Friend," exclaimed one, in answer, "it may be we can tell you when we know his name."

"I seek," said Jaufry, "Estout de Verfeil, and Taulat, called the Lord of Rugimon."

"Friend," said the knight, with courtesy, "from hence depart, and that with greatest speed; for should Estout but chance to meet you here thus armed, I would not give a denier for your life. He is so valiant and so stout of limb, that never yet hath he encountered foe who could make head against him. All these you see around are knights of proof, and can meet sturdy blows; natheless he hath subdued us all, and we are forced to follow him on foot wherever choice or venture leads him on. We're now engaged preparing him his food; so I advise you to depart at once."

"Not so, indeed," said Jaufry; "I came not here to flee. Before I turn my face, my shield shall be destroyed, my hauberk riven, and my arm so bruised it cannot wield a blade."

Whilst thus they held discourse, behold Estout arrived full spur, and, at the sight of Jaufry, cried aloud:

"Who art thou, vassal, who thus dar'st to come and meddle with my men?"

"And who are you," said Jaufry in reply, "who use such pleasant words?"

"Thou shalt know that anon."

"Are you Estout?"

"I am, indeed."

"Full long have I been seeking you throughout this weary night, without e'er stopping in my course or closing eye."

"And for what end hast thou sought me out?"

"For that I wish to know why thou hast slain the three knights on the road; which act I take to be a sin and wrong."

"And is it for this that thou art hither come? Thou wouldst have better done to stay behind, for to thy ruin do I meet thee here; thou shalt this instant lose that head of thine, or follow me on foot like yonder knights who patter humbly at my horse's heels. Deliver, therefore, up to me thy shield, thy breast plate, and they sword, and the bay horse that brought thy body here."

"My care shall be to guard them with my life," quoth Jaufry. "'Twas the good king bestowed this courser on me when he armed me knight. As to the shield, thou shalt not have it whole; nor e'en the hauberk, without rent or stain. Thou tak'st me for a child, whom thy poor threats can frighten: the shield, the hauberk, and the horse are not yet thine; but if they please thee, try a bout to win them. As to thy threats, I scorn them: 'threats,' saith the proverb, 'often cover fear.'"

Estout drew off his horse at these bold words, and Jaufry nerved him to sustain the shock; then ran they at each other with their utmost speed. Estout struck Jaufry on the shield's bright boss, and with such mighty strength, that through the riven metal went the lance, breaking the mail which guarded his broad chest, and grazing e'en the skin. Jaufry meanwhile had struck his foe in turn, and with so just an aim, he lost at once his stirrups and his seat, and rolled half-stunned upon the ground.

He rose again full quickly, pale with rage, and came with upraised sword towards Jaufry. The latter, wishing his good horse to spare, at once leapt on the sod and raised his shield. 'Twas just in time: Estout, in his fierce rage, brandished his sword with both his hands, and made it thunder down with such effect the shield was cloven to the arm.

"St. Peter!" murmured Jaufry, "thou dost covet this poor shield; still, if naught stay me, it shall cost thee dear."

Suiting to such words the act, upon Estout's bright casque he then let fly so fierce a downward stroke, that fire issued therefrom. But the good helm of proof was not a whit the worse. With gathering fury Estout came again, and with one stroke pared from Sir Jaufry's shield the double rim, full half a palm of mail, and the left spur, which was cut through as the blade reached the ground.

Wondering at the vigour of his dreadful foe, Jaufry, on his side, struck a second time his burnished helm; and with such force, his sword in twain was broken, yet left it not upon the trusty steel even the slightest dent.

"Heaven!" thought Jaufry, "what doth this portend? confounded be the hand that helmet wrought, whereon my blade hath spent itself in vain!"

Then Estout, uttering a fearful cry as he beheld Sir Jaufry's sword in two, flew straight towards him, and in his turn struck the son of Dovon on the helm, smashing the visor as the blow came down. Had he not raised in time the remnant of his shield, which that fell stroke for aye destroyed, the combat had been done.

"Knight," said Sir Jaufry, "thou dost press me sore; and I, good sooth, must be indeed bewitched; strike as I will upon that helm of thine, I cannot crack its shell."

As thus he spoke, he launched a desperate blow with what was left him of his blade; which, falling on the casque of his stout foe like hammer on an anvil, for the time deprived him both of sight and sound. With dizzy eye and tottering step, Estout, thinking to strike at Jaufry, whom he would have cloven to the heel had he received the blow, let fall his sword with such unbounded rage, it struck into the ground, and buried half its blade. Before he could withdraw it, the young knight, casting aside the battered shield and broken sword, seized with both arms Estout about the waist, and that with such good-will, his very ribs were heard to crack within. To cast him to the ground, undo his helm, and seize his sword to strike off his foe's head, were but an instant's work.

Estout, who moved not, cried with feeble voice:

"Mercy, good knight! O, slay me not, but take of me such ransom as thou wilt; I own that thou hast vanquished me."

"Thou shalt have mercy," Jaufry then replied, "an thou do'st that which I shall now command."

"It shall be done most willingly, my lord; thou canst not ask a thing I will not do."

"In the first place," said Jaufry, "thou shalt go and yield thyself a captive to King Arthur, with all these knights, to whom thou must restore what thou hast ta'en from them; and thou shalt then relate to that good king how I have thus o'ercome thee in the fight."

"I will do so full willingly, by Heaven!" Estout replied.

"And now," said Jaufry, "give to me thine arms; for mine have been all hacked and hewed by thee."

"Agreed, my lord. Give me your hand: the bargain shall be kept; and well can I aver, without a lie, that ne'er did knight boast armour such as mine. Many's the blow may fall upon this helm, yet never pass it through; no lance can dim this shield or pierce this mail; and for this sword, so hard is it of temper, iron nor bronze nor steel resists its edge.

Jaufry then donned these valuable arms; and whilst he buckled on the shining helm and burnished shield, and girded the good sword, the captives of Estout came up to do him homage. They were two score in number, all of price and lofty lineage, who addressed him, 'mid warm smiles of joy:

"Fair lord, what answer will ye that we make when good King Arthur asks the name of who sets us free?"

"You will reply that Jaufry is his name—Jaufry the son of Dovon."

This said, he ordered that his horse be led; for still he burned to overtake Taulat. And though Estout and all the knights pressed him awhile to tarry, yet he stayed neither to eat nor take the least repose: from squires' hands receiving shield and lance, he took his leave, and wandered on his way.

The day came on both clear and beautiful; a bright sun rose on fields humect with dew; charmed with the spring-tide and the matin hour, the birds sang merrily beneath the verdant shade, and conned their latin notes. Jaufry, natheless, went straight upon his road, still bent on finding Taulat; for to him nor peace nor rest nor pleasure can e'er come till that proud lord be met.

The Dwarf and the Lance.

After Sir Jaufry had rode on his way, Estout his promise kept, and to each knight restored both horse and arms. That evening he set out for Arthur's court, which he resolved to reach before the jousts and games and banquetings were o'er. Eight days had they been holden in those halls when he arrived there with his company. 'Twas after dinner, as the king was seated with his lords, lending an ear to minstrels' tales and the discourse of knights, who told of acts of lofty prowess done, that Estout came with that armed troop of knights. Having alighted at the palace-gates, they soon were led before the worthy king; when, kneeling at his feet, Estout expressed himself in terms like these:

"Sire, may that high King who made and fashioned all things— He, the Lord of every sovereign, who hath nor peer nor mate—now save us in your company!"

"Friend," the king replied, "God save you, and your friends beside! Who are ye, and what come ye here to seek?"

"My lord, I will recount you the whole truth: from Jaufry, son of Dovon, come we, to proclaim ourselves your captives, and submit to your just law. Sir Jaufry hath delivered all these knights, whom I had captured, one by one, and who were bound to follow me on foot—for they had mercy only on such terms: now he hath conquered me by force of arms."

"And when thou last beheldst him," asked the king, "by that true faith thou ow'st to gracious Heaven, say, was he well in health?"

"Yea, sire, by the troth I owe to you, believe, that eight days since, arise to-morrow's sun, I left him sound, robust, and full of fire. He would not even tarry to break bread; for he declared no food should pass his lips, no joy, no pleasure, no repose be his, until the knight named Taulat he had found. He now is on his track; and I engage, that if he meet him, and a chance do get to measure sword with sword, it will be strange an he not force him to cry grace; for I do not believe the world doth own a braver knight, or one more strong in arms. I speak from proof, who dearly know his force."

"O Heaven, in which I trust," cried Arthur, as he clasped his hands, "grant me my prayer, that Jaufry safe and sound may back return! Already is he known a doughty knight, and noble are the gifts he hither sends."

Leave we now bold Estout to tell his tale, and turn we to our knight. I have related how Sir Jaufry still went on seeking his foe by valley and by mount; yet neither spied nor heard he living man to give him tidings. He rode on thus, nor met he man or beast, till the high noon was passed. The sun had now become intensely hot, and hardly could he bear its burning ray; still, neither sun, nor hunger, thirst, nor aught beside, could cow his spirit. Determined not to stop upon his road till he had Taulat met, he still progressed, though ne'er a soul was seen.

As he pressed hotly on, some hours' riding found the youthful knight close by a gentle hill shaded by one of nature's finest trees. Pendent there hung from an outstretching bough a fair white lance of ash with point of burnished steel. Thinking a knight perchance was resting near, Jaufry in that direction turned his horse, and galloped towards the spot. When he had reached the bottom of the hill, he nimbly leapt him down, and walked to the high tree: but, to his great surprise, no soul was there, naught save the lance suspended to the bough. With wonder, then—asking of himself why arm so stout and good, the point of which like virgin silver shone, should there be placed—he took it down, and his own resting 'gainst the mossy trunk, handled and brandished this new dainty lance, which he discovered to be good as fair.

"Good faith," quoth he, "I will e'en keep this arm, and leave mine own behind."

Whilst making this exchange, a dwarf of frightful shape suddenly rushed from out a neighbouring grove. Stunted and broad and fat, he had a monstrous head, from which straight hair streamed down and crossed his back; long eyebrows hid his eyes; his nose was large and shapeless; nostrils so immense they would have held your fists; and thick and bluish lips rested on large and crooked fangs; a stiff moustache surrounded this huge mouth; and to his very girdle flowed his beard; he measured scarce a foot from waist to heel; his head was sunken in his shoulders high; and his arms seemed so short, that useless would have been the attempt to bind them at his back. As to his hands, they were like paws of toads, so broad and webbed.

"Knight," cried this monster, "woe befals the man who meddles with that lance! Thou wilt receive thy dues, and dangle on our tree; come, then, give up thy shield."

Sir Jaufry eyed the dwarf, and angrily replied:

"What mean you by such tale, misshapen wretch?"

At this, the dwarf set up so loud a cry that all the vale resounded; and at once a knight well armed, mounted upon a steed in iron cased, came, with high threats upon his lips, exclaiming:

"Woe to the man who hath dared touch the lance!"

Having the hill attained, he Jaufry saw; and thereupon he said:

"By Heaven, sir knight! to do what thou hast done is proof thou carest little for thy life."

"And why so, lord?" Sir Jaufry calmly asked.

"Thou shalt soon learn. No man doth touch that lance and get him hence without a fight with me. If I unhorse the knight so bold as dare to touch it, and conquer him by arms, no ransom saves his life—I hang him by the neck; and on my gallows which thou seest from here full three-and-thirty dangle in mid air."

"Tell me now, faithfully," Sir Jaufry said, "can he who sues for mercy gain it at thy hands?"

"Yea, but on one condition I have firmly fixed; which is, that never in his life he cross a horse; ne'er cut his hair or pair his nails; ne'er eat of wheaten bread, or taste of wine; and never on his back wear other dress than what his hands have woven. Should he such terms accept before the fight, he may perchance find grace; but naught can save the man who once hath fought."

"And if he know not how to weave such dress?" asked Jaufry.

"The art to weave, to shape the cloth, and sew, must then be learned," the knight replied. "Say, them, if thou consent; or if thou choose this hour to be thy last."

"I'll not do so," quoth Jaufry; "for too hard the labour seems."

"Thou'lt do it well before five years are fled; for thou art tall and strong."

"No, by my troth, I'd rather chance the fight, since 'twould appear I've no alternative."

"Take my defiance, then!" cried out the knight; "and bear in mind, the combat's to the death."

"So be it!" said Sir Jaufry; "I'll defend myself."

They drew apart some space with such like words, each thinking on his side a victim soon would fall. Then the knight came and thundered at his foe. In shivers flew the lance; but Jaufry bore the shock unmoved. Not so the knight; for Jaufry, his weapon planting at his shield, broke it right through; the hauberk too beside, and wood and iron, for a cubit's length, pierced through the shoulder.

He fell: Jaufry, with naked blade, was by his side; but as he saw him thus, so poorly sped—

"Knight," he exclaimed, "methinks thy hanging-trade is done."

"Lord," cried the wounded man, "unhappily 'tis true. Thou hast too well performed thy work for safety henceforth to be banished hence."

"I will not trust to that," quoth Jaufry; "or, at least, it shan't prevent my hanging thee."

"In Heaven's name, my lord, I crave thy grace!"

"And by what claim canst thou obtain it, thou who never yet hast granted it to man? Thou shalt find pity, such as those yonder found who once begged grace of thee."

"If, good my lord, my head have erred, my heart been black and habits villanous, guard thee from following in my steps. I ask for mercy—that should I receive. Wilt thou, a man of lofty virtue, choose that ever the reproach should come to thee of hanging up a brave and courteous knight, such as I once did bear the title of?"

"Thou liest in thy throat," Sir Jaufry said; "never couldst thou be prized a proper knight, but rather, I believe, an arrant knave. Who doth a villain's act doth forfeit rank and chivalry alike. In vain thy suit; no pardon shalt thou find."

Undoing his steel helmet as he spoke, he seized a rope and placed it round his neck; then, dragging him beneath the dismal tree, he well and fairly hung him up thereto.

"Good friend," he then apostrophised the knight, "the passage now may be considered safe, and travellers need fear little more from thee."

Leaving him hanging, upon such adieu, he rode towards the dwarf, as with intent to kill. But when the latter saw him thus return, crossing his arms full quickly on his breast—

"Fair sir," he cried, "I yield to you and Heaven; but grant me, pray, your pity. Of myself no evil have I done; since, had I disobeyed the knight, I should have lost my life. Maugre myself, for fourteen years I've watched this lance, which twice a-day I burnished. Woe had betided me if I had bilked such task, or failed by signal to advise my lord when it was touched by knight. This, fair my lord, hath been my only crime."

"Thou mayst have mercy," Jaufry said, "an thou dost that which I shall now command."

"Speak, good my lord; and God confound me if I lose a word!"

"Rise, then, and hie thee to King Arthur's court. Tell to that king the son of Dovon sends thee, and present this lance which he hath won, the fairest weapon eye hath e'er beheld. Recount to him beside thy lord's ill-deeds, how that so many worthy knights he'd hung, and how in his turn like meed was given unto him."

"My lord," exclaimed the dwarf, "all this I promise you."

And Jaufry made reply, "Well, then, begone!"

It was one Monday eve that this fell out, just at the setting sun. The night came shortly on serene and fair, and the full moon shone out as bright as day. Jaufry pursued his road—for naught could change his purpose—and dwarf prepared to execute his trust. At peep of morn he started for Carlisle, where, after certain time, he safely came. The king was breaking up his court, which for two weeks he there had held, and knights and barons all were going their way, content and glad, bearing rich guerdons from their noble lord, when curiosity their steps detained at sight of a strange dwarf, who in his hand a handsome lance did hold. This dwarf pushed forward to the palace-hall, where each with eager eye observed his shape; for never till that day had they beheld such wondrous man; but he, passing the gaping crowd without remark, straight to the monarch's throne his steps pursued; and there he said:

"May God, most noble sire, grant you weal! Albeit my form is strange, yet, please you, hear, for I do come a messenger from far."

"Dwarf," said the king, "God save thee, too! for thou methinks art honest. Speak without fear, and do thy message featly."

The dwarf preluded with a sigh, and thus began:

"Sire, from Dovon's son I bear to you this lance, which has been cause of mourning dire and great. Proud of his valour and his strength, a knight had hung it to a tree upon a hill, where I have watched it, burnished it beside twice evvery day, for fourteen weary years. If a knight touched it, I by my cry aroused my lord, who then, all armed, would rush upon the stranger; being vanquished, he was quickly seized and by the neck incontinently hung. 'Twas thus that three-and-thirty met their fate; when that the knight, whose messenger I am, conquered this lord and won the lance, hanging in turn its owner for his deeds. This is the lance that now he sends to you; and here and I, your vassal and your slave."

"'Tis well," the king replied; "but, dwarf, now give me, on thy faith, some news of brave Sir Jaufry: without a lie, say when thou saw'st him last."

"'Twas Monday evening, please you, my good lord; I left him when the fray was o'er and he had finished hanging up the knight."

"And was his health them good?"

"Yea, sire, with God's help, and well disposed and gay."

"Good Lord divine and full of glory," cried the king, with claspéd hands, "grant of your grace that I behold him safe; for scant my pleasure and my joys will be, till I have held him in these arms again!"

The Yeoman

We now return to Jaufry, who still wanders on, resolving not to stay for food or sleep before he meets with Taulat; for in his ears incessantly do ring the biting words of Quex: "Your courage will be higher when you're drunk,"—and he yet trusts to prove that lord did lie by beating Taulat fasting. Onward he therefore pricked till midnight hour, when he attained a narrow and dark gorge, shut in on either side by mountains high. No other passage was there but this one. Sir Jaufry gave his horse the spur; when, at the very mouth of the defile, before him stood a yeoman, active, of stout build, and large of limb, who held within his grasp three pointed darts that were as razors sharp. A large knife pended from his girdle, which enclosed an outer garment of good form and fashion.

"Halt, knight," he cried; "I'll have a word with thee."

Jaufry drew rein, and said:

"And what's thy quest, good friend?"

"Thou must give up thy horse and knightly arms; for upon such conditions only mayst thou pass."

"Indeed," quoth Jaufry; "dost thou mean to say an armed and mounted knight must not pass through this strait?"

"He might do so, but for the toll I've levied."

"To the foul fiend such toll! Never will I give up my horse or arms, till strength's denied me to defend them both."

"An that thou yield'st them not with gentle grace," the yeoman said, "I must use force to take them."

"And wherefore so? what harm have I e'er wrought thee?"

"Dost thou not wish to pass this gorge, and bilk the toll that's due save I use force to get it?"

"And what's the force thou'lt use?"

"That thou shalt briefly see; meantime I bid thee 'ware my hand!"

"I will do so," quoth Jaufry.

The yeoman now prepared himself for fight, and seized his dart as though in act to strike; but Jaufry, fearing for his horse, awaited not the blow, but galloped off amain. As o'er the road he sped, the man let fly the missile with just aim; it hit the shield, and that with force so great, red fire and flame forth issued at the stroke, which did not pierce it through. The sharpened point curled upwards on the steel, and the wood flew in shivers.

Sir Jaufry turned his steed at once and bore down on his foe, counting full surely that the fight was done; but, lo! at that instant he had leapt aside, and in the act discharged a second dart, which lighted on his helm; so fierce the stroke, the casque seemed all on fire; yet it resisted, though its lord was stunned.

The yeoman, seeing his second blow had failed, was a man possessed; so dread his rage as neither to have hurt the knight or broken his bright arms. Jaufry, whose senses had now back returned, thought only of his horse, which he rode here and there to guard it from the blow of the third dart. Not this, however, was his foe's intent, for he still thought to take the beast alive; like lightning swift he came, and whirling round the dart, launched the fell weapon, with these haughty words:

"By Heaven, slave, thou now shalt leave the horse, nor shall thy hauberk, helm, or shield protect thyself!"

Jaufry wheeled round his horse at this stern threat; and as the dart came hissing to its prey, he deftly bowed him down: it harmed him not, but striking on his mail. tore from the goodly arms a palm away, then bounded out of view.

"And now," cried Jaufry, the third dart being flung, "my lance's point shall give me my revenge."

With lowered lance he flew towards the man, trusting this time to pierce him through and through; but he was nimble as a roe or deer, and leapt from place to place to such effect, that Jaufry missed his aim; and as he passed, the yeoman seized a rock and hurled it at the knight, who, but for his shield, must fain have bit the ground. The mass in atoms flew; but such the force with which the blow was struck, it battered-in the shield.

Jaufry, enraged at following such a foe, now doubly maddened at this fresh attack, in wrath exclaimed:

"God, thou all-glorious King! how shall I meet this fiend? The world I'll hold not at a denier's price till he doth sue for grace!"

Then wielding his long lance—

"This time," he loudly to the yeoman cried, "or thou or I shall fall."

The yeoman from his girdle plucked his knife, and made reply:

"Ere that thou leave this spot thou'lt pay the toll!"

"Ay, that will I," quoth Jaufry, "take my promise on't; before we part, thou shalt have toll enough!"

He once again renewed a brisk attack, but still the other dodged; and ere that Jaufry could draw-in the rein, with mighty spring upon the horse he leapt and round Sir Jaufry's body twined his arms.

"Stir not, sir knight," he cried, "unless thou wish for death."

When Jaufry felt himself thus rudely seized, his mind was in a maze, and for a time incapable of thought. The yeoman held him with such strait embrace he could not stir a limb, while in his ear he hissed his future fate: how that a prison should his body hold, where tortures, griefs, unheard-of pains should vex him evermore. Till break of day, his arms were round him clasped; but when the stars were gone, then Jaufry communed with himself, and said:

"Better to die for God, who made this earth, than let my body be a dungeon's prey. We'll see what can be done."

Reflecting thus, he let his lance drop down, and as the yeoman's right arm pressed him most, with energy he clutched it in his grasp; so vigorous the attack, so nerved his strength, he forced the hand to loose the gleaming knife: then, when he saw the arm was paralysed and drooped inertly down, he fixed with both hands on the yeoman's left, which he then twisted till he caused such pain, its owner reeled in groaning to the ground. Dismounting from his horse, Jaufry drew near his foe, who lay quite motionless, crying for mercy in his agony.

"By Heaven! which I adore," quoth Jaufry, "ne'er will I pity show to wretch like thee."

And at the words, he cut off both his feet.

"I prithee, now," he said, "run not, nor leap, nor battle more with knights. Take to another trade; for far too long hath this one been thy choice."

He gathered up his lance and shield, and, mounting on his horse, prepared him quietly to go his way.

'Twas on a Tuesday, early in the morn, that Jaufry held this speech; but as he turned him from his footless foe—

"I have not yet inquired," he observed, "if thou perchance hold'st knights within thy walls?"

"My lord," the man replied, "full five-and-twenty are there held in chains beyond the mount where stands my dwelling-place."

"O, O!" said Jaufry, "these I must set free; it likes me not that thou shouldst guard such prize."

Without delay, he hied him to the house, whose massive portals were thrown open wide; and to a dwarf who stood before the gates he cried:

"Where lie the imprison'd knights?"

Replied the dwarf:

"Methinks you're all to rash to venture here. 'Tis more indeed than rashness—downright folly. You 'wake my pity; therefore take advice, and get you gone before my lord returns, save that you covet an inglorious death, or torments even worse."

Jaufry, with smiles, replied:

"Nay, friend, I want the knights; quickly lead on, that I may break their chains."

"An I mistake not, you will join their ranks ere you deliver them; and I must hold you as a fool distraught, not to have hied you hence; for should my lord chance meet you by the way, deeply you'll grieve that e'er you ventured here."

"Thy lord will ne'er return; I have deprived him of his nimble feet, and near his end he lies. The knights shall now be free, and thou, my prisoner, their place shalt take, save that thou goest where my bidding sends; then peradventure brief shall be thy thrall."

"Sir knight," the dwarf replied, "since, then, my lord is thus so poorly sped, I, by my faith, will follow your commands, and from great pain will draw those suffering knights, whose language is but moans; this featly will I do, who by coonstraint and fear was here detained. Truly, to God and you we should give thanks, and joyfully obey what you ordain."

"First, then," said Jaufry, "lead me to the knights."

The dwarf most gladly acted as his guide; and pacing on before, conveyed him to a hall where five-and-twenty knights were rudely chained, as each by turns had been the yeoman's prey. Jaufry, on entering, made them a salute, to which not one replied; nay, they began to weep, and mutter in their teeth:

"Accurs'd the day that yeoman was e'er born, who thus hath overcome so good a knight!"

But Jaufry, as he gaily drew him nigh:

"Why weep, fair knights?" he said, with courtesy.

"Go, madman, go," did one of them reply; "for sure thy senses must have left thee quite, to ask us why we weep, when walls like these rise up on ev'ry side. There is not one of us who doth not grieve to see the yeoman's prisoner in thee. Unhappy was the day that saw thy birth. In person thou art tall and fair to view, yet soon like ours will torments be thy lot."

Quote Jaufry, "Great is God; easy to Him can your deliverance be. Through Him my sword hath 'venged you on your foe, and now the yeoman lies deprived of feet. If, then, you see me in this weary spot, 'tis but to break your chains."

Scarce had the words escaped from out his mouth, when loudly did they call:

"Happy the day which dawned upon thy birth; for thou hast saved us all, and swept our pain and martyrdom away!"

Then Jaufry bade the dwarf set free the knights; the manikin obeyed, and with a hammer broke in bits their chains. They all arose, and bowed their heads in taken of submission, whilst they said:

"Lord, we are thy serfs; do with us as thou please, be it for good or evil, as is fit."

"Good knights," Sir Jaufry said, "whate'er of evil may henceforth betide you, none shall come from me. All that I ask of you is simply this, that ye betake you to King Arthur's court, and tell him all you know."

"My lord," they all exclaimed, "full willingly shall thy behest be done; but to the service rendered, add one more by telling us thy name."

"Barons," said Jaufry then, "tell him the son of Dovon burst your chains. Now quickly set ye out; and, mark, my friendship ne'er shall be bestowed, if that ye fail to tell the king each word."

The dwarf meanwhile had gone to seek the arms and fetch the steeds to furnish forth the knights. Each donned his hauberk, mounted his good horse, and then with Jaufry parted from that spot. He led them to the great highway, and in their company rode full a league. In passing by, he pointed to the place where, cold and motionless, the yeoman lay: they stayed an instant to observe their foe, then went upon their road. A little further Jaufry got him down, and tightened more his goodly charger's girths; then, his impatience to fall in with Taulat reviving in full force:

"God speed you, sirs," he said; "I can delay no more; already have I wasted too much time."

"My lord," replied the knights, as they presented him his shield and lance, "accept again our thanks: where'er we be, the service thou hast done in this great fight shall widely be proclaimed."

When that the band had watched him out of sight, they went their way until they reached Carlisle. They found King Arthur in his flowery mead, with five-and-twenty of his primest knights. There, kneeling at his feet, one of the troop was spokesman for the rest; and thus he fearlessly and sagely said:

"Sire, so please it the true God, who knoweth all that every creature doth, give you good luck, and guard from pain and ill the greatest king this world doth now contain!"

"Friend," the good king replied, "God and St. Mary keep thee and thy mates! Speak without fear and tell me what thou wilt."

"Sire, we come to yield ourselves to thee, from Jaufry, Dovon's son; he hath delivered us from durance vile."

"Good sir, give me at once your tidings. 'Tis long since you and he have parted company?"

"We left him, sire, on Tuesday morning last, both safe and sound, ardent and full of strength, tracking a lord with whom he seeks to fight, and to avenge thy cause."

"O Lord, thou glorious Sire," said the king, with joinéd hands, "grant I may Jaufry see unchecked, unscathed; for, an I hold him not within six months, I'll prize my fortunes as of nothing worth!"

Whilst that the dwarf in turn begins his speech, to tell the king how this adventure happed, we will go back to follow Jaufry's steps, who still, unwearied, presses stoutly on.

The Castle of the Leper

The knight had rode for great part of the day beneath the rays of a most burning sun, and horse and rider both alike fatigued, when he beheld a young and handsome squire running towards him at his greatest speed. Rent was his garment even to his waist; and on he came, with madness in his looks, tearing by handfuls his fair curling hair.

Scarce did he make out Jaufry from afar when he exclaimed:

"Fly, fly, brave knight, fly quickly from this spot, an that thou choosest not to lose they life!"

"And wherefore so, fair friend?" asked Dovon's son.

"Fly, for the love of God, say I; nor lose thou further time."

"Art thou, then, shorn of sense," exclaimed the knight, "such counsel to propose, when I behold no foe?"

"Ah!" cried the squire then, "he comes; he's there; nor think I in a year to cure the fright that he hath caused me! He hath slain my lord—a knight of price, who was conducting to his castle-home his lady-wife, a Norman count's most noble daughter. This wretch hath seized the bride; and to myself has caused such dire fear, that ev'ry limb still trembles at the shock."

"And is't because *thou* fearest," asked Sir Jaufry, red with rage, "thou counsell'st flight to *me?* By holy faith, I hold thee fool, and worse."

As he spoke thus, a leper came in sight, who sped along, a child within his arms. Its wretched mother, with dishevelled hair, followed with piercing cries. When she beheld the knight, she knelt down at his feet, and in a tone of agony exclaimed:

"Mercy, my lord; O, mercy! For the love of Heaven grant me help, and get me back the child yon leper bears."

"Woman," responded Jaufry, "wherefore takes he it?"

"My lord, because it is his wicked will."

"Had he no other cause?"

"No, by your glorious sire!"

"Since it is thus," quoth Jaufry, "he is wrong; and I will try to win it back for you."

He spurred at once his horse, she following; and cried aloud, with all the strength he had:

"Halt, leprous wicked wretch! and bring thou back the child!"

The leper turned his head and raised his hand, making the mark of scorn; which so enraged the knight, he swore the insult deeply to avenge. The hideous leper answered with a laugh; for he had reached the threshold of his door. He darted in for refuge, followed full speed by Jaufry; who, dismounting from his horse, which with his lance he left to the poor dame, dashed through the castle-gate with sword in hand and shield upon his arm.

As he was traversing the castle through, which he found vast and sumptuous to the view, he came into a hall where a huge leper, frightful to behold, had cast upon a couch a damsel in first youth, whose beauty in that age could scarce be matched. Her cheek was fresher than an opening rose at break of day, and her torn vesture half-betrayed a bosom snowy white. Her eyes were bathed in tear; her words, despair, and sobs, moved Jaufry's soul: but when the leper rose and seized his club, such feelings changed to horror and surprise.

He was in height more tall than knightly lance, and at the shoulders was two fathoms broad: his arms and hands were huge, his fingers crookt and full of knots, his cheeks were spread with pustules and with scales; a broken pupil, eyes without lids but with vermilion edged, blue lips, and yellow teeth, made up the portrait of this monster dread. Fiercer than living coal he flew on Jaufry, bidding him straight to yield.

"No, certes," the knight replied.

"Say, who in evil hour sent thee here?"

"No one."

"And pray what seekest thou?"

"A child, that from its mother hath been torn by lep'rous hands, which must give up their prey."

"Vain fool, 'tis *I* forbid—I, by whose mace thy fate shall now be sealed; better for thee thou hadst not risen the morn, since thou shalt now for ever lay thee down."

His club he raised in uttering these words, and on the shield of Jaufry then let fall so fierce a blow, the knight went reeling to the ground. Again that club was raised; but Jaufry rose and fled. Certes he had cause to flee the stroke he saw impending; for that huge mass of iron as it fell made the vast hall to tremble. Then Jaufry, with a bound, before the leper stood, and with firm hand dealt him in turn a blow which took a palm from off his raiment and the flesh behind. Seeing his blood, which fast began to stream, the giant uttered first a fearful cry, then ran at Jaufry, raising his knotted club with both his hands.

Scarce could the youthful knight evade the stroke and leap behind a column; the monster struck it with such dire strength, the massive iron crushed the marble plinth, and all the castle groaned.

Meanwhile the damsel fervently prayed Heaven, as humbly on the blood-stained stones she knelt:

"O, mighty Lord, who in Thy image didst great Adam make—Thou who hast done so much to save us all—now save me from this wretch, and let yon knight withdraw me from his hand!"

Her orison scare o'er, Jaufry stepped out, and ere the giant could again his heavy club let fall, he with his trenchant blade had severed his right arm. Being thus lopped, the monster in his wrath and agony so loudly groaned, the palace trembled to its very base and shook the outer air. In vain did Jaufry dodge his falling mace, it struck him to the ground; so that from nostrils, eyes, and mouth, the purple stream burst forth. The mace, in falling on the marble flags, now brake in twain, which Jaufry seeing, he uprose in haste, and newly struck the leper; at the knee-joint he aimed; the monster reeled, then fell like some great tree.

Prone as the leper lay, Jaufry ran up, his sword in air, and said:

"Methinks that peace will soon be made 'twixt you and me."

Then letting fall his sword with both his hands, he clove the monster's head e'en to the teeth. In the convulsions of his agony still fiercely strove the wretch, and with his foot hurled him so madly 'gainst the distant wall, Sir Jaufry fell deprived of sound and sight. His trembling hand no longer clutched his sword; like ruby wine, from nostrils and from mouth burst forth his blood, and motion made he none.

For an instant's space the damsel thought her champion was gone. In grief she hastened to undo the straps which bound his polished casque. The freshness drawing from his breast a sigh, she ran for water, and his face she bathed. His senses half-returned, he staggered up, and thinking still to hold his trusty blade, he struck the damsel—deeming her the foe—to such effect that both rolled on the ground. Like madman then he sped around the hall, and ran behind a column, where he crouched and trembled 'neath his shield.

'Twas there the damsel came; and in a voice of dulcet tone, she said:

"Brave knight, come, ope again those manly eyes, and see who 'tis that speaks. Forget ye what is due to chivalry, of which you are a lord? your courage and your fame? Recall yourself, and lower that bright shield: behold, the leper's dead!"

Jaufry recovered at this heart'ning speech, and finding his head bare—

"Damsel," he asked, "who hath removed my casque, and taken my good sword?"

"Myself, good lord, whilst you were in a swoon."

"The giant, what doth he?"

"Bathed in his blood and at your feet he lies."

Jaufry looked up, and when the corpse he saw thus shattered and quite still, he slowly rose, and sat him on a bench until his senses were again restored; then, when the dizziness had fled his brain, he thought upon the mother and the child, and straightway ran from hall to hall to search the infant out. But though he sought and ran and called aloud, neither the leper nor the child appeared.

"I will yet search and search," he then exclaimed; "or here or out the door they must be found; for I'll not hold me at a denier's worth till to the mother her poor child's restored, and I've had vengeance for that leper's scorn."

With such resolve, he strode towards the door; but though the portal was thrown open wide, he could not pass it through. Spite of his will, his efforts, and his strength, his feet seemed stopped before an unseen bar.

"Good Heaven," he said, "what! am I, then, entranced?"

He drew him back, and gathering for a spring, with wond'rous force he bounded to the door. Still all was vain, he could not cross the sill. Again and yet again he tried, till deep discouragement iced o'er his heart. Then tears broke from his eyes, and murmuring:

"Alas, good Lord," he said, "Thou gav'st me strength to kill yon wicked wretch; what boots it, if I here must captive be?"

'Twas as he thus bemoaned his adverse fate, there broke upon his ear from some nigh place a sound of infant tongues, which sadly cried:

"Save us, O, save us, mighty lord!"

Swift at the sound he roused his spirit up, and running, found at one end of a hall a close-shut door fast bolted from within. Jaufry called out, and struck it with great noise; yet answer none was made: enraged at this, he burst it in with force, and with his naked blade entered a gloomy vault. There was the leper found, with knife in hand, who seven infants had just put to death. Some thirty more there still remained alive, whose bitter cries went through the softened so.

Touched at the frightful sight, Jaufry struck down the wretch, who called his master's help; and the in wrath exclaimed:

"Thy master, villain, can no answer make; his soul this earth hath fled: and thou, for erstwhile making mock of me, shalt now thy meed receive."

Raising meanwhile his arm, the leper's hand he severed at a blow. The wretch upon the blood-stained pavement rolled; then crawling to his feet, he humbly cried:

"Mercy, good knight; in God's name pity me, and take not quite my life! 'Twas by constraint and force I killed these babes. My lord, who sought to cure his leprosy, bade me, with awful threats, each day prepare a bath of human blood."

"Thy life I'll grant," quoth Jaufry to him then, "an that thou give me means to leave this place."

"I can," the leper said; "but had you now deprived me of my life, not knowing of the spell, a hundred thousand years had rolled their course, and yet not seen you free."

"Haste thee, then, now," quote Jaufry, eagerly.

"Sir knight," the man with shining face replied, "you still have much to bear. Such is the fashion of this castle's spell, my lord alone could power grant to such as hither came to cross the threshold; but never did they pass it in return save dead or maimed."

"How, then, wilt thou succeed?" said Jaufry.

"Spy you, on top of yonder casement high, a marble head?"

"Yea, by my faith! And then?"

"Lo, reach it down; and break it fair in twain; you'll thus destroy the charm: but first your armour carefully put on; for when the spell is o'er, these castle-walls will crumble into dust."

Trusting not wholly to the lep'rous wretch, Jaufry then bound him by the feet and arms, and to the damsel thus confided him:

"If he hath lied," said he, "spare not his life."

Then he resumed his helm, took down the marble head, whose shape was fair and cunningly devised, and setting it near him on a wooden bench, discharged on't with his sword so great a blow, he clove it clean in twain. Sudden it shrieked, it moaned, it bounded up, hissing and growling as a thunderbolt; whilst the vexed elements at once unchained, and beam and stone at war with frightful din came crushing over Jaufry. Vainly his shield was raised to guard his head; Heaven's face was darkened o'er; an awful storm, where wind and lightning strove, bursting with ruin, 'mid the ambient air had borne the knight away, but for his orison to heaven's King. Huge clouds of dust rose upwards to the skies; while a fierce wind, in passing, swept away the last memorial of the magic work: of castle naught remained. Bowed down, and scarce himself, did Jaufry move his limbs. Bowed down and bruised and tottering, dragged he some steps, then fell. The maid, the slave, and mother with her child, who had sought refuge 'neath a huge rock's vault, found him at length outstretched upon the turf, his strength exhausted and quite motionless.

"Say, then, good knight," the damsel smiling spoke, "how fares it with you now?"

"I have no bruise that's perilous, nor mortal wound," replied the knight; "but such this latter strife, I find, indeed, I sadly lack repose."

The damsel then embraced him with her arms, and pressed

her lips upon his eyes and mouth. When Jaufry saw the mother—

"Woman," he said, "hast thou regained thy child?"

"I have, my lord; thanks, be it told, to you."

"An it be so, proceed then to Carlisle, with this fair damsel, babes, and leper—all. There I must beg you go, King Arthur thank, from Jaufry, Dovon's son, and tell him of this fight."

Thus speaking, he uprose; drew to his fancy his good horse's girths; and having consigned his friends to Heaven's care, resumed his quest of Taulat: albeit 'twas now with measured steps and slow; for this dread battle had worn out his strength.

Having obtained her mantle and her horse, the maid set out from thence at the like hour, and with her went the leper and the rest; nor stayed she on the way, but only stopped when she had reached fair Carlisle's lofty towers.

There all regarded her with wonderment.

"Whence can proceed," they said, "this strange cortège? whence come these people? and what want they there?" The curious crowd followed that damsel fair up to the castle-gates, and there the knights, who noble escort made, led her with all her troop before the king.

There bended she her knee, and as a dame of gentle breeding spoke:

"May He, the Lord of all and of all things, who in His hands doth justly hold the keys of good and ill, increase your fame, and keep in glory the knights of your Round Table!"

"And," said the worthy king, "may Heaven save you, sweet damsel, who are fair and good as courteous and well-bred!"

"Sire, from Jaufry, Dovon's son, I come, to thank you for my life; which to his mighty valour do I owe. I am the daughter of the Count Passant, whose name perchance hath reached your royal ear. A knight of high esteem, who sought adventure to display his worth, brought me from Normandy to these fair shores. For seven long months, by valley and by hill we wandered on, full many a snare escaping, and without check full many a weary fight. This land did hold, alas! a giant dread, of hideous aspect, and of awful strength, eaten with leprosy and fearful sores, whose thought doth make my very soul to heave. Before us suddenly this wretch appeared; and taking from his neck a monstrous club, struck at my lord with force so terrible, he stunned him with the blow. Like as a child then, clutching at his arm, against a rock he fractured every bone; whilst me he seized from off my palfrey's back, and to his magic castle quickly bore. There I had lost my life, yea, more than life, but that Heaven, whose justice I implored, in mercy sent Sir Jaufry to my aid. This doughty knight at length the monster slew; but ne'er can I with greater truth aver, such battle never did these eyes behold, or blows so great e'er given and received."

The mother and the handless leper told their tale in turn. But whilst they thus their message each relates, we will to Jaufry go, who onward still his course doth slowly take, without he yet a single soul described who could give tidings of the man he sought.

The Orchard of Brunissende

Harassed, fatigued, and sore with many a bruise, Jaufry was sinking too for food and drink; and yet the want of sleep—of all our wants the most imperious—so weighed him down, he scarce could keep his seat. Still he went on a quarter of the night with limbs benumbed and eyelids partly closed, taking such course his charger pleased to lead.

Serene and lovely was the atmosphere, and by the light the stars in shining gave, he by adventure a large orchard saw, shut in with marble walls and skirt with trees of umbrage such as earth scarce saw before. Flowers and fragrant herbs abounded there; and with each puff of wind there issued out a sweet and balmy breath like paradise. 'Twas thus that, as night fell, the birds for leagues around did hither flock, and perching on the leafy boughs, warbled their dulcet notes till matin prime.

This orchard appertained to a great dame, known as fair Brunissende. Within the castle of Montbrun she lived; and father, mother, husband, had she none; fine was her court and rich, of breeding high; and knights and burghers, minstrels, jugglers from all countries, hither trooping came. The palace, built of hewn and massive stone whereon the sculptor had employed his art, was flanked with towers blackened o'er by time.

'Twas in the centre Brunissende was lodged; and to it seven gates a passage gave, whereof the keepers could each one lead forth a thousand men.

Five hundred damsels waited her commands; but though 'twere rare to see such beauty met, yet Brunissende held empire over all in loveliness and grace: one might have sought throughout the realms of earth, and yet not found such high and gentle dame, or

one so fine in form. Her eyes and her sweet face swept from the
mind of those who gazed on her all thought of former charms.
She was more fresh, more fair, more purely white than snow that
lies upon the frosted dew, and rose that opens on a lily's breast.

But, ah, felicity did not attend her charms. Yielding to some
deep grief, four times a day she sadly wept and mourned; and
thrice she rose at night to mourn again. Her sole delight was
listening to the notes of those sweet birds which filled her
orchard near; which, when she had heard, she got some brief
repose—soon to awake again to weep and mourn; and all her
vassals, of each age and sex, little and great, at that same hour
of woe, uttered the self-same moans, and shed like tears.

Arrived, as we already said, before her orchard fair, Jaufry got
down; and seeing an open gate, he ventured in, removed the
bridle from his charger's mouth, so that he grazed at ease, and
his shield placing 'neath his weary head, his limbs outstretching
on the flowery turf, he soon most soundly slept. Just then did
Brunissende her footsteps take towards her chamber, followed
by her maids. Surprised, the birds no longer tuned their notes,
she straightway bade the seneschal appear, to whom she said
with wrath:

"Some creature surely must have passed the gates, and scared
my gently birds. Go, quickly find it out; and if perchance a man
it prove to be, he must be hither brought, alive or dead."

"Lady," the seneschal at once replied, "I go with speed."

Two squires preceding him, each with a lighted torch, his horse
he mounted, and rode down in haste, and in the orchard found
the weary knight, wrapt in profoundest sleep. He called him frequently, then shook him hard; but for a time in vain. His eyes at
length with effort he unclosed, when raising up his head—

"Fair knight," quote he, most courteously, "by thine attain-
ments and thy gentle birth, I do entreat thee, in God's name, to
let me here abide and sleep my fill."

"Sleep must you now no more," replied the chief, "but come
before my lady; she'll not rest until avenged on him who scares
her birds."

Quoth Jaufry:

"God permit, thou shalt not take me off without a fight!"

The seneschal, on hearing such resolve, called his squire to
bring him out his arms. Meanwhile the son of Dovon slept
again; so that the seneschal, when full equipped, was forced a
second time to wake him up, and roughly as at first.

"Knight," exclaimed Jaufry, as he then arose, "'tis a great sin to trouble my repose, for I am wearied out; but since thou hast chosen to accept the fight, wilt thou allow me to sleep on in peace if I do thee unhorse?"

"By Heaven's faith, I swear't!" laughing, the other said.

Jaufry then hastened to his house's side; replaced the bit, and tightly drew the the girths. Mounted, he galloped at the seneschal; who, having drawn him back a space, on rushing drove his lance at Jaufry's shield, but never harmed the knight. He, on the contrary, with happy stroke unhorsed the seneschal; who, full of shame, with head bowed down, and slow and thoughtful step, regained the castle and his lady's room.

"What is'it," asked Brunissende, "that there doth lurk?"

"A knight all armed, whose peer the world not holds, sleeping so soundly he would scarce awake."

"Why broughtst thou him not here? I wish him hither let; for, with God's help, no food shall pass these lips till that bold knight be hanged."

"Lady," replied the seneschal, "he would not come; nor could I wake him up."

"Indeed," quoth she; "then bid the tocsin sound, and rouse me up my knights."

The seneschal obeyed; the sound was heard, and straightway flocking came five hundred knights. The hall they entered, where their lady stood with spite and anger pale.

"Barons," she said, "a bold and wicked knight my grounds hath passed, and will not quit the walls; now if his head pay not this insolence, I never will hold land or honour more."

"Lady," replied a tall and proper knight of great renown— Simon the Red by name—"I will go seek him out, if such your wish; and thrust, alive or dead, to bring him here."

"So be it," said Brunissende.

Added the seneschal:

"My troth, good friend, I bid thee shield thyself He can most sturdily defend his sconce; and brave, indeed, I'll hold the happy knight who takes it off by force."

Simon, without a word, went on his way, and Jaufry found still sleeping; rudely he cried:

"Up, up, sir knight; arouse!"

Jaufry, who moved not more than any rock, received from Simon then so strong a kick, it woke him up in haste.

"Nathless thou promisedst to let me sleep," he then explained; "and 'tis a villain's act to break thy faith, when thus I'm over-come."

"Come, speak then to my lady," Simon said; "or I by force must take thee to the hall."

"We first will see who's strongest—thou or I," said Jaufry, in low tone; when, springing on his horse, he ran at Simon, who like haste displayed.

Bold Simon's lance was split on Jaufry's shield; but he was borne by that of his brave foe so swift to earth, it nearly cost his life. Jaufry ran up, as though to make it sure, when loud he called for grace.

"Wilt thou annoy me further in my sleep, if I do grant it?"

"No, lord, I promise thee."

"Go, then," said Jaufry, who again laid down, and quick reclosed his eyes.

Simon the Red, with flush upon his face amd shame at heart, slowly retraced his steps. Certes, did he make but half the noise he made on setting out; so that the seneschal, who watched him come, could not withhold his smiles.

"Lady," he said, "behold your champion; but with him comes no knight. I'd wage my spurs, like me, he has taken oath."

"Maugre this pleasantry," the dame replied, "ere I have rest, this naughty knight shall hang."

Hearing the words, one of the keepers of the seven gates descended to the orchard; but soon his troop returned, bearing him faint and bleeding on his shield. At such a spectacle, fair Brunissende could scare contain her rage—

"What! have I round me naught but coward folk," she loudly cried, "and knights without a heart? Go fifty; if it need, go thrice that number still; but bring this vassal, or no more return!"

At this reproach, the knights rushed off in troop, and to the garden hied with clash and din. When there, they Jaufry seized—some by the arm, and others by the leg; while some his shoulders held, and some his head—and brought him thus into that lordly hall without his being able to stir limb. On seeing them arrive, the dame impatient came with hasty step and bade them set him free. They loosed their hold, and Jaufry stood upright; nor could he think, as round his glance was thrown, 'twas sport that brought him 'mong such iron folk. Tall and well-shaped, his natural manly grace, set off with hauberk rich and burnished casque, struck Brunissende, who eyed him curiously.

"'Tis you," at length she said, "who all this ill have wrought."

"Fair lady," he replied, "so far am I from doing what you say, or causing you annoy, I would defend you with my utmost strength 'gainst all of mother born."

"In that you say not truth; for you erewhile have so misused my knight, that he may chance to die."

"I own it, lady fair, but he was in the wrong; having by oath engaged to let me slept, he thrice returned to wake me up, and struck me with his lance. Still, had I known him feoffee to you, never on him had risen this knightly hand, e'en for a greater cause."

"No matter! I can see," replied the dame, "we'll find in you—and that ere morning sun—a proper subject for the cord or worse."

Whilst thus she spoke, Jaufry regarded her; and ne'er had tired admiring her brow, her neck, her fair and sweet fresh face, her rosy mouth, and blue and loving eyes.

"Lady," quoth he, love gliding o'er his soul, "do with me what you will; for with no other arms than that rich robe, you would have vanquished me with greater ease than ten knights clad in mail. If, 'gainst my knowledge, I have caused you pain, wreak now your own revenge; and never 'gainst you shall uprise my sword, or lance or shield be used."

Hearing him reason thus so courteously, the dame forgets her wrath. Love with his golden shaft hath pierced her heart, and now she pardons all. Those lips still bear a menace to the ear; but those sweet eyes belie't.

Grown bold, the knight, who still did on her gaze, begged her to grant a boon.

"Let me," he said, "but slumber at my ease; then do what justice bids. Fear not that I shall hence seek means to fly; for, Heaven preserve me, you have somehow gained such power o'er my soul, that you alone are better guard than are ten hundred of your men with arms in hand."

Fair Brunissende retired with a sigh, leaving for sole adieu a look so sweet, that, spite of his dull sense, it filled his heart with joy. Meantime the seneschal, whose care it was, bade the attendants then prepared a couch in middle of the hall: he there conducted Jaufry, and then asked his name and country.

"I'm of King Arthur's court," quoth Dovon's son; "now prithee ask no more, but, in God's name, let me in quiet rest."

Full armed as he then was, he laid him down, and sleet his eyelids closed. Not so fair Brunissende. Love in her chamber had renewed the assault, and banished sleep away; and thus she mused, until the city-watch gave forth the accustomed sound. At that trumpet's call, each in the castle and the city rose; and all at once gave loose to tears and groans. High dames and damsels,

Brunissende in chief, clasping their hands in sigh of deepest woe, beat their fair breast and face; while the knights who guarded Jaufry made such dreadful din, it woke him up, and made him ask the cause.

All at the word rushed forward to the couch, and struck with lance and sword and iron mace. Well 'twas for him his hauberk was of proof; for the blows came just like to a storm of hail. Nor did they cease, thinking the knight was dead, until the doleful cries had died away. Then each resumed his post, and silence fell o'er all. Again, at mid of night, those cries uprose; but Jaufry, whom no sleep again had blessed, and whose cleared thoughts were fixed on Brunissende, took careful note to guard his curious tongue; holding his breath, he said within himself:

"Certes are these men no folk of flesh and blood, but demons hither sent to pester earth. With Heaven's help, to-morrow's blessed sun shan't light upon me here."

Persuaded he was dead after that storm of blows. the knights relaxed their watch, and slumbered at their posts; Jaufry then seized the chance, and noiselessly uprose. With shield and lance in hand, he left the castle-halls on tip of toe; by good luck found his horse, and mounting quick, at fullest speed set out. Had he but dreamt the love fair Brunissende conceived, not all her men-at-arms would from Montbrun have chased him but with slaughter. Little deemed he, as hill and dale he crossed with breathless speed, she at that hour was in her fancy musing how she might make him hers.

Who shall depict, as rose the sun next morn, fair Brunissende's dismay, when, of the first who to the hall came down, she heard of Jaufry's flight? As one deprived of sense, those hundred knights she loudly did accuse of treason to their faith; their negligence she banned; and to the seneschal in wrath exclaimed, that, if he found not Jaufry, he should by fire or cord full surely die, even if torments yet unheard were hers.

Whilst that this scene was passing at Montbrun, Jaufry already was well on his road. And shortly after rising of the sun, he met a neatherd, driving of a car laden with bread and wine and other things. This man invited him, by holy charity, to eat with him; and used such kindly words, that Jaufry yielded to his hearty wish, frankly avowing that for three whole days he had not tasted food. The neatherd therefore took his shield and lance, drew from his car good wheaten bread and wine, two roasted capons, three grilled partridges, and part of a wildboar; then spreading on the turf beneath a leafy tree a fair white cloth, a brook just bubbling by, he served the knight, and paid him great respect.

When they had eat their fill, and in their thirst emptied two bowls of wine, Jaufry prepared to go, thanking the neatherd for his welcome meal. This man was vassal to fair Brunissende, the lady of high worth; and as the knight was turning to depart, he drew the charger's rein and gently said:

"Good friend, one thing I fain would ask of you, which I had half-forgot: why do the people of this fair domain so weep and loudly moan?"

"Ah, rascal, wretch, thou traitor, and thou fool!" exclaimed the neatherd, bursting forth with rage, "thy wretched life shall answer for those words."

With all his strength he then at Jaufry cast the pond'rous axe he bore, which struck his shield and brought out fire and flame. The knight spurred on his horse and got clear off; but mid a storm of stones. The neatherd then, enraged at missing him, shivered his car to bits, and with his axe struck both his oxen dead.

In ignorance of the cause of all this rage, Jaufry at length relaxed his horse's speed; still as he went exclaiming, that he'd hold as naught all that he yet had done till he had met a creature who could tell the reason of what wailing. Busied with such-like thoughts and the remembrance of fair Brunissende, he rode the live-long day, spite of fatigue and heat. When daylight waned, two youths well-horsed, with falcon on the fist, and hounds and terriers running at their feet, came up to him; and after slight discourse, invited him to share their evening meal—and that so courteously, he could not make denial. The three young men then gaily went along, talking of love and battle's iron strife; when, as 'twas sunset, rose again that cry, at which the youths like madmen howled and wept.

"Good youths," quoth Jaufry, with astonishment, "what means this grief? What heard you, sirs, I pray; and why such noise?"

"Why? ask'st thou, foolish, treach'rous serf? that word shall cost thy life!"

And as one cast at him startled bird the other plucked his cap from his head and threw it madly 'gainst bold Jaufry's shield. Their fury and hard words finished as ceased that cry; when, quickly following the wond'ring knight, with honeyed phrase they charmed away his wrath, and to their habitation let the way.

This was a châtelet of graceful form, girded by lofty walls and outer fosse, through which a living stream for ever ran. Beside the bridge there sat an aged knight, listing a minstrel's song—"The

Lay of the Two Lovers." It was the father of the two young
men: beholding Jaufry, he in haste arose, and came to give him
welcome; saying, with joyful tone:

"I am beholden, lord, to those who've brought you: seven long
years have flown since stranger-guest hath this my threshold
crossed whose aspect pleased me so: God save you, sir!"

Thus speaking, by the arm knight escorted Jaufry to the hall,
where the two youths removed his armour bright. Soon there
came in a damsel fair, of fresh and smiling look, who brought
him a rich mantle, which when he had put on, she, on a cushion
placed beside him, sat. Then they discoursed on various pleasant
things until 'twas time for water to be brought. A well-bred page
did pour it o'er his hands, while the fair damsel held the ready
bowl; at which Sir Jaufry said:

"Maiden, I'll not this kindly act refuse; for should you e'er
need service at my hands, what'er the hour or place, you may
full surely call me to your aid."

They then at the table sat; and when the meal was o'er, the
cloth removed, the damsel went the couches to prepare, and left
her father and the knight alone. The old man asked his name,
and wept for joy to learn the son of Dovon was his guest—his
ancient friend in arms. He would have fain a month detained
him there; but Jaufry cleverly excuses made, and at the point of
day he in his saddle found himself again. The maid had given
him his shield and lance, and he his leave was then about to
take, when it occured to him to ask his host about that wailing
cry. Scarcely, however, was the question put when the old man
and his two sons alike assailed him with hard names: they called
him knave and wretch and villain's son; they tried to strike at him
with sturdy clubs, and tore their hair in that unseemly rage.

Jaufry by dint of spur escaped their wrath; and wond'ring saw
them on each other turn their fitful ire, and tear their clothes to
rags. Their fury spent, they called him back again; and Jaufry,
wishing to have news of Taulat, consented to return. As it fell
out, no man could give him more. The aged knight well knew
that champion fierce, and in these terms did tell him what he
sought:

"Follow," he said, "all day this very road; it leads across a track
of desert space, where ne'er are found or house or town, or bread
or wine, or man of mother born. If you should wish in passing
to repose, naught but the turf can be your host or tent. Go
onward thus until to-morrow's sun. Before the noon you will
have reached a plain, wherein is set a high and rugged mount.

There, at its foot, a castle you'll behold, pleasant and finely built; and round its moats a crowd of tents and huts, where harbour knights and lords of high descent. Pass stoutly on, nor speak a word to man; go to the castle without stop or stay, whatever may befall, and enter boldly in, leaving without your lance, and eke your shield. There will you find two dames—one old, one young—who watch a wounded knight. Go to the ancient dame, and to her say, that Augier de Cliart sends you there, that she may tell you why the people groan, and give you news of Taulat."

The Black Knight.

Well pleased at Augier's words, which seemed to raise his heart by full a span, Jaufry spurred bravely on, and by the morrow safely reached the spot his host had named. While he was passing through the scattered tents, the knights, who stared at him, exclaimed aloud:

"Behold a man who has ridden the night long, and hastens forward, but to seek his loss,"

Seeming as though he never heard the words, he to the noble castle straightway hied; which seemed most rich, and sculptured with fine art. Seeing a portal set with marble leaves and tinged of various hues, he there got down, secured his horse, and near him placing both his lance and shield, he passed within the door. At first his eyes no other forms beheld than those which orned the walls; but as he wandered on from room to room, he came at length where lay the wounded knight, and at his couch two dames in robes of woe, and tears upon their cheeks. As he was counselled by good Augier, then he to the elder went, and prayed her courteously, in Heaven's name, to tell him where was Taulat, and why the people of that land he left did day and night so weep.

Charmed with his breeding and his knightly words, the lady then explained that Taulat, whose brutality and pride exceeded bounds, would in eight days return.

"He comes," she said, "to glut his cruelty upon the wretched man who yonder lies. Seven years agone he with his lance did wound him cruelly; and when that wound is healed, each year, upon the feast-day of St. John, he has him fastened to a stake hard by, and beaten with a scourge until the wounds are opened once again. For this the vassals of the neighbouring land of Brunissende—whereof this knight is lord—weep and lament, and e'en do put to death those who would spy into their cause of grief."

"Lady," Sir Jaufry said, "pride slays its lord; and by that pride, I trust, will Taulat fall. In eight days' time to seek him I will come; and I can truly say that term will seem a year."

Commending her to Heaven, he left those halls, and took his way towards a neighbouring wood, where he did trust some man to meet to lodge him at his hut. The wood was gloomy, intricate, and dense; and at the first cross-road before him, he beheld, squatted beneath a pine, a hag, whose aspect struck him with surprise. Her head was larger than a portal's arch; her eyes were small as deniers, bleared besides and blue, misshapen, and deep-sunk beneath projecting brows. Her lips were black; teeth red as orpiment, which jutted out unseemly from her jaw. Her arms were sinewy, and her hands all knots; her face was colourless and wrinkled o'er; her body puffed; her shoulder round and high; her legs were skinny and of brownish hue; her knees were pointed; her toe-nails so long, no shoe could ever have enclosed her feet. A verdant wreath encircled her white hair, which stiffly stood on end. Her under-garment was of linen fine; her robe of ruddy silk; and over all a scarlet mantle fell, with ermine lined.

Jaufry saluted her; meanwhile with awe he gazed upon her figure strange, and ugly face. She turned her head, and without moving from her darksome seat, exclaimed:

"Retrace thy steps, sir Knight, and that at once."

"Not so, indeed," quoth Jaufry, "till I learn why thou dost tell me thus to fell away."

"Thou wilt repent it, then," the hag replied; "and death or dungeon shalt thou surely find."

"And wherefore so?"

"Go on, and thou wilt learn."

"Tell me, at least, with whom I'll have to strive."

"Those thou shalt meet will say."

"And thou, too; what are thou?"

"What thou beholdst!" the hag exclaimed, as, rising, she unfolded her huge length, tall as a knightly lance.

"Heaven!" Sir Jaufry cried, "in thee I trust; what figure have we here?"

"Dare to pass onwards," growled the wretched hag, "and thou shalt meet with worse."

"Nathless they stay not me: as to thy threats," he said, "I hold them as the wind, or nothingness."

Pricking his charger as he spoke the words, he passed along the path.

The hag, however, had but told the truth. For as he reached a chapel small, a holy hermit served, a knight of sable hue, mounting a sable horse, with sable arms, assailed him with such strength and unawares, that horse and knight were on the turf o'erthrown. Jaufry, all red with shame, at once upsprang, and, sword in hand, wished to avenge his fall; but, lo! no foe was there. He looked about, above, around, below, but horse and knight had vanished quite away. Again he mounted, his strange foe returned, with lowered lance, to strike at him again. Jaufry, prepared, now flew at him in turn; they midway met with shock so terrible, each rolled upon the earth. Half-wild with anger then, quick as the lightning Jaufry was afoot, with shield on guard and ready for the fight; but ne'er a foe was there.

"I will yet find him out," Sir Jaufry said, as in his saddle he again did leap. But scarce was foot in stirrup firmly set, when back returned the sable knight, hissing and growling as the thunder doth then tempests vex the air, and for the third time bore him to the ground. Jaufry, on his side, had so aimed his lance, it pierced his foe right through, and cast him on the turf. But when he wished to give the *coup-de grâce*, in vain he sought the knight, he neither saw nor heard.

"Good Heaven!" Jaufry cried, "where hath this recreant, this demon, fled? I drive my lance a fathom through his breast, I hurl him to the ground, and yet he flies, and doth escape my wrath! O gracious Lord, in Thee I put my trust!"

Again he mounted as he spoke these words; when the invisible once more appeared, unhorsing him anew. Why re-describe the scene? While daylight lasted, still this game went on. When off his horse, no creature did he see; but as he sat him on his charger's back the sable knight appeared to strike and hew. Weary of fight, Sir Jaufry then resolved to go on foot into the chapel-gate; but as he took his way, the spectre then his onward footsteps barred, so that the battle did again commence, and in the darkness without pause went on.

For half that night their swords and lances clashed, so that bright sparks of fire upward flew; fatigued at length to hear such din of arms, the hermit rose, and with his stole and cross and holy water, chanting a psalm, forth issues from his cell. The sable knight did not attend his coming; shrieking aloud, at once he disappeared, albeit behind him leaving such a storm as suffered no allay, until the chapel-bell rang out the matin hour.

Sheltered by this good man, Sir Jaufry asked, and thus obtained from him, the secret of the knight with whom he had fought so long.

"Friend, what thou ask'st I'll tell thee in few words: this knight in sable armour is a fiend, evoked from realms of darkness by a hag, whom thou perchance has met upon thy way. This hideous wretch once boasted as her spouse a monstrous giant, whose most wicked acts for twenty leagues around had spoiled the earth. As mortal, all-ferocious though he be, is ne'er without his peer, it happed this giant did return one night so grievously ill-used, that, at the end of three short days, he died. The hag, then, fearing for her own sad life and that of her two sons, called by her magic from the lower world that evil spirit who, for thirty years, these lands hath vexed. Meantime her sons have waxed in years and strength, and closely followed in their father's steps. Grown leprous, one, he dwelt within a house, built by his mother by the force of spells, whither his brother hath set out in haste, enraged and tost—for that the rumour saith a knight of Arthur's court the wretch hath slain. An it be true, may Heaven, all powerful, defend that knight!"

"He will endeavour to defend himself," quoth Jaufry smiling; "and the raged giant, if he held the wish, need not have gone so far to find him out: I am the man who did this brother slay, and by whose hand's the wicked spell was burst."

Eight days being fled, the hermit chanted mass, and at the altar prayed the holy saints to guide Sir Jaufry, and protect his life against the monster's wrath.

Having devoutly joined him in the prayer, the son of Dovon, like a valiant knight, did joyously set out; and scarce had ridden for an hour's space, when he beheld the giant swiftly come, bearing beneath his arm—with the same ease as he had done a child—a damsel, who did utter doleful cries. Her voice was hoarse from screaming out for help; her yellow hair, which sparkled in the sun, upon her shoulders all dishevelled fell like molten gold; her robe was torn, her eyes were swollen with tears; scarce, by Saint Mary! had she strength remaining to implore help of Jaufry.

The knight, with pity touched, heard not in vain the prayer. His shield advanced, his lance within the rest, he at the giant rode, and called aloud that he should loose the maid.

Letting her truly for an instant go, the giant ran towards the nearest tree, and pulling at the trunk, unearthed it, roots and all. Before, however, he had done so quite, Jaufry had plunged his lance into his side. Checked by the stroke, and trembling in the hand, the giant's blow lost half of its effect, yet ne'er the less it bore to mother earth both Jaufry and his steed. The knight full quickly leapt upon his feet; and with his ready sword struck at the monster with such vigorous hand, he sliced from off his flank a palm of flesh; and through the gaping wound one might behold his beating heart, whilst streams of blood poured through. Exhausted, tottering, still the giant overthrew the knight by striking with his fist upon his helm; but though his sword escaped from Jaufry's grasp, it was too late for harm—the giant fainting fell. On this, the knight hewed off his monstrous feet; when, in all gentleness, the maid he raised, for she had kneeled at her preserver's side, and thus did say:

"Accept, my lord, a thousand grateful thanks; for more than life have you preserved for me, in saving me from him!"

"Damsel," Sir Jaufry answered, "God for ever aid you! But explain how is't I find you here?"

"My lord, 'tis easy to relate the tale: but yesterday, I in an orchard strayed, to which my mother had conducted me; it was our usual walk; when, as we left the gates, behold your giant suddenly appeared, seized me at once, and to his castle now was bearing me away, when you, sir knight, so happily stepped in."

"I thank great Heaven, it was just in time! But where, I pray you, was you worthy sire, and where your brothers, when this giant came?"

"Hunting within the forest, good my lord: but you surprise me, asking me of them. One fain would say that you did know all; and yet, methinks, I ne'er have seen yourself."

"Sweet damsel, yea, and that few days agone. 'Twas at your father's, Augier good house, where I, at need, so courteously was served by you and all of yours."

"Blest be the hour, gentle lord an knight, you harboured 'neath our roof; and we, how happy to have you for guest."

"By this you see, my fair and courteous maid, how meet it is that we should service do, even to those unknown. One knows not who shall go or who shall come, they who do hold or they who hold them not, or what the future keeps for in store. Well it becomes us, then, to render help where help we can; welcome with courtesy, and honour guests with shelter and with food, whom chance may send us as they onward go."

"And where, Sir Jaufry," then inquired the maid, "if I ask, do you direct your steps?"

"I will explain as we do ride along. But I must haste: time presses; and e'en now I greatly fear me I shall come too late."

Remounting quickly, as these words were said, he then good Augier's daughter lifted up and placed upon his horse; for he resolved she should not quit his sight until he put her in her father's arms: this done, he rode apace towards the spot where lay the wounded knight.

Taulat de Rugimon

Never did help come more in time of need. Returned that very morn, Taulat had bound his prisoner to a stake; and four stout ploughmen, each armed with a strap, already raised their brawny arms to strike and ope the closèd wounds. But as Jaufry came, they stayed their hand to gaze awhile at him; nor less surprised than they, Taulat, who on the castle-terrace stood, descended in hot haste, and thus accosted Jaufry:

"Sir knight, I fain would learn what madness or what pride hath thus conducted thee into my lands. Dismount and doff thine arms, for thou art prisoner henceforth for ay."

"My Lord," the knight replied, "methinks you practise an unseemly haste. Give me, I beg, the time to tell my errand. I come to speak in favour of the knight you knaves were going to strike; and I entreat you, for the sake of me, to grant unto him grace."

"May Heaven help me!" Taulat answered him, "but sure thou art distraught: such words deserve the rope—a peasant's death."

"'Twould be a grievous wrong, my lord, the words being good and wise; again I do repeat them, praying grace for yonder knight, who seven long years hath groaned."

"Go, churl; too long I've listed; go and disarm thyself, if thou wilt live, and to my squires give up the girl with thee."

"If she's dishonoured and I put to shame, this arm, by Heaven, must indeed be weak."

"What! wouldst thou fight with me?"

"E'en unto death, before I suffer shame."

"Vain fool, beware; when on my neck I've put my shield, thou'lt find but little grace."

"Mine ear," quoth Jaufry, "hath been oft assailed by higher threats than these. I do reply, that, by the faith of Him who built this world, you shall set free you knight, and to the court of good King Arthur go, to pay the felony you there have done; or you shall fight with me, till you or I be vanquishèd and slain."

"Know'st thou then not, I've fought and conquered full five hundred knights, all better men than thou?"

"It may be so," quoth Jaufry; "now for proof: go get your arms, and God's high will be done!"

"No other armour," proudly Taulat said, "do I require than my good lance and shield: seven of thy strength might then come on, and I'd defy you all."

"'Tis madness," did Sir Jaufry make reply, "to enter fight unarmed. But since your pride doth blind your senses so, e'en have it as you will."

Furious at the words, Taulat addressed a squire:

"Go to the castle, quickly as thou canst; bring me my lance and shield, and tell the knights I've conquered one by one to meet me here, that they may witness a base peasant's death, as with a single blow I do intend, through shield and hauberk, to find out his heart. And at the instant, should this not be done, may I lose arms and chivalry and lady's love!"

The squire ran quickly to the scattered camp, where lodged the captive knights—who all were grieving for the wounded man, bound to the stake and waiting for the scourge—to them he briefly said:

"Barons, my lord attends you there beyond, that you may see him battle with a fool, who comes to seek his death."

Mounting then speedily the castle-stair—amid the tears and murmurs of the dames who ceaseless mourned—he took him down the shield and lance suspended to the rack, and bore them to his lord, who, vaulting on his horse, nor stopping to don breastplate or aught else, cried in a haught tone:

"Come to thy death, thou churl, whose sight offends me!"

Sir Jaufry, angered at the insult, then dashed at full speed upon the haughty knight, who like a lion came: so fearful was the shock, no saddle, girth, or art, availed Sir Jaufry. Down to the earth he rolled beneath the stroke. But not alone; for Taulat, on his side, by blow as vigorous and deftly put, at the same instant fell, his shield pierced through, and Jaufry's lance within his side.

A shout of joy unsprang from those good knights:

"Good Heaven, but this day thou chast'nest Taulat, and dost break that pride which long hath vexed the land!"

Jaufry meanwhile, his sword within his grasp, ran to fierce Rugimon, fast pinned to earth, as though some snake he were; but as he came, Taulat, in humble tone, exclaimed:

"For God's love, knight, O do not end thy work; for 'tis my folly that hath brought my death."

"Thy folly, true, was great," Sir Jaufry said; "but ere we part, I count on curing thee. Too long this pride endured, it now must have an end. Thou deemd'st this morn no knight was in the world who in address and strength could vie with thee. Most brave, no doubt, thou wast; but thy consuming and most wicked pride exceeded far thy valour, and 'tis a vice God neither loves nor bears. Thou now canst learn that, but for His resolve to chasten thee, this youthful arm—certes less robust than thine—would ne'er have cast thee down. 'Tis but the punishment for thy fierce pride, the outrage thou to good King Arthur didst—that flower of chivalry, whose uprightness god loves. And thus it fares with those who seek his shame: sooner or later will the knights, who sit at his Round Table famed, mete out their punishment, save 'neath the earth they hide. What they can do in fight, thou mayst surmise by me, a novice, scarcely two months armed, and who have sought thee day and night until this hour when thou does find the guerdon of thy deeds."

"All that thou sayst, sir knight, is but too true," Taulat replied, in weak and failing voice; "but mercy grant me, as thy conquered foe, as dying man, and who doth yield to thee."

"The mercy that thou prayst for, thou shalt have," Sir Jaufry said; "but upon certain terms: first, thou shalt go to good King Arthur's court, there yield thyself a prisoner; he will take such vengeance on thee as his honour claims."

"That will I do; but now, for Heaven's sake, permit the leech to bind me up this wound."

"No leech shall come, nor e'er shalt thou uprise, till, by St. Thomas, thou hast let go free the knight who's bound to yonder cruel stake, and all the captives thou hast ever made."

"Do as thou wilt, my lord, with them and me."

Jaufry at once did sheathe his own good blade and take the sword of Taulat. Then he allowed the squire to fetch the leech, who probed his master's hurt and washed the wound with water and white wine, when on a couch he had him gently laid, and borne within the gates.

Jaufry meanwhile set free the wounded knight; and having extorted from the captive lords their promise that they'd hasten to Carlisle, and to King Arthur his affair relate, he was about to leave them to God's care, when the wounded knight—lord paramount of all those gentlemen—most humbly to him said:

"Good sir, to you I yield, and with my person offer men and

lands. Most nobly have you won all this and more, in freeing me from all the pangs I've borne for seven weary years. So great those pangs, so cruel was my lot, better for me had death relieved my woes. Taulat, without a cause of enmity, hath tortured me full long; but now, by God's grace, and, sir knight, by yours, at length his reign is o'er."

"Good lord," responded Jaufry, "pray retain your having; naught do I wish for your deliverance, save that, with these brave knights, you do proceed to good King Arthur's throne, and there explain you owe your liberty to Dovon's son."

The knight such promise gave; when Jaufry, calling for his horse, which all prepared they brought, while Augier's daughter mounted by his side, he took of all farewell, and then set out for the fair damsel's home; his thoughts, in sooth, turning to Brunissende, towards whom he felt his heart most sweetly drawn.

When he had gone, Taulat returned the knights their steeds and arms, and, by the compact made, departed in their train for fair Carlisle. There they arrived upon the eleventh day. The worthy king gave audience to a dame, who, bathed in tears, her castle was to lose within a week, if she no champion found to meet her foe. When he had listed to her dolorous words, the king aggrieved replied:

"Lady, were Gawain here, most willingly would he defend your cause; but he is not: nor have I Dovon's son, nor Ivan bold, nor any of the braves of my Round Table. If of the knights who here surround my throne, there's standing one who'll venture you defence, great is the honour that shall be his meed."

But no one made reply. In vain the dame, turning to spurrèd heels, with warmth exclaimed:

"'Fore Heaven, brave knights, shall it be said a woman came to seek in this high court for aid, yet found it not?"

Still no one made reply.

'Twas at this moment Taulat's troop appeared; himself upon a gilded litter laid, covered with sumptuous cloth, and gently by two snowy palfries borne. Five hundred knights, he had in fight o'erthrown, armed *cap-à-pie*, followed in his train, each mounted on a charger richly decked. Their lord was at their head, who, as they reached the king, knelt humbly down before that monarch's throne, and thus addressed him:

"Sire, may He who for our weal came down on earth, which eke His blood bedewed, now grant you joy, and double your renown!"

"And you, friend, may He save!" the king replied. "But what,

I pray, are these, who seem so stout and good? And what the wounded man that litter holds?"

"My lord, the man is Taulat."

"Taulat de Rugimon?"

"My lord, the same; Jaufry, the son of Dovon. bravely vanquished him, and hither sends him to the queen and you; so that you may, my lord, such vengeance take as in your wisdom your consider fit, for the same outrage, now two months agone, he did to you."

"Heaven and earth," King Arthur then exclaimed, "how well hath Jaufry served me! Friend, tell me truth: when last you left him, was he safe and sound?"

"Great lord, he was, as doth comfort such honoured and brave knight, who hath nor grief nor fear. Naught else but good can harbour with his name; and it were sweet to laud, if that his acts did not upraise him more than words can ever reach. When you shall know from what most cruel fate his valour hath snatched *me*, you will indeed be full of wonderment. But this recital must before the queen and all her dames be made."

The king at once commanded unto Quex to go and seek the queen: the seneschal obeyed, when meeting her—

"Lady," said he, "if it so meet your wish, the king, your Lord and mine, bids you to come and list a message brought by valiant knight who heads a great escort."

The queen at once proceeded to the hall with all her dames and damsels; and when she placed herself besides her spouse, Melyan, the worthy knight, addressed them thus:

"Lady, from brave Sir Jaufry, Dovon's son, I bring high reparation to yourself and all your train. I bring you Taulat, hight of Rugimon, that you may vengeance take for the affront that he hath done to you, and for the cruelty he's heaped on me. Learn, without motive he my father slew, and me he wounded with such grievous hurt, that ne'er shall I be healed. I was his captive in his castle kept; and when my wound had closed, he too a stake did have me bound, and scourged by cruel hands until the wound again was open laid. Each month did I this martyrdom endure; which caused such dire despair throughout my lands, that, thrice by day, and thrice by night, they gave aloose to tears and doleful cries."

"By Heaven," exclaimed the worthy king at this, "what Felon act!"

"By all the saints of heaven," said the queen, "this was the reign of haughty pride run wild!"

"Yea," from the litter did Taulat respond, "I had, good sooth, most wicked, foolish pride; but I have lost it all. A leech appeared, who in a space most brief did work a cure. I sought in vain a knight who could make head against me, and I've found my match. Never did better jouster wield a lance: modest as brave, and generous as good, spite of my insults—which did merit death—Sir Jaufry gave me grace, and granted pardon. You, noble sire, who are the best of kings, deign but to imitate his clemency, and pardon give for that most foolish crime I here did madly do."

The worthy king, alway to good inclined, his pardon freely granted to the knight; any more, he used such reasons, with the queen, that Guenever, as generous, noble dame, her pardon likewise gave. Melyan alone remained inflexible. Rejecting all entreaty, he resolved, as was his right, since his was *corporal shame*, that Taulat should be judged by legal court.

At once they called a hundred legists in, who, when they'd heard the cause, the following sentence did at once proclaim:

"Taulat to Meylan shall be given up; who, month by month, shall bind him to like stake, and by like hands on him inflict like punishment. The court doth grant this power unto Meylan for seven years; with liberty albeit in him to set his prisoner free whene'er he feel inclined to grant him grace."

Brunissende and L'Ondine

AT the same hour the legists sentence passed, Sir Jaufry, riding quickly with the maid, before the towers of Augier arrived. Warned of his coming by the vassals' cries, who gave him joyful welcome and warm thanks for having set their lord and suzerain free, Augier mounted quickly on his horse, and with his sons came out to meet the knight. Beside Sir Jaufry he perceived the maid, guiding with sweeter grace than I can tell her gentle palfrey; but he knew her not, for she was veiled. Descending from his horse as he approached the knight, who eke alighted as he saw him come, he seized his hand, and with a trembling voice—

"My Lord," he said, "within my castle come, as you did promise me. We will most gladly there a welcome give, albeit my heart is melting with its woe. Since last we two did meet, a monster hath my daughter carried off, and with her all my joys."

"You did not guard her with sufficient care," Sir Jaufry mildly said, "since she is gone. What now remains to do? It was to be. None can avert his fate; so be consoled, and dry at once your tears. Some days agone, I won a maid in fight, gentle and lovely as a maid can be; and if you will, to you I'll give her up, that she may take the place of her that's lost."

"Alas, my Lord," good Augier replied, "where is the damsel or the dame that can compete with her in grace, in gentle manners, gaiety, and love? Her like is still unborn; and for my rest of days this world to me can naught, alas, afford of happiness or ease."

"And I do still the contrary affirm; and more than that, declare that you this damsel shall her equal find in beauty and in love."

In speaking thus Sir Jaufry raised her veil; and Augier looking, his sweet daughter knew. When he had pressed her often in his arms, a thousand grateful thanks bestowed on Jaufry, and listed to the tale of his exploits with Taulat and the giant, he to the castle led the way, the serfs and vassals following in troops.

Great was the honour they there showed the knight: the brothers poured the water for his use, the damsel served him with her own fair hands a roasted peacock nobly bedecked, and Augier fain had kept him there a month; but Jaufry, frankly owing that his heart allured him to Montbrun, set out the morrow morn. Escorted by his host and his two sons, he took his way, musing on Brunissende; when, at the hour of noon, he met her seneschal, just then returned from fair Carlisle, where he had Taulat seen and Melyan and the five hundred knights from bondage freed. He still was seeking, by his dame's command, brave Dovon's son; but half-de-spaired success. Scarcely, however, did he learn the truth, that Melyan's saviour and the weary knight who in the orchard slumbered were the same, when, urging his horse, ne'er did he stop until Montbrun was reached, where travel-soiled he came to Brunissende.

"Where is the knight?" asked she, before the man could e'en unclose his lips. "Cometh he on? shall I soon seen him here?"

"He follows me, fair lady," he replied; "but such his deeds, whereof the saving of our lord from pain and torment is but one, that I do think 'twere well you met the knight, and with a hundred damsels formed escort."

The thought pleased Brunissende. She orders gave to deck the roads with green, to hang rich stuffs and silk, damask and cloth-of-gold, upon the castle-walls; while she herself, mounting her palfrey white, with all her court and knights and damsels fair, went out to meet Sir Jaufry. Arrayed most richly in a silken robe with trimmings of pure gold, she had upon her blondin tresses placed a gorgeous wreath, where peacock's feathers shone; while in her hand she bore the choicest flowers from her garden culled. No wonder, then, if Jaufry were surprised to see her come thus lovely, full of grace, and smiling as the queen of the sweet south. With courteous words they met, and side by side to Montbrun's lordly halls together they returned.

I leave you to surmise the games and joy which at the castle on that day were seen. Jaufry and Brunissende the fair alone nor ate nor oped their lips. The lady glanced at Jaufry with a sigh, and each sweet glance shot through his softened eyes and fell into his heart; while Jaufry, on his side, at every moment blushed, and through the very marrow of his bones, by dart invisible, did feel that he was pierced. Musing of love, the live-long night, they watched till rosy morning came. In her chamber the fair lady, and Jaufry on his gorgeous couch, thought but of the gentle speeches they would make the morrow morn; and, when once the sun had risen, they were up and quickly clad; and when mass at length was over, side by side they sat them down in the great hall of the castle, where they oped their swelling hearts.

'Twas Brunissende who first the silence broke; for, dazzled by her beauty, Jaufry lost in gazing on her face the pretty speeches he had framed o'ernight.

"My lord," she said, in voice of sweetest tone, "your coming brings us joy and happiness; no service could be higher than the one you've rendered us; and bless we good King Arthur in his knight, bless we the land which claims so brave a man, and—bless we, too, the lady for whose sake such noble acts are done."

"Alas," sighed Jaufry, at this latter phrase, "no lady cares for me."

"You speak in jest," said then fair Brunissende; "your sense and valour raise you up too high for noble lady not to care for you."

"I care, perhaps, for her—not she for me."

"Knows she at least of this your love for her?"

"I cannot say, fair lady, if she guess; but I ne'er told my love."

"No blame can then at least alight on her: if you ne'er seek where lies the remedy of that same evil whereof you complain, who is in the wrong?"

"'Tis I, sweet lady, I. Her greatness curbs me, fills me with strange fears; I cannot ask her love, for ne'er an emperor who trod this earth but by that love were honoured—such is the height, above all other dames, to which she's raised by sovereign grace with wealth."

"What you now say is folly, gallant knight, emperors and Kings ne'er won in true love's lists a greater prize than brave and courteous man: such love holds not to riches; noble heart and gentle grace have in his court more power than lands and titles. How many folks there are of high descent whose worth is valued highly at a groat! How many others rolling in bright gold whose value would not buy a coat of mail! Hide, then, no longer in your single heart the thought with which it's filled; your valour and your deeds give you a claim to match upon this earth with the most fair, most high."

Sir Jaufry heaved a sigh, and thus, much moved, replied:

"Lady, forgive, I pray you, the avowal which you, forsooth, are destined now to hear—avowal that no torture e'er had drawn, but which is due to those sweet words of yours. You, then, are she for whom my heart doth melt; she whom I love and fear and I implore; she who doth hold the keys of all my joys, my pains, and who can make of me, even at her will, foolish or wise, a coward or a brave."

At length had Brunissende the fair attained the sum of her desire; yet she her joy concealed, and in a tone of playfulness exclaimed:

"Sir Jaufry, you are pleased to banter me; ne'er can I think I have the power you say."

"A thousand times more power, you may believe, than I can ever tell."

"That we shall prove right soon," she made reply. The age is spoiled by wicked usages: true courtesy is lost, and he who warmly vows that he doth love too oft but utters lies. If you full truly wish to have *my* love, I must be wed as well as wooed, my lord."

Sir Jaufry cared not, you may well believe, such offer to refuse. He had just vowed by Peter and St. Paul naught upon earth such joy could give to him, when a knight entered, beating on his shield, to announce the coming of the Lord of Brunissende.

"To horse, good knights, to horse!" the lady cried; when lords and damsels, mounting in hot haste, went out to meet their suzerain.

As thus the cavalcade rode gaily off, headed by Jaufry and fair Brunissende, they saw approach two ladies dressed in black, with eyes all red and swimming with fresh tears. Jaufry saluted them, and then inquired for tidings of Lord Melyan; but one of them in under-tone replied, and with a sigh, that of Lord Melyan nothing did she know; she thought but of her woes.

"Tell us," said Jaufry, "why you shed these tears."

"Since you do wish to know, my lord, I'll speak the truth. A knight, misshapen, and ill-bred to boot, wishes to force on me his odious love; and I in grief have left King Arthur's court, where I have neither found advice nor aid."

"You do astonish me," Sir Jaufry cried; "where was Sir Gawain then? Ivan the courteous, Coedis that brave knight, Tristrem and Calogrant, Lancelot du Lac, Eric and Caravis, and bitter Quex—pray, where were they?"

"I know it not, by Heaven, good my lord; nor have I any trust but in Sir Jaufry, that most famous knight whom now I seek, that he may turn my fate, and my good right maintain."

"I will maintain it, certes," then Jaufry said; "for I am he, the Jaufry whom you seek; but I must first conclude a matter here which before all things claims my every thought."

The mourning lady wept and urged her suit, spite of the angry looks of Brunissende. Sir Jaufry would not yield, but to Montbrun with Melyan straight returned. The lady there, giving all cause to think that to her suzerain she bowed her will, was for long time entreated she her hand should give to Dovon's son; then they set out for Carlisle's gallant court, and in their train were twice twelve hundred maids, and full three thousand knights in brilliant arms.

The three first days of travel naught occurred; but on the fourth, having pitched their tents in a green mead, balmy with flowers, and shut in with trees, Jaufry and Melyan suddenly did hear a voice which help implored in piercing tone. The son of Dovon called for horse and arms, and would alone go seek this cause of wail. He thus arrived upon the borders of a pond of some extent and limpid water, where a damsel stood tearing her hair and robe, and, in her grief, her face.

"My lord," she cried, as Jaufry hastened up, "have pity, for St. Mary's sake, upon a dame who in this pond is drowning; she was the best, the wisest of her sex."

Jaufry advanced; and there, in truth, he saw, within the waters battling with death, a dame, who now appeared, now slid beneath the wave. He soon alighted, and his efforts used to save her with the butt-end of his lance; but whilst his arm was thus outstretched, and he stood by the brink, the damsel pushed him with such hearty will, at once he toppled in, which she perceiving, leapt in after him.

Drawn downward by the great weight of his arms, Sir Jaufry disappeared with those two dames. The neighing and the rage of his good horse, which pawed the ground and madly bit the earth about the pond, announced this dire mischance to Melyan. He hastened there; and finding Jaufry drowned, he swooned away. 'Twas then the rest, 'mong whom the news had flown, galloped full speed towards that fatal pond. Force was required to drag Lord Melyan off; for, when restored, he tried to drown himself; and, for fair Brunissende, she by her seneschal was barely saved, since, Jaufry lost, she would not him survive.

Joining her cries to dames' and damsels' moans and to the lamentations of her lords—

"O Jaufry, Jaufry!" sobbed she wildly out, "frank, generous knight, all-powerful at arms, who then hath ta'en thy life? Some traitor-blow hath struck thee by surprise; for living man could ne'er have fairly won. O Jaufry! lone on earth, what good am I? Worthless is life, which keeps me far from thee. I pray for death, which comes not at my call. Where shall I seek this truant sense-less death, which will not reunite me to my love? There 'neath yon water doth his body lie, which calls me, waits in vain."

Then suddenly upspringing, lost, and mad with grief, she to the treach'rous water wildly flew; and 'twas by dint of strength they dragg'd her back. Then she her tresses tore, her lovely face, till in a swoon her woe and sense were numbed.

Good Augier had her carried to her tent, where on her couch the damsels laid her down; then he returned, and with the other knights around the fatal wave did weep and groan. Such were their tears, their mourning and their cries, that the archbishop learnt the fatal news, and to console that doleful train proceeded to the mead.

With wisdom there he preached, and in his sermon said:

"My friends, the Scripture teacheth us that God is master of all things, and when He pleaseth can again resume those gifts He hath bestowed. If, then, Sir Jaufry hath been ta'en by Him, He, as His work, might freely call him back; and it were sin to find such judgment ill, and felony towards our Sovereign Lord. They among you who held this brave knight dear, should now to heaven pray he may be saved; and should at once give o'er these cries of woe, as vain rebuke towards your Heavenly King."

The Giant

WHILE the archbishop preached beside the pond, Sir Jaufry found himself with those two dames in a delicious land. Valley and plain, water and shady grove, city and castle—all was charming there. Before he well recovered his surprise, the lovelier of his two companions said:

"I now, sir knight, do hold you in my power; perchance this time you'll not refuse to do the service which with tears I begged of you some three short days agone."

"Lady," Sir Jaufry wondering replied, "methinks I ne'er set eyes on you before."

"I am that weeping dame who did entreat you to defend her rights 'gainst Felon d'Albaru, a wicked wretch, whom God confound! This monster, who doth not deserve the name of knight, since he doth naught but plan most villain acts and set vile snares, bears on his shoulders more the head of horse or bull than that of living man. His eyes are large as eggs; his features horrible; his lips are thick and black; his fangs project from out his mouth, which is itself huge as a leopard's jaw; and against nature are his frightful shape, distended body, and misshapen legs."

"'Tis not to fright you, good my lord, I draw this portrait of my foe—your heart ne'er harboured fear: but true it is, he doth all men alarm; so that his aspect, at a distance seen, doth scare away all such as would defend my cause. As yet in fight invincible, he hath despoiled my lands and all the country round; I but my castle now have left to me, and that to-morrow must be given up, if God and you oppose not such decree. But I would rather suffer torture, death, than fall into his power."

"Is all this true?" asked Jaufry.

"Yea, lord, by the faith!"

"Since yours the right, I'll battle with this foe; but you have wrong'd me, and fair Brunissende hath certes her thoughts on death."

"She," said the lady, "fear not, will not die; and you will me have saved."

As thus discoursing, they the castle reached; a building strong, surrounded by good walls, with fosses, cut from out the solid rock, filled with a living stream. Jaufry was there most grandly entertained by that fair lady's vassals; and, morn come, when he had dressed and armour buckled on, bathed well his face and hands, and prayed to Heaven to give him grace that day and strength to uphold the right of the oppressed, he with humility attended mass, and gave seven marks of silver.

When mass was done, he to the terrace mounted with the dame and with her damsels, and watched for Felon's coming. Short space elapsed during their stopping there, he suffering in his heart for Brunissende's just grief, ere a bright band of knights appeared upon the plain.

"Lady," he then inquired, "is this our foe?"

"'Tis he, my lord, with all his train. He rides ahead of them."

"Let him then come, and we will hear his cause."

Felon came gently on, bearing upon his fist a hawk most rare as it was beautiful. It had a slender neck, a large beak sharper than a razor's edge, long wings, a tail a palm at least in length, a sinewy leg, and strong and shapely foot.

Just as he came beneath the castle-walls, Felon perceived some hundred cranes all grouped about the grass of a small verdant close; at once he loosed the hawk, which flying off, began to wheel about the grassy spot, then rose up in the air to such vast height, scarce could the eye detect his presence there. Some time elapsed, then straightway down he shot, and pounced upon the cranes with cry so dread, that, fluttering and hiding in the grass, they let themselves by Felon's men be caught without attempting to escape away.

When they had thus some dozens of them ta'en, Felon recalled the bird, which on his fist again returned to perch.

"By Heaven!" quoth Jaufry, muttering half-aloud, "that man possesses a right precious bird; never was finer seen or one more stanch; and could I win it, and return above, 'twould be a worthy present for the king."

"You shall return full soon, my gentle lord," the lady smiling said, "and shall bear with you, I have little doubt, both Felon's bird and arms."

During this time, the giant had drawn near; and when he stood before the castle-bridge, with all his strength he cried:

"Come down all you who there above do stand; and with you bring along that idle jade, whom I will make the servant of my squires."

"My lord," said Jaufry calmly in reply, "if you left here the jade whereof you speak, pray you to point her out, and none will strive such person to detain."

"You know full well the meaning of my words. Give up the dame and castle, as agreed."

"All covenant is sacred."

"So give up the dame."

"But if you please, my lord," Sir Jaufry said, "where is the right by which you claim such prize?"

"The right of my good pleasure, signor knave; who soon shall dangle on a hempen rope."

"'Tis an ill answer, savouring great pride. But all injustice doth not win its end. You would abuse your strength against a woman having no defence. Go arm yourself; for Heaven hath sent her one who will maintain her right."

"An the saints help me," Felon then replied, "you shall pay dearly for those words of yours."

Giving his squire the hawk, without delay he donned his hauberk and his armour rich, buckled his helm, and seized his lance and shield; when out he cried:

"Let that pert knave descend who wants to fight: we soon shall see upon this very spot how he doth wield his arms."

Sir Jaufry went to put his armour on, and as he did so, made to God his prayer; crossed he the drawbridge without noise or vaunt, while the fair lady and her vassals knelt and made this orison:

"Thou, Lord, who didst thy hands upon the cross permit Thy foes to nail, and let an infidel pierce through Thy side, now grant to Jaufry strength to conquer Felon!"

The champions met within the verdant close where the hawk chased the cranes. And when the giant did Sir Jaufry see, fiercely he cried:

"Hast thou thy senses, fool, to dare meet such as I?—I, who could vanquish full a score like thee?"

"High vaunts like these," Sir Jaufry calmly said, "I hold as little worth; for idle words are but as empty wind. Now list: if thou wilt render back unto the dame who owns yon castle even the smallest thing thou hast unjustly filched from her away, thou mayst depart without a scratch or wound."

"Find bargain, on my faith," the giant said; "thou dost pretend to grant me thy good grace: and I affirm I will not quit this spot till with this hand I've torn thee limb from limb."

"Now I no more can list; pride blinds thy sense. Henceforth, then, beware of me!"

And Jaufry at these words wheeled round his horse to give him a broad field, when at full gallop he did rush at Felon. Seeing him come, the latter grasped his shield, and flew to strike him with such dire shock, both horse and knight were thrown. But in the encounter Jaufry's steady lance had broken his shield and pierced the arm right through. Like lightning Dovon's son was on his feet, his good sword firmly grasped. Mad with his wound, Felon came running up, and loudly cried:

"'Fore Heaven, villain, thy last hour is come, and without mercy shall thy carcass swing!"

It was his thought to pin him to the earth; but Jaufry dealt his horse so true a blow, it clean shaved off his head. So both were now afoot, and front to front with the same arms: now we shall shortly learn which is the better knight.

Felon, all pale, with foam upon his lips, struck with his sword upon Sir Jaufry's helm a blow so strong, it paired the visor off; the latter dealt him in his turn a stroke which made his shield-arm droop. But such the force with which he gained this point his sword escaped his hand. This Felon seeing, he his foot placed on't, so that the knight might not resume the blade; then he assailed him with such strength, fire flew from out his helm.

"Yield thee, sir knight!" the giant fiercely cried, "since thou are now disarmed."

Sir Jaufry answered not, but raised his shield to ward a blow that seemed intended to conclude the fight; for Felon's sword fell on it with such force, it shivered it in bits, and full two feet the blade struck in the earth.

Quick as the lightning's flash the youthful knight darted to raise his own, which when he held, he turned again on Felon. He, humbled in his pride, exclaimed aloud:

"Mercy, sir knight; O, mercy! pray restrain thine hand, and hold me at a ransom!"

"Since you speak thus," Sir Jaufry made reply, dragging the giant's sword from out the ground, "render yourself to *her* you have so oppressed. As for myself, no ransom do I wish saving yon hawk which chased erewhile the cranes."

Felon then called about him all his knights, who bore him to the castle. There, when the leech had bound his gaping wounds, they laid him on a couch borne by two quiet steeds; whilst the fair dames, followed by numerous train, led Jaufry back to where they brought him from.

The Court of Carlisle

LORD MELYAN and his troop were still encamped upon the borders of the magic pond. Judge their surprise, their shouts, their whirl joy, when, 'mid a numerous train, Sir Jaufry rose!

As for fair Brunissende, so great the emotion which such change produced, it found no vent in words, but in a swoon she fell into his arms. Jaufry related how the fairy's art had to her country led him through the deep and darksome waters; how he had vanquished her great giant foe, and gained the wondrous hawk for the good king. Then, the recital o'er, they gaily took their way, and at the peep of the next following morn, they saw fair Carlisle's towers. Leaving their train a little way behind, Jaufry and Melyan, clad in armour bright, pranced on the glacis with eight chosen knights. Such a bravado at King Arthur's court could not unnoticed pass. Quex, the high seneschal, soon crossed the bridge, and meeting Jaufry cried:

"Good sooth, sir Knight, thou shalt repent thy coming."

"'Tis thou shalt feel repentance more than I," responded Jaufry, who divined the man, and meeting him full speed, did with such strength and art assail Sir Quex, he hurled him to the ground.

As he essayed to struggle to his feet, he reeled a pace, then fell, while Jaufry cried:

"Why, how now, jolly Quex? What say'st, art drunk?"

Gawain had now appeared upon the field, spurring his horse to join in the affray. Sir Jaufry went to meet the worthy lord, and as he yielded up Sir Quex's horse:

"To you alone, good knight," he said, "I yield."

Gawain then knew the voice of Dovon's son, and pressed him in his arms; which, when his squire had learnt, he flew to take the tidings to the king. Good Arthur overjoyed then left his halls, and with a gallant host of knights and lords came forth to honour Taulat's vanquisher. Fair Brunissende he courteously did greet with all her train; then, smiling, said to Jaufry:

"Hath, then, our seneschal on you his horse thus gen'rously bestowed?"   "My lord," the son of Dovon made reply, "perchance you may remember, on the day I begged you arms to follow Taulat's track, Sir Quex exclaimed, I'd fight him better drunk. 'Twas then my wish to teach him, good my lord, how I can strike when fasting."

"He is well struck, methinks," the king replied; "and may the lesson stead him!"

"Saying the words, he led Sir Jaufry in to good Queen Guenever, who, as she tended him her rosy cheek, thanked him with warmth for having 'venged her cause on Taulat. King Arthur on his side did give him thanks for all the precious gifts he there had sent—the fair white ashen lance, the yeoman's dwarf and e'en the leper's too, Estout de Verfeil and the captive knights, Melyan, and Taulat's numerous prisoners, with Felon d'Albaru; then was the convent-church most richly decked, to which the king in pomp conducted him with the fair Brunissende.

More than a score of thousand gallant knights the fair betrothed accompanied. The good archbishop, who had chanted mass, before the altar joined the happy pair; then to the palace back again they came, and the great feast began. At trumpet sound, Lucas the royal steward, with twenty thousand pages clad in vests of scarlet silk, bearing fine snowy cloths, vases of silver and rich cups of gold, flocked to the hall to furnish forth the boards. Already harps had tinkled, minstrels tried to charm their hearers with the gay romance, when straight into the hall a squire rushed, crying aloud:

"To arms! good lords, to arms; defend your lives!"

"What hast thou seen, good friend?" King Arthur said.

"O sire, I've seen a bird, a wond'rous bird, which never man of mother born described. He hath a beak at least ten palms in length, and a huge head large as a fisher's boat; his eyes like carbuncles or diamonds shine; and then his feet, good sooth, without a lie they are as big—as big as yonder door. I know not how I did escape his maw; but ne'er methinks was I so near my death."

"Bring me my arms," exclaimed the gallant king, "that I may learn whether this squire hath lied."

Gawain, Sir Jaufry, and Lord Melyan, fain would follow him to help; but he forbade, and thus alone did quit the castle. Scarce had he crossed the bridge, when he beheld this marvellous great bird. He quietly drew nigh, his shield on arm, his sword within his hand. But, spreading its grand wings, the bird escaped a blow full promptly aimed; and by both arms embracing tight the king, rose with its prey full swiftly in the air. Ladies and knights despairingly rushed out, and o'er the country spread with rending cries. The bird still rose; and when in bulk it seemed no bigger than a crane, it then the king let go. The crowd, all breathless, hastened to the spot, where they expected that their king would fall crushed from that dizzy height. Not so! ere that he reached the ground the bird had deftly seized on him again, and to the summit of a lofty tower borne him in ease away. Reposing there a space, with rapid wing it flew towards the wood, wheeled with a graceful flight, then to the palace brought the king again; itself returning to a human shape, that of the fair enchanter, whom Arthur pardoned, as he'd done at Pentecost, the fright his trick had caused. And thus did close the joyous nuptial feast of brave Sir Jaufry and fair Brunissende. The morrow-morn they left the merry court; and all the train, which called Sir Meylan lord, escorted back in triumph to Mountbrun that happy pair, meeting upon their way the lady of the pond (she was in fact the fairy of Gibel), who there had come to bless their life and love.

SON OF THE MORNING
by Ian McDowell

We now enter the start of the dark days of Arthur's reign as Mordred appears on the scene. Mordred was the incestuous son of Arthur and his sister Morgause, but at the outset Arthur did not realise Mordred was his offspring. He was raised amongst his elder brethren Gawain, Agravain, Gaheris and Gareth, but the moment had to come when his true origin was learned by Arthur. This was the situation that attracted Ian McDowell who, with his first sale, 'Son of the Morning', considered the situation from the point of view of the young Mordred.

I sat on the cold cliff and squinted out across the water, absent-mindedly trying to drop stones on the heads of the squawking terns that nested on the tiny beach so very far below. I'd been waiting for a long time—my nose felt full of icicles and my backside was almost frozen numb. It was all a rather silly vigil: sea voyages being what they are, Arthur might not make landfall for the better part of a week. Still, I waited there, naively expecting to see the speck of his ship approaching over the dark swells. Time is nothing but an inconvenience when you're fourteen years old.

It was all so exciting. My uncle Arthur was coming to our island to do battle with a giant he'd driven out of his own realms the year before. My Da, King Lot of Orkney, had sent a rather sharp letter to his brother-in-law when Cado (that was the monster's name) turned up on our shores and started terrorizing the peasantry. Not being one to leave such things half done, Arthur

322

responded with a promise to come to Orkney and settle Cado's hash just as soon as he was able.

Lot hadn't given much thought to Cado when his depredations were confined to the Pictish and Dalriadan Scottish peasantry, but that changed when the giant swam the eighteen miles or so of stormy water between those territories and our island and announced his presence on our shores by wiping out three entire farmsteads down on Scapa Bay. And although royal search parties had found the remains of over two dozen gnawed skeletons, they'd not come across a single skull. Cado evidently had the charming habit of collecting his victims' heads.

I thought about all of this as I sat on the cliff at Brough's head. I'd never been particularly worried about the monster, for he had confined himself to the less-settled end of the island—and what were a few rustic peasants more or less? And I enjoyed the embarrassment that my father suffered for being unable to cope with the menace, for I harbored little love for Lot. Still, I looked forward to Arthur's coming. His battle with Cado was sure to be more exciting than a mainland boar hunt. And I did love my uncle. I loved him very much.

Suddenly I spotted it, the tiny speck that could only be a distant ship. I rubbed my salt-stung eyes, but it stayed out there; not wishful thinking but the hoped-for reality. Beyond the toy-like sail, dark clouds tumbled low across a sky as cold and gray as old, unpolished iron. The ship seemed to be riding before a storm. Evidently, they'd decided to chance the weather and made for Orkney rather than turn back to the mainland coast they'd surely been hugging during their long trip up from Cornwall.

I leapt up with a whoop and started scrambling back away from the cliff. The jagged stones, wet and black and speckled with bird dung, gave me poor footing, and several times I stumbled and fell before reaching the sand and turf. Over the rise bulked Lot's palace, squatting there in the lee that gave it some scant protection from the sea and wind. It might not have been much by mainland standards, but it was the grandest building in all the Orkneys. A twenty-foot ditch and two earthworks encircled a horseshoe-shaped two-story stone and timber hall. I dashed across the plank bridge that spanned the ditch and waved up at the soldiers manning the outer earthwork. Those that weren't busy playing dice, sleeping on the job, or relieving themselves waved back.

Mother's tower was on the opposite side of the inner courtyard from the Great Hall. Picking my way through milling clusters of chattering serfs, grunting pigs, squawking chickens, honking geese, and other livestock, I skirted the deepest mud and the piles of fresh excrement until I arrived at the tower's slab-sided foundation. The brass knocker stuck out its tongue and leered at me. "Who goes there?" it demanded in a tinny soprano.

"Mordred mac Lot, Prince of Orkney," I snapped, trying to sound smart and military. The door made no response. "Open up, dammit, I said I'm the Prince!"

The knocker rolled its eyes nonsensically. "I heard you the first time," it trilled, "and I don't care if you're the Prince of Darkness himself, I'm not opening this door until you've wiped your filthy feet!"

It was futile to argue with something that wasn't even really alive. I scraped the heels of my boots against the doorstep while muttering a few choice curses. When I was finished, the door swung wide without further comment. But I knew that it was snickering at me behind my back.

The stairs were steep and winding, which was one reason why King Lot never came here, though they didn't bother Mother, who had the constitution of a plow horse. The room at the top was high and narrow and all of gray stone. It had one window, large and square, with an iron grille and heavy oaken shutters. A ladder connected with a trap door that opened up onto the roof. In one corner was a brick hearth with a chimney flue, not so much a fireplace as an alcove for the black iron brazier that squatted there like a three-legged toadstool. Flanking the alcove were imported cedar shelves lined with animal skulls, a few precious books, rather more scrolls, netted bunches of dried herbs, and small clay jars containing rendered animal fats and various esoteric powders. In the center of the floor was an inlaid tile mosaic depicting a circle decorated with runic and astrological symbols. Off to one side of the mosaic stood a low marble table where Mother sacrificed white doves, black goats, and the occasional slave who'd become too old, sick, or just plain lazy to be worth his keep.

Today it was a goat. Queen Morgawse was bent over the spread-eagled carcass, absorbed in the tangle of entrails that she carefully and genteelly probed with the tip of her silver-bladed sacrificial dagger. From the expression on her sharp, high-cheekboned face, I knew she'd found a particularly interesting set of omens in the cooling guts.

"Hullo, Mother."

She looked up, straightening to her full, considerable height.

I may have gotten her black hair and green eyes (I'd seemingly inherited nothing of Lot's appearance, thank the gods), but that impressive stature had all gone to my older brother Gawain, though he'd added to it a broad beefiness that contrasted with her willow slimness. She was dressed in her standard magical attire: an ankle-length black gown that left her arms bare. On her head was a silver circlet, and her long, straight hair was tied back with a blood-red ribbon.

She smiled. "What is it, sweets?"

"Arthur's here. I saw the ship."

She frowned. "Is he now? And me such an untidy mess." She wiped her bloody hands on the linen cloth she'd laid out under the goat. "Do me a favor, love. Clean up this mess while I go change to greet our guests. Do you mind?"

"No, Mother."

After giving me a quick kiss on the cheek, she hurried down the stairs, leaving me alone in the room. I bundled the goat into the stained dropcloth and stumbled with it to the window. That side of the tower was built into the earth and timber wall that formed the fourth side of the courtyard square. With a heave I got my burden through the aperture. It landed on the other side of the wall. Immediately a battle for possession of the carcass broke out between a pack of the palace dogs and several of he serfs who had hovels there.

A wet whistling sound came from somewhere above me. "Hello, Young Master. Please give me something to eat."

I looked up at Gloam where he clung to the ceiling directly over the magic circle. "No, I don't have time. Arthur's here."

Gloam resembled nothing so much as a pancake-shaped mass of dough several feet in diameter, his pale surface moist and sweaty with small patches of yeasty slime. Offset from his center was a bruise-like discoloration about the size of a head of lettuce. Only when its round mouth puckered open and its wrinkled lids parted to reveal eyes like rotting oysters did it become recognizable as a face. Gloam wasn't much to look at, but then, few people keep demons for their beauty.

"I know all about Arthur," he gurgled in a voice like bubbles in a swamp. "Your mother and he. . ." He broke off, looking suddenly uncomfortable.

"What was that?" I asked, curious despite myself.

"Oh, nothing, nothing at all. Forget I even said it."

I sighed impatiently. "Are you trying to trick me, Gloam?"

He darkened to the color of the old buttermilk and faded back to his normal pasty hue, always a sign that he was enjoying himself. "No, not at all. I just know something that I'm not allowed to tell you."

"Something about Arthur, I take it."

He whistled and expelled gas. "Well, yes, and rather more than that. Have you ever wondered who your father is?"

My patience was wearing thin. "He's the King of Orkney, you stupid twit."

"Haven't you ever considered the possibility that King Lot might not be your da?"

Hadn't I ever. I suddenly felt a strange gnawing in my guts, as if I'd swallowed something cold and hungry. Not that Lot not being my father would make for any great loss, but if he wasn't, just who was? Finding my voice again, I asked Gloam as much.

"I can't tell you that," he gurgled in reply. "Your mother doesn't want you to find out until after you've reached manhood."

"I'm fourteen, dammit," I snapped in my best regal manner.

"Well, yessss," he mused, "and there was the serving maid with whom you tried to. . ."

"Never mind that!"

"And that is one common definition of initiation into manhood," he continued. "Not that you managed it very well."

Enough was enough. "Listen, you stinking, slimy mollusk, if you don't tell me right this very moment what it is that you've been hinting at, I'll. . ."

"Oh, all right," he said before I could come up with an appropriate threat. "But you must find me something to eat first. A dog, perhaps. Or a cat. A child would be best, really. A tender little milk-fed babe."

"Oh, stuff it," I snapped, "I'll go catch you a chicken."

He smiled, never a pleasant sight. "A chicken would be very nice."

So I ended up chasing chickens through the deep mud of the inner courtyard for several frustrating minutes. Finally, I caught a fat rooster. Tying its legs together with a strip torn from the hem of my surtunic, I puffed and panted my way back up the stairs with the protesting cock tucked securely under one arm. It shat on me, of course, but my clothes were already so soiled that it hardly mattered.

I tossed the bird onto the tiled circle. Gloam detached himself from the ceiling with a loud sucking noise and fell on the hapless fowl, his jellyfish-like substance hiding it from view. After a brief struggle, the thing that moved under that white surface lost all recognizable shape and there was only a sort of pale sac that quivered slightly beneath its coat of frothy perspiration. The inflamed face erupted from his upper surface and grinned at me, the toothless mouth slack and drooling.

"Well, out with it, you repulsive greaseball!"

Gloam frowned. "All right, Mordred. Arthur's your father."

I didn't understand. "But he's my uncle!"

"Oh yes, that too."

"Oh." My mind felt blank; I didn't know what to think or feel. "How?"

Gloam sighed. "Your mother will have my arse for this."

"You don't have an arse. Now, tell me how it happened."

His face flushed from dark purple to bluish green. "Fifteen years ago Arthur was little more than a green boy with his first command. No one knew who his father was: he was a landless bastard of a soldier. But he was very handsome. It happened during the Yuletide feast at Colchester, when the King and Queen of Orkney were paying their seasonal visit to Uther's court. Arthur had just had his first taste of battle and it had gone very badly. He drank too much. Your mother was tired of her dry little stick of a king, so she paid a midnight visit to Arthur's tent. It was dark and he never knew that she was the Queen of Orkney, much less that she was his own sister. When they met some years later he thought it was the first time. That's all there is to tell."

Arthur was my father. It was dizzying to go from being the son of a cold and loveless island lord to being the son of the best man in the known world. What would he say if he knew he was my da? My understanding of his Christian morality was dim at best, and, foolish as it sounds, the incest taboo never entered my mind. I'd had no formal schooling in *any* religion, and had no idea what the followers of the crucified carpenter thought about such things.

Arthur had hardly ever spoken of his faith. That was understandable: he'd come to power in a realm that was at least half what he'd call pagan, and no doubt he'd had to learn tact. Certainly, he'd never held being a nonbeliever against my brother, nor had he tried to repress the worship of Mithras, the Roman soldier's god, among his mounted troops.

But tolerance of different religions hardly meant that he'd welcome an illegitimate (and incestuous, but I still wasn't thinking of that) son with proverbial and literal open arms. Still, there was the chance he might. I suddenly found myself wanting that very much. He was unmarried, and according to gossip had not left behind the usual string of bastards that would be expected of a thirty-two-year-old bachelor king and former soldier. Though it was said that he'd shown more than a passing interest in Guenevere, the reputedly stunning daughter of the Cornish lord Cador Constantius.

The sound of sudden commotion outside broke my reverie. "That would be Arthur's arrival," commented Gloam dryly, as he flopped over to the wall and began to climb it, leaving a sluglike trail across the tiles and flagstones.

I was out of the room and down the steps in a trice, for at least action would keep me from having to think. Indeed, the yard was a confusion of babbling serfs, barking dogs, and clucking chickens, all frantically trying to stay clear of the muddy wake churned up by the two-dozen riders that came pounding under the fortified gatehouse. A trim man on a magnificent black gelding rode at their head, snapping off orders with the practised ease of long command.

Arthur was dressed for rough travel in an iron-studded leather jerkin and knee-high doeskin boots. His head was protected by an iron-banded cap of padded leather, lighter than the conical helmet he'd wear on campaign, and a sopping cloak was draped around his shoulders and saddle like limp wings. Obviously, his ship had passed through the storm I'd seen brewing.

He was of medium height, with broad shoulders and a barrel chest. His brown hair was cut short and his face clean-shaven in the Roman manner. Although this tended to emphasize his rather large ears, he was still a handsome man. For the first time I realized that his slightly beaky nose was almost identical to my own.

He vaulted down from his tall horse and clapped me on the shoulder. With his crooked grin and easy manner, he was still more the soldier than the king.

"Hullo, laddy-buck, you've become quite the man since I saw you last." I started to bow, which was rather hard with him standing so close. "No need for that," he laughed, "we're all bloody royal here."

"Actually, they're always saying Gawain got all the height and I'm the puny one," I replied to his compliment.

"Are they now? Well, a lad's growth is measured in more than the distance from his head to his heels, and that's the truth of it."

I saw no sign of Gawain. "Did you bring my brother with you, sir?"

He shook his head. "His squadron's manning the Wall, keeping an eye on our Picti friends."

Lot's acid bark cut through the brouhaha. "Mordred, get the hell out of the way, you're as filthy as a Pict! Change before supper or eat in the stable: by Mannanan and Lir, I'll have no mud splattered brats in my hall."

I quickly stepped back out of reach as the thin, stooped form of my nominal father came gingerly through the clinging mud. Arthur's formal smile was as cold as the sea wind. "Give you good day, my Lord of Orkney." To me he whispered, "Run along now before your Da starts to foam at the mouth. We can talk later, when we're out of this forsaken gale."

"Gale, hell, this is a slight breeze for this place," grumbled one of his captains who'd overheard the last sentence.

I scurried through the crowd to the entrance of the Great Hall. Brushing past clucking servants, I entered the building, shut the stout oak doors behind me, and crossed the huge room to the stairwell, where I started bounding up the steps two and three at a time. As I ran down the hall to my room, I began stripping off my filthy clothes. Once in my chamber, I tossed the soiled garments out the narrow window, shouting down instructions to the slave whose head they landed on to have them patched and laundered and to send someone up with a bucket of hot water. After washing with more than my usual care, I donned a fresh linen shirt, cross-gartered wool breeches, a long-sleeved and high-undertunic, a short-sleeved and v-necked surtunic, and calfskin shoes. That done, I went downstairs to the feast.

Lot sat at the head of the table with his back to the roaring hearth, Mother at his right and Arthur at his left. The King of Orkney had dressed for the occasion in a purple robe trimmed with ermine fur and there was fresh black dye in his thinning hair. The beard that he wore to conceal his lack of a chin was more clipped and clean than usual, but the barbering only emphasized its sparse inadequacy.

By contrast, Arthur's garments were of plain wool and bare of any fashionable embroidery at the neck, sleeves, or hem of his surtunic. His brown breeches were cross-gartered with undyed strips of dull leather and he'd changed to a clean but far from new cloak that was fastened at the shoulder with a simple bronze brooch. Although he'd been on his throne for almost three years, he'd never learned to dress like a king.

Mother had saved a place for me on her left. Lot glared but said nothing as I sat down and Arthur winked. The first courses were just being served: salads of watercress and chickweed, heaping piles of raw garlic, leeks, and onions, hardboiled auk and puffin eggs, and smoked goat cheese. Usually Lot tended to serve guesting lords niggardly meals of boiled haddock, salt herring, and the occasional bit of mutton stewed in jellied hamhocks, leading Mother to the frequent observation that we might be better off as Christians, for they observed their Lent only *once* a year. But he dared not be stingy with his royal brother-in-law, High King of all the Britons. This time there'd be real meat to come, and plenty of it.

Arthur's men and the household warriors sat on sturdy, rough-hewn benches, quaffing tankards of ale and wine while the palace dogs and a few favored pigs milled about, waiting patiently for the scraps they knew were soon to come. The wall tapestries had recently been cleaned, fresh rushes were strewn on the floor, and the long wooden table was spread with that ultimate luxury, a snow-white linen tablecloth. More courses began to arrive: dog-fish and grayfish in pies, whale flesh simmered in wine, smoked plovers and shearwaters, and a whole roasted ox and boar. Individual servings were shoveled out onto trenchers of hard, crusty bread and each man was given several small clamshells to use as table implements, though most preferred to stick with their knives and fingers. Most of the guests did respect the tablecloth and instead wiped their hands on their clothing or on the backs of passing dogs.

Lot was actually trying to keep up a polite facade. "Of course, good Artorius," he was saying (he always called Arthur by his formal Latin name), "I'll be more than happy to help fortify the northern coast of the mainland—assuming, of course, that you can force a treaty on the Picts."

Arthur nodded. "The Picti are half-naked savages, but they're natives just the same as us and we could use their help against the Saxons."

"Ach, I thought you'd finished them for once and all at Badon Hill, back before you'd even ascended to the throne."

Arthur shook his head. "Not by half, I didn't. Oh, it will take them a few years to mount a new invasion, but they'll be back. They can't get it out of their thick heads that this isn't their land; do you know what they're calling us now? *Welshmen*, their word for foreigners. Foreigners, in our own forsaken country! Well, either Briton and Picti will find a way to stand together, or they'll go down separately under the Saxon yoke!"

Lot sipped his wine. "Of course, as an outsider, I can see certain virtues in them that your folk can't. For instance, their kings are very brave."

Arthur looked at Lot sharply. He knew as well as I did that the King of Orkney wasn't one to be praising others unless he had an ulterior motive. "Lord of Orkney," he said softly, "I came here to rid your land of a dire menace, not to hear you sing the virtues of my enemies."

"Well spoken," replied Lot easily, "but I was simply remarking on a fact. Take old Beowulf Grendelsbane, for instance. He took on the monster that was menacing his people alone, and with bare hands, besides. Grabbed the beastie by the arm and pulled it off as easily as I tear the wing off this bird's carcass."

"I am familiar with the story," said Arthur dryly. "What's the point?"

Lot smiled. "Just this. Though you've never said as much, I do believe that it would please you to see these islands convert to Christianity."

Arthur nodded warily. "It would do my heart good to see my nephews and sister living in a Godly household." Mother cleared her throat and made a point of looking down at her hands.

"But you must understand," continued Lot, "my people find it hard to be impressed with your faith when you must bring with you over a score of armored men to do the sort of job that Beowulf of the Geats was able to do with his good right arm."

One of Arthur's men spoke up. "Sire, this is boastful nonsense! That Saxon oaf could never have. . ."

Arthur silenced him with a gesture. He turned back to Lot. "Lot Mac Connaire, if I go against Cado tomorrow all alone, taking none of my men with me, and if I bring you back his head, do I have your word that you will accept Holy Baptism?"

Lot nodded. "If you can manage that, I'll build a church on every island."

I felt stunned. Such a deed would be appropriate to a classical hero, but it could hardly be expected of a flesh-and-blood man. I looked carefully at my father. He was clearly not a fool. "Uncle Arthur," I said softly, "you are the greatest warrior in all of Britain. But is this wise?"

He looked at me solemnly. "You're a good lad, Mordred. Some day you'll be an excellent king. I would see you brought into the Faith."

I felt uncomfortable under his gaze. "I was thinking of your realm, sir. Your people need you. Such a risk puts them in danger, too."

He grinned his lopsided grin. "Well, they'll just have to cross their fingers and hold their breath, won't they? Don't be a worrywart, lad, I do know what I'm doing. My God defended Padriac against the serpents of Ireland, and Columba against the dragon of Loch Ness. He protected Daniel in the lion cage and lent needed strength to little Daffyd's good right arm. He will not fail me, not if I'm half the man I must needs be if I'm to call myself a king."

Mother cleared her throat. "Tell me, brother, has that kingship become a bore yet, or do you still like the office?"

Arthur laughed. "It's been far from dull. Before I learned of my paternity, I thought I'd be a simple soldier all my life and that all my difficulties would end once I beat the Saxons. Then came Badon Hill, where I did that very thing, and I dreamed that I might retire in peace and quiet." Several of his men snorted at that, but he ignored them. "Don't laugh; I even had visions of becoming some sort of gentleman farmer, as larky as that sounds. But then Uther opened his deathbed Pandora's box and there were suddenly at least ten thousand voices crying 'Artorius Imperator! We want Arthur for our king!' and who was I to say them nay? My first year on the throne was all fighting. The Picts had to be driven back across the Wall, the Irish were making pirate raids, and every local king with a cohort to his name thought it worth his while to challenge my right to rule. Such a bloody mess you never saw and I imagined I'd be old and dying like Uther before I had it straightened out."

He motioned for a slave to refill his goblet. "But that was just the easy part. The fighting's been over for two years this winter and since then I've spent half my days haggling like a fishmonger and the other half wearing as many masks as a dozen troupes of actors. But I can't complain. It's been fun for all of that."

Mother laughed sweetly. "I'm sure it has." She smiled icily at her husband. "Isn't it refreshing to listen to a ruler who takes his duties seriously and doesn't look upon his office as his gods-granted excuse for never having to sully himself with a day's honest work?" Lot's only reply was a belch. His flushed and sweaty face indicated that he was getting very drunk.

Mother turned back to Arthur. "You must have future plans."

He nodded. "Trite as it sounds, peace and prosperity are the first things that come to mind."

"That's a rather vague agenda."

The King of Britain smiled. "Isn't it just? I'm afraid that my ideas of good government are not particularly complex. I'll die happy if I can just maintain a nation ruled by the principles of Roman law and Christian virtue."

Lot hiccuped explosively. "I thought it was Roman Law that nailed your Christian virtue to a bloody tree."

The room went very quiet. More than ever, I was glad that Lot was my father, but I felt ashamed of him just the same. Arthur's face seemed to freeze over like a winter loch, but he kept his voice calm. "I'll ignore that remark, Lord of Orkney. Some men are always fools and others need a touch of strong drink to bring it out."

Once again, Mother saved the situation. She clapped her hands for Fergus, the court bard. The little Leinsterman strutted out, bowed, and began to pluck his gilded harp. Lot and Arthur's eyes gradually unlocked while they listened to those soothing melodies. Skilful harpsong can calm a Brit that way, and even when drunk Lot was too much the coward to meet Arthur's gaze for long. Arthur's men relaxed and took their hands away from their swordbelts, causing our household guardsmen to breathe sighs of deep relief. Though the numbers were on their side, they knew full well that Arthur's crack troops could carve them up like so many feast-day bullocks. I understand that the Saxons consider it in bad taste to wear steel at the table, and in this regard I've come to suspect that they may be a bit more civilized than we are.

Soon it was time for all to say goodnight. Arthur's men trooped out to the barracks (in deep winter weather they'd have stretched out before the hearth, sharing the floor with the dogs and pigs and the household guard), while Arthur himself had been granted an apartment at the far end of the upper hall. I paid my respects, trudged up the stairs, and settled wearily into bed without bothering to remove my clothing.

I had the oddest dream. I was standing below the crest of a steep hill, where a tall wooden cross loomed against an inky sky. A corpse had been crucified there in the old Roman fashion. After awhile I somehow realized that it was the *Cristos*. Although the birds had had his eyes and lips, I still recognized his face as being Arthur's.

I awoke all drenched with sweat, and found it hard to relax and sleep again.

Despite my lack of rest I managed to rise before dawn and dress in new and heavier woolen clothing, to which I added other-skin boots with the fur inside, a hooded cloak, and a leathern jerkin with protective bronze scales. Then I strapped on a shortsword and slung a bow and quiver over my shoulder. These might not be much protection against Cado, but only fools take extra chances when such monsters are about. I knew my way well enough to navigate the upper floor and the pitch-black stairwell, but right after reaching the lower landing I tripped over a sleeping boar-hound, who put his considerable weight on my chest and began to wash my face with his enormous tongue. After I'd cuffed him in the nose several times, he finally realized that I didn't want to play and released me. There was nothing left of the fire but embers, but those gave me enough light to tiptoe through the sleeping forms until I reached the outer door.

The yard was empty, for all the livestock and the serfs were huddled in the barns, and the mud was frozen solid by the evening chill. The dawn was close at hand, and enough light leaked over the horizon to see by. Squaring off in front of one of the wooden practice posts that stood between the barracks and the stables, I drew my sword and began to hack away. Despite the cold and the usual fierce wind, I'd actually started to work up a sweat when the door to the great hall opened and Arthur emerged.

Like me, he'd dressed for travel in a fur-lined cloak and high boots. Instead of the iron-studded leather he'd worn the day before, he was now clad in a mail hauberk: a thigh-length coat of inch-wide steel rings, wherein each metal circlet was tightly interlocked with four others. This was the sophisticated modern gear that, along with the recent introduction of the stirrup, had made his mounted troops the terror of the Saxon infantry. On his head sat a conical helmet with lacquered leather cheekguards and a metal flange that projected down over his nose. The sword at his side was at least half again as long as the traditional German *spatha,* and it had a sharpened point like that of a spear, as well as an efficient double edge. He also carried a sturdy iron-headed cavalry spear and a circular white shield embossed with a writhing red dragon was slung across his back.

He seemed surprised to see me. "Practicing this early?"

"Every day," I gasped between strokes. "Gawain won't be the only warrior in the family."

He leaned on his spear and watched me with a critical eye. "Use the point, not the edge: a good thrust is worth a dozen cuts. That's it, boyo, but remember; a swordsman should move like a dancer, not like a clod-hopping farmer."

Exhausted, I sat down on the cold ground. The post was splintered and notched and my sword was considerably blunted. No matter, it was just a cheap practice weapon.

"I rather foolishly forgot to ask your father for directions to Cado's lair," Arthur was saying.

"I know," I panted. "I'll take you there. Folk say he's made himself a-den out of the old burial cairn of Maes Howe, down on the shore of the Loch of Harray."

He shook his head. "It would be too dangerous for you to come along."

I'd known he'd say that. "You need a guide. I know the way, because I used to play down there when I was just a kid." Time for the baited hook. "Don't you want me to witness the power of your God?"

He looked very grave. "Would the deed convince you of the correctness of my Faith?"

No, my faith was in him and not his *Cristos,* but I could hardly say *that.* "It would be something to watch," I said truthfully, "and I'd like very much to see a miracle."

His frown finally worked itself into a grin, as I'd known it would. Even then I must have partially realized just how vain he was of his faith, for all that he tried not to show it. "Saddle up," he said, pointing towards the stable. I readied his horse and mine while he went back into the great hall to steal bread and smoked cheese from the kitchen. The sun was only beginning to peek over the horizon when we rode across the plank bridge and skirted the nearby village's earth-and-timber palisade.

We passed fallow fields strewn with dung and seaweed, thatch-roofed stone cottages where the crofters were just rising for their daily toil, and low hills bedecked with grazing sheep. The Royal Cattle ruminated unconcernedly in pastures surrounded by nothing but low dikes of turf and stone. On the mainland the local kings and lordlings considered cattle raids to be good sport and engaged in livestock robbery with the same gleeful abandon that they brought to deer or boar hunts, but our island status protected us from that sort of nuisance.

Keeping in sight of the ocean, we rode between wind-shaped dunes and rolling slopes carpeted with peat and stubby grass. The sun rose slowly into view and shone golden on the water.

There was a whale hunt in progress beyond the tip of Marwick head. Men in boats chased the herd towards a sand bar while beating pitchers, rattling their oarlocks, and shouting in an attempt to terrify the creatures into beaching themselves. The women and children who waited in the shallows would then attack with harpoons and makeshift weapons that ranged from peatforks to roasting spits. As they died the whales made shrill, whistling cries and strange humming noises that sounded like distant pipes and drums. Ordinarily I would have stopped and made sure the royal share was put aside for the castle household, for whale flesh was always a welcome treat. However, today there wasn't time.

It was over six miles down the coast to the Bay of Skail. We soon passed all signs of human settlement. The tireless wind actually seemed to get fiercer as the morning warmed. My feet itched from the otter fur inside my boots and not being able to scratch made for a decided nuisance. For once, I could smell no sign of rain. The great clouds that raced overhead were as white as virgin snow.

"Arthur," I said, breaking a long silence, "were you glad to find out that Uther was your father?"

He took no offense at what might have been an impertinent question. "Yes, though the old sinner wasn't the sort I might have chosen for my da. Still, I'd been conceived in wedlock, and knowing that took many years' load off my mind."

"Why? Is that important to a Christian?"

"Very. Bastardy is a stain that does not wash off easily. Being born that way just makes the struggle harder."

This was getting rather deep. "What struggle?"

"To keep some part of yourself pure. A man has to look beyond the muck he's born in."

For some reason I wanted to keep making conversation. "Is it hard, then?"

He was looking out at the waves but his gaze was focused on something else entirely.

"Always. I remember my first battle. A fog had rolled in from the coast and hid the fighting. Men would come stumbling out of the mist waving bloody stumps or with their guts about their feet."

I'd never heard war described that way. "But you won, didn't you?"

He nodded. "The first of many 'glorious victories.' I was as green as a March apple and could no more control my men than I can command the sea. They burned three Saxon steadings with the men still in them, British slaves and all. The women they crucified upside down against a row of oak trees, after they'd raped them half to death."

I didn't want to hear this, but he kept on. "There was a celebration at Colchester in honor of our triumph. Your parents were there, I think, though my rank was too low for me to sit at the royal table and so I didn't meet them. I messed with the junior officers, got more drunk than I've ever been since, and committed all the standard soldier's sins. When I sobered up and decided I would live, I made a vow to never again become what I was that day."

Later, we dismounted and devoured the bread and cheese while taking shelter in one of the stone huts of Skara Brae, the ancient remains of a Pictish village that stood half-buried in the sand beside the Bay of Skail. The meal done, Arthur stood beside his gelding and gazed inland, scanning the treeless horizon. Gesturing out at that rolling emptiness, he said, "For all its smallness, there's none that could accuse this island of being the most *crowded* kingdom in the world. Not to worry; some day you'll be lord of more than this."

"What do you mean?"

"The time will come when you take your father's place upon the throne of Orkney."

"I don't know," I said doubtfully. "It's bound to go to Gawain, not me. After all, he's the oldest."

Arthur clapped me on the shoulder. "Not if I have anything to say about it. Your brother's a good man and I love him dearly, but he doesn't have the makings of a king. Too thick-headed. The Saxons will return someday, and when they do I may be too old or too tied down by royal duties to lead the war host into battle. I'll need a good *Dux Bellorum,* and the role of warlord fits your brother like a glove. Lot will proclaim you his heir if he knows what's good for him, and that's the truth of it."

I gave up on all attempts at idle chatter as we rode inland for the Loch of Harray. Arthur remained outwardly calm, but I was beginning to feel the first gnawings of anticipation in my churning stomach. Ach, but I was so sure that I was about to see a deed the like of which had not been witnessed since the days of Hercules himself.

At last we spied Maes Howe. It was a huge green mound over a hundred feet in diameter and as high as a two-story dwelling. Here and there the great gray stones of the cairn's roof poked their way above their covering of grass and soil. I knew from my boyhood explorations that there was an exposed passage on the other side of the barrow that led to a central chamber about fifteen or twenty feet square. If Cado was as large as he was reputed to be, he obviously did not object to cramped living quarters. Of course, giants were probably used to things being too small for them.

Arthur reined in his horse at the edge of the broad but shallow ditch that surrounded the mound. "I assume that this is it, then."

"Aye. The only entrance that I know of is on the other side."

His eyes scanned the great mass of earth and rock. "I think you'd best keep back a ways, so that that if I should fail you'll have time to wheel your horse around and escape."

And in that moment Cado walked around from behind the ancient pile.

Arthur and I gasped in unison and I actually came close to shitting in my breeches. The giant was at least eight feet tall and tremendously broad, with ox-like shoulders and a barrel torso. In fact, he was so stumpy that if seen at a distance he might be mistaken for a dwarf. His filthy, mud-colored hair blended with his equally filthy beard and fell to his knees in matted waves. Woven into this tangled mass were the scalps and facial hair of his victims' servered heads, so that he wore over a dozen mummified skulls in a sort of ghastly robe. This served as his only clothing. From the mass of snarled locks and grinning eyeless faces protruded arms and legs as massive as tree trunks, all brown and leathery and pockmarked with scrapes and scratches that had festered into scabby craters. Even at thirty paces his stench was awful, a uniquely nauseating combination of the smells of the sick room, the privy, and the open grave. His appearance alone was so formidable that the weapon he held easily in one gnarled hand, a twenty-foot spear with an arm-length bronze head, seemed virtually superfluous.

Ignoring me, his gaze met Arthur's. "Ho, Centurion," he boomed in surprisingly pure Latin. "How goes the Empire?"

This was the real thing, with no safe gloss of legendary unreality. I found myself wanting to be hunting or fishing or snatching birds' eggs from the cliffs, or doing anything as long as I was far away from here. It was a shameful feeling, and I did my best to ignore it. Arthur at least seemed to be keeping his cool.

"No more Empire, Cado, not for years. And I'm no centurion. You must know that."

Cado squinted at him with red-rimmed eyes the size of goose eggs. "Aye, the Empire's dead. And so are you, *Artorius Imperator*."

Arthur wasn't taken aback. "You know me, then. Good."

Cado snorted. "Oh, I know you well enough, Artorius. How could I not know the man whose soldiers have harried me across the length of Britain. You're mad to come here without them, *Imperator*. Do you wish your son to see you die?"

I was suddenly unable to breathe. How could Cado know?

How could he *know*? By the very look in his eyes, I was suddenly sure that he did.

Arthur stiffened. "He is not my son. And I do not intend to die."

Cado's black-lipped mouth spread out in a face-splitting grin, exposing a double row of square yellow teeth that might have done justice to a plow horse. "I think he is, Artorius. I can smell you in his sweat and see you in his face. Like all immortal folk, my kind can sense things that humans cannot. He's your seed, or I'm the Holy Virgin."

Arthur looked at me. Afraid to meet his eyes, I tried to turn away, but I felt frozen by his expressionless gaze. Before I could speak, he turned back to Cado and laughed out loud.

"You can't confuse me with such paltry tricks, monster. And don't make it any harder on yourself with blasphemy. I don't profess to know whether or not you have a soul, but if you do you'd better make your peace with God."

Cado never stopped smiling. "Don't you know where giants come from? We're descended from the ancient *nephilim,* the sons of the unions between the *Elohim* and the daughters of Adam. I need no peace with God—my blood is part divine!"

Arthur lowered his lance and unslung his shield. "More blasphemy, Cado? You might face your ending with somewhat better grace."

Cado growled, a low rumbling that spooked my horse and made him difficult to control. "Tell me one thing," said the giant. "Why have you hounded me these many leagues? What am I to you now that I am no longer hunting in your lands?"

"You know full well what you are," said Arthur grimly. "Your actions have made you an abomination in the eyes of the Lord."

Cado began to laugh, an ear-splitting sound like a dozen asses braying all at once. "Little man, your puking Lord fathered all abomination. I see his world as it truly is and act accordingly."

Couching his lance, Arthur spurred his horse forward with what might have been a prayer and might have been a muttered curse. The sun gleamed on his polished mail as he emerged from the shadow of a wind-driven sweep of cloud. Lugh and Dagda, but he looked magnificent in that brief moment.

Cado casually lifted his spear and thrust out with the blunt haft, catching Arthur squarely in the midriff before he was close enough to use his lance. Torn from the saddle, he seemed to sit suspended in the air for a brief eternity. As he crashed to the sward, his horse shied past Cado and went galloping away in the direction of the distant loch.

Cado bent over him, reversing his spear so that his spear head just touched Arthur's throat. For a measureless time they seemed locked in that silent tableau. My brain screamed that I should do something, but my body showed no interest in responding. The two combatants were frozen and so was I, and I lost all sense of myself as my awareness shrank to nothing but those still and silent figures.

At last Cado spoke. "Now would be the time to look me in the eye and say 'kill me and be done'—I do believe that that's the standard challenge. But you can't say it, can you?" He laughed even more loudly than before. "They all tell themselves it's victory or death, but in the end they find those two limited alternatives not half so attractive as they'd thought."

Arthur hadn't moved. I was suddenly abnormally aware of my physical sensations: the itchy fur inside my boots, the sting of the cold air upon my raw nose, the spreading warmth at my crotch where I'd pissed my breeches, and the mad pounding of my heart. Arthur was down. He wasn't moving. I knew that I must do something, and it seemed incredibly unfair for such responsibility to have fallen upon my puny shoulders.

I've always been good with horses. Urging my mare forward with my knees, I unslung my bow and drew an arrow from my quiver. The trick was not to think about it, but to act smoothly and mechanically. If I thought about it, I'd fumble. Cado was within range now. He looked up just as I pulled the string back to my ear and let the arrow fly. The feathered shaft seemed to sprout from his left eye socket. I'd already drawn again, but all my instinctive skill left me and the arrow went wild. Not that it mattered. My impossibly lucky first shot had done the job.

Cado stiffened and groaned. He shivered all over, causing the heads in his hair and beard to clack together like dry and hollow gourds. When he fell over backwards it was like a tower going down.

As suddenly-clumsy as a six-year-old, I half-fell out of my saddle and ran to Arthur. "Don't be dead," I pleaded like a stupid twit, "please Da, don't be dead."

He groaned. "Too big. Sometimes evil's just too damned big. And I'm too old for this."

"Are you all right?"

He sat up painfully. "Rib's broken, I think, but I can still stand." With my help he did. "My horse has run off."

I pointed to mine. "Take the mare. I'll search for your gelding."

He clapped me on the shoulder. "You're a good lad. I was an arrogant fool today—I hope you can forgive me."

I didn't know what he meant. "Of course," I muttered, cupping my hands and helping him into the saddle. From this vantage point, he surveyed Cado's corpse.

"Like Daffyd and Goliath. The Lord works his will: I'm taught humility and Cado is destroyed."

I looked him in the eye. "Are you saying that your god guided my arrow?"

He shrugged. "Perhaps. Not that it takes any of the credit away from you. I'm very proud, Mordred. I pray that someday the Lord will give me as fine a son as the one he gave to Lot."

I'd been trying to find an opening all day. My heart was in my mouth—this was more frightening than confronting Cado. "Arthur, there is something you must know."

Something in my voice must have warned him, for he looked at me very oddly. "And what would that be?"

No hope for a smooth tongue: I had to be blunt and open. "You're my father."

"What?"

"You're my father."

I knew it then: I'd blundered. His face wore no expression, but the words hung between us in the heavy air. I tried to laugh, but it was a forced, hollow sound. "I was just joking," I stammered, desperately trying to unsay my revelation. "I didn't mean. . ."

He reached out and gripped my shoulder. His clutch was firm, painful. And his eyes were cold and hard as Lot's. "You're lying now. I know that much. And Cado called you my son, too. How could it be true?"

I tried to pull away, but he held me fast. Now my terror was of *him*, of the man himself. This was a side of Arthur that I'd never seen. "Please," I said, "it's all a mistake. I. . ."

He shook me. "What makes you think you are my son? Tell me now, the truth, and all of it."

I could no more refuse that command than I could up and fly away, though I would have been glad to do either. "Mother's familiar told me."

"A demon? And you believed such a creature?"

"I asked Mother, and she said that it was true."

He shook his head. "How? It's impossible. We've never. . ." He broke off then, but his eyes were still commanding.

"It was at Uther's court after your first battle. She came to your tent in disguise."

The silence that followed that statement was as cold and painful as the bitter wind. He mumbled something that might have been a prayer, and his expression resembled that of a man kicked by a horse. His hand slipped from my shoulder. "It's sin," he said at length, his eyes not meeting mine. "It's mortal sin."

This was worse than I'd feared. Bloody gods, but why couldn't I have kept my foolish mouth shut? "She didn't know you were her brother. It's not her fault."

"No, for she's a pagan, and lost anyway. I'm the one to blame."

"It wasn't your fault either. It wasn't anybody's fault."

He shook his head sadly. "Ach, no, it's always someone's fault. Always." Straightening up, he reined the mare towards Cado's still form. "You knew, monster. You knew what I was. Perhaps you should have killed me." His shoulders slumped, and he looked so *old* as he sat there swaying in the saddle. "But no, then I'd have died in ignorance, unshriven, with no chance at repentance. No wonder that I lost today. My own sin rode beside me."

"Don't talk like that!" I shouted, suddenly angry as well as hurt.

He ignored my protest. "Come up behind me. I won't leave you here, no matter what you are."

No matter what you are. Words that have haunted half my life.

"Go on with you," I snapped. "I said I'd fine your goddamned horse."

He didn't react visibly to my profanity. He just sat there, slumped in the saddle, the wind tugging at his cloak. His eyes were focused in my direction, but it was as if he was looking through me at something else. At length he spoke. "All right, Mordred, suit yourself." with that he spurred the mare into a gallop. I suppose that in that moment I became the only thing he ever fled from, but that distinction does not make me proud. I stood there, watching him ride away, while the wind whispered in the grass.

"Thrown it all away, then!" I shouted when he was well beyond hearing. "Damn you, Da, it wasn't my fault either!"

I never did find his bloody horse.

And so, the end of this testament. Why did I tell when even, the young fool I was then might have guessed how he'd react? I don't know. It's all very well for Socrates to maunder on about how one should know oneself, but sometimes the water is just so deep and murky that you cannot see the bottom. I didn't hate Arthur, not then, but the love was all dried up.

I'd never asked to be made the symbol of his own imagined sin.

It was a long walk home. A storm rolled in from the ocean long before I reached my destination. The rain was curiously warm, as if Arthur's god were pissing on his handiwork. Wrapped in my soggy cloak, I trudged back to Lot and Mother's world.

THE LADY OF BELEC

by Phyllis Ann Karr

Phyllis Ann Karr (1944–) is probably still best known for her series about the sorceress Frostflower and the swordswoman Thorn who first appeared in Frostflower and Thorn *(1980). She has also written a number of Arthurian stories, as well as the fascinating novel* The Idylls of the Queen *(1982) which opens with the poisoning of Sir Patrise as part of Mordred's plot to reveal the adultery of Lancelot and Guinevere. The following story takes place some while later in the grim days at the end of Arthur's reign.*

U ntil after the birth of their third child, her lord had locked her into a chastity belt each morning, hanging the key around his neck before opening the door of their bedchamber. At night, he would relock the door with a large key and hide the key somewhere about the chamber while she undressed by rushlight, with her back to him, her eyes seeing only his shadow moving on the tapestry. When all was ready, he would summon her to the bed, unlock the chastity belt, and pull her under the linen sheets and the covers of animals furs to him.

The Lady of Belec did not complain. The chastity belt was a symbol of his love for her. She was his jewel, to be guarded as carefully as a soft, white pearl from the depth of the sea, or the golden amber that hyenas emitted from their bodies and buried jealously in the sand to keep it from mankind, or a great ruby like the Heart's Blood of Jesu, crystallized in the holy chalice. She might have asked to wear the belt on the top of her gown, as she heard some of the high Ladies did at court, especially when it became fashionable after the goblet of Queen Morgan le Fay showed the unfaithfulness of womankind in the courts of King Mark and King Arthur. But the Lady of Belec was not quite clever enough with her fingers to make the slits that would be needed in order to fit the metal through her skirt, nor quite bold enough to have worn a gown so perforated. Sufficient that the Lord of Belec wore the small iron key in plain sight against the murrey brown cloth of his surcoat.

Nevertheless, the symbol of his love was not comfortable, and she was glad each time he laid the belt aside for a few months in consideration of a child swelling within her.

The first two babes were daughters, coming little more than a year apart; and, after the birth and the churching, the chastity belt. The third child was, at last, a boy; and, after his birth, the Lord of Belec brought out the belt no more, except when he left the castle to hunt or to visit some old friend or kinsman. It was as if by giving him a son she had at last proven her faithfulness, as if only now did the Lord of Belec consider their marriage fully sealed.

She rejoiced in the freedom with which she could now move by day—freedom all but forgotten since her girlhood years. And yet, conversely, now that he seemed satisfied with their union, she felt less secure, and thought wistfully sometimes of the old nightly rituals. . .as she thought wistfully of so many things in her past.

Once, when she was a girl not quite fifteen, Sir Gawaine had visited this castle of Belec, her father's castle then. Sir Gawaine of Orkney, Sir Gawaine of the golden tongue, Sir Gawaine the favorite nephew of the King himself, Sir Gawaine with the golden pentangle, the symbol of perfection, on the crimson of his shield and surcoat. The great Sir Gawaine, in his early manhood then, looking to her mature, strong, ageless, and, with his fine golden hair falling to his shoulders, his fine golden beard, his kind brown eyes and ready smile, seeming to her much as she thought sweet Jesu must have been when He walked among the unbelieving Jews of the Holy Land. Gawaine's voice seemed to her like Jesu's also—or at least, since Gawaine spoke in pleasantries instead of holy parables, like the voice of an angel fay.

The Damsel of Belec waited on her father and Sir Gawaine as they sat at table and talked of things she could not understand, things she could partly understand, and things she might have understood if she had not had to pour ale or replenish a platter of meat and bread. Often enough to nourish her, though not enough to sate her, Sir Gawaine had looked in her direction, either full in her face or with a soft, sliding glance that showed his awareness of her and appreciation of her efforts, and spoken of matters she could perfectly understand, comparing the flow of life to the flow of the seasons. . .or telling short tales of the bravery, fellowship, and love at court. . .or likening glory to the sun and the sun to the King, love to the moon and the moon to the Queen and the Queen to all good and beautiful womankind.

The old minstrel of Belec had been sick that week with the beginnings of the fever that was to kill him, but Sir Gawaine had shown her a few new bransle steps as well as he could without music. Afterwards, they sat together by the fire in her father's chamber (a rare honor for her, to be allowed to sit here with a guest). Sir Gawaine had drawn out Excalibur to show them, holding him up full in the firelight, hilt flashing like the sun and blade gleaming like the moon, and told them the tale of how Arthur had received the great sword from the Lady of the Lake and later given it in trust to his nephew.

Before the Damsel of Belec left them, Sir Gawaine had taken her in his arms, in sight of her father, and kissed her gently on the forehead. For a few moments, her hands felt the beat of his heart beneath the crimson silk of his surcoat; for half a heartbeat, his lips touched her skin.

He had left the next morning before daylight; but often, during the months that followed, she pressed her fingers to her forehead and then to her own heart until she seemed to feel him again, as clearly as when it had truly happened. And, indeed, those few heartbeats had never truly ended for her.

A few years later, feeling his end draw near, her father arranged her marriage with the third son of an old friend. Thus she would gain a lord and protector, and her husband would gain a wife and the castle and the lands of Belec. So far as she knew, only one obstacle had threatened the union.

Her father used to boast of the occasion when they of Belec had entertained the greatest knight of the land and favorite nephew of the King. Her bridegroom-to-be seemed to find displeasure rather than satisfaction in the account. Once the Damsel had heard angry words between her father and her future lord, the younger man hotly demanding proof that his bride was unstained, the older as hotly protesting her honor and his own. This happened in the garden, and they seemed not to be aware she sat in her arbor, enjoying the thick green of summer.

"If any other," she heard her bridegroom say, "*any* other—even the King himself—were to touch. . ."

Her father began to interrupt with a shout, but it turned into choking. Hearing another fit in his cough, the Damsel rushed from the arbor where she had sat innocently concealed. Her future bridegroom did not seem embarrassed.

Her father recovered. The marriage was read and sealed. The next morning her new lord pronounced himself satisfied of her virginity on the bridal night. Yet quarrels continued, long and heated, between her husband and her father. Those which she overheard seemed to be of foolish matters, and she tried to beg her husband not to cause her father more fits. Her husband seemed sincerely to repent of his hot temper; but he could not control it. Some of the folk of Belec whispered that the new lord's temper hastened the old lord's death, and perhaps it was so. But her father was old and ill, and would have died soon in any case.

Once, shortly after the birth of their first son, she ventured to ask her lord, "What would have you done, that first night, had you not found me. . .to your taste?"

"Had I not found you to my taste," he replied, kissing her and trying in his way to make a pleasantry, "I would still have done my duty and given you children, but I would also have taken a paramour."

She suspected he had a paramour already, in the castle of one of those old friends he visited thrice or four times yearly; but all men could not be like holy priests or knights of the King's court, sworn to perfection. "If I had been otherwise to your taste, but not a virgin, my Lord' would you have abandoned me?"

"I would have taken a burning brand from the fire," he said, "and thrust it through your foul body."

She did not mention such things again. Nor did she ever give him cause to quarrel with her. When he sought to quarrel, she was silent, or answered him only with agreement, even when he abused her. Sometimes he would stalk out and quarrel with another; several times over the years there were servants with cracked heads to mend, and three of four times there were dead knights to bury, after her lord indulged his temper. But never did he beat her, as she heard some lords beat their wives. And if sometimes, in temper, he put sword or spear through a retainer or a passing knight-errant, that was less than she heard of other knights doing in sport and honor.

On the whole, she did not regret her marriage. She was practical enough to realize that not everyone could go to court, and that not all loves were for wedding, nor even for bedding. Her lord seemed a good husband to her, in most ways; and even if he were not, he would still have been her father's bequest to her, and precious on that account. She was faithful to him in body and intent; and, when she noticed that those servants and retainers to whom she spoke most often were those with whom her husband was most like to quarrel violently, she learned to keep her eyes lowered at all times except when alone with her husband and children, and to give what few orders she issued through the lips of one of her two damsels.

Always, however, she kept just below the skin of her breast, where he could not see it, a thin line in the shape of the golden pentangle that Sir Gawaine of Orkney wore on shield and surcoat. The five-pointed star was to her more than the symbol of all perfection and all true love, as the memory of the sword Excalibur shining silver and brilliant summed up more than beauty and honor. Together, the sword, the pentangle, and especially the man reflected a glory too bright for the world, a perfection that, being too noble to remain on earth, must rise to Heaven of itself, and in rising draw all the rest of mankind up with it, at least partway. She thought of the other knights, of Sir Gawaine's brother Sir Gareth Beaumains, of his favorite cousin Sir Ywaine of the Lion, of the great Sir Lamorak de Galis, or of Sir Lancelot, of whom Sir Gawaine had spoken as his special friend, giving Lancelot praise that in the opinion of the Damsel of Belec could belong only to Gawaine himself. All other great knights, the King himself, even Jesu in her prayers, all had Sir Gawaine's face, above their various shields and surcoat which her imagination could not quite fill in from the descriptions she had heard.

For thirty-five years, the feel of Sir Gawaine's lips upon her forehead and Sir Gawaine's heartbeat beneath the silk of his surcoat never faded, though the skin that remembered was growing wrinkled and mottled.

From the time of his visit until the time of her marriage, she had counted the days and months, hoping he would come again. Even after marriage, though her mind willed him to stay away—for her husband's sake, not for Sir Gawaine's, who could have defended himself at need against any three other knights who dared attack him in enmity—her heart raced and her hands trembled when she heard of his being anywhere within two days' ride of Belec. But the King's knights must do the King's good work; and the greater the knight, the more he must do. It had been a priceless gift that he came even once, all the more precious in that he came so early in her life, leaving her so many years to cherish the memory.

Belec lay on the way between London and Dover. Surely, she thought, the King's work must bring one of his knights past them here again sooner or later. Whenever, from crenel or thin, deep-set window, she glimpsed some strange knight or party of knights ride by, the blood throbbed in her neck. Even a visit from some lesser companion of the Round Table or the Queen's Knights would be a thing to savor, a second glimpse of the great, noble world beyond the walls and fields of Belec.

No other knight was Gawaine, but another knight could, perhaps, tell her news of him. She was old enough now to sit as mistress, helping entertain visitors; and surely not even the Lord of Belec could grow jealous of hospitality offered to one Arthur's own good knights.

The Lady of Belec realized unbelievingly that she had been old enough for most of her life, now, to sit as mistress in her father's hall, and never another knight from Arthur's court had she helped to entertain, nor any strange knight at all—only, from time to time, a minstrel, or a wandering holy man, or an old friend of her husband's. Her children, those who had survived childhood, were grown and gone, the last daughter married at an earlier age than her mother had been, the last son killed in the great tournament at Winchester. Unlike their mother, the daughters had left Belec for the castles and manors of their own husbands, where, perhaps, some of them might entertain knights from Arthur's court, or see tournaments. The Lady of Belec had never seen a true tournament, only a small one her father staged at his own castle even before the visit of Sir Gawaine. The thought that her sons had died in the exercise of glory somewhat eased the pain of their deaths. She had never, in any event, felt as close to her sons as to her daughters.

She thought, sometimes, of holding another tournament at Belec. Perhaps it would bring back Sir Gawaine for a day or two. But her lord would never have permitted so many strange knights so close to her; and, moreover, a tournament at Belec could only be a tawdry mockery of such great tournaments as those of Winchester, Lonazep, Surluse, or the Castle of Maidens. Better not to lime the twig for Sir Gawaine at all, than to lime it with such bait!

And then, too—she looked at herself in the water of her small garden pond—she was growing old. If he came now, he would be disappointed in her. Then she remembered that he would have grown old, too. . .ten years older than she. Perhaps it was best that he never return, best to keep the memory of him always as he was thirty-five years ago.

But no. He could never grow old, any more than Jesu in her book of hours could grow old. Or, if he did grow older, it could only ennoble him still more.

The Lady of Belec heard rumours sometimes, news that was months or years old and distorted beyond measure. There was talk that King Arthur's great court was not as it should be, that adultery was more common than faithfulness, that the Queen herself had taken a lover, or several. Now love, now jealousy of the Queen was said to have driven Sir Lancelot mad more times than once. An angel, or several angels, had appeared in the guise of knights and led the companions of the Round Table in search of the Holy Grail; only half these knights had returned to the King, but none had come past Belec.

Then Lancelot had actually been found with the Queen, in her chamber. The Queen had been burned at the stake and Lancelot driven into exile across the sea. Then the Queen had not been burned, but cast off and put into a convent. Then the King himself had crossed the sea, shipping with his host from Cardiff or another port far to the north, to make war on Lancelot for stealing the Queen from him. Then the Queen had not been put into a convent, nor carried over the sea with Lancelot, but was to marry the King's nephew, Prince Mordred, in London; and folk said that Prince Mordred was trying to raise the country to his own banner and soon would be here in the south.

The Lady of Belec sat in her small garden, enclosed by the walls of her father's castle, watching the spring herbs turning into summer herbs and the summer ones into fall, and trying to reconcile the reality of Sir Gawaine's visit thirty-five years ago with the impossibility of what was said to be happening now. All her life she had lived within an area of land that she could have walked across in half a day. One time only had the greatness of King Arthur come into her life. Sir Gawaine's visit was truth to her, and all the rest was falsehood.

Then a great host passed by on its way south to Dover, and folk said it was the new King, Prince Mordred, and that he would have come aside to claim more men from the Lord Belec, but was in too great haste.

Three days went by, then four, and there came rumors of a great battle at Dover, half on the land and half in the sea, with ships sinking for the weight of the blood that was spilled within them.

Close on their heels of these newest rumors, Sir Gawaine came again to Belec.

He came in the night, and he came with thirty men around him, knights, squires, and yeomen. He came with a crowd of country folk following him. The Lady of Belec heard their voices and woke before her husband. She rose, climbed to the narrow window, looked down and saw their torches on the other side of the moat. She did not see Sir Gawaine. She only saw six men carrying a long litter, and a throng of men and torchlights surrounding them. She woke her husband.

The Lord of Belec would not permit her to come down to greet the party of knights. He shut her in the bedchamber, and she heard the heavy bolt fall on the other side of the door.

She could not return to bed. With great care, she dressed herself in her best gown. It was more than twenty years old, older than her youngest daughter, who was not three years away from home; but she rarely had occasion to wear it, and it was still unfrayed, though somewhat faded, like her hair. She plaited her hair slowly, noticing by the firelight that there were still a few strands of black among the long, gray ones. She twined it up on top of her head, and she rubbed her face and neck with the precious, perfumed ointment she used only on the highest feast-days. Then she sat beside the fire and waited.

Soon she heard the bolt withdrawn. She stood, her blood throbbing, wondering what she would say, how she would persuade her lord to allow her to descend to the hall, why it even seemed important that she go.

There was knocking on the door. The Lord of Belec would not have knocked for permission to come in to his lady. She called out that whoever was without should enter.

He entered, a strange knight, almost as old as her lord, with an animal she thought might be a lion or a gryffon embroidered on his surcoat. Its colors were hardly visible for the dust. "My Lady?" he said.

"I am the Lady of Belec."

"My cousin visited your castle once, my Lady. He spoke highly of it. Perhaps that was before you came here. . ."

"I have always been here." She would not ask who this knight was, nor who was his cousin; but she thought she could trace a faint resemblance, through the years and the shadows. "Is your cousin below?"

He nodded and stepped aside. She crossed to the open door, and the strange knight, the cousin, escorted her down. Was this, she wondered, the courtesy that fine ladies enjoyed at court? No, it was the poor shred of an ancient garment that the last wearers were trying vainly to hold together in the face of a freezing wind. The spirit. . .aye, she could feel what must have been the old spirit of the cousin knight, struggling to walk steadily beneath grief and weariness. But the grace was lacking.

He led her into her own hall as if she, and not he, were the stranger. She knew her husband must be here, frowning at her. She wondered, very briefly, how the strange knights had persuaded him to allow her presence, to permit her to be brought down by one stranger. Then she forgot the Lord of Belec. For the table was raised on the trestles, and on the table lay a tall man in a crimson surcoat.

She stepped forward. His hands were folded in prayer, the fingertips partially covering the golden pentangle on his breast. No man, how saintly whatsoever, slept with his hands folded in such rigid, motionless prayer. She moved her gaze slowly up to his face.

The silver did not show so clearly in golden hair as in black, but the face was sunken and withered with more than age, the lips were beginning to pull back despite a cloth tied around the jaws, and a gold coin weighed down each eyelid. The Lady of Belec screamed.

Then she stood for several moments, panting, listening to the echoes of her shriek die away in the high beams of her hall. Sir Gawaine of the golden tongue had returned to her at last, and brought with him the reality of all the rumors of these later years.

"Where is the sword Excalibur?" she said. "He should be holding the cross of the sword Excalibur."

"He gave the great sword back to the King when he was dying," said the cousin of Sir Gawaine. "During the battle at Dover, a wound he had from fighting Sir Lancelot reopened."

"Sir Lancelot? He would not have fought with Sir Lancelot." That much remained of the old vision, a memory of how Sir Gawaine had praised Lancelot as his truest friend. They could not have fought, unless in friendship and mere testing of arms.

"Lancelot had killed Gawaine's brothers, rescuing the Queen from the stake."

She screamed again, a longer scream, and fell to her knees, clutching the table, not quite daring to reach farther and touch his hands.

Footsteps approached her. Her husband's voice came down from somewhere above her, angry, but low—unusually low, for his anger. "Stand up. You disgrace my hall."

She stood, but she did not turn to face the Lord of Belec. She gripped the edge of the table and stared down at her other lord, the lord of thirty-five years of hope and trust. "Ah my lord Sir Gawaine!" She reached out at last and seized his folded hands. "Ah my Lord, my noble Lord, the only Lord I have ever loved in all my life!"

It was not only for the death of one man alone that she cried, but for the death of honor and glory and nobility, for the decay of every true and good ideal from within, for the loss of the calm center of her soul.

The sudden shuddering pain in her neck seemed for an instant merely the natural extension of the storm within her. But the strange, dizzy angles at which her eyes met the whirling walls and floor—Mercifully, her consciousness was extinguished before she fully realized what had happened.

Gawaine's cousin, Sir Ywaine of the Lion, and his companions had among them some of the finest of those few who remained to Arthur and all of the Round Table. They cut down the Lord of Belec with immediate justice.

Then they carefully bound the head of the Lady of Belec back to her body. The top bandage was a band of crimson velvet, tied with threads of slightly tarnished gold. They carried her body back with that of Sir Gawaine. Thus, at last, the Lady of Belec came to court with the lord of her true soul, to be buried beside him in the same tomb.

ARTOS, SON OF MARIUS
by André Norton

And so we come to the final days of King Arthur when he faces civil war with his own son and nephew Mordred. André Norton (1912–), one of the legends of fantasy fiction, here considers the historical context and tells the tale from the point of view of another and much younger Arthur, or Artos, son of one of King Arthur's troop commanders. André Norton, who like Joy Chant and so many other good writers, was for many years a librarian. She has been writing since 1934 and now has well over one hundred books to her credit, the majority being science fiction or fantasy, including the notable Witch World series. She has used Arthurian motifs in several of her books including Merlin's Mirror *(1975), one of the few successful science fictional treatments of the legend. The following story is an episode from* Dragon Magic *(1972) wherein a group of children each experience an adventure in the past.*

It was harvest time and most of the war host were scattered, out in the fields where the barley stood high and ready for the cutting and the grain was as golden as the sun was hot. A good harvest, as all had hoped, for it had been a bad year earlier with the cold, and there had been scant gleanings from a too-wet summer last year. Men had gone with empty bellies through the last of that cold and had sown grain they would joyfully have crammed by

354

fistfuls into their mouths and chewed raw, even threw it into the waiting earth.

Not only in Britain had hunger pinched, but overwater, too. So that all men knew the winged-helmed invaders were on the prowl, and a coast watch had to be kept even though the men were needed in the fields.

Artos smeared the back of his hand across his forehead and tried not to wince as he straightened his aching back. Field work was harder than the training in the war band, though he had not had too much of that yet, just enough to prove how much he had yet to learn. He glanced now to where his shield mates were strung out in a straggling line along the field. It did not matter if one's father was Marius, troop commander under the Dragon himself. A man was matched against his own deeds, not by what his father, or his father's father, had done before him.

Artos had been named for the High King, Caesar of Britain, but he took his turn in the fields all the same. Just as he suffered the hard knocks of the wooden training sword when he was awkward or unlucky, or stupid enough not to be able to defend himself against Drusus' attack. Drusus was old now, but he could remember seeing the last of the Legions go down to the sea, taking the might of Rome with them, leaving Britain open to the sea wolves.

The High King had ridden north five days ago, to visit the post manned against the Scots and the painted men in the north. And he had taken most of the Companions with him. Modred ruled here in Venta.

Artos scowled and kicked at a clod so that it crumbled under the toe of his boot. It was the High King (though Father always called him Caesar) who held Britain together. He had been just an army officer at first, but he had been loyal to Aurelianus, whom the real Caesar overseas had made Count of Britain. They had called Artos "Pendragon" and "Dux Bellorum" (Commander of Battles). Artos shaped the words though he did not speak them aloud; they had a ring to them. Men did not speak the true latin of the empire any more, but added British words to everyday speech. Marius, like the High King, believed they should remember the past, and one way of doing that was to keep the language of men who had lived in cities and known the old lost days of peace.

For years now life had been only fighting. Men kept swords ever to hand, listened always for the roar of war horns. It was do that, live armed, or die under a Saxon ax—or worse, live a Saxon slave. The cities the Romans had built were mostly destroyed. Saxons hated cities and, when they could, reduced them to ruins. But Venta was where a Roman governor had once lived, and there were hill forts from the old days, which the King's men had rebuilt, forts which had once sheltered men from attack long before the coming of the Roman Legions.

Modred did not believe in keeping to the old ways. He smiled sneeringly behind backs—yes, and even to the faces of such as Marius and others of Caesar's men who wore short hair, went shaved of cheek and chin, carried the old Roman shields and armor. His men said openly now that it was better to forget Rome, to make peace with the Winged Helms, maybe even to give them some coast lands and swear blood-brother oaths with them, rather than fight forever.

Modred spoke only the British tongue, pretended not to understand Latin. He feasted the petty kings and chieftains of the north and the tribes. Marius, and the others like him, watched Modred with care. But many of the younger men treated Modred with deference, listened to him.

Artos bent back to his work. He hated the field more with every hour he was forced to spend in it. Why could he not have ridden north with Caesar's guard, with his father? He swung the harvest knife as if it were a sword, cutting the stalks raggedly. The furrows were endless and the sun hot, the day long.

One of the house slaves bought around the leather bottle of vinegar and water, and Artos drank his share. It was then that he saw the riders on the sea road. Their vividly colored cloaks were bright, thrown well back on their shoulders; in this heat they must be wearing them only for show. There was no mistaking Prince Modred as their leader.

Artos watched as they passed. But he was startled to see what the Prince wore about his arms just below the edge of his summer tunic's short sleeve. He would take oath that it was the Dragon armlet of the High King! But only Caesar, Artos Pendragon, had a right to that, and he had worn it himself when he had ridden out of Venta.

And Modred was not even the High King's heir by right, though men whispered that by some chance in the past he was truly the King's own son. But he was unlike Caesar in every way.

For Artos Pendragon was as tall as one of the forest trees, or so he looked among lesser men. And his hair, though he was now nigh an old man, was still the color of that rich gold which comes from the Western Isle. He wore his hair short and he shaved as did the Romans, which made him look younger than his years.

Whereas Modred was a good handsbreadth or more shorter, and dark of hair, the locks curling to his shoulders. Also he had wings of mustache curving on either side of his thin-lipped mouth, so that he looked as any of the tribal kings. He wore also their brightly colored clothes, cloaks woven in checkered patterns of green, red, and yellow, with like tunics and breeches, wide belts of soft leather studded with gold, a jeweled dagger, and a long sword.

Artos watched the party move on until they were hidden in the dust cloud. He longed to be a horse and riding with them. No man could deny that Modred was a good fighter, and now he had been chosen by Caesar himself to hold Venta. He commanded all the forces except the Companions, who remained here, and the school for their sons, both of which were under the orders of Kai.

At the thought of Kai, Artos bent to work again, his shoulders hunching as if he already felt the sting of a willow switch laid smartly across them. Kai was a fighter, one of whom Marius thoroughly approved. You never won more than a grunt of half-satisfaction from Kai. But a grunt from that battle-scarred warrior was perhaps equal to half a Roman Triumph. Artos grinned. But still he remembered that armlet shining on Modred's darkly tanned arm and it cast a small seed of uneasiness into his mind.

It was his turn that night to wait upon the high table, bring in the drinking horns, set out the spoons and table knives. Modred's chair remained empty, as did two others, those of his close officers. Only Kai and Archais (who had come from overseas and was much learned in the healing of wounds) and Paulus, the priest, were there.

Artos listened to their talk, but there was little new to hear. Paulus was old and thought of little but the Church, and he disliked Archais, as he made very plain, because the healer did not believe what Paulus taught. But this the priest could not say openly, because the High King had long since made it plain that what god a man chose to serve privately was his own business. This made the priests angry and they muttered a great deal, though there was naught they could do. However, lately they had been very bold about the need for peace, and Modred had those among them who talked so—too much, Marius said.

When the thin beer of the past year had been poured and the platters taken from the table, Archais spoke: "Our Lord Modred rides so far abroad that he cannot return for the evening meal?"

Kai shrugged. "That is his affair," he replied shortly. But the tone in his voice made Artos listen closely.

"The Winged Helms have been reported offshore. That fisherman from Deepdene reported sighting at least ten ships. It must be a raider with reputation to bring such a fleet. One thinks of Thorkiel—"

"No, no." Paulus shook his head. "Thorkiel would not dare. Did not our Lord King give him so grievous a beating yesteryear as to send him in fast flight?"

"These Winged Helms," growled Kai, "are like ants, Father. One can stamp out a scurry of them here, another there, yet there are always ants, and no end to them! They are only quiet when they are dead, but that takes a deal of doing. Good fighters they are, with their berserkers and their shield walls. Our Lord King knows the way to deal with them. Men sometimes laughed straight to his face in the beginning. But he went ahead with it, by Aurelianus' favor. He got horses, big ones—mostly before that we had just ponies, nothing to mount a grown man. And he found how to make armor for them and for their riders. He did not gather a big army such as is hard to feed and easy to ambush—even the Legions learned that there were newer and better ways of fighting, good as they had been in their time.

"No, he took the horse companies and he was here, there, riding hard. We were so much in the saddle in those days that we got hard skin on our bottoms like calluses on the hands. And where the Saxons came, there we were—before they could expect it. Yes, the horse and the Companions cleared the land and kept it cleared.

"I remember the day they brought him the Dragon banner. It was new, a queer strange thing. Let the wind catch it rightly and it snapped out like a great red worm, its claws reaching for you. With that over a man's head, he got heart in him. Yes, we had the Dragon—'til it was cut to pieces. Seeing it seemed to send the heathen wild, and they would aim spears at it every time. But we just got us another, and another—all made the same. When the war horns call, the Dragon answers them!"

Artos knew the banner. There was a small one like it that flew from the watchtower of Venta when the High King was here and was carried with him when he traveled. But the big Dragon was kept safe until needed for battle. They called Caesar "Pendragon"—even just Dragon. And some of the people who did not know much actually thought he had a real dragon to help him in battle.

"But for all your valiant efforts, still these Winged Helms come," Archais observed.

"They come and they die." Kai pushed away from the table. "Always they come—it is a way of life."

"But need it be?" Paulus' voice sounded thin, almost like a whisper after Kai's deep-chested tones. "There is a way to keep peace and all men living in fellowship."

Kai laughed. "Cry 'pax' to a Winged Helm who has just beaten in your door, Father—one who has his ax ready to cut you down. There is only one *pax* for such." His head swung to Artos, who had been very still and thought he was forgotten. "Youngling, get to your bed. Before cock's crow you'll be needed in the field again. With luck we'll be able to get in the rest of the barley before nightfall."

"With God's grace," Paulus corrected him. But Kai paid no attention to the priest as he stretched wide his hard-muscled arms.

Only, Artos was never to work in that barley field again. And it all came about because of the need for a drink of water.

He was tired enough to sleep soundly, but he roused out of a confused dream which afterward he could never remember; only, it left him feeling afraid. He sat up on the pallet which was his bed, feeling thirsty. Around him was the heavy, even breathing of the other sleepers. A thin sliver of moonlight shone in the hall without.

Once this maze of rooms, hallways, courtyards, had been the home and headquarters of a Roman governor. Now it was a rather badly kept palace, which few living within had ever totally explored.

The nearest water was in the great hall and Artos debated going after it. He ran a dry tongue over cracked lips and thought that he must. He had worn his breeches and leggings to bed, he had been so tired, and he did not wait now to pick up his tunic as he padded across the chamber, careful to avoid the pallets of the others.

In the hall the moonlight came through the window. There was another source of light, too, a dim glow in another chamber. Artos was curious. Who could be there? It was well away from any place where the guards were on watch duty. That curiously sent him to see, creeping up with caution toward the half-open door.

He passed the shut door of Kai's chamber. Beyond it were two empty rooms, usually occupied by men who were now riding north with the King. That left only the arms room. But why—?

Artos edged his way along, close to the wall. He could hear a very faint murmur of voices, sounds of men moving about. He reached the place where the door swung out, shielded himself behind it to peer through the crack.

Modred—there was no mistaking the young man who sat at the table where the armorer kept his supply lists. But beyond him were three men wearing the scale armor of the Companions—young men. Artos knew two of them by name as clansmen who had been recruited a couple of years ago. The third was Argwain, who prided himself on being blood-kin of Modred through one of the complicated clan reckonings.

Artos could not believe what he saw. They had opened the dragon chest. Its lock was broken—Kai had the keeping of the key. And now they were pulling out the coils of the Red Dragons, folding the banner with more haste than care, to cram into a bag Argwain held ready. Torchlight glinted on Modred's arm as he changed position. Artos saw his guess proven true. That was a king's royal arm ring, twin to the one Caesar wore.

The Dragon, the armlet, Modred— How those fitted together the boy did not know. But there was evil here, like black smoke curling from a fire.

"—to the west. Show him this and bid him land where the four torches move right to left before full moonrise." Modred was speaking.

"You." The Prince turned then to Argwain. "Take the signal to Maegwin, to Caldor. We shall so cut the land apart before they can drag themselves out of their fields and take up sword to front us. And with that"—he nodded to the bagged Dragon banner—"and such news as we can proclaim, there will be few swords left to them. Men shall not be sure what is true or false until it is too late!"

"No man can say that you do not plan well, Lord King," Argwain nodded.

"This has been long in planning, but now we act. Let us go."

Artos had only time to push away from the door, dodge into one of those empty rooms. He stood in the gloom within, his heart pounding, rubbing sweating palms against his breeches, trying to make sense of what he had heard.

Modred had the armlet and the banner, and Argwain had called him king. He smoke of torches to signal a landing. And this talk of peace-making with the Winged Helms—their ships reported offshore— All made so ugly a pattern that Artos could not believe it added up as he feared. He must tell Kai!

The men were surely gone from the arms room now. He crossed

the hall to the closed door of the commander's chamber, pushing it open only wide enough for him to slip through. The moon shone through a wonder to show a low bedstead, and he could hear the rumbling snore of the sleeper who lay there. Artos laid a hand on the man's bare shoulder.

Kai had the warrior's trick of waking instantly, his wits alert, and as he raised himself on his elbows Artos crouched by the bed, spilling out what he had seen and heard. There was a muffled exclamation from Kai, and he sat fully up, his feet meeting the floor with a thud.

"What this may mean," he said, "is not to be judged hastily. But that the High King must know goes without arguing." He rubbed fist against fist, and in the moonlight Artos could see the scowl on his face.

"Listen, you" he spoke then directly to the boy. "This must not be done openly. A known messenger riding forth would give away that they had been discovered, if he were not also followed and cut down."

"I ride light and I ride as Marius taught," Artos dared to say.

"Ay, and the High King lies at the hill camp near Fenters Hold. The Roman Way runs north to the Wall, and it is cut by a traders' track to the sea. It is a clear way."

"And I have ridden part of it," Artos was proud to say. "I went to the Wall two summers ago when my father held truce meeting with the Painted People."

"So you did. Which is another piece of fortune." Kai pulled at his thumb, turning the circlet there around and around to free it from its long grip on his flesh. It was a giant's ring to look at, broad and heavy, with a queerly shaped red stone showing the head of a man with horns. Paulus said it was evil, but Kai said that it had belonged to his father, and *his* father, and that it had come overseas in the far-off days, before the Legions set foot in Britain.

He worked it free with an effort. "This is known, boy. Do not take any horse from the stable here, you would be marked and questioned. Slip into town and on to the post of the first hill watch. They keep messenger mounts. Show this and take the road north. Change at any hill fort when your beast begins to fail. For it is time which draws sword against us in this matter. Now—let us go."

Artos slipped from shadow to shadow across the streets of Venta. He wore a tunic and cloak now, as well as his own sword belted heavy against him. Marius had traded for that sword two years ago at the meeting with the Painted People. It was a Legion sword, Marius said, loot from some long-ago battle along the Wall perhaps. But the blade was good and Artos' father had haggled for a long time to get it. It was shorter than the swords the Companions favored, but it was just right for Artos. He had a pouch of rations, too. And Kai's ring was slung on a thong around his neck for safekeeping.

He might have been questioned if he had not had the ring to show when he reached the hill watch. The horse they brought him—stripped to a light saddle pad for speed—though undersize in comparison to the chargers of the Companions, was picked, he knew, for the steady, mile-eating pace it could keep. And he pounded off along the road, thankful for the smooth pavement the Legion had built.

The road ran due north, and though more years than Artos was old had passed since it had been repaired, it was still good footing. Sun rose, and midmorn came. He changed mounts at another of the hill forts. The men here were from one of the tribes, as their plaid tunics made plain. They rained questions upon Artos as he leaned against the log wall, gulping down mouthfuls of bread with just enough barley beer to make it swallowable. To all he only shook his head and said he was on the High King's business and the message he carried was not of his understanding.

Once more, afternoon, when the sun was hot and he had to fight against nodding in the saddle, he changed mounts. This time the watchers were in a crumbling Roman tower. They wore no armor, nor even the brilliant dress of the tribes, but rather had tanned hides on their small, dark bodies marked with blue tattoos. They had bow and arrows, and they spoke in a soft, clipped speech to one another. But their leader—who had a cloak of wolf skin in spite of the heat, the wolf's head with its upper jaw resting on the man's head, dozens of ivory fangs necklaced about this throat—spoke Latin, though in a strange singsong.

Though Artos had never seen these people so closely before, he knew them to be Picts from over the Wall—who served not the land of Britain but rather one man alone, the High King. For Artos Pendragon had in some way won their favor and they came to his call.

Tribesmen, Picts, and a small handful of men who, like Marius, still called themselves "Roman" with harsh pride—these made up the High King's army. Among themselves they would have been sword against sword, knife against arrow. But under Artos Pendragon they were one. His greatest gift was that he could make a victorious army out of such normally divided forces.

Soon after he left the watchtower, Artos swung into the west way. Here he had to slacken pace, since this was no paved road but a wandering tract which turned and twisted with rough footing. There were no grain fields to be seen and here the King's peace was more often broken than kept.

The moon was once more up when the boy saw the scarlet leap of campfires. He slid from his mount, so stiff he could only walk with his hand laid in support against the shoulder of the stumbling horse. His throat was dry with dust as he croaked an answer to the sentry. And he was never quite sure how he came into the High King's chamber.

"It is young Artos! But what do you here? Call Marius."

"Lord king." This time Artos managed better than the croak, found a horn pushed into his hand, and drank some of the bitter beer before he went on. "Lord King"—he fumbled for Kai's ring—"Legatus Kai has sent me."

"To come in such a plight smells of trouble. What manner? Do the Winged Helms— But then the alarm torches would have flamed across country to warn us long since. What is it?"

Then those big, strong hands lay gently on his shoulders, drawing him closer, supporting him. Artos spilled out word after word of what he had seen and heard. There were confused voices about him, but they meant little. Then, somehow, he was lying on a camp pallet, and his father's dark, clean-shaven face, surmounted by a plumed helm, was close to his. He knew he had done what he had come to do.

So the dark time began, and afterward Artos sometimes wondered what might have happened had some small chance led them in a different way.

He was not the only messenger Kai sent, but his forewarning gave the High King some precious hours, which he used well. Other riders went out with the warn-call. Harvest time—Modred had chosen the time for his treachery well.

As men straggled in, a handful here, a better-disciplined war band there, they learned that Modred had indeed raised the Red Dragon and taken a blood oath with the Winged Helms. Ten ships had the fisherman reported off the coast, but now came tales of twenty, more at the sea edging in. It would be such a bloodletting to come as would crush all the High King had fought for, unless he could hold the invaders to the coast.

"But Modred is mad—!" Artos, now his father's trumpeter,

watched Marius bring his bronzed fist down upon the table, setting the drinking horns shaking with the force of his blow.

"No, far from mad," the High King replied. "Remember Vortigen? Modred is of his line, and so sees himself more truly King of Britain than I. By the reasoning of half the tribes I have no right to this." His hand twitched forward a fold of the purple cloak draped across the back of his seat. "Until Aurelianus gave me power I was no more than a man with a plan and a dream. Though now that seems long ago. However"—now he spoke more briskly—"no matter how royal Modred deems himself and is hailed by those deluded enough to believe that his time they can play Vortigen's game with the Saxons and win, I am not about to let the axes of the Winged Helms bring down what is left of life and light in this land.

"Therefore—" He began to talk briskly of men and the movements of an army, those about him listening carefully. Artos saw his father nod once or twice, heard an assenting grunt from Bedivere, who ordered the left wing when the Companions charged.

In the end the High King made a small gesture and the serving men hastened to fill the drinking horns, not with the usual thin beer but rather with the strong-smelling mead of the northlands. Then did Artos Pendragon raise his horn high, get to his feet, the others scrambling up to join him.

"Comrades, it may be that this time we go into dark ways. But if that be so I will say it now—we cannot go in better company! If Modred would buy the kingship, and the Winged Helms this land, then let the price be high!"

There was an answering growl as men drank and threw the horns from them, to roll empty across the table.

When Artos and his father went back to their own quarters, Marius stood for a moment eying his son.

"I would have you ride now to Glendower."

"No!" For the first time in his life Artos found the courage to say that to his father, and in spite of the other's deepening frown he hurried on. "Is this army so great a single sword can be spared?"

"A boy's sword? You are no man to ride—"

"And if—if Modred's men come to Glendower? What of our neighbour Iscar? He has long wanted our lands. You can send me forth only bound and gagged and under guard!"

Marius must have read his son's determination, for suddenly he looked very tired and gave a small shrug. "So be it. But if you stay you are under my orders."

Artos drew a deep breath. "That I know."

Thus he was one of the army that marched south and west. Army? It was hardly a full troop to begin with, though men continued to gather and add to the number as they went. More messengers arrived with ill news of the Saxons pushing inland and of Modred setting up a camp to which came men of the tribes, swearing blood oaths of loyalty under the stolen Red Dragon.

The High King laughed harshly when he was told of this.

"Blood oaths, is it? Do they remember that in the past such oaths were also given to me?"

"But the priests say that they are absolved of them, since they were given to one who did not hold the true church in reverence," observed Bedivere with a twist of lip. It was well known that he was one who followed the old gods, and that the High King had many times been urged by the priests to turn him away for that very reason.

"Men cannot be absolved from treachery so easily," was all that Pendragon answered.

But it seemed that traitor or not, Modred was gathering the greater host. And only half of it marched under the horse-tail standards of the Saxons.

Artos rode as Marius' trumpeter and messenger, always at his father's back as he cantered alone at the head of the troop. Most of them were of the old Roman breed. They used the shorter swords of the Legions, and their faces, overshadowed by the old crested helms, differed from those of the tribesmen. Their standard was an Eagle, mounted on a pole, its wings outspread.

Caius carried it, and his place, too, was behind his commander. Artos envied him that honor. The war horn bumping at his own hip was not nearly as fine a symbol as that Eagle.

There came a time when at last they could see the fires of the enemy camp. But between lay a swampy, broken land, unfit for horses.

"Modred has chosen well," Artos heard his father say to the first Centurion, Remus, as they looked down from a hillock.

"Traitor though he be, he is still a fighting man. But then he has not yet met Caesar in battle." There was confidence in Remus' answer.

They had further additions to their force. Kai came out of Venta with what was left of the defenders there. Artos saw among them a sprinkling of his in-training comrades, so the old and the very young had closed ranks together. Yet no Red Dragon led the van now.

The High king would not let them use the pinion symbolic of his rulership. Instead he gave orders that each man break a handful of barley in stalk from the fields as he marched (so many fields were left without reapers now) and bind it to his helm in sign that he fought not for any king's honor but for his own land. So it was that a large tuft was on the haft of a spear carried behind the High King as he rode, and a twist about the Eagle carried by Caius.

That night came a sounding of horns for parley across the broken land, now well lighted by torches. Then came a band not of fighting men but of priests, craving speech with the King. They were led by Imfry, one of those who had argued in the past with Pendragon because he would not give more power to the church. Yet the High King had ever treated him with courtesy.

Of that meeting Artos heard only what his father told later—that the churchmen urged a truce wherein Modred and the High King might meet face to face, and perhaps the land escape a bath of blood.

"What of the Saxons?" Artos asked.

Marius laughed harshly. "Ay, the Saxons. But the priests are ever hopeful for the winning of their souls. Their leader, Bareblade, has listened to Imfry, it seems. Well, Caesar will grant them their truce meeting. That will gain us more time, which is our greatest need. There is no trusting in the promises of either Modred or Saxon. Each is to bring an armed following of ten, but with strict orders not to draw blade for any reason. To show steel is to break peace."

"Do you go?" To Artos' relief Marius shook his head.

"Caesar takes only two of his captains, Kai and Bedivere If it be a trap he must not lose all of us. And meanwhile, truce or no, we shall be battle-mounted when they go."

The sun was well up when the High King and his selected followers rode out from the lines of his war host. From those other ranks, where the horse tails of the Winged Helms were insolently planted and the Dragon shaft stood, came others.

"Their Dragon sulks," Caius murmured to Artos.

That was true enough. The red banner was not proudly bellied out in the wind but hung limp as a tattered rag about its standard. Perhaps it was an omen that the banner of the High King would come to life for him alone.

As the two parties met, the priests to one side changed a hymn, which reached the watchers as a faint murmur of sound. The sun grew hotter as they waited. Now and then someone in the company spoke in a low voice to his neighbor. But the stamp of a horse because of the flies, the grate of armor as someone shifted position, broke the silence more noticeably.

The ground before them was heath, bog in some patches, ill footing for mounted men. There were some scattered clumps of stunted firs, but mostly coarse grass, sun-browned until it was near the color of ripe grain.

Artos saw a flash of light. One of Modred's men had drawn sword, was stabbing down at the ground. His steel was bare.

"Truce broke! Truce broke!" The cry began low, but swelled into a roar as man after man took it up.

Below was a tangle of men, swords out, clashing—

"Sound!"

Artos did not need that order, the war horn was already at his lips. Its harsh call was lost among other sounds. And then began the charge the High King had planned, the men of the company shouting "Ave, Caesar!" as they rode.

The rest of it was a madness which Artos could never remember except in small snatches. For he was swallowed up in it, swinging the Roman sword. There were distorted faces which came into view and vanished, then once or twice a breathing space when the men of the troop came together and re-formed, to be sent to charge again.

Artos saw Caius go down under a Saxon ax and grabbed the Eagle before it was lost, using its pole to drive against the head of the man who had killed its bearer, knocking him from his feet so that the horses went over him. Each time the troop re-formed the lines were thinner, more men in them were wounded, some clinging to their saddles only by force of will.

The sky darkened, but yet there was light enough to see about them. The High King, his Caesar's purple cloak a ragged fringe; his shield, its garnet-eyed dragon's head half shorn away, still on his arm; and that great sword about which there were such awesome tales, red in his hand—the High King, Artos of Britain!

Fronting him was Prince Modred, all his royal finery spoiled by this day's foul work.

"No!" The Prince's voice rose in a great cry, as if to see that the King still lived was more than he could bear. He rushed forward, his sword ready. The King prepared to meet his charge.

Modred struck first at the horse and it reared screaming, while the Prince dodged those flailing hoofs. Artos Pendragon came out of the saddle, but he landed badly, stumbling, so that Modred, low like a serpent, thrust around his shield. His blade caught on the rent rim and he could not withdraw it quickly for a second stroke. The High King struck in return, a mighty blow across the other's body where neck met shoulder. Modred staggered to one side, dead before his body crumpled to the ground.

But the High King wavered on a pace or two, until one of the kicking legs of his dying horse hit him and he, too, fell.

"Ahhhh"—a moan came from the bloodied and battered men near the King. Artos lurched out of the saddle, tottered on to pull at the High King, trying to drag him away from the horse, others elbowed him aside, unheeding of the enemy, to free their leader.

Then a shout warned them and they looked up to see Saxons running toward them. They fought a wild, desperate battle around Pendragon. And so great was their grief and rage that they paid no heed to wounds. But as if they were men of iron, who could take no hurt, they cut down the Winged Helms.

When that swirl of battle had subsided there remained only five of the Companions still on their feet. Artos crouched beside the King where he had tried to shield that body with the hacked and splintered pole of the Eagle and his own flesh. The standard was shorn of a wing and blood ran warm from his arm. His fingers were numb, unable longer to grasp a sword hilt.

The King stirred and moaned. Somehow they got him out of the press of the dead, to where he could lie straight on the ground. Artos looked around, dazed. Kai lay, his sword deep in a Saxon, but his own craggy face empty of life. Marius? Where was his father? One of those bending over the fallen king looked upon.

"Artos?"

The boy could not answer aloud. Using the staff of the Eagle as a support, he hobbled to where the King lay with those others gathered around him. It was Marius who said, "This is a grievous wound, but we must get him into hiding. There is no way yet of telling how this day has gone. And they would rejoice greatly to set his head on one of their spears."

Among them they carried him away. It was hard labor, for he was a large and heavy man and they were all spent, no man without some wound. Artos stumbled along in their wake, still leaning on his pole. But as he circled to the left to avoid a tangle of dead men and horses he came upon the Royal Standard. The pole had been planted firmly in the earth. About it the Red Dragon hung limp and lifeless, as if it would serve none but its true master. Artos could hardly see it in the twilight. He pushed the broken end of the Eagle shaft into the ground to keep it upright and pulled at the Dragon's pole. It had been too firmly set to yield to his weak tugging. At last he went to his knees and dug in the earth with his belt knife until he could pull it free.

It was heavy and he had to rest it across his good shoulder. The folds, smelling of wood smoke, draped about his head. But he brought it with him, trailing those who carried the King.

They found a rough little hut, perhaps the shelter of some holy man who had chosen to dwell in the wilderness alone, as some did nowadays. Someone had kindled a fire, and by its light they were easing off the King's armor to examine his wound.

No man with the true healing knowledge was there. But they had been long enough at war to know the look of hurts men could take. Marius sat back on his heels, his face a dark mask. Artos turned away his eyes.

"Marius?"

"Caesar!" He bent again over his lord.

"This is my death hurt—"

I have seen men take worse and live."

"Use such words for a child, Marius. This is the dark road after all. But truss me up as best you can. I shall hold to life until I know—know how it fares with Britain. Let me know how went the day—"

"Be sure you shall" Marius turned to the others, all wounded. "Sextus, Calyn, Gondor—see what you can learn!

They were the least hurt of that company and they went swiftly.

"At least that traitor Modred is dead!" Marius spat.

"All deeds—bring—their—own—reward," the High King said. "Is——there—aught—to drink?"

"There is a mere beyond." Marius got to his feet. "It is doubtless scummed, but it is still water." He pulled off his helmet, crestless where its plume had been cut away, and went out. Artos leaned the heavy pole of the banner against the wall, slipped down to sit with his back against the rough surface. His wound had stopped bleeding, but his arm was till numb.

It was a long night, but the king spoke now and then. Sometimes Artos could hear his words clearly, sometimes they were only a murmur, faint and faraway. Marius tended his son's wound and bound it with a strip torn from his cloak, ordering him to sleep if he could.

Men came, to glance within the hut and look upon the King. Some he greeted by name, one or two came to kneel beside him for a space. But they all remained without as a guard about the hut. Slowly news came, too. Modred's forces had melted away when the story of the Prince's death reached them. The Saxons had been driven back to the shore by fresh troops come too late for the real battle. But the war host that had followed the Caesar of Britain, the Companions of the Red Dragon, had been so rent and destroyed that it could never ride as an army again.

When the dawn came, and with it the news that the Saxon host was taking to ship under the harrying of the new levies, the High King listened greedily. Then he turned to Marius and spoke, his voice a little stronger, as if he had been hoarding his strength against this time.

"I made the war host, and now it is broken. But my name may hold men together yet awhile so you can gain time. A dream it was, a good dream—of a Britain united against the dark night of the heathen. We made it live, if only for a space, but now it dies. Do the best you can, Bedivere Marius, those like you, to remember the dream in the coming night. Now, that I may serve dead even as I served living, do not let any save those in this hut known that I die. But say rather that I go to be healed, that my wound, though it be deep, is not fatal.

"We are not far from the river. Get a boat, if you can, and lay me on some island there, making sure that there be no marking of my grave. Swear this to me as the last loyal oath I ask of you."

And together they swore. He did not speak again, but a little later Marius, leaning over him, laid hand on the King's forehead, rose, and nodded. Then he came swiftly to the great Dragon banner and slashed at the cords which bound it to the pole, cutting it also as it lay flat upon the ground. Into it they laid the High King. When they carried him forth they said to the waiting guard that they would take him now to the holy men who lived downriver, who knew the healing arts.

Marius and Bedivere found a boat and put the King in it, Artos crept behind his father. Sextus rowed and the boat answered well. Then they were caught in the current and let it bear them along. At last they came to an island covered with brush and small trees, some of them bearing small, half-ripe apples. Who had planted them in this wilderness, Artos could not guess.

Breaking through the barrier of reeds and brush, Marius, Bedivere, and Sextus carrying the King, they came to an open space in which stood a small building of rough stone. The carven statue of a woman was just within its portal, two others, though smaller, standing a little behind her. That it was a temple of the old days Artos guessed, but honoring what goddesses, British or Roman, he did not know.

There before the temple, with the three statues seeming to

watch, they dug into the earth with their swords, Marius' blade broke against a stone he was trying to lever away. He reached within the roll of the Dragon banner and drew forth the King's longer and heavier weapon, to hack at the clay. Meanwhile Artos pushed away the loosened soil the others tossed out of that cutting.

It took them a long time, for the swords were unhandy spades, and Marius and the others sought to make the hole a deep one. Then they pulled fresh reeds from the shore, and leaves, which, when crushed in their soil-grimed hands, gave forth clean smells. Artos found a bed of small flowers by the temple and jerked them up. From these they made the bed of him who was the last Caesar of Britain. Then, well wrapped in his war banner. Artos Pendragon, the High King, was laid in his hidden grave.

They worked long once more to fill in and cover the place. When they had done and were ready to go, Artos suddenly saw the King's sword lying where his father had dropped it. That should have been buried, too, in the hand of its owner.

He held it out to his father in mute question. Marius took it with a sigh, ran his hand along the scarred, notched blade.

"It is too well known. So it must also disappear. For no man would believe that Caesar would willingly let it go form him."

He went down to the river bank and whirled it above his head with all the force left in his tired arms, letting it fly out over the water and splash into the dark flood. So it was gone, the last tie they had with Artos Pendragon, Dux Bellorum, Caesar, High King of Britain. And the sun went down.

AN ENTRY THAT DID NOT APPEAR IN DOMESDAY BOOK
by John Brunner

The memory of Arthur and his mighty deeds lived on after his death, although it would be nearly six hundred years before Geoffrey of Monmouth recreated the Arthurian word in writing. In the intervening years, tradition and word of mouth kept the legend alive. Did the Norman scribes encounter it when sent out by William I to survey the land and compile the Domesday Book? John Brunner explores that idea here. Brunner (1934-) is one of Britain's leading writers of science fiction, but he has occasionally turned his hand to fantasy with marked success, especially The Traveller in Black *(1971). He has produced other Arthurian fiction, including* Father of Lies *(1962) a short science fiction novel about a boy with such strong psi powers that he can recreate his own Arthurian world. In this story, however the legends can do that for us.*

Along a causeway that the Romans had originally built, half as wide again as a man's height but in poor repair and sometimes overgrown, the King's Inquisitors headed north amid the mists of early autumn, following a local guide and escorted by half a dozen surly, footsore English soldiers.

Attired in his hauberk, but with his conical helmet slung at his saddlebow along with his great sword, his kit-shaped shield hung slantwise at his back, their leader was Count Robert de Bernay. He, and the two similarly accoutred men-at-arms who rode beside him, had come to England in the train of the Conqueror and shared his victory at Hastings. Buy that had been twenty years ago, and – like William himself – they were none of them any longer in their prime. Nonetheless, despite his grizzled beard and balding pate, the count still made a most impressive figure.

Speaking Norman French as they did, neither he nor his companions had more than half a dozen words in common with their guide, but for the most part they made shift with signs.

In their wake, attended by his clerk, Walter of Gisor, and two monks also a-horse – though his mount was the finest – rode the chief investigator of this commission, Abbot Henry of the monastery at Rougemont, or Redhill as the native tongue would frame it, an outpost of Christian civilisation in the distant wilds of Surrey. Compared to the dense forest of Andredeswald, this flat plain verging on the western sea looked as though it ought to make for easy going and swift travel in any direction. That, though, was a treacherous illusion. Here and there among the reeds and marsh grass glinted pools of standing water, betraying the fact that they were crossing a virtual swamp. Without a guide the riders could have found themselves floundering up to a horse-belly height after straying a dozen paces from the causeway. Indeed, they had been told at Summertona, their last stopping place, how during the winter this whole area was so widely inundated that the local peasants gave up farming and turned to fishing and wildfowling instead.

Distantly visible was the sole prominence in the area, a nearly round hill crowned with a rudimentary chapel: the tor dominating Glastingberie, the town where they were next to carry on the king's investigations.

Eventually, when the standing water beside the track almost matched the area of visible land, they approached an oaken bridge across the river that had created this floodpain: insignificant in itself, but only because its waters were not channelled. They had been told that northwest of here, at a place known – reasonable enough – as Mere, its flooding sometimes formed a lake five miles around.

Near the bridge, moored to oaken stanchions, lay half a dozen boats of the crude local type, beside which scrawny men, in ragged clothing kilted nearly to their waists, were mending nets, making fish traps of woven osier, and caulking the flimsy hulls, which were apparently of the same material. Doubtless they were farmers preparing to change to their winter occupation. On sighting the strangers, they broke off their work and drew together suspiciously into a tight group.

Beyond, a short distance downstream, could be seen an island, partly veiled by the drifting greyness.

For some reason it attracted the abbot's attention. Just as the men-at-arms reached the bridge, he shouted out for them to halt.

"Walter!" he added to his clerk. "Give me the record that describes this area."

After some searching of his pack – which also held the tools of his calling, goose-and swam-quills, trimming knives, and a bag of oak-galls like tiny brown apples, for making ink – the relevant document was produced. Taking it, the abbot spurred forward to join the country's party, and they conferred while the others waited nearby, chilled by the all-pervading mist. Finding their reins slack, the horses bent their heads to crop at the coarse grass.

The younger of the monks trembled visibly, and his companion gave a harsh laugh.

"So you can't stand the weather of your own country, is that it?"

"Not at all!" The boy bridled. "But it had just struck me that – well, we're on holy ground!" He crossed himself, and an act in which he was automatically imitated by the footmen. "Jesus Himself may have trodden this same path!"

He believed the legend because he was English and bore an English name: Edward, like the Confessor King. But the other monk, Udo, was Norman, inclined to make mock of all such claims. He promptly did so.

"You'll not deny that Joseph of Arimathea came hither!" Edward countered hotly." And brought a staff cut of that very tree from which they wove a crown of thorns to mock Our Lord, which he struck into the ground on yonder hill where to his day it bears wondrous blossom every Christmas-tide, be it never so hard a winter!"

So much they had been told at Summertona last night. This was a resumption of the argument that had followed as they retired to bed.

At a sign from Abbot Henry, Walter the clerk snapped at the quarrelling monks.

"Hold you your tongues! Holy ground or not, such bickering between brethren is unseemly!"

Edward fell obediently silent, but Udo muttered something, and the abbot rounded on him.

"What did you say?"

With veiled defiance: "Nothing, my lord abbot. Save that I wish we might have more proof of such a story than the unsupported word of a few Englishmen."

"We shall lodge at Glastingberie tonight, and remain there several days. You'll have plenty of time to be convinced or otherwise, Brother Udo! Meanwhile, we have a commission to perform for the king. Since you appear to have forgotten what duties are assigned to us —"

"My lord abbot, I have not!" protested Udo.

"Rehearse them, then!"

The monk sighed, but did as he was told.

"We are to confirm the accuracy of the return made by the local tenants-in-chief, shire-reeves and other officers, stating how many hides of land they hold in this area, how many plough teams of oxen and how many other animals, as horses and swine, how many men owe duty to them, whether bond or free, what manner of dwellings they reside in, what mills and fisheries they have, what forests and who claims the pannage of them and the like, all to be certain what taxes are raisable and whether they are paid in full and in due time."

"Fair, if not exact," allowed the abbot. "And at this moment that's precisely what I'm doing! So have the goodness not to distract me with you squabbling!"

"So far, my lord," Edward ventured, "we have found no worse mistake than honest oversight."

He was always prompt to defend the honour of his people, conquered and humiliated though they were.

"Say you so?" countered Henry. "Then tell me why that island goes unmentioned in this report!" He thrust the parchment into Edward's hands, well knowing he had scarcely learned as yet to decipher Caroline minuscule, the standard clerkly style of writing. "Maybe your young eyes are sharper than mine, hm? I find no trace of it, but suppose you can!"

Dreadfully embarrassed, Edward suggested, "Perhaps it isn't always an island. At the time the return was made out, might the water not have been lower, so that it was linked to the mainland?"

"Ingenious!" Henry granted. "Unfortunately, the return was *not* compiled at the height of a dry summer. Any more ideas?"

Sweating despite the chill, Edward cast around frantically in his mind.

"Well, then, perhaps they thought it too small to be worth mentioning. Perhaps it's uninhabited and worthless."

"It's a fair size," grunted Count Robert, staring across the water. "And it bears what look like fruit trees. I swear there are yellow apples hanging from their branches."

He was given to bragging about how, as he grew older, his ability to discern objects at a distance had improved, With this went mockery of those who concerned themselves about clerkly marks on parchment; those he disdained, on the grounds he could not distinguish them at all.

"Moreover," he appended, "I detect movement, and not just of wild birds, or a breeze ruffling the reed beds. If there are people or cattle there, they owe taxes to the king, and if there's game, it properly belongs to him. Either way, we need to find out. Am I not correct?"

"Entirely," Henry murmured, reclaiming the parchment from Edward's nerveless grasp and returning it to his clerk.

Count Robert shouted at their guide. "What can you tell us about that island? You – what's your name – Edward! Come here and translate for me!"

Sighing, the young monk urged his horse forward.

The man answered in the local dialect that even Edward – born as he had been on the far side of England – found difficult to follow. What he said, after many misunderstandings, amounted to the fact that he had never seen it before.

"But you boasted that you knew this country well!" said the count as he descended from his horse and belted his sword around his waist. "Well, it won't take long to cross to it and see what's to be seen. The water here looks too deep to ford, even on horseback, so we'll requisition some of those boats. I don't suppose they can carry more than a couple of us apiece, but on the other hand there's no need for us all to go. I suggest you and your clerk, Lord Abbot, and myself, and Brother Edward in case we run into someone else who doesn't speak a civilised language."

Walter, looked a trifle nervous. "Should we not take a couple of soldiers, too?"

But the abbot - he was still a young man, under thirty, and well set-up-scoffed at the clerk's fears as he likewise dismounted.

"Walter, you're insulting the prowess of a warrior who fought at Hastings! Where do you think we are – the eastern fens? And even there the followers of Hereward have been scattered by the might of the king!"

Walter swallowed hard, but all he said in answer was, "We also ought to list those boats. I don't believe they were included in the original return either."

"Save that until afterward," rumbled the count. "They may sink under us, in which case there'll be no point."

His jest did nothing to reassure the clerk.

The boat-owners were most reluctant to convey the strangers to the island, but Count Robert forwent Edward's services as interpreter and cut the Gordian knot in the ancient way, by brandishing his sword, whereupon they gave in. A few minutes later, leaving the other boats and boatmen under guard, the investigators embarked on their brief voyage.

To the plashing of paddles, Edward sat in the bow of the one he shared with the count, this time frankly shivering, not so much from anxiety – though the craft did feel alarmingly fragile and unstable – as from mere cold. The fog seemed to grow abruptly denser as they drew away from the shore, so that there was a brief interlude during which they could see neither the island nor the mainland; he had missed his footing when trying to get aboard and was soaked to the knees. As soon as possible, he reminded himself, he must re-tie his sandals, or their rawhide thongs would shrink and bite into his flesh. But while they were actually afloat, he had no wish to do anything that might capsize them, not even wring out the hem of his robe.

Mercifully soon, however, the bow grounded on soft silt, and the scowling boatman held his craft steady by clutching at alder branches while his passengers clambered ashore. The other boat had kept pace, and the abbot and his clerk joined them within moments.

They stared about them, finding that they were indeed surrounded by apple trees, neatly arrayed in a small grove. But there was not a sign of the creatures Count Robert claimed to have spotted. Nothing moved here save the shifting river mist.

This was much to Edward's relief. He had not seen, but he had often heard, what vengeance the king's troops could wreak on those who tried to resist or deceive him. Were not entire counties in the north of England returning reports that said of once-rich farmland, once-populous settlements, "*Wasta est* – it is a desert"?

Then, all of a sudden, the count let out a great roar.

"Stop them! Traitors!"

While their attention had been distracted, while Edward had been refastening his sandals, the boatmen had pushed off again and were vigorously padding away. The count rushed after them, but halted, panting, when he was over ankles in the water, by which time the boats were already lost to view.

"We're stranded!" Walter moaned, and even the abbot looked dismayed.

But Count Robert snorted. "Ah, what matter? There are more boats. As soon as they realise what trick has been played on us, no doubt my men will commandeer them and row to the rescue. We'll probalbly find them waiting for us when we finish our circuit of the island. Come along! Let's see what's to be seen! I wager there'll be something – I doubt these apples plant and tend themselves."

It was obvious from Walter's expression that he would far rather have stayed put. However, had he done so, he would have been left alone, since Edward, though he felt the same way, was pledged to obey his abbot. That prospect did not appeal. So they all set off in the count's wake.

Soon enough, though – reluctant as the count would have been to admit a mere Englishman, and a youth at that, could have been right when he was wrong – they established that, the island was smaller than he had assumed: perhaps no more than a tenth of a hide in total area, and low-lying. But for a few trees at its centre, veiled in the obscuring mist, a tall man might have looked clear across it from the spot where they had landed. They trudged completely around it, having now and then to splash through rivulets that soiled them to the knees with mud, without discovering any sign of habitation or even use of it for pasturing animals. Relaxing, Edward concluded that his guess about the reason for it not having been reported to the king must be correct, since there was obviously nothing to tax. Apart from the mysterious apple trees, they had found only reeds, rushes, willows, alders, scrub grass, and a few wild birds and water rats. The movements Count Robert claimed to have spotted must after all have been a trick of the mist.

However, when they regained the place where the boats had rounded, there was still no sign of rescue. Worse, the mist remain as thick as before.

And into the bargain it seemed to soak up sound. When the count bellowed at the top of his voice towards the mainland, his call seemed to die aways unnaturally soon – and he had been able to rally his men on the field of battle without relying on a hornman.

Even this tough old warrior, Edward judged with dismay, was growing worried.

Typically, though, he concealed his anxiety behind a bluff veneer of confidence.

"Mayhap the fog's too dense just now," he grunted. "In a little while they'll come for us. Meantime, we need not lack for sustenance. Apples are no proper meat for a man, but in time of need worse nourishment than that has stayed the grumbling of my belly. You, boy – pluck us some!"

Unwillingly the young monk complied, reaching on tiptoe to a high branch where the largest grew: no bigger than a man's fist, but nonetheless remarkable. Moreover they appeared to be at the pitch of ripeness, with a sheen between russet and gold.

But he picked only three, greatly tempted though he was by the warm colour of the fruit. Some impulse stayed his hand before it touched a fourth. This much amused the count, who demanded whether he was afraid of being taken for a Norman thief – a common term among the English, never used save at the speaker's peril in earshot of one of the new overlords.

Annoyed with himself, Edward was about to seize one after all, when harsh words assailed their ears.

"Who are you, and by what right do you rob apples from our trees?"

The voice was a woman's, high and clear, but steely, like a knife blade turned to glint in sunlight. As one they gasped and swung around. From the corner of his eye Edward noticed how Count Robert's hand fell reflexively to the hilt of his sword, but he had only half-drawn it when he realised who was confronting him.

Standing among the swirls of mist, that seemed to have parted either side of her like curtains, tall, stern of countenance, she wore the habit of a nun. Her expression was of noble defiance; she had the air of a lady owning lands in her sole right, used to command, used to obedience. Edward had met a few of those, visitors to the abbey at Redhill, and wondered whether he, were Heaven one day to grant him the privilege of exercising authority, would be able to match their sense of assurance.

But her manner made no impression on Count Robert. He parted his lips in a wolfish grin.

"We are on the king's business," he retorted. "We have his authority to go everywhere and pry into everything."

"Not here," countered the nun.

"How dare you claim so?" Abbot Henry barked, striding forward alongside the count. Walter scurried after, leaving Edward apart.

"I have heard of your king," the woman said. "A usurper

and an upstart, who neither reigns here, nor does he rule."

"Treason!" shouted the count. "Were you not a woman, I'd smite your head from your shoulders! All the lands of England belong to him by right of conquest! And all things in it, too – including these apples!"

To underline his boast, he raised the one he held to his mouth and crunched it. Thanks to his age his teeth were few and caried; Edward fancied he saw him wince, as though he found the apple hard and would rather have cut it with a knife, but he bit down defiantly. Henry did the same at once, and not to be shamed Walter imitated them.

At the same moment came a sound like the tolling of a brazen bell.

And they stood frozen, as though struck to stone.

For a long appalling instant Edward imagined he, too, had been rendered statue-rigid. He could neither move, nor cry out, nor even breathe.

After a few seconds, however, his teeth began to chatter. No sensation in his short life had ever been more welcome. The nun was turning away, about to disappear among the mist again. Gasping to fill his lungs, he managed to shout after her, but she affected not to hear.

His companions' faces might have appeared comical in their uniform expressions of surprise and shock. But to Edward they were purely terrifying. All he could think of was that he did not want to be left alone in this fog-shrouded place where – plainly – the old magic ruled. He glanced around frantically in hope that the count's men-at-arms might be approaching in the other boats, but there was nothing to be seen save the grey vapours.

He could hear something, though. In place of the bell's tolling, music: the chanting of a splendid choir. And to his nostrils wafted a perfume whose sweetness outdid the finest incense in the richest cathedral of the land.

Yes – *magic!*

A heartbeat later, babbling a frantic prayer, he was running in the direction taken by the nun.

And, so soon he could truly not believe it, caught up with her before a building that he also could not believe. It was – it had to be – a chapel, for above its peaked roof there swung the bell that he had lately heard.

But where had it sprung from? Why had they not seen it before?

It was not large, but it was magnificent. No rough-hewn stone formed its walls, or daub-and-wattle such as he was used to; instead, he saw polished and seamless plaques of minerals he had no name for, that seemed to glow with inner luminance. As for its roof, it glistened like silver – but was there so much silver in the world? All the pence of the kingdom, melted down, would not suffice to layer it with such a sheen, untarnished even by the mist!

And behind the nun, who had turned to confront him, rose a two-leaf door of smooth dark-gleaming wood within a rounded arch. She stood before it, though it was closed, as to deny him entry.

Yet somehow he knew he *must* find out what lay within. Perhaps the music, perhaps the delicious fragrance, perhaps the glow emitted by the very stones – something, at any rate, made him convinced that were he to die the moment he set foot upon the threshold, it would have been worth it. For nothing else, though he should live to be a hundred, would match what the parting of those doors would show. . . .

Ought he to drop to his knees and plead? Or should he boldly ask her to step aside, as though he were her equal rather than a humble monk barely out of his postulancy? While he was still dithering, she spoke again.

"You may not enter, brother. Even though you wear your order's habit, this is not a chapel you may worship in."

Her tone, to his surprise, was not commanding. It was regretful. But determined.

The poignancy of the music was agonising now. Clinging to a straw of hope, he begged, "Sister! May I not a least . . . look?"

She pondered a moment. "You're no Norman," she said at last.

"I? No! I have to serve our conquerors, for they have ruled the land since long before my birth, and there's no other path to learning now save through the abbeys and monasteries they approve. But I do so with a heavy heart, and yearn for a time when England shall be England once again, when English shall be spoken in the court, and courts of law, as in the time of the Confessor King whose blessed name I bear . . . Oh, Sister, grant me this boon! I shall remember you forever in my prayers!"

This time she paused so long before replying he grew afraid she might have disbelieved him. What should he swear by to persuade her of his sincerity? His hope of salvation?

While he was still hunting for words, however, she gave a slow and thoughtful nod.

"It is perhaps as well that, now and then, one of the ancient stock should be permitted to bear witness to the world. . . . I warn you, boy! The burden of knowledge that you crave is not lightly to be undertaken. Speak of it in the hearing of those who do not love this ancient land, and mockery will be your lot. Mayhap they'll call you mad, and chain you up. Mayhap they'll dub you heretic and traitor, and put you to the sword. Are you prepared to run that risk?"

"I am!" cried Edward with all fervency at his command.

"Kneel, then, and watch. But do not try to pass within. It may not be."

As he obeyed, she turned her back. Without her touching them the double doors swung wide, and he was unable to repress a sigh of amazement at the brilliance revealed. He had to raise a hand to shade his eyes, for indeed it was such light as might make stone glow inwardly. At the same time the music swelled to a climax, and the perfumes grew overpowering.

In a little, though, he was able to see more clearly. And what he saw . . . extremely small and far away, as though the chapel were far bigger than it looked outside, yet they were sharp so that he made out the pettiest detail. He saw . . .

To either side of an aisle, most of them hidden because the doors did not span the full width of the chapel, robed figures: nuns, like the one he had had speech with, singing in supernal voices. There seemed to be no words to their anthem – that, or it belonged to no language he had heard before.

For an instant he recalled Count Robert's gibe about meeting someone who did not speak a civilised language, and wondered what tongue the nun had addressed them in. Disturbingly, he realised he had no idea. More magic? No! He must think rather in terms of miracles!

Then the thought faded like smoke, and he went on drinking in the marvels before him.

The floor of the aisle was inlaid with jewels, as though a rainbow had been fetched from heaven and struck solid. Yet even that magnificence paled beside what stood before him.

In this chapel its place was taken by a catafalque, apparently carved from a single gem, whose hue was never the same from one instant to the next. He began to feel dizzy and had to wrench his eyes away, upward to the figure that lay on it: an effigy of a tall bearded man in kingly robes, reposing on his back, his hands crossed on his breast and grasping – yes – an empty scabbard.

And on his forehead there was the scar of a most dreadful wound.

The hint of a whisper of a suspicion of what he was beholding crept into Edward's mind and brought with it such naked terror as, he thought, a sinner's soul might feel as it was cast into the depths of the abyss. He clung with might and main to his conviction that this was holy ground, that Jesus Himself had walked nearby, that no power of evil might hold sway where the Saviour had passed. . . .

And his resolution almost failed in the moment when he realised: that was no effigy!

For the tall man's chest, albeit slowly, was rising and falling as he breathed.

Full knowledge came to him. That catafalque could be none other than the altar known as Sapphire, that floated on no matter how turbulent a sea! The more-than-earthly glow must emanate from the Cup of Cups, the one so many noble knights had sought life-long, abandoning all earthly love and loyalty in quest of it. And the unconscious man –

He could control himself no longer. Leaping to his feet, he shouted out the truth.

"*Non mortuus est sed dormit! Rex quondam, rex futurus, et rex meus!*"

And made to rush into the chapel.

But there was no chapel. No more fragrance, no more chanting nuns. Only the grove of apple trees, into one of which he seemed to have run full tilt and banged his head so that it rang. Only a dazzling brightness in his eyes so that for a while he could not clearly see, and a sense of dreadful loss that tore his heart.

"Faugh!" said Count Robert, spitting out the chunk of apple he had tasted "They 're sour as crabs despite their pretty colour!"

Doing the same, Abbot Henry confirmed, "Fit for making cider, maybe, but no more."

As for Walter, he glared at Edward as though suspecting it was all a plot on his part, or some other Englishman's, to make the Normans look like fools.

The bleariness was fading from his sight, the memory of music from his ears. Edward, glancing uncertainly around, noticed that the fog was dissipating. Moreover, he could make out the plop-plop of paddles.

"What's got into you?" Count Robert growled. "You look as though you've had the fright of your life."

Edward disregarded the question. "They're coming for us!" he answered, striding to the shore. "Can't you hear?"

At the same moment there was a shout from the water.

"My lords! Answer us! Are you well –? There they are! I spy them now!"

And four boats emerged from the swathes of mist.

A few minutes later they were all embarked again, amid a stream of threats from Count Robert concerning what he was going to do when he caught up with the boatmen who had stranded them. He paid no attention when his men-at-arms apologetically admitted that they had made good their escape in the fog.

Only when the count finally ran out of ingenious punishments and tortures could their rescuers pose the crucial question. It was, in fact, Udo who uttered it.

"My lord abbot, what of the island? Did you find anything worth recording?"

"Not a thing," Abbot Henry grunted. "Miserable place! Mostly marsh and puddles. Walter, don't bother to make note of it. It probably doesn't even have a name. . . . Did you say something, Brother Edward?"

Nearly. He had been about to burst out, "Yes, it does! And I know what it is!"

But it the nick of time he had kept the knowledge to himself – as he must for the rest of his life, save in the most trustworthy of company. Nonetheless, as he and the others remounted for the ride to Glastingerie, he could not avoid whispering, unheard, so that his lips and tongue might relish the shape and texture of the words:

"He is not dead, but sleeps, the once and future king."

"In Avalon!"

MIDNIGHT, MOONLIGHT, AND THE SECRET OF THE SEA
by Darrell Schweitzer

So we come to the end. When Chrétien and Malory created their Arthurian worlds, it was not the historical past from the sixth century of which they wrote but a magical never-never land set in the Middle Ages at the time of the Crusades. This is the true Arthurian period, albeit seven hundred years after the historical Arthur existed. Are the knights of that period any less Arthurian? To close this volume I have selected one of Darrell Schweitzer's stories about Sir Julian, a hapless, dispossessed knight wandering through an Arthurian Middle Ages. Only when you reach the final line will you see real reason this story is here. Darrell Schweitzer (1952) is a prolific American writer, critic, editor and literary agent in the fields of fantasy, horror and science fiction.

I

I lost my faith on a foreign shore, in the shade of the conscience tree. In the shade of the conscience tree, on a foreign shore, where the sand ran wet with the blood of children.

385

II

There is something about the number three. . . . Three encounters started my adventure off.

First: Ragged and tattered and starving I came, my mind filled with a thousand ghosts and shadows, into a land where it was always raining, raining until all color had been washed out of the land, save for muddy brown and the grey of the sky. Nothing grew. The earth slept beneath dead leaves, the branches of the trees bare of them. It was late in the year, almost to Yule, and yet nowhere did anyone sing the carols of the Child Christ, or allow themselves to be seen, or stir unseen. It was very quiet, almost without sound. The constant voice of the rain was too universal, too interwoven with the fabric of existence to be considered a sound. After a while, the ear shut it out.

There I arrived, I Julian, called apostate, second of that name, formerly a knight of God and his holy crusade, shunned and shunning. Once more stepping into Europe and the realm of my own people. I found a newly slain knight lying under his shield in the middle of a meadow, already beginning to decay. Despite the rain, two large black birds perched on his face, pecking at his eyes. I drove them away and stripped him of his sword, his shield, his coat of mail, and his helmet, for I had lost all of mine. I couldn't recall where. In desert or in sea, in waking dream or in sleep.

I found his horse nearby, mounted, and rode away. I examined the shield. On it was the sign of the Endless Knot, an emblem of great potency. But the blow of a sword had dented the metal, scraped away a bit of paint, and broken the knot.

All around me the ground seemed to boil with mist; the air was damp and bitterly cold, filled with pestilent humors and dead souls.

Second: In an ancient wood, where pagans long ago had carved idolatrous faces in the trunks of the trees, near the ruin of a charcoal burner's cottage, I heard a cry of distress. I spurred my steed ahead through the underbrush and came to a clearing, where I found a lady writhing on the ground in agony.

"The bite of the serpent!" She pointed to twin wounds on her ankle. "Quick! Tie a string around my leg, lest the venom spread through my whole body." And her speech broke into inarticulate screams, and she moved her head from side to side rapidly in her pain.

I dismounted. Right by her was a huge tree, around which was tied a red cord. Without thinking I yanked it away—it broke easily—and knelt to bind her wound, when suddenly something stirred in the leaves and a tiny, dry voice said, "Did I do well, mistress?"

"You did very well," said the damsel.

I looked down, astonished, just in time to see the snake whiplash away. Then I turned my gaze to the lady, who was gazing beyond me at the tree, and laughing. She seemed entirely recovered.

I leapt to my feet, whirled out, and beheld six old women sliding down from the branches, slowly as a slug oozed rather than as a human climbs, as if they were growing from the boughs like obscene, overripe fruit. Six more were emerging from the roots of the tree, burrowing up out of the ground like worms, mud on their faces, and spitting up filth.

"He cannot stop us," they tittered. "He has not the cross. His magic sign will do him no good without it."

"*Who are you?*"

"Hail, anti-Merlin, brought to us in the fullness of time. Hail, liberator. Hail, fool."

"*Who are you?*"

"Who are we? Who are we?" Their voices slid into chant, into singsong. "We are all the evils of the world, all the lusts, all the fears, all the secrets concealed in the unredeemed dark. A great one bound us with mighty enchantments, and now you have undone his work. What is let loose may never be bound up again."

"*Who are you?*"

"Who are we? Who are we? We are who. We are who. We are who we are." They joined hands, the twelve of them, and danced in a ring around the tree, cackling, and I knew them to be witches, but older, more powerful than a common village hag who sells her soul to the devil for the power to send pains and poison wells.

The laughter of the damsel stopped, and I glanced back to where she had been. A fat toad hopped between my legs and into the circle. One of the crones scooped it up and placed it underneath her clothing, against her breast. Furious and frightened, I drew my sword, let out a battle yell, and charged. They scattered like startled pigeons, running between the trees in all directions with startling agility. For an instant there seemed to be a hundred witches, an army of them; my horse reared and bolted at the sight of them; and then I was alone, in the rain, with the final echoes of my voice coming back to me from the depths of the forest. I felt very cold and exhausted and began to shake.

I asked myself, how can I know this thing has happened, or where it has happened, or whether or not it is a vision of the future? Were my eyes closed to these things, or open? How can I ever know if I wake or dream?

The answers: There were still holes in the mud at the base of the tree, rapidly filling with water, their sides collapsing. On the ground nearby was a broken piece of red twine.

Third: I waded to my thighs in a frigid stream where a bridge had washed out, then clambered up the muddy bank, stumbling over loose stones. I splashed through once tilled fields, now bare of all but a few dead stalks. The rain made little lakes, and the soil ran away in brown rivulets. Beyond the fields, another stream, another ruined bridge, and a mill with its wheel moss-covered and rotting and motionless. Beyond this, roofless cottages and a manor house, which seemed abandoned, but at least might provide me with dry shelter.

The great hall within was empty, and the rooftree sagged. Boards and beams had fallen across the tables. The hearth was cold, and tiny waterfalls were everywhere. I explored other rooms, and found them likewise fallen down and sodden, but then I came upon one which was not, and in it were the four inhabitants of the place.

Three were bald, white-bearded men who wheezed and shuffled, servants to a younger master, or at least one who might have seemed young once before suffering had wasted him. His eyes were sunken, his face all but a death mask. His hair was falling out in patches, and it was streaked with grey. The skin of his hands seemed exquisitely white, like carven marble.

He sat in a high-backed wooden chair, hunched forward with a soiled blanket in his lap, and his three bent servants at his side. He was paging through a mildewed book, carefully separating the damp leaves with a thin knife, so as not to tear them.

When I had introduced myself and explained the circumstances of my coming—or at least as much as I cared to let him know—he said, "You were destined to arrive here, as my savior." And he told me his tale:

"My name is Gottfried. I was called Gottfried the Bold at one time. I was a bold, proud knight, a champion always in joust and battle. I wore a blue lily on my shield, and the scarf of my lady in my helm. Yes, I was to marry a great lady—more than that even, a vision of the Ideal made incarnate—but first I swore, for the honor of my Lady of us all, by which I mean God's Mother, that I would go to the East and fight in the crusade. There I would cleanse the land of pagan evil and win free all the holy places, even the sepulcher where Christ slept for two nights and a day, and the hill of Golgotha where he died. I fought long and well with the army. God was with us, but then, as we approached the Holy City, a herald of the enemy came to us, saying that the gates would be opened and the city surrendered if one of our number could defeat one of theirs in single combat atop a nearby mountain. I think it was my pride—and this whole thing a device from on High to show me the folly of that pride—which made me accept the challenge. On the appointed morning I climbed the mountain. I labored all day in the hot sun, burdened by my armor and weapons, inching my way up the nearly sheer stone face. It was nearly evening when I came to the top, a wide plateau, and met my enemy. He had been waiting for me all day, it seemed. I don't know how he could have gotten there. The way I went was the only one possible for an earthly man, unless one could drift to such heights in the heart of a cloud.

"He was a giant. His armor was a shiny black, brilliant in the orange glow of the fading sun. I fought with him, and the struggle was over with painful swiftness. His arm moved faster than the eye could see. I was like an untrained boy with a stick against him. Before I could scarely draw two breaths he had dealt me a wound on the thigh, but he did not follow it with another blow. He left me there, and vanished into the oncoming night. He seemed to walk right off the edge of the cliff.

"The city was finally taken, as you know. Thousands died in the battle, thousands more from heat and foul water, but I saw little of this. At dawn my comrades came in search of me, and there they found me, suffering from a wound which never healed. I hired the most learned men of physick, but they could do nothing. It was beyond the power of leeches to draw the evil out. This work was the Lord's. Priests sang masses for me, and the whole of the army prayed, but it did no good. At last I had myself borne home, where I found my lands in ruin and decay, under a curse of endless rain, as you see them now. I have been waiting here ever since, waiting for sluggard death to come, or a miracle."

"Alas," I said. "I can work no miracles."

"But hold," said he. "Hear the rest: At long last I heard of a holy anchorite who had walled himself up in a cave and gained much wisdom in the dark. I went to him, and spoke through a tiny portal where a stone had fallen out. I saw nothing within, but heard a voice serene with confidence, saying, "Until the ungodly is removed from your domain, you shall not be healed." And thus it is my hope, brave sir, that you can bring about my salvation. I no longer am able to move from my dwelling, but you are strong even yet, and you can go forth and root out whatever evil there is to be found."

I could not bring myself to answer, and he did not press me. The servants fetched a meager meal, which I ate gratefully. The two of us spoke for a while of other things, of poetry and strange dreams, and of impossible tales written in books.

III

That night I was shown to a bed in a room filled with cowbeds. When I slept, I swam backward in time through seas of memory, and saw clearly the tale I had been unable to tell in reply to Gottfried's.

I saw again the morning when the holy Tancred, Bishop of Anjou, Averoigne, and Poictesme, stood before the troops in the dim light of dawn with the walled city at the back. There was complete silence, save for the cawing of expectant crows and the flapping of banners in the brisk wind. He spoke:

"Soldiers of Christ, in yonder city wait ten thousand pagans, idolaters, devil-worshippers, atheists, and Jews, each of them by every breath he breathes an affront to the God who created him and a triumph for the Adversary who corrupted him. This is your task, mighty men of valor and virtue, your task set for you by God on high, to rid the land of this infection, to cleanse with fire and sword the very pavement on which the unclean ones walk. I have prayed for victory this day, and just before I came to you I had a vision. I saw in the sky, above the hills and above the pagan city, the great sign of the Cross, blazing as it did for Constantine when he embraced the Saviour, in this sign we too shall conquer. Jesus looks on. His Holy Mother waits to take any who die today in her own arms into Paradise. *Onward! For Christ and the Cross!*"

"Christ and the Cross!" The cry returned from every throat, and the host surged thunderously forward like an inexorable tide. The first wave broke against the stone walls of the city, and the battle was joined. "Christ and the Cross!" men shouted as they fell screaming beneath curtains of molten iron poured from above. "Christ and the Cross!" resounded once more as mangonels, catapaults, and ballistas filled the air with death. The fighting went on without pause until midday, and then there was a brief respite, scarcely long enough for both sides to wipe sweat from brows, and then the fury was renewed. In the purple evening the huge siege towers rumbled forth, and it was in full darkness that I clambered over the walls with the rest, too filled with wrath and battle lust to even think of waiting for the morrow.

The city was taken. The battlements were cleared of every foe, then the nearer streets, and eve before the gates could be opened they were smashed from without by boar-headed battering rams. From above it must have looked like the flood of Noah, inundating the world. On the ground, a nest of hornets, stinging with steel.

When resistance was reduced to small pockets, the slaughter went on like an avalanche which grew and grew with each new falling stone and could not be stopped. Now mounted knights ran down women, old men, and children. Some laughed, thinking it a merry hunt as they speared the fleeing pagans. Anything which were insatiable, famished for death. In narrow alleyways soldiers waded ankle-deep in gore. Once a group was found meekly sitting in the middle of a square, waiting for the end. There were priests and scholars present, staring with hopeless resignation, a few of them paging slowly through books. Women sat among them, young and old, with barefoot urchins in their laps. Only a few looked up as the vanguard of the conquerers halted before them. And I and the others, without hesitation, and rejoicing that God had granted us this chance to avenge our fallen comrades, dismounted and ran among them, hewing off heads and splattering brain as methodically as reapers in a field of grain. Bishop Tancred was there too. Forbidden by holy law to shed blood, he used a padded club which did just as well.

Later, as each man went his separate way in search of booty, I came to a holy place in the center of the metropolis, a vast structure of domes and delicate towers. I was at first reluctant to enter, lest I find Mahomet's coffin just inside the door, floating between floor and ceiling, but then I said to myself, "God is with me, and has triumphed this day," and I went in. In a wide, torchlit hall were three maidens, naked and headless. Outside the riot of shouting, occasional screams, doors being smashed, and the roaring of flames, but here it was quiet. I explored other rooms. The soothing darkness swallowed me up. Everything else seemed a remote dream.

Eventually I came to a place filled with books. Someone had been through it before me, and most of the volumes were in heaps on the floor, as if eager hands had sought treasure behind them on the shelves. Bloody fingerprints defaced some of the leaves. In the middle of the room was a coal-filled brazier which provided light. Miraculously it had not been overturned. At the base of it lay a dead man. His turbaned head was cloven messily in twain. An arm raised in futile defense lay severed at his side. Yet in the other hand he still firmly clutched a thick volume. I pried it from his already stiffening fingers and looked through it. I could not read the script, but the diagrams seemed to suggest a treatise on magic. I knew it for a devilish thing, but was attracted by the sheer forbidden mystery of it. I resolved to keep it, perhaps have it read to me by a learned prisoner, if there were any.

And then I dropped it with a start, and my heart leaped with sheerest terror as something clamped onto my ankle with the grip of a steel trap. I jumped away and looked down, and it was there still—the hand of the hewn off arm, clinging to me with more than human strength. I kicked and stamped and struck the thing with my sword, nearly chopping my foot off, but it would not let loose. An observer might have thought I was dancing a bizarre jig. I was only free of the thing when I had reduced it to such a pulpy ruin that it was more liquid than solid. I stood gasping, staring down in revulsion, and involuntarily I said aloud, "By the wounds of Christ!"

"Yes, the wounds of Christ and the hand of Christ and the face of Christ shall haunt you forever." A new dark miracle was upon me. The corpse sat up, and the lifeless lips on the ruined face spoke impossibly. "This curse I place upon thee, infidel, man of Europe—the burden of your own conscience. Let your eyes be opened for the first time, and from this day hence you shall find no rest, your pride and your remorse warring endlessly within you. Hated and hating, outcast before your God and your folk, you shall wander over the face of the earth in the face of death and fleeing the iron face of your Christ, and death shall precede you and follow after, bringing ruin to all things you hold to be holy, until you hold them holy no longer—"

"No more! Say nothing!" In a blind, tear-filled fury I struck off the head of the apparition, and hacked and hacked at the body until no part remained joined to any other. I sank my hands into the reddened sea of its breast—if only, if only I could hold the heart in my hands, then I would be sure my will had overcome the other. So I took out the very core of the monstrosity, impaled it on my sword and held it aloft, but there was no comfort in the action. Disgusted I flung it to a far wall, where it splattered like on overripe fruit.

And the voice spoke no more, and panting, ready to faint. I knelt there, leaning on my sword in a parody of prayer, breathing with labored gasps. All the accumulated weariness of the day seemed to fall on me just then. I barely managed to crawl a short space away and sit down, my back against the shelves. I stared dumbly at the ceiling until some traces of reason returned, and then I retrieved the grimoire.

As did I heard someone coming. I leapt to my feet, sword in hand, ready in case the newcomer should be a foe.

I knew the man. He was Robert of Tharras, a gallant knight who had saved my life in battle once when the enemy had me surrounded and unhorsed. I lowered my weapon at the sound of his familiar voice.

"Ho, Julian! You won't find any gold there. I already looked."

"So I. . .see. . ."

"There's nothing worth half a penny in this whole accursed place. No vessels like in our churches. But look—here's a prize."

He held up his spear to my face so I could see in the half light what he had. It was an infant, impaled on the point, covered with blood and trailing guts.

"One less devil-lover to grow up and trouble us, eh? And yet another goodly deed for saintly me." He laughed and rolled his eyes up to heaven in jest. When I said nothing he shrugged and went away, brandishing his trophy aloft.

I was without words. The sorcerer's curse had taken effect even there in the dim silence, revealed on the tip of a spear. It was as if the vast cathedral doors of my mind had opened for the first time, flooding daylight in on my unborn conscience. I asked myself, *What am I doing here? Are these deeds really pleasing to the Living, Loving God and his gentle Mother to whom the courtly heroes pray? And if they are, is He not more rightly to be called Moloch?*

There were no answers there in the room filled with loose papers and the smell of blood, no answers at all as Sir Robert's footsteps faded away and I was left alone, alone as I knew myself doomed forever to be.

The memory faded, but the final image would not. "Take it away!" I screamed, and the spear was still before me. I awoke screaming in the sodden, musty room, and when I had regathered my wits I knew what I had to do. I needed a ritual penance, an exorcism, a laying to rest of unquiet souls. I had to bind what I had loosed, heal what I had wounded, rebuild what I destroyed.

I went at once to the chamber of Sir Gottfried. He was awake with his books. It seemed he never slept. The pain, he said, was too great for that.

I knelt down before him, presented him my sword for him to touch and bless, and swore to fulfill his quest. At this he took great comfort, and I a little, although I knew I could not be saved as easily as he. My enemy was far, far greater, if closer at hand.

IV

I was unable to see the maimed knight again to exchange blessings before I set off. His servants said he was asleep, truly asleep for the first time since his misfortune had begun. They dared not wake him. Hope had brought him this far, and they would not interfere.

The three of them brought me not my own sword and armor, but more splendid gear.

"These alone of all his treasures our master has been able to save. He bids you take them."

"I shall return them when I am done."

"There is no need! If you are successful, all things shall be awarded to you, and if you are not, alas, Sir Gottfried will have no used for things of war except for be buried in them."

They helped me on with steel shoes first, then greaves, knee pieces, cuisses, a mailcoat of brightly polished rings, encasing me in steel from toe to head with practiced skill. Fingers knew their tasks, even if faces seemed blank and distracted. I considered these three, and thought it strange that I had never come to know them as persons, just the three, the identical three, like bewitched vegetable men pulled from the root of a single mandrake.

Over the coat of mail they placed a surcoat, covered with intricate designs, like a thing worn by the pagans in the East. Here, lions and elephants ran. There, a castle and a dragon in the sea, and all these things circling about the great sign of the blue lily across my chest. I was given a shield rimmed with rubies, on which the emblem was repeated, and a jeweled sword too, something I had never thought even to touch, too exquisite for a king, fit only for one of the Nine Worthies. I placed a golden helmet on my head, took a long white spear in hand, and mounted my horse, which now wore a saddle rimmed with silver tassels. Thus equipped I set out, while behind me the old men raised their hands aloft to wave me Godspeed. Soon they and the house were swallowed up by the mist and distance.

It continued to rain. Among the clouds overhead, sheets of lightning flared faintly and there were distant hints of thunder. For a while I was comfortable beneath my clothing, but in time the dampness and chill crept in, and then, as if to celebrate this victory, the storm suddenly increased in fury. The light, steady downpour became a torrent, and the wind whipped spray through the opening in my helmet, into my eyes. A veritable river ran under my collar and down my back. Above me, naked branches swayed and huge limbs creaked. I began to look around for shelter from the worst of this squall, but found none. In all directions the leafless forest stretched, barren, wet, and hostile, writhing like a tormented thing beneath the rippling blankets of rain. And as I searched I wondered what it was I hoped to accomplish. What "ungodly" thing was I to find, which was the cause of all Sir Gottfried's woes? If there was any such thing, it would have to find me. I might not recognize it even if I did come upon it. If not, what then? I could not return to the manor house and say I had failed. From the surety of such tidings the knight would certainly die. No, I would continue on, out of the country until I came to some more hospitable part of the world. Perhaps he would think I had been slain whatever it was I was supposed to fight, and had offered my life up for his. In the soil of this delusion might be planted the very real seed of hope, from which his cure would grow. Under any circumstances, I would continue on my way.

As it happened, my circumstances were these: I rode until nearly nightfall, bend against the rain. I turned in a different direction, but the wind changed to meet me head-on, as if directed by will and intelligence. Beneath my splendid helmet, my teeth chattered. I was as cold and miserable as a grandfather abandoned in an unheated hovel in the dead of winter.

Then suddenly my horse whinnied and reared up, and I found myself staring ahead at two intense green eyes, floating in the mist. And the mist moved toward me, and assumed a shape out of the shadow of the trees—a huge grey dog-like thing as large as a bull, with massive, hunched shoulders and a tail as long as a man's leg. Its paws were a span or more wide, and its fearsome jowls were lined with teeth like dirks of ivory. The monster padded stealthily over the mud and leaves, completely silent.

Yanking hard on the reins, I forced my steed to obey me, lowered my lance, dug spurs into flanks, and raced forward. The hellish face loomed before me, mouth stretched wide in a soundless snarl, and the lance-tip struck something solid. The shaft broke—and this was a war weapon, not something designed for jousting—and there was another shock too quick for me to comprehend, as both I and my mount were flung up into the air, over and backwards into the mud.

Luckily I fell clear of the saddle and was not crushed by the weight of the horse. But still I hit hard, and lay stunned beneath a bush, conscious but unable to move. This was the end. Any second now I would feel one of those massive paws on my chest, and there would be a brief instant of pain and terror as the hot breath enveloped me, the teeth sank into my flesh, and I was torn to pieces. Yet nothing happened. I sat up and looked around, and saw the creature was gone. A dream? No. My horse was still there, still twitching, its ribs and bowels torn out by a single swipe of grey limb. And my shattered lance lay nearby. These were concrete proofs of the encounter. I had been deliberately conquered, then spared. But why?

With the jeweled sword I released the dying horse from its agony. I walked on through the underbrush. After a while my spurs became tangled in sticks and vines; I nearly tripped a dozen times; and so I took them off and threw them away. I plodded through the mire for hours, it seemed, with sword drawn and shield ready to ward off any foe. Evening approached. It began to get dark. There was no sound, save for the whisper of the rain, and the splashing and sucking of my footfalls, but this was not to be for long.

The forest cleared into a plain, in the middle of which was a gently rising hillock. Twelve figures stood atop it, and when I went to see who they were, I came upon a group of fantastic beings, shaped like old women from the neck down, but with the heads of hairless, grey dogs. I raised sword and shield, ready to do battle, and the heads came off—they were masks of leather, with glass eyes and carven teeth of wood—to reveal faces I knew.

The twelve witches from the tree, laughing. The answer was clear to me. These were the ungodly things. I was sure, I had released them. Now I would put them to rest. I charged up the slope, sword swinging.

"Ho! Ho! Look, sisters! He threatens us!"

They were too quick for me, faster than earthly things. As before they scattered, but this time they did not flee. They were all around me, behind me, their shrivelled hands clutching, and yet my sword's edge sliced only air.

Then—my senses were confused from this point and I cannot be sure of the details of my history—one of them was on my back. Hands tore away my helmet and grabbed my ears, and one witch, or two, or three rode me as Tom O'Bedlam rides his jackass to death when racing after the moon. Icy, dagger-like fingers clamped into my brain; dirty heels banged against my sides; and we were off, down the far side of the hill and through more woods, into fields, up to my shoulders in a murky stream, with all the other hags flying alongside in the air like predatory birds on the wings of nightmare. How far we went, I can never know. We ran until my legs seemed ready to break, till I was past all pain, over the threshold of delirium, and the blurred landscape seemed to jump and whirl before my weary eyes. We traveled throughout the night, perhaps covering a hundred leagues, perhaps a thousand, or some other impossible distance. At times we seemed to sink under the earth and wriggle like worms, only to escape into darkness and sail through the sky like bats, seeing nothing and yet knowing what invisible things passed before us. And I think for part of the time we were accompanied by wolves and stags and beasts far more fantastical, dragons, hippogriffs, and even the *glimmich,* which plays with dragons as cats do with wounded mice before devouring them. But I am sure that it was nearly dawn when we came to the sea and danced on the sandy beach. The one who was riding me at last let go, and I collapsed in weariness, then fought my way to my feet, feeling around for a sword or dagger. All were gone. A dozen pairs of hands dragged me into a circle, and once more my body was not my own. We formed a circle and whirled around and around, and then we were not on the shore but the ocean, dancing lightly over the waves, until the solid land was a dim line far away. I, numb with terror and exhaustion, could not find the strength of thought to question this new wonder.

At last? At last? At last we came to a place in the sea where a white colossus stood above the waves reaching into the lightening sky, a figure carven from a mountain of salt by demon sculptors. It was not an ugly figure, but majestic, almost beautiful, a superbly formed and muscled man with flowing beard, wild hair, and a crown of seashells on his head. One arm was outstretched, holding a trident. And looking on this giant I understood what it was—not the form of a man at all, but of a god.

We formed our ring around the figure and were still. The water around us was still too, like a plain of glass. Rain splashed onto it.

One of the witches spoke.

"Now may all be revealed to you. Now may you know that we are not truly as we appear, old, yet younger in our first shapes. We were bent thus only by a force more powerful than ourselves, which bound our hands and cast us down. And *yet that force does not touch you!* The stain of baptism is erased from your soul, and we can see, feel, and touch you as a thing real. Behold! There shall be an exchange of burdens, then a new chain forged with living links, then a new life. We take only a worthless thing from you, the weight of your conscience and your offense against your God. To ours this is naught, and onto your shoulders we place what you would call our heathenness, which we call the wholeness of our god's spirit, which has never known the Christ. To one outcast such as you, this likewise is without further injury. By the exchange of sins, both are cancelled out."

All of them cried out, "Let it be so!"

And, astonishing myself as I spoke, I replied, "Let it be so."

And even then I felt a new strength coming into me, my weariness of soul and body draining away. I felt younger, as if dark, painful years were being stripped away. If two men meet on a road, each with a heavy bundle to carry, and each takes the load of the other, the work seems less somehow. It was like that.

All of us, thirteen of us, placed our joined hands against the thighs of the salt giant—I filled with a joy I could not understand—and shouted in a single voice, *"Live! Live!"*

The giant lived. The whiteness faded into brown, then green, then grey, then the color of living flesh. The hard salt became flexible and soft to the touch. The enormous limbs began to move. The penis rose erect. All of us released our hold and ran back a few paces. Still in a circle, and in the midst of us the thing sank down into the sea, slowly, slowly, like an avalanche without end. When at last the head was submerged the water began to bubble and foam, and rise, as if a whale were about to breach. An enormous tail broke the surface, all covered with glistening silver scales, then sank down again.

In a moment we were alone.

"He is free at last," one of the witches said. "Now a new age begins."

As she spoke, I noticed that all of them had changed. They were no longer crones, but beautiful maidens, each with a face round and glowing like the moon, each with a tiara of stars in her hair, each with a cloak of purple sky about her shoulders.

Surely Sir Gottfried's wound would be healed by now, for I had, albeit inadvertently, accomplished my mission. Now there was not one among the company save myself who could be recalled ungodly.

V

The rain stopped. In the east, over the sea, was the glow of the arriving sun behind the clouds. Then the clouds broke overhead, revealing constellations not yet ready to fade.

Out of the sunrise came a white ship with sails of shining silk, gliding swiftly over the water. The twelve stood and waited till it drew near. As it did I could make out its features clearly: on the prow the face of a blindfolded woman, and an arm outstretched to grope the way. On the stern, two faces with wide eyes, and a sword bedecked with flowers.

They left me standing there and went to embark. In my confusion and wonder I realized slowly that this was my chance, my only chance to get free of all I dreaded. Everything was reversed. If I went with what I had feared I would have no fear. If I went with gods I would escape the one God.

"Wait!" I shouted. "Take me with you! I have served you well, have I not? Take me with you!"

The last of them to climb aboard turned and said sadly, "But you are a man, a mortal man of numbered years. It is not for you to drink the milk of paradise."

And a wind filled the sail, and the ship was carried away with the same rapid grace it had shown in coming.

The sky faded from black to purple to blue. The sun showed its full disc above the horizon. It was going to be a brilliant morning.

Suddenly, standing alone on the water, I felt myself beginning to sink. The reverie was over, and the danger immediate. I turned and ran toward the shore, all the while sinking lower and lower, to my knees, to my waist, to my shoulders, till the water brought me to a stop. Some stray rational thought saved me. I tore off all my armor, right before the magic which held me up failed completely, and I went under, but surfaced again, and began to swim desperately in the direction of land. Each stroke was an agony, as my weariness returned tome. My arms seemed to encumber me as if they were tied down with steel. Yet somehow I survived, and was rolled onto the beach by the surf, where I slept for a long time.

Later I awoke and wandered, and came upon a fisherman, who was preparing to cast his net. I bade him good day, but he spat and said, "Bah! It is a terrible day. The sea is more bitter with salt than ever before, and the fish elude me. It seems the world has turned its back on Christian men."

L'ENVOI

So what could I do? I continued questing, and journeyed as a knight errant to the farthest lands. And it happened that on the highway out from the City of Stars, which stands nigh unto the world's rim, I met three knights.

They were coming from the city, and I was going toward it. The sun was down; the stars were out in a windy sky; and by the light of stars and the moon I saw them, resplendent in their polished armor, with elaborate insignia on their shields and long lances in their hands.

I reined in my steed, and sat tarnished and begrimed before them.

"Hail," said one, a broad man with a drooping moustache. "We have not seen a Christian man in many months."

"Nor have I." Such irony. I laughed within, but without mirth.

"We are far from home."

"Why have you come so far?" I demanded, before they could put the same question to me. The dolorous history of Julian the wanderer I did not want spread any farther than it already had been.

The first knight fell silent, and another, younger and fair of face, spoke.

"We seek the Holy Grail, from which all peace of the spirit flows."

My astonishment registered.

"You are surprised?" asked the third of them.

"The Holy Grail? I've heard the stories, but I can't think anyone really—"

"Sir, the Lord God On High sent us on this quest, and we cannot sleep two nights in the same place until we have found the Grail."

"How long have you been looking?"

"A long time. We've lost track."

"And what are your names? Are you men of great renown?"

"I am Sir Bedivere. To my right is Sir Gawain, to my left Sir Galahad. We serve the greatest of kings, Arthur of Camelot, of whom you have no doubt heard."

"Yes, I have heard of him." I struggled with words, speech eluding me. "The stories of him are told. I heard them from my father, he from his, he from his. . .many years, hundreds. . .it is written in the ancient books of Arthur. . ."

Worry showed on their faces. Perhaps they took me for a lunatic, but I don't think it was that. For a full minute no one spoke, and then the youngest, Galahad, broke the silence.

"If this be true, and you don't seem to lie—if this be true, tell us, we beg you, what the year is."

"Why—I don't know. I stopped counting long ago."

"Please! Something! The century at least. What century is it?"

"I don't know. I'm sorry, but I don't know."

Together they let out a cry of despair, and they spurred their horses and raced past me, vanishing down the road in a cloud of dust and shadows.

I looked after them and felt the full weight of eternity upon me, then ahead toward the City of Stars and the earth's end, and I think I understood. Not to them, but to me some trace of enlightenment came. I think we have all lost touch with time. History has passed us by, and we are tossed like corks on the tempest of years, unable to touch the shore. Perhaps, like the fabled Merlin I live backwards, growing younger to die in my mother's womb when at last I meet her, but I think even that is taken from me, and from the rest. Men remember us dimly, and glimpse briefly into our faces in the depths of dreams, and do not understand as we spread ourselves upon the centuried wind like smoke and eventually are no more.

We have all become legends, I think.

THE PENDRAGON CHRONICLERS
A Survey of Arthurian Fiction

Legends are full of heroes: the Greeks had Achilles and
Heracles and Theseus; the Nordic Eddas had Sigurd or
Siegfried and Loki; the Sumerians, whose legends are as old as
time, had the mighty Gilgamesh, the first hero of all. And yet in
literary and romantic terms these heroes shrivel to nothing beside
King Arthur and his Knights of the Round Table. More tales
have been written about their exploits than any other characters,
real or fictional. Hope and strength come from association with
Arthur's sense of mission and his weaknesses and the tragedies
that ultimately befall him and the fellowship earn our sympathy.

To appreciate and enjoy the Arthurian world it is not necessary
or important to know who the real King Arthur was. It does not
matter if he was Riothamus (d.470) king of the Britons, as suggested by Geoffrey Ashe in *The Discovery of King Arthur* (1985),
or if he was Arthwyr ap Meurig (503–579), 61st hereditary king
of Glamorgan and Gwent as convincingly argued by Alan Wilson
and Baram Blackett in *Artorius Rex Discovered* (1985), or even
if he was Gwenddolau ab Ceidio (d.573) king of the Selgovae in
south-west Scotland and identified as the patron of Merlin by
Nikolai Tolstoy in *The Quest for Merlin* (1985). In all probability
the legends that have grown about him are drawn from all three
kings plus the exploits of other heroes and princes. What does
matter is the image projected by the fictional portrayal of Arthur.
For here was a unity and strength defending Britain against all
oppressors in dark times, our one true national hero.

The first full history of Arthur as we now know it was written
in Latin by a Welshman, or at least a man born and raised
in Wales, Geoffrey of Monmouth (*c.* 1100–1155). It forms a

large part of his *History of the Kings of Britain* written down in Oxford and completed in about 1136. At this time Britain was descending into civil war between King Stephen and the Empress Matilda over the right to the throne. How much did the pedigree given to Britain's kings by Geoffrey inspire the British nation during those dark days? Whatever the immediate cause for its popularity, Geoffrey's *History* rapidly became a national classic helped on its way by retellings and adaptations by other scribes includes Walter Mapes, Geoffrey Gaimar and, in particular, Wace. Wace added his own embellishments in his *Roman de Brut* (1155) and this was in turn rendered into Anglo-Saxon by a Worcestershire priest called Layamon in *Brut*. Layamon worked on his version during the absentee reign of Richard I, although his final manuscript was not completed until 1205. By then the name of Arthur was already a by-word for national success, and it was no coincidence that the name selected by Henry II for his grandson who should have become king when he came of age was Arthur. However, this Prince Arthur, died, probably by the order of King John, in 1203.

Although Geoffrey had formulated much of the basic Arthurian legend he was drawing upon a wealth of oral tradition which at the time of his youth was beginning to be written down, usually by unknown scribes. The bulk of this tradition was of Celtic origin, from Geoffrey's native Wales. The very first mention of Arthur had been in the *Historia Brittonum* attributed to a Welsh monk called Nennius who chronicled the deeds of this fellow men in the ninth century. Nennius described Arthur as a warlord or general, not as a king, and links him with the great battle of Mount Badon which took place, according to the Welsh annals, in the year 518 A.D. Badon was the last great victory of the Britons against the Saxons and ushered in a period of relative peace, a Golden Age, linked to the reign of Arthur, that lasted for twenty years until his death at the battle of Camlann.

The greatest collection of Welsh legends is the *Mabinogion*, which brings together eleven traditional tales first written down over a period of years and not the work of a single chronicler. Several of the tales concern the deeds of Arthur with "Culhwch and Olwen", dating from the tenth century, being the earliest Arthurian tale in Welsh. "The Dream of Rhonabwy" is from the twelfth century, and there are three later tales, "Peredur", "The Lady of the Fountain" and "Gereint Son of Erbin" which show traces of Norman influence. Because these tales were of Celtic origin, they were also known to the Bretons in France and the

French contributed much to the development of the Arthurian story. Marie de France, for example, a half-sister of Henry II, rendered into French a number of Breton tales that she heard at court. These "lays', or narrative poems, were taken up by the minstrels and troubadours of the twelfth and thirteenth centuries and Arthur's fame spread across Europe. Marie de France's main contribution is the introduction of the story of Tristan and Iseult, which was originally a Celtic legend known as early as the tenth century, but then with no Arthurian connection.

The real father of the Arthurian romance, however, as opposed to history, was Chrétien de Troyes (*c*. 1130–1190), a French poet and favourite at the court of Louis VII, who entertained Louis's daughter, Countess Marie, with tales of knightly deeds. Five of these survive: *Érec et Énide, Cliges, Lancelot and Yvain,* all composed during the period 1170–77, and the unfinished *Perceval, or the History of the Grail,* started in 1182. Chrétien was the man who gave the name Camelot to Arthur's court, who introduced us to Lancelot, and who first sought to unify the many legends of the Holy Grail which had abounded for centuries. And it was Chrétien more than any other early poet who developed the concept of courtly chivalry and so flavoured the Arthurian romances to the form in which they are remembered today.

And so the tales spread. The Tristan story was translated into German by Gottfried von Strassburg (d. 1220) as *Tristan und Isolde* around 1200. His contemporary Wolfram von Eschenbach completed his epic of the Grail Legend, *Parzival,* at about the same time. Other poets whose names have not survived contributed their own versions from oral tradition. *Jaufry the Knight,* reprinted in this volume, surfaced at the court of Aragon at about this time. The greatest of all the anonymous works is that of *Sir Gawaine and the Green Knight* composed some time around 1380 and believed to have been commissioned by John of Gaunt, fourth son of Edward III. This poem has come to be regarded as one of the highlights of medieval English literature.

By the end of the fourteenth century there was a substantial body of Arthurian literature and it remained for someone to bring it all together into a unified form. Several tried but it was left to an English knight, Sir Thomas Malory (d. 1471) to bring about this final transition and produce the masterwork of Arthurian literature, *Le Morte d'Arthur.* The identity of Malory is still uncertain, although the likeliest candidate is a Sir Thomas Malory of Newbold Revel in Warwickshire who, unlike the chivalrous deeds that he liked to portray, was an accused murderer, rapist and thief who spent most of his final twenty years in prison, where he may have composed *Le Morte d'Arthur*.

The time of writing is significant. During Malory's life England was split by the Wars of the Roses (1455–85) between the Houses of Lancaster and York. Malory had sided with the Yorkists and his political views were probably the main reason for his imprisonment. It is easy to imagine, therefore, that his imagination would return to the days of England's past conflicts and especially the days of Arthur when a strong king had brought peace and harmony to the land. Equally significant is the date of publication. Malory's work came into the hands of William Caxton and was one of the first books printed in England. It appeared in 1485 at the same time as Richard III was slain at Bosworth and Henry Tudor succeeded to the throne as Henry VII. Henry made much of his Welsh ancestry and, if some chronologies are to be believed, his descent can be traced from Arthwyr ap Meurig, one of the claimants for the original King Arthur. With the succession of Henry VII, England was again united and perhaps the prophecy came true after all and Arthur had returned. Certainly, Henry VII firmly believed the legend. His eldest son, born in September 1486, just a year after Caxton published *Le Morte d'Arthur,* was called Arthur. Alas, he died in 1502, and it was Henry's second son who succeeded to the throne as Henry VIII. I have no doubt that Henry clearly had it in his mind to live up to the legend of Arthur and the greatness of Britain as a world power dates from Henry VIII's reign.

It would be nearly four hundred years before there came a major revival of interest in Arthurian literature. In the Victorian era England was again under seige, not from rival armies, but from industrialism and social discontent. The Victorian romantics cast their minds back to a Golden Age that never really existed but which was felt to have done so and which was certainly preferable to the darkening skies of industrial England. The wonder of the Arthurian age was expressed in verse and paintings, and the major force in the movement was Alfred Tennyson (1809–92). Tennyson followed the lead set by Sir Walter Scott (1771–1832) in the popularisation of medievalism, but brought the Arthurian age into focus. Starting with his poem "The Lady of Shalott" in 1832, Tennyson began to pen a cycle of poems around the Arthurian heroes which eventually led to his *Idylls of the King*. The first volume of the Idylls appeared in 1859 and they were added to over the next twenty-five years. Other romantics contributed to the growing movement. Matthew Arnold with his *Tristram and Iseulte* (1852), the great William Morris with *The Defence of Guinevere* (1858) and Algernon Swinburne with *Tristram of Lyonesse* (1882).

The poetical and artistic form only gradually gave way to the narrative form, and it is clear that the Arthurian legend was sufficiently well established by 1889 to be spoofed by Mark Twain in *A Connecticut Yankee in King Arthur's Court* which ushered in the modern era of Arthurian fiction. During the last one hundred years the treatment of Arthurian fiction has followed several paths. There has always remained the traditional approach which was adapted with consummate skill by T.H. White in his *The Sword and the Stone* (1938) and successive works. There has also been a trend toward realism, either in the hard-bitten direct historical approach with Arthur as a warrior king, or by blending the realist and traditionalist with a more mystical approach, sparing the savagery for a more romantic flavour. Of the former, the works of Henry Treece and Victor Canning stand out. Of the latter, those by Mary Stewart and Marion Zimmer Bradley.

There has been such a growth in Arthurian fiction in recent years. especially with the post-Tolkien interest in fantasy fiction, that it is impossible to discuss it all here. I have instead prepared a bibliography listing the most important works of Arthurian fiction published in the last one hundred years. It could not be complete, but concentrates on narrative fiction—novels and short stories—and excludes all poetry and drama. I have excluded most retellings of Malory (usually for younger readers) and I have also excluded stories where the appearance of Arthur or Merlin or the Knights is gratuitous and of little relevance to the plot. Finally, I have excluded most symbolic or allegorical stories using Arthurian images in contemporary settings. What remains is a core of Arthurian fiction which I feel would interest all readers of this anthology. The listing is in order of publication so that you can rapidly find recent works and also chart the growth of Arthurian fiction during the century. As a guide through the mass of fiction I have provided some form of identification and the occasional plot summary where necessary. The following terms are used:

Historical—means the story sets Arthur in an historical context and includes no fantasy elements.

Historical Fantasy—as above but with fantasy elements.

Historical Romance—means an historical setting but idealised and romanticised.

Traditional—means the story is set in the traditional never-never world of the Arthurian romances.

Contemporary—means the story is in a modern-day setting.

All the other descriptions, such as allegorical or satirical. are, I hope, self-explanatory when read with the plot summary.

100 YEARS OF ARTHURIAN FICTION

1. *1889* Twain, Mark *A Connecticut Yankee in King Arthur's Court* New york: Harper's, 1889. Satirical/ Traditional.

2. *1898* Babcock, William H. *Cian of the Chariots* Boston: Lothrop, 1898. Historical.

3. *1902* French, Allen. "Sir Marrok", *St. Nicholas Magazine* May 1902. Also as book, New York: Century, 1902. Children's historical romance.

4. *1903* Deeping, Warwick. *Uther and Igraine* New York: Outlook, 1903. Historical

5. *1905* Housman, Clemence. *The Life of Sir Aglovale de Galis* London: Methuen, 1905. Traditional.

6. *1906* MacLeod, Fiona. "Beyond the Blue Septentrions" in *Where The Forest Murmurs* London: Newnes, 1906. Mystical; Arthur adopts his name from the constellation of the Great Bear.

7. *1907* Sterling, Sara Hawks. *A Lady of King Arthur's Court* Philadelphia: George Jacobs, 1907. Historical   romance; Holy Grail.

8. *1908* Senior, Dorothy. *The Clutch of Circumstance; or, The Gates of Dawn* London: Black, 1908. Historical.

9. *1909* Machen, Arthur. "Many Tower'd Camelot" in *T.P.'s Weekly* April 2, 1909. Later retitled "Guinevere and Lancelot" in *Notes and Queries* London: Spurr & Swift, 1926. Traditional.

10. *1911* Dawson, Coningsby. *The Road to Avalon* London: Hodder & Stoughton, 1911. Allegorical.

11. *1913* Tatum, Edith. "The Awakening of Iseult" in *Neale's Monthly* August 1913. Traditional.

12. *1914* Wodehouse, P.G. "Sir Agravaine" in *The Man Upstairs and Other Stories* London: Methuen,

1914. Traditional; spoof.

13. *1921* Broun, Heywood. "The Fifty-First Dragon" in *Modern Essays* edited Christopher Morley, New York: Harcourt Brace, 1921. Satirical; Gawaine at the knight school believes he is protected by magic.

14. *1926* Erskine, John. *Galahad: Enough of His Life to Explain His Reputation* Indianapolis: Bobbs - Merrill, 1926. Traditional.

15. Hamilton, Ernest. *Launcelot* London: Methuen, 1926. Historical romance.

16. Moore, George. *Perronik the Fool* Mount Vernon, NY: Rudge, 1926. Traditional; retelling of Parsival.

17. *1927* Bradley, Will. *Launcelot and the Ladies* New York: Harper's, 1927. Contemporary/Historical; explores ancient and modern parallels.

18. *1930* Faraday, Wilfred B. *Pendragon* London: Methuen, 1930. Historical romance.

19. Marquis, Don. "King O'Meara and Queen Guinevere" in *Saturday Evening Post* March 15–22, 1930. Historical spoof.

20. *1932* Erskine, John. *Tristan and Isolde: Restoring Palamede* Indianapolis: Bobbs-Merrill, 1932. Traditional.

21. *1935* Lindsay, Philip. *The Little Wench* London: Ivor Nicholson & Watson, 1935. Historical romance.

22. *1938* White, T.H. *The Sword in the Stone* London: Collins, 1938. Followed by *The Witch in the Wood* Collins, 1939; *The Ill-Made Knight* New York: Putnams, 1940. These three revised and collected with the previously unpublished "The Candle in the Wind" as *The Once and Future King* Collins, 1958. Traditional, though contains contemporary idioms. See also no. 73.

22. *1939* MacCormac, John. "The Enchanted Week End" in *Unknown* October 1939. Contemporary; Merlin revived; light-hearted and shallow.

23. Munn, H. Warner. "King of the World's Edge" in *Weird Tales* September–December 1939. As a book, New York: Ace Books, 1966. Historical fantasy; post-Arthurian, survivors of Arthur's warriors under a Roman centurion sale West and discover America. See also no. 52.

24. *1940* Erskine, John. "Seven Tales From King Arthur's Court" in *American Weekly* February 4 – March 17, 1940. [Titles, "The Tale of King Arthur's Sword Excalibur", "The Tale of Sir Tristram and the Love Potion", "The Tale of the Enchantress and the Magic Scabbard", "The Tale of Sir Galahad and the Quest of the Sangreal", "The Tale of Sir Launcelot and the Four Queens", "The Tale of Merlin and One of the Ladies of the Lake" and "The Tale of How Sir Launcelot Slew Sir Agravaine".] All traditional.

25. *1943* Kuttner, Henry. "Wet Magic" in *Unknown Worlds* February 1943. Contemporary fantasy; Merlin released.

26. *1944* Frankland, Edward. *The Bear of Britain* London: Macdonald, 1944. Historical.

27. *1947* Roberts, Theodore Goodridge. "Strike Hard! Bite Deep!" *Blue Book* December 1947 and "A Quest Must End" *Blue Book* April 1948. Traditional; quest of King Torrice and the Mazed Knight Lorn.

28. *1949* Sharpe, Ruth Collier. *Tristram of Lyonesse* New York: Greenberg, 1949. Contemporary/ Historical romance; interchange between two periods.

29. *1950* Johnstone, Paul. "Up, Red Dragon!" *Blue Book* March 1950. Historical (504 AD); Artorius battles the Picts.

30. Roberts, Theodore Goodridge. Sir Dinaden series all in *Blue Book*: "A Quarrel For a Lady" February 1950, "A Purfle For a King" July 1950, "A Quest of the Saracen Beast" November 1950, "The Madness of Sir Tristram" December 1950, "Sir Dinadan and the Giant Taulurd" April 1951, "The Goose Girl" August 1951, "For To Achieve Your Adventure" October 1951 and "A Mountain Miracle" December 1951. All traditional and humorous.

31. *1951* Powys, John Cowper. *Porius* London: Macdonald, 1951. Historical (499 AD).

32. Sturgeon, Theodore. "Excalibur and the Atom" *Fantastic Adventures* August 1951. Contemporary; Arthurian characters recreated in modern lives.

33. *1952* Brooke, Maxey. "Morte d'Alain" *Ellery Queen's*

Mystery Magazine December 1952; also "Morte
d'Espier" *Ellery Queen's Mystery* Magazine June
1955. Traditional; murder mysteries.

34. *1953* Green, Roger Lancelyn. *King Arthur and His
Knights of the Round Table* London: Pen-
guin Books, 1953. Traditional; retelling of the
Arthurian legends.

35.   Roberts, Dorothy James. *The Enchanted Cup* New
York: Appleton-Century-Crofts, 1953. Historical
romance; Tristram legend.

36. *1954* Roberts, Dorothy James. *Launcelot My Brother*
New York: Appleton-Century-Crofts, 1954. Historical romance.

37.   Treece, Henry. *The Eagles Have Flown* London:
The Bodley Head, 1954. Children's historical.

38. *1955* Borowsky, Marvin. *The Queen's Knight* New York:
Random House: 1955. Historical.

39.   Mitchison, Naomi. *To the Chapel Perilous* London:
Allen & Unwin, 1955. Contemporary/Historical
romance, satirical.

40. *1956* Ditmas, E.M.R. *Gareth of Orkney* London: Faber,
1956. Historical romance.

41.   Mitchell, Mary. *Birth of a Legend* London: Methu-
en, 1956. Historical.

42.   Treece, Henry. *The Great Captains* London: The
Bodley Head, 1956. Historical; life of Arthur. See
also no.51.

43. *1959* Marshall, Edison. *The Pagan King* Garden City,
NY: Doubleday, 1959. Historical; first person narrative by Arthur.

44.   Wibberley, Leonard. *The Quest of Excalibur* New
York: Putnams, 1959. Contemporary/Satirical;
Arthur returns to modern Britain.

45. *1961* Manning, Rosemary. *The Dragon's Quest* London:
Constable, 1961. Children's fantasy.

46. *1962* Brunner, John. "Father of Lies" in *Science Fantasy* April 1962; as book, New York: Belmont,
1968. Contemporary science fiction: child with psi
powers creates Arthurian world.

47. *1963* Roberts, Dorothy James. *Kinsmen of the Grail* Boston: Little, Brown, 1963. Historical.

48.   Sutcliffe, Rosemary. *Sword at Sunset* London:
Hodder & Stoughton, 1963. Historical.

49. *1965* Fry, Colin R. "The Purpose of Merlin" in *Fantastic* April 1965. Historical with mystical/science fiction undertones.

50. *1966* O'Meara, Walter. *The Duke of War* New York: Harcourt, Brace & World, 1966. Historical.

51.   Treece, Henry. *The Green Man* London: The Bodley Head, 1966. Historical; Arthur's last days. See no. 42.

52. *1967* Munn, H. Warner. *The Ship From Atlantis* New York: Ace Books, 1967. Historical fantasy (616AD), sequel to no. 23, the two books later reissued as *Merlin's Godson,* New York: Ballantine, 1976. See also no. 63.

53. *1968* Turton, Godfrey. *The Emperor Arthur* Garden City, NY: Doubleday, 1968. Historical.

54. *1970* Robbins, Ruth. *Taliesin and King Arthur* Berkeley: Parnassus Press, 1970. Traditional.

55.   Stewart, Mary. *The Crystal Cave* London: Hodder & Stoughton, 1970. Historical romance; life of Merlin. See no. 62.

56. *1971* Sutcliffe, Rosemary. *Tristan and Iseult* London: The Bodley Head, 1971. Traditional, retelling of legend for younger readers.

57.   Taylor, Anna. *Drustan the Wanderer* London: Longman, 1971. Historical, based on Tristan legend.

58.   Turner, Roy. *King of the Lordless Country* London: Dennis Dobson, 1971. Historical; Arthur's rise to power.

59. *1972* Norton, André. "Artos, Son of Marius" in *Dragon Magic* New York: Ace Books, 1972. Historical; death of Arthur.

60. *1973* Laubenthal, Sanders Anne. *Excalibur* New York: Ballantine, 1973. Contemporary fantasy; Excalibur in modern Alabama.

61.   Norton, Andre. *Here Abide Monsters* New York: Atheneum, 1973. Children's fantasy; alternate world of Avalon.

62.   Stewart, Mary. *The Hollow Hills,* London: Hodder & Stoughton, 1973. Historical romance; Arthur's youth. Sequel to no. 55. See also no. 82.

63. *1974* Munn, H. Warner. *Merlin's Ring* New York: Ballantine, 1974. Historical fantasy, travels of Merlin's

godson, Gwalchmai, around the ancient and medieval world. See also no. 52.

64. *1975* Chapman, Vera. *The Green Knight*, London: Rex Collings, 1975. Followed by *The King's Damosel* Collings, 1976 and *King Arthur's Daughter* Collings, 1976, all later reissued in single volume as *The Three Damosels* London: Methuen, 1978. Traditional.

65. Johnson, Barbara Ferry. *Lionors* New York, 1975. Historical romance.

66. Norton, Andre. *Merlin's Mirror* New York: DAW Books, 1975. Science fiction treatment of Geoffrey's *History*.

67. Viney, Jayne. *The Bright-Helmed One* London: Robert Hale, 1975. Historical.

68. *1976* Canning, Victor. *The Crimson Chalice* London: William Heinemann, 1976. Followed by *The Circle of the Gods* Heinemann, 1977 and *The Immortal Wound* Heinemann, 1978, all later reissued in a single volume as *The Crimson Chalice* Heinemann, 1980. Historical, life of Arthur.

69. Steinbeck, John. *The Acts of King Arthur and His Noble Knights* New York: Farrar, Straus & Giroux, 1976. Traditional; retelling of Malory.

70. *1977* Carmichael, Douglas. *Pendragon* Hicksville, NY: Blackwater Press, 1977. Historical

71. Gloag, John. *Artorius Rex* London: Cassell, 1977. Historical.

72. Monaco, Richard. *Parsival, or a Knight's Tale* New York: Macmillan, 1977. Followed by *The Grail War* New York: Pocket Books, 1979, *The Final Quest* Putnams, 1980 and *Blood and Dreams* New York: Berkley, 1985. Historical; Parsival series.

73. White, T.H. *The Book of Merlyn* Austin, Texas: University of Texas Press, 1977. Traditional, originally written as part of no. 22.

74. *1978* Berger, Thomas. *Arthur Rex* New York: Delacorte Press, 1978. Traditional but more bawdy and humorous.

75. Christian, Catherine. *The Sword and the Flame* London: Macmillan, 1978; retitled *The Pendragon* New York: Alfred Knopf, 1979. Historical romance.

76.   Haldeman, Linda. *The Lastborn of Elvinwood* Garden City, NY: Doubleday, 1978. Fantasy; Merlin.
77.   Hunter, Jim. *Percival and the Presence of God* London: Faber, 1978. Traditional.
78.   Nye, Robert. *Merlin* London: Hamish Hamilton, 1978. Erotic fantasy.
79.   Vansittart, Peter. *Lancelot* London: Peter Owen, 1978. Historical.
80. *1979* Drake, David. *The Dragon Lord* New York: Berkley /Putnam, 1979. Historical fantasy.
81.   Greeley, Andrew M. *The Magic Cup* New York: McGraw Hill, 1979. Historical fantasy; Celtic version of the Grail legend.
82.   Stewart, Mary. *The Last Enchantment* London: Hodder & Stoughton, 1979. Historical romance, Arthur and Merlin. Follows-on from nos. 55 and 62. See also no. 97.
83.   Sutcliffe, Rosemary. *The Light Beyond the Forest* London: The Bodley Head, 1979. Children's traditional; retelling of the Quest for the Holy Grail.
84.   Zelazny, Roger. "The Last Defender of Camelot" in *Isaac Asimov's SF Adventure Magazine* Summer 1979. Contemporary fantasy.
85. *1980* Bradshaw, Gillian. *Hawk of May* New York: Simon & Schuster, 1980. Followed by *Kingdom of Summer* Simon & Schuster, 1981 and *In Winter's Shadow* Simon & Schuster, 1982. All collected into one volume *Down the Long Wind* London: Methuen, 1988. Historical fantasy; retells the Arthurian legend through the eyes of Gwalchmai/Gawaine.
86.   Godwin, Parke. *Firelord* Garden City, NY: Doubleday, 1980. Historical fantasy; life of Arthur. See also no. 98.
87.   Jakes, John & Gil Kane. *Excalibur!* New York: Dell Books, 1980. Historical fantasy; novelisation of film about Arthur and Merlin.
88. *1981* Newman, Sharan. *Guinevere* New York: St. Martin's Press, 1981. Followed by *The Chessboard Queen* St. Martin's Press, 1983 and *Guinevere Evermore* St. Martin's Press, 1985. Traditional; the life of Guinevere.
89.   Schweitzer, Darrell. "Midnight, Moonlight and the

Secret of the Sea" in *We Are All Legends* New York: Bluejay, 1981. Traditional; post-Arthurian.

90. Sutcliffe, Rosemary. *The Sword and the Circle* London: The Bodley Head, 1981 and *The Road to Camlann* The Bodley Head, 1981. Traditional; retells the life and death of Arthur for young readers.

91. Taylor, Keith. *Bard* New York: Ace Books, 1981. Historical fantasy; novelisation of five stories of which "Buried Silver" from *Fantastic* February 1977 is the most Arthurian.

92. *1982* Bradley, Marion Zimmer. *The Mists of Avalon* New York: Alfred Knopf, 1982. Historical romance; major retelling of the life of Arthur as seen through the eyes of Morgan Le Fay.

93. Karr, Phyllis Ann. *The Idylls of the Queen* New York: Ace Books, 1982. Traditional; events following the murder of Sir Patrise.

94. Monaco, Richard. "Blood and Dreams" *Elsewhere* Volume II edited by Terri Windling & Mark Arnold, New York: Ace Books, 1982. Historical; advance excerpt from the Parsival novel *Blood and Dreams* (see no. 72).

95. *1983* Chant, Joy. *The High Kings* London: Allen & Unwin, 1983. Traditional; retelling of Geoffrey of Monmouth's *History* culminating in the story of Arthur.

96. McDowell, Ian. "Son of the Morning" in *Isaac Asimov's Science Fiction Magazine* December 1983. Historical.

97. Stewart, Mary. *The Wicked Day* London: Hodder & Stoughton, 1983. Historical romance; death of Arthur. See also nos. 55, 62 and 82.

98. *1984* Godwin, Parke. *Beloved Exile* New York: Bantam, 1984. Historical fantasy; life of Guinevere. See also no. 86.

99. *1985* Aquino, John T. "The Sad Wizard" in *Fantasy Book* December 1985. Medieval fantasy; Merlin's grand design on history.

100. *1986* Hanratty, Peter. *The Last Knight of Albion* New York: Bluejay, 1986. Traditional; after Arthur's death Percevale seeks revenge.

101. Yolen, Jane. *Merlin's Booke* New York: Ace Books,

1986. Fantasy; a collection of nine stories and four poems a few with prior publication during 1983–1985.

102. *1987* Lawhead, Stephen. *Taliesen* Westchester, Illinios: Crossway Books, 1987. Followed by *Merlin* Crossway, 1988 and *Arthur* Crossway, 1989. Historical fantasy; Pendragon Cycle, follows the survivors of Atlantis down to the days of Arthur.

103. Woolley, Persia. *Child of the Northern Spring* New York: Poseidon, 1987. Historical romance; life of Guinevere. First volume in a series.

104. *1988* Brunner, John. "An Entry That Did Not Appear in Domesday Book" in *Amazing Stories* March 1988. Medieval; survival of Avalon.

105. Coney, Michael G. *Fang, the Gnome* New York: New American Library, 1988. Science fantasy; an alternate Arthurian world created by Nyneve fosterling of Avalona, wife of Merlin.

106. Dickinson, Peter. *Merlin Dreams* London: Gollancz, 1988. Traditional. Eight tales as remembered by Merlin, plus illustrations by Alan Lee.

107. Gemmell, David. *Ghost King* London: Century Hutchinson, 1988 and *Last Sword of Power* Century Hutchinson, 1988. Historical fantasies; life of Uther Pendragon.

108. Godwin, Parke (editor). *Invitation to Camelot* New York: Ace Books, 1988. Anthology of eleven Arthurian stories by Morgan Llywelyn, Tanith Lee, Phyllis Ann Karr, Elizabeth Scarborough, Parke Godwin, Susan Shwartz, Gregory Frost, Madeleine E. Robins, Chelsea Quinn Yarbro, Sharan Newman and Jane Yolen.

109. Paxson, Diana L. *The White Raven* New York: William Morrow, 1988. Historical fantasy; the story of Tristan and Iseult.

110. Pollack, Rachel. "The Three Cups" in *Merlin and Woman* edited by R.J. Stewart, London: Blandford Press, 1988. Mystical. [Volume also contains two other mystical stories of only borderline Arthurian interest.]

111. Tolstoy, Nikolai. *The Coming of the King* London: Bantam Press, 1988. Historical/Mystical; the First Book of Merlin.

112.   Van Asten, Gail. *The Blind Knight* New York: Ace
        Books, 1988. Historical fantasy; post-Arthurian,
        twelfth century with an ancient Lord of Faërie who
        claims to be Uther Pendragon.

113.   Wolf, Joan. *The Road to Avalon* New York: New
        American Library, 1988. Historical ro-
        mance.

114.   Yolen, Jane. "The Quiet Monk" *Isaac Asimov's SF
        Magazine* March 1988. Historical fantasy. Year
        1191 A.D. Lancelot still wanders the Earth sear-
        ching for the grave of Guinevere.

115.   Kats, Welwyn Wilton. *The Third Magic Toronto:
        Douglas & McIntyre, 1988. Contemporary/Alter-
        nate Fantasy; young Morgan LeFerre is summoned
        to an alien buy Arthurian world.*

116. 1989 Sampson, Fay. *Wise Woman's Telling* London:
        Headline, 1989. Historical romance; story of Morgam
        LeFay. First of Daughter of Jintagel series, with
        White Nun's Telling, Headline, 1989, second volume.

ACKNOWLEDGEMENTS

In addition to general texts the following books were consulted in the preparation of this volume.

Ashe, Geoffrey. *The Discovery of King Arthur* London: Debrett's, 1985.

Barber, Richard. *The Arthurian Legends*, Woodbridge: The Boydell Press, 1979.

Brengle, Richard L. *Arthur King of Britain*, Englewood Cliffs, NJ: Prentice-Hall, 1964.

Chrétien de Troyes. *Arthurian Romances* translated by D. D. R. Owen, London: J. M. Dent, 1987.

Goodrich, Norma Lorre. *King Arthur*, New York: Franklin Watts, 1986.

Jenkins, Elizabeth. *The Mystery of King Arthur*, London: Michael Joseph, 1975.

Jones, Gwyn & Thomas. *The Mabinogion*, London: J. M. Dent, 1974.

Malory, Sir Thomas. *Le Morte d'Arthur* edited by Janet Cowen, Harmondsworth: Penguin Books, 1969.

Malory, Sir Thomas. *Le Morte d'Arthur* translated into modern idiom by Keith Baines, London: George Harrap, 1962.

Matthews, John. *An Arthurian Reader*, Wellingborough: The Aquarian Press, 1988.

Matthews, John & Caitlin. *The Aquarian Guide to British and Irish Mythology*, Wellingborough: The Aquarian Press, 1988.

Taylor, Beverly & Elisabeth Brewer. *The Return of King Arthur*, Woodbridge: D. S. Brewer, 1983.

Thompson, Raymond H. *The Return From Avalon*, Westport, CT: Greenwood Press, 1985.

Tolstoy, Nikolai. *The Quest For Merlin*, London: Hamish Hamilton, 1985.

Whitlock, Ralph. *The Warrior Kings of Saxon England*, London: Moonraker Press, 1977.

Wilson, Alan & Baram Blackett. *Artorius Rex Discovered*, Cardiff: King Arthur Research, 1985.